Juliet E. McKenna

THE RIVEN KINGDOM

ANGRY ROBOT

ANGRY ROBOT
An imprint of Watkins Media Ltd

Unit 11, Shepperton House
89-93 Shepperton Road
London N1 3DF
UK

angryrobotbooks.com
No Three Rules

An Angry Robot paperback original, 2026

Edited by Simon Spanton
Cover by Alice Coleman
Set in Meridien

Map artwork designed by Oisín McGann.

ISBN 978 1 83673 037 8
Ebook ISBN 978 1 83673 038 5

Printed and bound in the United Kingdom by CPI Group (UK) Ltd, Croydon CR0 4YY

The manufacturer's authorised representative in the EU for product safety is eucomply OÜ - Pärnu mnt 139b-14, 11317 Tallinn, Estonia, hello@eucompliancepartner.com; www.eucompliancepartner.com

9 8 7 6 5 4 3 2 1

MIX
Paper | Supporting responsible forestry
FSC
www.fsc.org
FSC® C013604

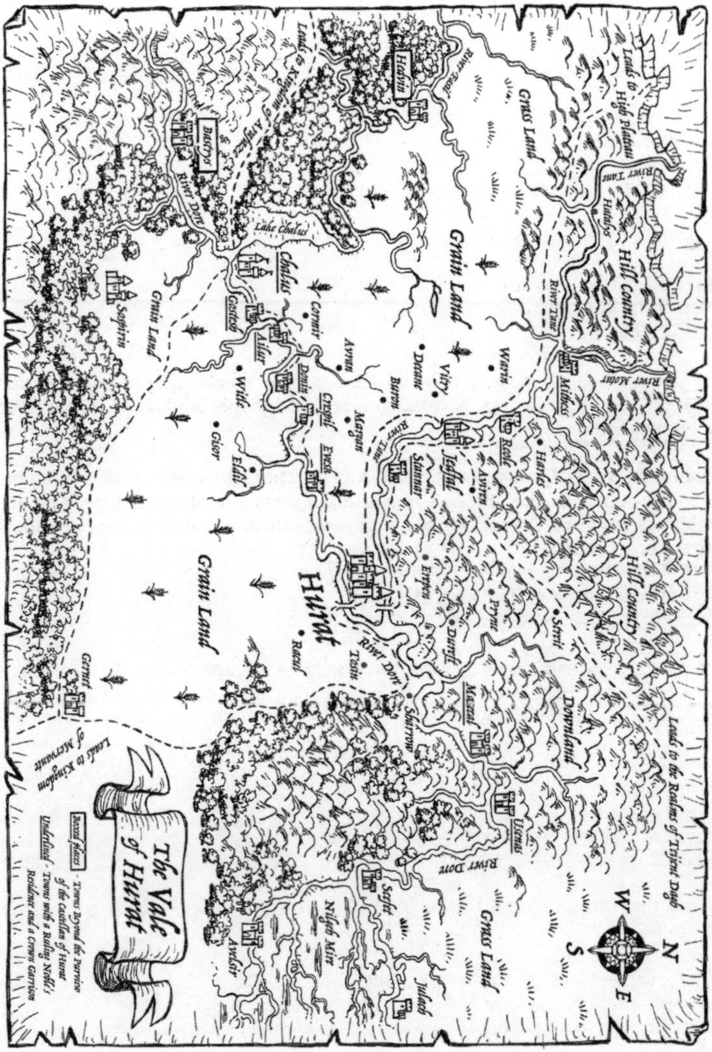

Illustration by Oisín McGann

Monarchs of Arafaze
holding court in the city of Velasta

King Ganirin the Bold
King Serken, his descendant in the seventeenth generation
Queen Misene, King Serken's wife

King Fedrin, King Serken's son
Princess Alriad, King Serken's daughter, married to Earl Lystro of Coylure

Queen Sefriya, King Fedrin's wife
King Venais, King Fedrin's son
Princess Idelina, King Fedrin's daughter, married to Earl Maren of Evarise

Significant Nobles of Arafaze and Attendants

Earl Lystro of Coylure
Earl Maren of Evarise
Lord Padran of Evarise, brother and heir to Earl Maren
Nindera Kyse, scrivener and advisor

Earl Debin of Shirlat
Reske Masol, enquiry agent

Baron Lebarre of Hedvin
Baron Zavire of Bastrys

Notable persons in Hurat Castle

Castellan Maixen, commander of Hurat's crown forces across the province
Senon, the castellan's chief steward
Mistress Zile, the castle's chief scrivener
Master Byen, her deputy
Brother Delnor, priest-physician in charge of the castle's Infirmary

Notable persons in Hurat Town

Quenild Ditayan, respected and prosperous merchant
Ticosa Reture, her wife and business partner
Ristal, their long-standing and trusted employee
Yanter, a young employee learning the river trade

Significant Priestesses Serving the Temple of the Sun Goddess in Hurat

Mother Finevre, sworn to the Secret Sisterhood
Sister Jadewin, sworn to the Secret Sisterhood, recently arrived from Velasta
Sister Deyadir, sworn to the Secret Sisterhood
Sister Meida, sworn to the Secret Sisterhood

Significant Priests Serving the Shrine of the Moon God in Hurat

Father Memlin
Brother Archivist Praidel
Brother Talaven, sworn to the Hidden Brethren
Brother Cavore, sworn to the Hidden Brethren
Brother Alory, newly sworn to the Hidden Brethren
Brother Augol, sworn to the Hidden Brethren
Brother Belid, sworn to the Hidden Brethren

Significant Nobles in the Vale of Hurat Ruling Lands along the River Dore and the River Tane

Baroness Karlin of Evesk
Baron Lensin of Chalus
Baroness Gossen of Sospirin

Margrave Vauset of Jedfal
Margrave Antrem of Reole
Margrave Satrel of Stannar

Lord Romer of Sharrow

The Calendar
customarily used in the Vale of Hurat
and across the Kingdom of Arafaze

Wolf Moon
Snow Moon
Thaw Moon
Spring Equinox festival
Blossom Moon
Hare Moon
Flower Moon
Midsummer Solstice festival
Thunder Moon
Hay Moon
Harvest Moon
Autumn Equinox festival
Stag Moon
Frost Moon
Ice Moon
Winter Solstice festival

Chapter One

HURAT

7th of the Snow Moon

'Have you seen it?' They met at the crossroads. Jadewin's breath clouded the crisp, cold air, catching the light from the lamp over a house's locked door.

'I caught a glimpse of her in Serrit Place.' Alory shifted his feet, rubbing gloved hands up and down his arms.

'It.' Jadewin rebuked him. 'You've seen ***it***. Do not grant the thing more substance or reality than it has already gained.'

'Of course.' The young priest ducked his head, apologetic.

'That will become second nature.' Jadewin smiled to reassure him. 'Lead on. This is your town's recurrent phantasm.'

She followed Alory, huddled in her felted wool cape. The heavy cloth was as pale as the winter sun that was a token of the Goddess's promise her blessed warmth would return with lengthening days. These couldn't come soon enough for Jadewin.

The priestess walked cautiously on the treacherous cobbles. She had arrived here midway through the Ice Moon and learned that lesson the hard way as the days grew colder. Through the Wolf Moon following the Winter Solstice, the weak sunlight struggled to melt the trodden snow on Hurat's narrow streets.

Wearing the black of a Moon God's servant, bulky in a long-sleeved jerkin lined with sheepskin, Alory moved like a shadow ahead of her. Tall and broad-shouldered despite his youth, his heavy boots crunched on dark smears of ash strewn by householders mindful of Hurat's by-laws.

They soon reached Serrit Place. The public fountain was dry, with its statue wrapped in sacking and straw to protect the finely carved stone from these months of shattering cold. Jadewin laid a gloved hand on Alory's arm and pointed.

The figure on the far side of the square wasn't someone returning late from revelry. Hurat's townsfolk stayed close to their firesides in the depths of winter. These days, with rumours of horrors stalking the streets, no one went out after the shrine and temple bells marked the Sun Goddess's rule over the day passing to the Moon God's command of the night.

'What do we do?' Alory's shiver had nothing to do with the cold.

Jadewin pushed back her hood. The waxing Snow Moon shone above them in a cloudless sky. Its light burnished threads of silver in her dark, coiled braids. 'We take note, first of all. A phantasm's form tells us about those whose fears and spite have spawned it. Where the thing goes and where it lingers will tell us more. We have to find this apparition's source if we're to extinguish it for good. I don't propose to banish it tonight to see it return tomorrow.'

Alory watched the phantasm walk back and forth across the square, like a dog casting for a scent.

When she had first seen the apparition, Jadewin could see the buildings behind it, as though she were looking through smoke. As it drew closer, the phantasm become more solid, more horribly real. The semblance of an age-withered woman approached; a short, hunched figure with toothless gums drawing its nose into a hook above a pointed jaw.

'Someone fears growing old and poor, outliving husband and children or perhaps never marrying to have a family,' the priestess observed calmly. 'She needs reminding that solitary and destitute women will find shelter in the Sun Goddess's almshouses.'

Alory didn't say a word. Jadewin glanced at him and saw the Horned God's young servant stare at the phantasm, wide-eyed.

'This is no living soul,' she said sharply. 'Old women walk slowly and carefully, often with sticks and pain. This phantasm moves like a girl. It doesn't fear slipping on ice-glazed cobbles. This is a vile mockery of life, and we will dispel it.'

Alory squared his shoulders.

Jadewin continued. She was here to teach the boy. 'What can we learn from its clothing? A full-skirted sleeveless gown over a high necked under-dress is the latest fashion for the wealthy in Velasta. Whoever's embittered dreams are dwelling on some grievance to call this phantasm forth, I'd say their family visits the capital regularly.'

'That's another sign.' Alory cleared his throat. 'No one real would venture outside in this chill without a cloak.'

'It might still attack if we do something foolhardy to get its attention.' Jadewin removed a glove and reached inside her cape. Her fingertips found her gold sunburst pendant on its chain around her neck.

'Can it hurt us?' the boy asked, apprehensive.

'Not as long as our faith holds steady,' the priestess assured him.

Moving with sudden purpose, the wandering apparition headed west.

'Come on.' Jadewin didn't wait to see if Alory followed.

As it left the square, the phantasm studied the shuttered windows of the houses' upper floors. Their glass-fronted balconies were thickly curtained against the cold. A short distance further on, it stalked towards a particular house.

Jadewin had been in and out of Hurat's homes serving the goddess since she had arrived in this far-flung town. The dwelling's heavy double doors would open into a flagstoned entrance hall which would store day-to-day deliveries, perhaps also a handcart or a carrying chair if some elderly family member needed help to get from place to place. Stone steps on one side of the hall would go down to the cellars. A carved wooden staircase opposite would lead up to comfortably furnished rooms for socialising and dining, with bedchambers on the floors above.

The creature ran its hands over the painted doors. It was gaining a firmer foothold in this world. Jadewin could see its colourless talons; a manifestation of this recurring apparition's name, whispered behind fearful hands. The Icicle Witch. The phantasm's claws bit deep into the wood. Its triumphant hiss echoed in the empty street.

'Alory, now!' Jadewin drew her sunburst pendant out, its sudden radiance warming her hand.

The monster spun around, snarling, and strode toward the priestess. growing taller. It hissed louder, showing murderous fangs. Its clawed hands reached out to seize her.

Jadewin forced away thoughts of those talons tearing her clothing and digging into her flesh. 'In the Golden Mother's name, I deny you form and substance. I banish you to the unseen realm.'

She recalled the indistinct shadow she had seen on the far side of the fountain, spawned by a tissue of lies. The Icicle Witch was a spiteful story to scare children into a sham of good behaviour. A shaft of golden light from her pendant pierced the Icicle Witch like a sunbeam cutting through cloud.

'You have no breath, no blood, no flesh,' Jadewin declared. 'You are not of this world.'

The phantasm froze. Alory stepped behind it, raising his hand. Moonlight coalesced into a long silver blade. The sword's hilt formed as he closed his fingers. Alory slashed downwards, cutting deep into the apparition's shoulder.

'The peace of the night is the Moon God's gift to the living,' he said, furious. 'You will not pollute his restful darkness with your terrors.'

The apparition shimmered, as translucent as clouded glass. Jadewin directed her pendant's radiance into its snarling face. Alory hacked with his sword, again and again. The phantasm's clawed hands hung limp and useless. Any living creature would have collapsed, writhing in agony.

Jadewin stared into the phantasm's inhuman eyes. She denied its right to exist with every beat of her heart. They had to rid Hurat of the monster before some householder was roused by their voices and opened a window's shutters. If anyone glimpsed this walking nightmare, their efforts could be undone. 'Return whence you came!'

The creature squirmed, trying to turn to attack Alory. Jadewin's magic held it skewered. The young priest put his strength and faith into a two-handed stroke. The moon blade sliced through the phantasm's midriff. The monster broke into fragments vanishing like leaves scattered by a wind.

'Lord of Secrets!' Alory heaved a shuddering sigh.

Jadewin looked into the intangible realm, holding her pendant tight, alert. She was the interloper there, to be attacked and driven out. The unseen world belonged to phantasms and apparitions.

At first glance, the houses and cobbled street appeared much the same. Stone, wood and glass, everything inanimate, existed across both realms. Jadewin watched the Icicle Witch stagger away, reduced to a shifting misshapen shadow.

The priestess stifled her disappointment. It had been too much to hope that a single night's work could destroy a phantasm deeply rooted in local folklore. They had damaged the creature though, with her focused fury and Alory's untutored strength. If the apparition had retained its shape and intent when they had forced it back to the intangible realm, malicious daydreams and tormented nightmares would summon it back to the living world all the sooner.

She returned her gaze to reality and studied the house the phantasm had sought out. 'Phantasms like that are drawn to the fears and hatreds of the unconscious minds that spawn them. Vain and selfish young women dread losing their beauty to old age. When they resent older women in authority over them, they scorn them as ugly and decrepit.'

She pulled on her gloves. 'Most likely, some quarrel stirred up resentment in a girl who lives here. She will have an unsuspected, minor talent for magic which created this manifestation.'

Identifying the family would be easy enough. The temple in Hurat banked prosperous households' coin and validated business dealings. Material wealth stemmed from the Goddess's bounty after all. In every province across the realm, priestesses assessed the taxes owed to the Arafaze crown. In Hurat, a proportion was paid in silver and gold to the castellan as the king's representative. Letters of exchange sent to distant Velasta accounted for the rest.

Jadewin turned her back on the silent house. Her sisters would tell her this family's history, tensions, friendships and rivalries. As midwives and nurses, priestesses attended childbeds and deathbeds. As teachers, they instructed the young in their letters and numbers, hearing artless childish confidences about homes and families.

'What will happen to her?' Alory tried to hide his misgivings.

Jadewin wondered what dark hints he had heard about the Sun Goddess's wrath from the priests who trained him. 'Barely one man or woman in a hundred has any talent for magic. Of those, barely one in a thousand has an instinct for the unreal which is strong enough to be trained. There's every chance we'll only need turn tonight's malcontent towards some positive purpose to focus their mind on the here and now.'

If not, if whoever had unknowingly summoned the phantasm turned out to be powerfully talented but proved stubborn, or unteachable, their fate would be one of the Moon God's secrets which Jadewin didn't want to know. Alory would learn whatever the Hidden Brethren chose to tell him of the justice they delivered in the Lord of Mysteries' name. Right now, her feet were so cold that she couldn't feel her toes, even wearing two pairs of thick stockings. 'Let's get—'

Bells rang out from temple and shrine. Alory stared at her, aghast.

'Wait.' Jadewin raised a calming hand, even though her own heart was pounding. 'That's not an alarm.'

The bells would be ringing frantic and haphazard if some fire were raging. No unforeseen flood could have surged down the two rivers that flanked this point of land where Hurat's walls defied all-comers. The waters were frozen solid for a start. No invaders could have got so close to the town to attack unseen. No, this was something far worse. The temple's bell was tolling steadily, answered by the Moon God's shrine.

She clapped her gloved hands to get Alory's attention. 'What's the quickest route to the crescent gate?' The boy had lived here all his life and they had no time to waste. The shrine was much closer than the temple.

'This way.' Alory led her a short distance before cutting along an alley to a broader thoroughfare. The young priest zig-zagged along footpaths between the blocks of tall houses to reach another street.

A crowd had already gathered in the square in front of the Horned God's shrine. Some people were dressed for the bitter cold. Others had snatched up clothes closest to hand and would soon regret their haste. Lanterns and candles kindled in windows overlooking the square glowed golden with an illusion of warmth.

Beneath the great hammered silver crescent, the gate swung open. Shrine Father Memlin in his long black robes walked forward with a parchment in his hands. Jadewin noted the profusion of lead seals dangling from braided ribbons threaded through the document's lower edge. Speculation scurried around the square.

'That has to be news from Velasta.' She instantly regretted speaking to Alory as anxious faces turned towards her. To her relief, Father Memlin raised his voice.

'Good people of Hurat! A crown envoy has brought grievous tidings.' The veteran priest shook his grey head, unable to deny this news. 'I must tell you, with the most profound sorrow, that our beloved King Venais is dead. He died on the twenty-second day of the last Ice Moon.'

Every voice in the crowded square fell silent. For a long moment, it seemed nobody even drew breath. Then Father Memlin turned back to the crescent gate. Questions and protests bombarded him. King Venais was a young man! What calamity could have befallen him? Had he been stricken by illness?

Father Memlin offered no answers. The shrine's gate closed behind him. Shocked townsfolk turned to each other, trying to make sense of this tragedy.

Jadewin tapped Alory's forearm. 'Join your brothers.'

She watched the boy hurry across the square to knock on the small door set into the tall crescent gate. It opened a crack and he was recognised. As Alory slid through, Jadewin walked briskly away, avoiding anyone's gaze. No one approached her as they would have done in Velasta. That was one good thing about being a stranger here.

Jadewin walked through the icy streets as fast as she dared. Temple Mother Finevre must know more than the brief announcement Father Memlin had shared. Those official parchments would be sent to every temple and shrine. Medicine's mysteries fell within the Moon God's purview, but ever since the Golden Mother and the Horned God had divided day from night, the deities worked together to ensure the world they created prospered. Their servants did the same.

Whatever had happened, the king had died while she was travelling to Hurat. This must be the last place in the realm to receive the dreadful news. The remote border province was more than five hundred leagues from Velasta. With the river Dore frozen solid, no courier boats could bring news downstream. Those parchments, heavily weighted with so many noble seals, would have been carried by successive crown couriers risking the hazards of winter roads.

She still couldn't understand this. Whether the king had suffered some injury, or fallen ill, how could the Moon God's servants have failed so completely? The capital's priests were the realm's finest physicians. Then another question struck her so forcefully she skidded on the ice and nearly fell over.

Why didn't the proclamation declare Princess Idelina as the new monarch? The line of succession was clear, even if no one would ever have expected to see King Venais's sister wear the Arafaze crown. Why hadn't Father Memlin reassured the horrified populace by announcing their new queen's reign, blessed by Velasta's high temple and high shrine?

Chapter Two

VELASTA

18th Day of the Snow Moon

'The princess won't see anyone from the high temple, or the high shrine?' Reske cradled his glass in his blunt-fingered hands. The liquor's aroma promised fragrant warmth sliding down his throat. Not that Chamberlain Korel's luxurious sitting room was cold, even on this bitter winter evening. A log crackled softly on a bed of embers in the fireplace.

'We have orders to turn away anybody serving the Goddess or the God.' Facing Reske across the polished rosewood table, Korel didn't take offence at being asked to repeat himself. 'What do you suppose the High Priest and the High Priestess think of that? How do the realm's nobles feel about the princess's retreat from public life?'

Reske took a sip of the barley sunshine and rolled the smooth spirit around his mouth. He wasn't only taking time to think. Korel enjoyed gifts of the finest delicacies and expensive liquors as Velasta's merchants competed to supply Princess Idelina's household.

Korel also dealt in information. Reske owed his long-standing friend answers, and not merely because, newly sworn to the crown's service, they had been casual, youthful lovers twenty or more years ago. After he had served his twenty years, first as a cavalry trooper and then as a courier, Reske had given his oath to the Earl of Shirlat as a liegeman. His lord wanted to know what was going on inside Princess Idelina's sprawling mansion. That's why Reske was here.

Unfortunately, Reske had more questions than answers, multiplying like the rats in Velasta's sewers. He put down his glass. 'Has any noble lord or lady tried to visit her highness in recent days?'

'We've seen no one since the middle of last month.' Korel's beard bristled as he pursed his lips. 'Those in court circles are doubtless respecting the princess's grief. Everyone saw she was overcome at the late king's funeral.'

Overcome was one way to put it. Reske would have said Princess Idelina had been furious. Nobles and commoners alike had witnessed her vehemently reject the high temple mother, and the high temple father, as they tried to offer solace.

Shock on Velasta's streets at such impiety had swiftly yielded to sympathy. The princess and her little daughter hadn't only lost her adored brother Venais. Her beloved husband Maren had died in this tragedy too. All the same, Reske knew the common folk's patience wouldn't last. Talk in taverns and stable yards was already turning to speculation about Princess Idelina's coronation.

'Is there any sign of the princess's mourning running its course?'

'Who can say?' Concern shadowed the chamberlain's eyes. 'My mistress has no one to comfort her since her royal mother left yesterday. At Princess Idelina's insistence,' he added with a grimace.

'Is that so?' Reske wanted to hear more about that. Dowager Queen Sefriya's carriage had left the city when the sun had barely risen above the rooftops. Rumour ran rife around Velasta, with people of every rank debating how the strong-willed princess and her meek and gentle mother had fallen out this time. Reske wondered how soon they might be reconciled without King Venais to play peacemaker?

'I wonder when Princess Alriad will emerge from her mourning.' The chamberlain reached for the bottle and topped up their glasses. 'I gather she receives regular visitors from the high temple offering counsel for her loss.'

'So I hear.' Reske understood Korel wanted to know well ahead of time so his mistress could be forewarned of her royal aunt's intentions.

Reske and Earl Debin had discussed how soon Princess Alriad might send out invitations to a poetry reception or a musical performance for select guests. The late King Fedrin's sister had been the arbiter of fashions and trends among the noble and influential since her own girlhood. After her wedding to Earl Lystro of Coylure, her patronage had made dressmakers, musicians and artists rich. Withdrawal of her favour could beggar them. She had married later than most, but the Goddess had blessed her with healthy sons and daughters. They were now grown to within a few years of marriageable age, making Princess Alriad the foremost hostess of noble gatherings in Velasta.

Reske had no doubt Princess Alriad grieved for her nephew as sincerely as she had mourned her brother's death barely a decade before. But as voices in taverns across Velasta agreed, every family from highest to lowest suffered unexpected deaths. The Moon God alone knew his reasons and the Sun Goddess's blessings ensured that life went on.

Korel looked Reske in the eye. 'Word of the king's death will have reached the furthest provinces of the realm. Riders will be coming from the western baronies with letters from their suzerains to the high temple, the high shrine, and to anyone else who those noble lords and ladies can ask why they weren't told the full story from the outset.'

Reske nodded. He and Korel had agreed that initial despatch was woefully ill-advised, sharing a bottle of wine on the dreadful evening when King Venais and Earl Maren of Evarise had been brought back dead from their hunting expedition. Not saying plainly how the monarch and his closest friend had died had been a foolish, pointless error. The most distant nobility had their own ways to get news from the royal court and the capital. So did the merchants who traded up and down the great rivers flowing through the realm. They were bound to be wondering what else they weren't being told.

'You think there's some threat in the west? From the principalities between Arafaze and the ocean coast?' Reske wasn't convinced. 'That declaration of King Venais' death may have lacked crucial detail but it was signed and sealed by the realm's most powerful nobles.'

Korel shook his head. 'The first proclamation lacked the seals of the high shrine and the high temple. It didn't proclaim Queen Idelina's reign with the blessing of the God and the Goddess. The Arafaze crown's ties to the western principalities aren't so strong these days. Not since the old king turned his back on generations of tradition, and let his children marry to suit themselves instead of serving the interests of the realm.'

Since the two of them were much the same age, Reske knew Korel meant King Serken, father to Alriad and Fedrin, grandfather to Venais and Idelina. Before he could answer, an urgent knock rattled the door.

'Enter.' The chamberlain was ready to glare at whoever was interrupting his leisure between overseeing the princess's dinner and securing the mansion for the night.

'She's here again.' The harassed maidservant was as incensed as she was out of breath from running. 'That woman with the hand. She's pestering Brother Haber.'

'Is she now?' Wrathful, Korel stood up and rebuttoned his russet velvet doublet. He shot a brief glance across the table as the maidservant left. 'I must deal with this.'

'I'll be on my way.' Reske drained his glass and got to his feet.

'We'll talk again tomorrow.' Korel was already at the door, smoothing the lace edging his shirt collar. The chamberlain hurried away without a backward glance.

Reske made his way through the servants' domain to a narrow door that opened into the mansion's vast grounds. A lackey sitting glumly on a stool roused himself to find the key. Reske took his cloak from the peg where he'd left it and found the closely woven wool was nearly dry.

As the door closed behind him, he glanced towards the mansion's encircling wall. Even with the intermittent moonlight misted by winter's incessant drizzle, the dark outlines of sentries patrolled the high walk at a measured pace. With their halberds sloped over their shoulders, they looked outwards for sneak thieves hoping the cold and damp might blunt the guards' alertness.

Reske raised his hood. He didn't head for the great gate which admitted carriages bringing noble guests to enjoy entertainments in the opulent reception rooms or the formal gardens. He made his way through the cobbled yards and outbuildings tucked behind the mansion, where day-to-day necessities were delivered and stored, linens were laundered and ale was brewed. Countless mundane tasks kept this household running, no matter who lived or died.

Since this was a crown mansion, Korel could call on a resident priest-physician to treat illness or injury among the servants. Reske guessed Brother Haber was staying out of Princess Idelina's sight, to avoid being sent back to the God's shrine. Hearing angry voices as he approached the servants' main entrance, Reske pushed back his hood to hear and see more clearly, making sure he stayed hidden.

A tall woman in a long dark cloak stood toe to toe with Brother Haber. Her braided grey hair was uncovered despite the mizzle. Reske didn't recognise her. Whoever she might be, she was used to being obeyed.

'I demand to speak to the groom who witnessed Earl Maren's death. You have no right to deny me. I must know what he saw in exact detail.' She loomed over the balding, mild-faced priest.

Brother Haber wasn't remotely impressed. 'He is my patient and I will not allow it. Asking the poor child to revisit those dreadful deaths will cause him further distress.'

'I am Earl Padran of Evarise's personal representative. The noble lord has the right to know precisely how his brother died.' The woman brandished a letter in the light of the oil lamp hanging over the door. 'The boy wasn't injured. The lightning strike didn't touch him. Now the shock has faded, he may recall further details of that day. I insist on asking him myself.'

'You may consult his account of that day held by the high shrine's infirmarians. They wrote down the recollections of everyone they treated who witnessed the tragedy.' Brother Haber tucked his hands inside the sleeves of his thick black robe. 'I can vouch for the boy's honesty.'

No one could argue with that. The Moon God granted his priests the power to hear falsehoods. Everyone saw such magic at work when the nobility held assizes to punish criminals within their fiefdoms, where the justiciars delivered their verdicts in the crown's name. A priest was always on hand to unmask anyone telling lies. Just as a pale-robed priestess used the power the Goddess granted her to endorse truth.

'Your obstruction is unacceptable.' The woman took a half-step sideways.

Startled, Reske thought she was going to force her way past the priest. Korel appeared at Brother Haber's shoulder. He might have been wearing a tailored doublet, velvet breeches and soft leather shoes, but he drilled daily with the weapons he and Reske had mastered in their youth.

'You have already been turned away twice.' The princess's chamberlain didn't hide his disdain. 'I don't know why you expected a different answer if you called at this late hour. Did you hope to bully your way past some hapless lackey? Never mind. Please leave and do not come back with this request. If your master sends you on other business, kindly call at a more civilised time.'

For a moment, Reske thought the woman was going to threaten Korel with some retaliation. Instead her heavy cloak flared as she spun around and stalked away.

Korel stepped aside to allow a liveried man out through the door. 'Go with her. Make sure every guard knows to hold her at the gate if she turns up again. Whatever the hour, and whatever she says brings her here.'

As the guard hurried after the unknown woman, Brother Haber turned to Korel, troubled.

'I don't understand why she's so insistent on interrogating the boy. Granted it's rare for lightning to kill, and rarer still for a single strike to hit two people, but such deaths have been recorded. There were plenty of other witnesses besides the lad.'

The priest closed the door on their conversation. Reske hurried after the guard following the unwelcome visitor. Anything out of the ordinary deserved a closer look at present.

As the stranger approached the back gatehouse in the mansion's encircling wall, the guard called out. 'Open up the wicket and let her pass!'

The sentry promptly obliged. The woman's long strides hardly slowed as she passed through the narrow portal. The double gates for wagons and carriages had been barred at dusk.

She turned right to follow the lane running alongside the wall. The liveried guard was repeating Korel's instructions to the sentry. They barely glanced at Reske as he left. Everyone knew he was the Earl of Shirlat's liegeman, and their chamberlain said he could be trusted.

Outside the mansion, Reske pulled up his hood and kept to the shadows. The woman turned into a wide, tree-lined road. When Princess Idelina's great-great aunt's new home had been built outside the ancient city walls, this had been a district of glades and grazing. Within a generation the royal mansion was ringed by luxurious houses where noble families from distant provinces would spend the spring and autumn. Sons and daughters mingled at dances and entertainments while their parents discussed more serious concerns. The spring equinox feast would see these thoroughfares and side-streets busy with carriages and crossing-sweepers while the flower gardens perfumed the evening air.

For now the roads were deserted. Reske followed the woman past silent houses with dark, shuttered windows. He was ready to dodge behind a tree or a gatepost, but the woman didn't glance over her shoulder once.

He wondered how many barons and baronesses ruling fiefdoms within easy reach would come to Velasta as soon as the worst winter weather was over. Those in the city when the coronation date was declared could be the first to congratulate the new queen, well-placed to gain her favour. Reske decided to check for signs of the servants who tended these properties lighting fires to drive out the damp and taking delivery of provisions.

As the woman kept walking, he wondered where she was going. This wasn't the way to Earl Maren's – Earl Padran of Evarise's residence. Artisans lived among their workshops in this district, alongside those skilled in less honourable trades.

The woman accosted an urchin with a candle lantern loitering outside a tavern. She flipped the child a coin, but she wasn't hiring the light to see her home. The woman shoved the urchin towards the tavern door. Reske waited in a dark alleyway on the other side of the road. The child soon reappeared, followed by four individuals wearing heavy boots and thick jerkins, with hard faces and suspicious eyes. Three men and one woman, Reske reckoned, though at this distance he couldn't be certain.

He could only watch as the tall woman handed over what must be a purse of coin. She issued instructions with swift gestures. One man shook his head and turned away. She challenged him with a jabbing forefinger, stepping so close she could have poked him in the eye. Reske recalled the maidservant mentioning the woman's hand. She only seemed to use her right arm.

He saw the hireling's shoulders slump. Whoever she was, these ne'er-do-wells believed she would make good on whatever she had just threatened. A dray rumbled past, blocking Reske's view. When the heavyset horses and the barrel-laden wagon passed by, he couldn't see the woman or her hirelings anywhere

Reske cursed the bad timing. He'd visit the tavern tomorrow and spread some silver around to see what he might learn. He walked quickly through the city to the Earl of Shirlat's residence. The salon windows were lit and the last of the evening's guests were leaving. As one of old King Serken's inner circle, Earl Debin had grown accustomed to wintering in Velasta decades ago.

This house would have fitted into a single wing of Princess Idelina's mansion. Reske had a key to the door from the yard at the side. He made his way to the earl's private sitting room. The oil lamp had been lit earlier together with the fire. Reske would never get used to such extravagance. He threw some wood into the hearth and draped his cloak over a stool to dry.

As he helped himself to a glass of the clean spring water, Earl Debin came through the door. Lean and hatchet-faced, he was old enough to be Reske's father, if Reske was a younger son in a long family. The earl kicked off his elegant shoes and unbuttoned his silk doublet. Walking to the sideboard in his embroidered stockings, he poured himself a glass of wine.

'Well?' His hair shone white in the lamplight as he took a seat at his writing desk.

Reske summarised everything he had learned, though not who provided these insights. Earl Debin never asked, just as he never asked who Reske told the things he learned in this room.

The earl took a sip of wine. 'Idelina's refusal to engage with the crown's obligations is testing everyone's patience. Her rejection of the shrine and the temple's envoys is troubling many people too. She cannot be crowned without the Goddess's blessing and the God's. Someone needs to talk some sense into the girl, though I don't know who can do that, since Queen Sefriya has left the city.'

He gestured at a pile of unfolded letters with broken wax seals. 'That inadequate declaration is still causing trouble. Though I have finally found out what happened. Customarily, when a monarch dies, the leader of the crown council takes charge of such matters, instructed by the heir, but with Idelina incapacitated by grief...'

His exasperated gesture was eloquent. 'Earl Lystro and Earl Padran were too busy quarrelling over whose name and seal should be attached to the parchments first to agree on a fuller account of the tragedy. Naturally the noble earls are now blaming each other.'

'I see.' Reske noted Lystro of Coylure had got the upper hand in that argument, with his name and seal heading the list of those signing the declaration. He would be regretting his victory now.

'At least we don't need to fret about trouble from the west, and we can thank Lystro of Coylure for that,' Earl Debin went on. 'If he hears a whisper that his cousins and nephews and nieces married into the western baronies are seeking advantage from this calamity, he'll remind them it will serve their best interests to have Princess Alriad's husband as a friend rather than an enemy.'

The earl sighed. 'I'm more concerned about the east. Venais's promise to wed the King of Mervante's daughter is as dead as mutton, but King Tadiri won't shrug off his disappointment.'

Reske had wondered about that. The betrothal had been announced over a year ago, but there had been no hint of wedding preparations.

Earl Debin looked grim. 'He'll seek some other route to influence over Hurat. We can be thankful he is cautious and that winter lingers so far from the ocean. We have some time in hand.'

Reske tried to recall what he knew of Hurat. He'd been sent to the realm's most easterly province maybe a handful of times in his courier days. As with any other such journey, he only recalled crown way-stations, highways in good and bad repair, and delivering his message to someone in crown livery.

'Earl Padran of Evarise has no wife.' he observed. 'Would King Tadiri accept the queen's brother by marriage for his daughter? Especially if Padran has ambitions to take his brother's place as Queen Idelina's foremost counsellor.'

Earl Debin shook his head. 'His weaselness wants a grandchild wearing the Arafaze crown. Besides, even if Padran of Evarise was willing, Lystro of Coylure would rouse opposition to the match.'

Reske couldn't argue with that. The Earl of Coylure had spoken constantly of the perilous consequences if Venais were to die with his heir still in swaddling clothes. The young widow would surely turn to her father for guidance in her grief.

'At least he can't claim his weaselness had King Venais poisoned.' Coylure's associates were the first to repeat rumours of Mervantese fondness for poison whenever some notable in King Tadiri's court fell ill and died. The younger nobles of King Venais's inner circle countered with the undeniable fact that Mervante had more than its share of fatal pestilence.

Earl Debin drummed wrinkled fingers on his leather-topped desk. 'Mervante has claimed Hurat's grainlands south of the river Dore since time out of mind. Once Venais had a child with Mervantese blood, I imagined King Tadiri would propose the Dore as the new boundary between the realms. He has always been willing to play the long game. Many of the crown council would glance at a map and agree, between filling their bellies at a noon banquet and dressing for their evening's entertainment. It would put an end to the bloody skirmishes between Hurat's cavalry patrols and King Tadiri's scouts for a start.'

The white-haired earl grimaced. 'Now? I suspect Tadiri will stir unrest. The hill-country hotheads are always ready to make trouble as soon as the thaw arrives. Then there's no knowing what mischief the marsh-dwellers in the Nilgeh Mire might make, with the nobility of the Tane and the Dore looking westward to Velasta.'

Earl Debin broke off. 'You have no idea what I'm talking about. You're not alone.'

'I'll learn.' Reske disliked having his ignorance exposed.

His liege lord had moved on. 'We have more immediate concerns. This rift between Princess Idelina and the shrine and the temple has to be mended. To do that, we must learn what's caused it.' He yawned. 'But I am ready for my bed. That can be your task for tomorrow.'

'Good night, my lord.' Reske stood up, bowed, grabbed his cloak, and left the residence by the side door. He headed for Princess Idelina's mansion. Korel wouldn't be going to bed before midnight. Reske would share what he had learned from Earl Debin, and he'd try to talk to Brother Haber. Perhaps the priest could shed some light on Princess Idelina's hostility to the God's and the Goddess's servants.

Reske had concluded long ago that even the crown's couriers couldn't rival the speed and accuracy of the shrines and temples for gathering and sharing information. The brothers of the crescent gate shared improved treatments for the injured and ailing across the realm. Priestesses travelled widely as guardians of the wealth flowing from the Golden Mother's blessings. Her daughters recorded all but the most trivial payments and debts in their ledgers. They safeguarded the passing of wealth from generation to generation by attending women in childbed, and witnessing deathbed wishes as they eased suffering and distress.

The rain fell more heavily and a strengthening breeze emphasised the chill. There were fewer folk on the streets. Reske walked fast. He'd run this errand and then he'd sleep soundly. The earl's housekeeper, his current lover, would have had a maid tuck a flannel-wrapped hot brick under his blankets.

He reached the tree-lined street leading to the lane that circled the princess's mansion. Scudding clouds obscured the moon, making a cluster of figures ahead no more than shadows. One wore a long, dark cape, backing away, raising pleading hands. ,The others spread out, brandishing cudgels, and with scarves wrapped around their heads.

As they attacked, their victim hunched desperate shoulders, arms raised to protect their head. Cries of pain cut through the night as blows landed hard and fast. An attacker laughed as the victim's knees buckled. Now the attackers could use their boots.

Reske was running, reaching for a specially tailored pocket in his breeches. This wasn't some street robbery. As he got closer, he realised the attackers were the grey-haired woman's hirelings. Hired to do what?

Intent on their victim, none of the brutes saw or heard him approaching. His short cloak and breeches were sewn from charcoal-grey broadcloth to merge with the shadows, and he had long ago mastered the skill of moving quietly at speed.

Reske kicked the closest man hard in the back of one knee. The brute staggered and went sprawling over the victim. The other attackers stared, momentarily confused.

Reske moved first. The woman to his left instinctively raised her weapon. Before she could strike, Reske stepped closer and slammed his cosh into her forearm. It was barely twice the length of his hand, but the tightly stitched leather was packed with lead shot.

Bone cracked. The woman yelped and dropped her club. Reske grabbed her by the throat, forcing her backwards. She staggered, pressing her broken arm to her chest.

The first man to fall was getting to his feet. Reske threw the woman at him. Tangled together, they knocked the next man off his feet. The woman screamed. The last man leaped backwards to save himself. Dropping his club, he ran off into the darkness.

Reske scooped up the nearest cudgel and assessed his choices. He couldn't detain these three on his own. He could stop them running by breaking their knees, or with a potentially murderous blow to the head, while he fetched Princess Idelina's guards. But he would have to answer for his actions in open court when the brutes were brought before a justiciar. Reske's usefulness to the earl relied on going unnoticed.

The figure huddled on the ground raised himself up on one elbow and his hood fell back. Bother Haber's bald head was smeared with blood from a ragged gash. 'What—?

'How badly are you hurt?' Reske demanded.

The priest gasped with unexpected pain. 'My ribs.'

The scrape of a boot on the cobbles betrayed an attacker edging away on his arse. Reske watched him, ready to defend the priest. The man shuffled further off. Reske didn't move.

If the princess's guards seized these three, he'd have no chance to question them. If he let them run, he knew where to pick up their trail. Track them down, and he could learn what they knew by calling in this debt.

The woman whimpered, cradling her broken arm. The other man's scarf had been ripped aside, stained with blood from a split lip. As they found their footing, Reske's cold stare made it clear, if they tried to rush him, he would crack their skulls and the Moon God could decide their fate.

The cold wind plucked at the bloodied attacker's scarf. The priest's laboured breath rasped in the silence. Reske sprang forward with a wordless yell, brandishing the cosh and the club. The cowering brutes fled.

'What—?' Brother Haber coughed wetly.

The priest's unfocused eyes worried Reske. 'Can you stand?'

Haber spat blood onto the cobbles. 'I think so.'

Reske offered his hand. 'Let's get you safe and warm.'

The priest struggled to his feet. 'Who attacks the Horned God's servants?'

Reske didn't answer. He knew who was behind this, even if he didn't know her name, her allegiance or her reason for this outrage. As the Father of Night was his witness, he was going to find out.

Chapter Three

HURAT

10th of the Thaw Moon

Jadewin passed through the open gate in Hurat town's great western rampart. When Mother Finevre had first shown her around, the older priestess had explained this mighty wall of earth and stone ran from the southward bank of the curving Tane to the northerly bank of the Dore. It cut off this entire spearpoint of land thrusting eastwards until the two great rivers met at its tip. She crossed the wooden bridge over the great ditch in front of the town gate, where stone for the rampart had been quarried, according to Mother Finevre.

Jadewin walked briskly towards the castle, mindful of slippery mud underfoot. The Goddess's business hadn't brought her outside the town before now and she was curious to see the vast fortress built by King Venais' famous ancestor, King Ganirin the Bold. He had led Arafaze's armies east of the Bastrys mountains, to drive back the marauding Mervantese before they could reach the Hedvin Gap. The Vale of Hurat's noble families had fought alongside Ganirin and sworn fealty to him after their victory.

The castellan held Hurat as the king's proxy in the province. He commanded the crown's cavalry, cannoneers, and the foot soldiers who kept the peace in the town and guarded the ferries. These forces wore the crown's insignia. In that way, Hurat reminded Jadewin of Velasta, where no other livery challenged the crown's authority. No one set foot within the capital's ancient and crumbling walls wearing the colours of whichever earl or countess commanded their liege lord or lady's fealty.

Which was all very interesting, but Mother Finevre had sent her to the castle to find out what might be of use here and now. She rounded the outwork that defended the main entrance and saw two footsoldiers standing on either side of the gate with their halberds at rest. Both young men dutifully bent their heads as she approached the tunnel that cut through the rampart.

The elder greeted her politely. 'Good morning, sister. Please, proceed.'

'Goddess bless you.' Jadewin could see daylight at the far end of the tunnel. Torches burned in brackets to banish the shadows, and a guardroom had been built into the rampart's thickness, halfway along.

A grey-haired, liveried soldier stepped through the guardroom door. 'Good sister, may I know your name and your business?'

Jadewin quelled an impulse to glance over her shoulder, to see if those lads were blocking her escape with their halberds.

'By all means, sergeant.' She offered him Mother Finevre's unsealed note. 'I am here to see Castellan Maixen.'

The sergeant snapped his fingers before reading the note. A young woman appeared in the guardroom doorway and waited. When he was done, the sergeant passed her the paper. 'Find the commander.'

As the footsoldier ran off, the grey-haired man grinned at Jadewin. 'He could be anywhere and we'd waste half the morning wandering around. Let's see how soon the lass can find him while I give you the tour.'

'Thank you, Sergeant...?'

'Sergeant Lund, sister.' He escorted her into the castle's courtyard.

Jadewin blinked as they emerged. The sky was cloudless and the sun was bright. Well-worn paving drew a line across the cobbles from the castle's entrance to the great square keep. Sergeant Lund pointed to a modest stone building half way along the path. Its iron-bound wooden door stood open with hospitable benches on either side. 'That's our sanctuary, sister. If you wish, we can wait there for Jorin.'

'The Goddess has sent us a sunny day. Let's enjoy it.' She gazed around. 'This is my first visit. Tell me more about your castle.'

Sergeant Lund pointed to a small building to the right of the keep. 'That's the well house.'

Jadewin could have guessed that. Castle servants swung empty buckets as they approached, while others emerged carrying full ones away with more care.

Lund indicated a battered cannon some way beyond. 'The artillery training ground.'

Youthful cannoneers clustered around a formidable weapon. Their sergeant's barked commands echoed across the extensive enclosure.

'Swab! Charge! Wad! Ram! Ball! Again!'

The wooden hafts of long tools clashed as the young cannoneers got in each other's way.

'New recruits.' Sergeant Lund chuckled. 'They've got a lot to learn before they'll be trusted with firing-powder and shot.'

'Where will they do that?' Jadewin couldn't imagine such risks were taken here.

'In the old castle quarries,' the sergeant assured her. 'Well away from the town.'

Footsoldiers were drilling with halberds on the open ground beyond the sweating artillery recruits. In the other direction, Jadewin saw stables, workshops and storehouses beyond the keep, and ranges of accommodation in the distance. Pruned trees hinted at a garden over that way. People came and went everywhere.

'Let me show you the sanctuary,' Sergeant Lund suggested.

'By all means.' Jadewin took the hint this time.

Reaching the open door, she looked inside. The Sun Goddess's altar faced the one dedicated to the Moon God. The Golden Mother's icon smiled with arms outstretched to embrace her children. The Father of Night's presence was marked by a twice life-size copy of the smooth silver mask his priests wore to hear sins confessed or when they stood witness as crimes were judged. Every sanctuary was laid out the same, while different artisans made each one unique.

'There's Jorin.' Sergeant Lund was looking outward from the threshold.

Jadewin saw the young woman leaving the keep through a door in the closest tower. The priestess took the opportunity to glance into the unseen world. The castle buildings were unchanged, and as far as Jadewin could see, the unreal realm was deserted. That was good to know.

Jorin reached them and saluted the sergeant before turning to the priestess. 'Castellan Maixen's compliments, sister, and you are invited to join him in his audience chamber.'

'Thank you.' Sergeant Lund dismissed the footsoldier with an approving nod. 'This way, sister.'

As he led Jadewin towards the keep, a lean, bald-headed man opened the tower door. The sergeant introduced him. 'Steward Senon.'

'This way, sister.' The steward stepped back to let her enter. 'The castellan is upstairs.'

'Thank you.' Jadewin walked up stone spiral steps. The first door she reached stood open into an airy chamber with wide, mullioned windows. Pale wood panelling reminded her of prosperous houses in Velasta. Two cushioned chairs stood on either side of a low table, set at a comfortable distance from a fireplace. On the other side of the room, a long, polished table flanked with bench seats would suit larger gatherings with some sterner purpose.

Castellan Maixen stood by the low table and chairs, holding Mother Finevre's note. From the silver glints in his dark hair, Jadewin guessed he was much her own age. She noted the plain cloth and cut of his dark grey crown livery. The military's senior echelons in Velasta favoured expensive tailors, claiming they must dress to equal their noble rivals for the king's attention at court.

Mother Finevre had assured her Hurat's castellan was no fool, and nor were the officers he commanded, for the most part anyway. That would make a refreshing change. Jadewin had long ago concluded that eminence and influence in Velasta's court circles was too often won by skilful flattery instead of proven achievement.

'May I take your cape, sister?' the steward Senon asked.

'By all means.' Jadewin stuffed her gloves into the pockets and unfastened the clasp.

'I'll fetch refreshments.' The steward draped her cape over one arm and withdrew, closing the door behind him.

'Shall we sit?' Castellan Maixen refolded Mother Finevre's note.

'Yes please.' Jadewin was glad to get close to the warmth. She managed to restrain herself from stretching her hands out to the modest flames.

The castellan took the other seat. 'The cold takes some getting used to.'

She matched his friendly tone. 'Aren't you used to it? Someone told me you were Hurat born and bred.'

Maixen was caught unawares. 'I suppose that's true. I was born on this side of the Bastrys mountains, in a tiny village in Sospirin's hinterland. But I enlisted in my fourteenth summer, and I've served the crown across Arafaze. I had forgotten how cold winters here can be until I was given this command.'

'Let us be thankful for the Goddess's gifts of firewood and for the Dark God's gift of coal.' Jadewin settled comfortably in her chair. 'So, Mother Finevre is curious to know what you might have learned of recent events in Velasta. Confidentially, of course. Similarly, she has sent me to share news which you might find of use.'

'Please assure her the Goddess can trust my discretion, in the name of the Keeper of Secrets.' Maixen's face was as serious as his words. 'I receive letters from a friend in Velasta who I will not name, so do not ask.'

'Of course.' Jadewin agreed. 'What have you been told about the king's death?'

'We know King Venais went hunting. What hasn't been widely shared is he insisted on riding out for the thrill of the chase even with foul weather threatening.' Maixen shook his head. 'The sky turned black with thunder clouds far sooner than anyone expected. His party was caught in the storm and a bolt of lightning struck the king and Maren of Evarise who was riding beside him. Both died in the single strike.'

The castellan leaned forward, resting his elbows on his knees. 'As soon as the dead men were carried back to the palace, Earl Maren's brother Padran claimed the Evarise seal as heir to the earldom. His brother's marriage settlement relinquished all claims there on behalf of any children the princess might bear him. It seems Padran is now issuing orders to the crown forces and the crown couriers in Princess Idelina's name, even though she has still not been proclaimed as queen by the high temple or the high shrine. Can you shine any light on that?'

Jadewin shared what she and Mother Finevre had agreed Hurat's castellan needed to know. 'Princess Idelina has more to contend with than the double tragedy of losing her husband and her beloved brother. She is pregnant.'

'That would ordinarily be cause for congratulations.'

Maixen's tone was neutral, but Jadewin noted the shrewd alertness in his dark eyes. She explained.

'Three years ago, after Princess Olyshai's birth, Idelina's life hung in the balance. She was advised by the high temple's most experienced midwives not to risk bearing another child. As you know, such prudence is within the Goddess's gift. Princess Idelina chose to ignore this advice. More than that, she rebuked Velasta's priestesses for their lack of faith and has refused to let them attend her. We can only pray the Golden Mother protects her and the unborn child.'

Jadewin tried not to sound too critical. She didn't doubt the power of the divine. How could she, when the Golden Mother had blessed her with insight and influence in the unreal realm? Even so, Goddess and God alike expected their mortal creations to use the common sense they were given.

'Do we know when she's likely to be brought to childbed?'

Jadewin could see the castellan was making the obvious calculations

'If we assume the princess conceived shortly before her husband died, the child should be born in the latter days of the Thunder Moon, or the early days of the Hay Moon. The princess may not survive, and there is no way to know if the baby will live to take its first breath. Mother Finevre believes Velasta's high priestess and high priest are waiting for the Goddess and the God to decide Idelina's fate before temple or shrine makes any declaration.'

Maixen grimaced. 'So we could be looking at half a year of uncertainty. If Princess Idelina doesn't survive her ordeal, the crown will pass to little Princess Olyshai, and the realm will be ruled by a toddler still learning to count.' He made the sign of the crescent moon with his left hand to avert misfortune. 'No disrespect to the Goddess, but it's a shame King Fedrin and Queen Sefriya didn't have more children. And King Serken and Queen Misene, come to that.'

'That was none of the Goddess's doing,' Jadewin said tartly. 'You started your career in the cavalry. You should know the consequences when bloodlines are bred too closely together, one generation after the next. Let us be thankful that King Serken had the sense to ensure his own children did not marry their cousins, after everything Queen Misene suffered through miscarriages and stillbirths.'

She cleared her throat. 'Let us pray for the best possible outcomes. If the worst should happen, a regency council would be formed, presumably led by Earl Padran of Evarise as the little queen's uncle.'

'What about Earl Lystro of Coylure?' Maixen countered. 'His wife, Princess Alriad is – was – aunt to both King Venais and Princess Idelina.'

'Indeed.' Jadewin remembered that extravagant wedding two decades or so ago, when the princess had finally chosen one of her many suitors. Half of Velasta's populace had eaten and drunk themselves cross-eyed at the crown's expense. Venais had been hailed as the heir apparent, newly released from his nursemaids' care to begin his education with a succession of tutors. Everyone had expected another glorious feast in another decade or so, when the young prince chose his bride to continue the royal line.

The priestess chose her words carefully. 'When King Fedrin gave his beloved sister's hand in marriage – his twin sister, no less – to his closest friend, Lystro, Earl of Coylure was brought into the heart of the realm's councils and decisions. After King Fedrin's untimely death, King Venais preferred to seek advice from his own friends. Lystro of Coylure has been quick to criticise the judgement of Venais's inner circle, though never rebuking the king himself.'

'Indeed,' Maixen said wryly. 'Did King Fedrin really die of a winter fever?'

Jadewin blinked, surprised. 'Yes, of course. Putrid congestion ravaged his lungs despite the high shrine's finest physicians' endeavours. It was only by the God's grace, and the Goddess's love, that Queen Sefriya survived.'

Though the dowager queen had suffered enduring fatigue ever since. Jadewin knew that was one reason Sefriya preferred to live in the countryside.

'Is Princess Olyshai a robust child?'

'I believe so.' Jadewin understood the castellan's concern. So many children, however cherished, died in their first half-decade despite every care temple and shrine could offer. 'Let us pray for the Goddess's blessing, so Queen Idelina sees her children grow to adulthood in peace and prosperity, educated in their duties and responsibilities long before the crown passes to Princess Olyshai.'

'From your lips to the Moon God's ears,' Maixen agreed.

'Meantime,' Jadewin prompted, 'we wonder what King Tadiri of Mervante will make of this ongoing uncertainty?'

'Trouble,' Maixen said frankly. 'Somehow, somewhere, sooner or later. Most likely sooner.'

'How well prepared is this province to repel an attack?' Jadewin was concerned for her sisters first and foremost. Together with the Moon God's sons, they would tend the wounded on any battlefields. She and Alory would have different duties, alongside those other sisters and brothers with magical talents. Supposedly the Mervantese knew nothing of the unseen world. Perhaps she would learn the truth of that, one way or the other.

Maixen got up to stare out of the closest window. 'The nobility of the Tane always look south with suspicion. If the Mervantese so much as hint at making a move, the margraves and margravines will follow Vauset of Jedfal's lead. He's shrewd and sharp-witted, and don't believe anyone who tells you he's too old to lead a campaign. His years give him a wealth of experience. His wife is – was – the last-but-one Margrave of Reole's cousin, and his eldest son married the heiress of Mithess. I believe his elder daughter is promised to the second son of the Margrave of Stannar—'

'Please.' Jadewin raised her hands to ward off this bombardment of names. 'Slower, and do you have a map to hand, so I can get my bearings?'

Maixen grinned. 'Come with me.'

As Jadewin stood up, the door opened to reveal the steward Senon carrying a tray of tea and cakes.

'We're going to the gallery,' Maixen told him. 'Please, bring that with you.'

'Castellan.' Senon stepped back to let them go ahead down the spiral stair.

Jadewin presumed they weren't leaving the keep since Maixen hadn't called for a cloak or her cape. She still felt chill drafts from doors she could hear opening and closing as they walked along a long corridor between this tower and the next. She realised the wall to their right hand was in fact a wooden partition. A section had been folded back to reveal a wide, hammer-beamed hall with ornate stained glass windows.

'That's where we'll have the coronation feast,' Maixen commented. 'Eventually.'

Jadewin imagined the dark oak tables draped with crisp white linen and garlands of flowers. The massive chandeliers would have to be lowered so their crystal lustres could be polished and the candles replaced. That wouldn't be an easy job. Nor would taking down those hanging banners to be beaten free of dust.

They reached the next tower and the castellan headed up the spiral stair. He passed one door and opened the next to reveal the uppermost floor of that side of the keep. Sunshine flooded the single long room, thanks to tall windows reaching to the rafters. Glass cases on tables on either side were opaque with reflected daylight, so Jadewin walked closer. She was astonished.

'Relief models of every town and fortress in the Vale of Hurat,' Maixen explained. 'Precise and accurate to the last hedgerow, and kept scrupulously up-to-date. My garrison captains and their cavalry patrols report any changes, when new houses are built or old wells are dug deeper, so on and so forth.'

'Remarkable.' Jadewin had never seen anything like them.

'If I ever send forces to fight the Mervantese, my captains will know every detail of the ground before they arrive.' Maixen walked along the central aisle, gesturing at the end wall. 'And here is our map.'

Jadewin turned her attention to the painted plaster. The castellan's huge map held far more detail than anything inked on parchment in Hurat's temple. She followed the line of the river Tane flowing south from the hill country beneath the sharp escarpment of the high plateau in the far north. The town of Jedfal was about halfway to Hurat, on the Tane's western bank. Painted fortresses upstream and down were identified with some of the names Maixen had mentioned. Mithess, Jedfal, Reole and Stannar.

On the eastern side of the river, starting opposite Jedfal's castle, a broad road headed north-east, dividing the hill country from gently rolling downland. Jadewin recognised the names of several towns scattered across those pastures. One reason she had been sent to teach young Alory to manage his magic was because Hurat shrine's Brother Cavore was travelling in that region, pursuing rumours of monstrous wolves. Securing the boundary between the unseen realm and the everyday world required constant vigilance.

Of course, as far as Father Memlin was aware, unable to see the unknown world, Brother Cavore was collecting records of death and disease compiled by the priests in the downland's sanctuaries. Just as Jadewin's excuse to journey out from Hurat would be auditing their financial records.

'Jedfal's influence east of the Tane runs deep,' Maixen observed, seeing where she was looking.

'Good to know.' Jadewin turned her attention to the broad waters of the Dore. She followed that wider, slower river upstream from Hurat to the rocky gorge slicing through the Bastrys mountains. That marked this province's western boundary. Jadewin used a finger to trace a line through the air, from the town of Chalus in the far west all the way to Usenas, far to the east of Hurat and a long way downstream from the confluence of the two rivers.

'What can you tell me about the barons and baronesses who rule along the Dore? Come to that, why are they honoured as barons and baronesses in the Arafaze style, rather than as margraves and margravines according to Hurat's ancient tradition? Oh, thank you.'

Senon the steward offered her a fragrant cup of silver tea. Jadewin sipped, grateful for the perfumed warmth.

Maixen swallowed a mouthful of spiced cake. 'The nobility of the Tane were still holding their own when King Ganirin and Arafaze's armies arrived to force the Mervantese back over the Dore. By then, every town along both banks of that river been razed to the ground. Anyone making a stand against the invaders had been slaughtered. As King Ganirin retook each town, he granted suzerainty over the ruins to a hand-picked commander from his army. Then he ordered Hurat and its castle to be built as the keystone in a new line of defences.'

'I see.' That was presumably why those families ruling along the Dore visited Velasta more often and had more friends in court circles than the nobility of the Tane.

Jadewin knew King Ganirin's interest in the Vale of Hurat had not only been to defend its people. Even in distant Velasta, the Goddess's daughters were aware of the wheat, barley and oats sent by the wagonload from the grainlands north and south of the Dore. Raw wool and finished cloth came from the flocks of sheep grazing the downs east of the Tane while the grasslands' herds sent salt beef, leather and horses to every province of Arafaze. Iron, steel, copper and tin came from the hill country's mines. Saltpetre and other mysterious minerals were hewn from still more distant valleys.

She pointed at the easternmost edge of the great map, where three fortresses bracketed an expanse of tufted green threaded with broken blue lines. 'Why are those castles painted in a different style?'

'Because those garrisons answer directly to me.' Maixen held out his cup and Senon refilled it from the slender-spouted silver teapot. 'When the Mervantese last invaded, they sent forces to circle around that higher ground you can see there, on the southern bank just beyond Sharrow.'

He waited for Jadewin's nod to confirm she was looking at the substantial outcrop of sharp peaks with trees cloaking their lower slopes. 'The Mervantese sneaked north along the edge of the marshes. They didn't cross the river to try to take Masecal or Usenas. Instead, they marched west as fast as they could to attack Hurat's flank, The bog-trotters let them pass through the Mire and fought alongside them. That's not going to happen again.'

'I see.' Jadewin squinted at the lettering and realised the vast marsh was in fact the Nilgeh Mire. She had known that was the source of many valuable herbs, medicinal and culinary, and a wide range of dyestuffs, but she hadn't realised where the near-mythical marsh was to be found.

'Thank you.' She took a spiced cake from the plate Senon offered and contemplated the map as a whole. Low in the south-west corner, she noted Sospirin tucked close to the edge of the forests of the Bastrys foothills. Far from any significant trade route. No wonder Maixen had sought better prospects for advancement elsewhere.

'You're welcome to study our map whenever you wish.' Maixen smiled at her. 'Since you're here, why don't I show you where to find each town's temple or sanctuary in our models? We have this tea to drink, and the cooks will scold Senon if he takes any cakes back to the kitchen.'

'Why not?' Jadewin felt a frisson of interest as she met Maixen's intent dark eyes. He was an agreeable and courteous man as well as a source of information. It was in her interests to get close to him, to learn whatever news he got from Velasta. He would be equally keen to learn what the temple might hear. Jadewin found the prospect of such give and take appealed.

Chapter Four

VELASTA

29th of the Thaw Moon

Kings might die without warning but some things never changed. Quenild had seen a good many of these Velastan merchants when she'd first visited the city as a girl, watching her father and learning his skills. He'd shown her the profits to be made by the first sail barges forcing their way upstream in the spring, as soon as the ice broke on the Dore. The trick was to offer rarities as lightweight as they were valuable.

Tables lined the Merchant Voyagers hall. Apprentices offered samples of wares to be felt, smelled or tasted with boasts and inducements. Swatches of warm woollen cloth lay alongside cool cottons and shimmering silks. Shallow bowls offered ground spices whose muted colours gave no hint of their potency. Those who traded in leathers and metals displayed finely crafted pieces showing the quality held in their storehouses.

Quenild noted which merchants had swapped a rabbit-trimmed jerkin for a velvet doublet since her last visit, and who wore satin skirts instead of a homespun gown. She also looked for those beguiled into employing some young relative with no talent for commerce. Hapless fools could be comprehensively bamboozled. As her father had said, anyone letting sentiment make business decisions deserved to pay for their folly. How else would they discover their error?

The wealthiest merchants stood aloof in sable cloaks and ermine-trimmed gowns. When an apprentice won someone's interest, their masters and mistresses stepped forward to bargain, low-voiced amid the bustle. Once offer and counteroffer reached mutual satisfaction, their clerks opened their ledgers and recorded the details. Contracts were drawn up and exchanged.

Quenild frowned. Priests should be sitting at the far end of the hall, to compare and validate those agreements with the Moon God's seal. Each merchant would take a signed and sealed copy to be lodged in their chosen shrine's archive, in case of defaults or disputes. The Horned God was the Keeper of Secrets and the Bane of Cheats.

And where were the priestesses who witnessed merchants pressing their seal rings into hot wax on letters of credit or payment, in the all-seeing Goddess's name? The holy sisters should be recording those transactions. How else could each merchant's holdings in silver and gold, shared between different temples, be reconciled?

These Velastans must know what was going on, but Quenild didn't want to betray her ignorance by asking. Showing weakness invariably had a price.

'Sun in your eyes?' Ticosa arrived and kissed her cheek.

'More like morning fog.' Quenild drew her wife to one side of the hall's double doors. 'How have you got on?'

'I've agreed excellent prices for the speckled pepper, feery root, and astanis,' Ticosa said with satisfaction as she opened her ledger. 'Though the price of silver tea has gone up again. Regardless, I bought the quantities we agreed.'

Quenild nodded. Bulk and burden were far less of a consideration travelling downstream on the Dore's steady flow.

'The rest was much as we expected.' Ticosa ran a blue-varnished fingernail down the closely-written columns on her page.

'The silver tea will sell, at whatever price.'

No notable who valued their reputation would go without the delicate, fragrant refreshment to offer their guests. As for the rest, Quenild's swift calculations indicated a healthy profit. With the cold lingering before the equinox, Hurat folk were eager for spices to liven up meals of pease and beans, shrivelled root vegetables, dried fish and salted meat.

'What about the apothecaries and scent merchants?' Ticosa asked, expectant.

'See for yourself.' Quenild opened her own ledger.

Ticosa studied the figures. 'That trip to Scefet was worth every midge bite and water-nettle sting.'

'Just as you told me, dearest.'

There was no denying it, however reluctant Quenild might be to repeat the journey. Velasta's dyers, distillers and tincture makers had snapped up the dried herbs, flower heads and seed pods from the reputedly impenetrable Nilgeh Mire. Better yet, Velastans were still willing to pay the old prices, from the days when bold venturers had braved the trackless swamps themselves. The merchant women had simply traded with the bog-trotters in the new marketplaces overlooked by the castles on the edge of the marsh's braided streams.

Ticosa stowed her ledger in the satchel slung over her shoulder. 'Let's check the price of copper tea once we've had something to eat.'

'And let's see if we can get everything delivered and loaded by dusk tomorrow,' Quenild suggested. 'I don't imagine the lads will object to heading home early, now the equinox feasts and fairs have been cancelled.'

Ticosa was bemused. 'What are folk supposed to do? Stay home and be miserable?'

King Venais's death had been a horrible shock, but life had gone on much as usual in Hurat. The merchant women and their crew had been startled to find Velasta was still observing the deep mourning decreed by the crown council. The taverns closed their doors at dusk, while the dance halls and gambling dens stayed shuttered.

Quenild had spent their first night here pacing the wharf while Ticosa snored in their cabin. If the market halls were closed, this journey would have been for nothing. Thankfully, by the Goddess's grace, trade continued. Though not quite as usual.

'I still need to get our contracts drawn up and certified, and have our letters of exchange sealed under the Goddess's eye. I don't know—'

'We have to go to the closest temple, and then to the nearest shrine to find a priest.'

'Why?' Quenild didn't bother asking how Ticosa learned this. Her wife's heart-shaped face and limpid eyes frequently prompted people to offer their help. She also knew her own strong features and opaque expression didn't encourage casual conversation. That didn't bother her in the slightest. Being hard to read was useful for a merchant.

Ticosa shrugged. 'No idea. Let's ask Alory when we get home.'

'You think he'll hear the latest news from Velasta while he's washing bedpans?' Quenild was fond of her nephew, and proud he served the Horned God, but that seemed unlikely.

'He's not working in the Infirmary now. Prylla said he's been assigned to the shrine library. Oh,' Ticosa suddenly remembered. 'Did you remember to buy her beads?'

'And the embroidery floss.' Quenild was looking forward to sitting quietly with Ticosa on the voyage home, companionably intent on their needlework. How her sister Prylla found time for bead work with six children and a fractious husband to placate was an enduring mystery.

Ticosa chewed her lip inelegantly. 'Let's eat, then I can go to the Cooper Street temple while you try the shrine in Meek Straight.'

Quenild pointed towards The Sundial. 'Let's see what's on offer there.'

Entering the tavern, she saw most tables were taken. Scriveners and merchant apprentices snatched bites from their plates as they copied ledger entries.

'Over here.' Ticosa moved fast, sliding onto a vacant bench as soon as its occupant left.

A sharp-eyed servitor came over. 'Ladies?'

Quenild decided they deserved a modest celebration. 'Wine, red, from Tierna if you have it.'

The servitor shook his head. 'No wine. Golden ale or winter dark?'

'There's no Tiernese red available?'

The servitor scowled. 'No wine from anywhere for anyone. The city is in mourning, by Earl Padran of Evarise's decree.'

'The winter dark brew, if you please,' Ticosa said quickly, 'for us both, and thank you.'

'May we have some food?' Quenild lifted her satchel's strap over her head and shed her cape.

'Pease pudding and rye bread. Cheese and vegetable pasty.' The man's face made it clear nothing else was on offer.

'Pease pudding, if you please.' Ticosa smiled at him.

'I'll have the pasty, thank you.' Quenild hoped one meal or the other would be more or less edible.

The servitor didn't move. 'Are you for Coylure or Evarise?'

That question made no sense to Quenild. 'We live in the Vale of Hurat, beyond the Bastrys mountains.'

Surely their full skirts and warm winter bodices marked them as provincials. Velasta's tavern staff were normally much more observant.

'Who is the true queen?' the servitor demanded.

'If you please, I don't understand.' Ticosa's eyes widened, anxious.

The servitor stepped closer. 'You tell Hurat folk the Father of Truth will uphold Princess Idelina's rights. Lystro of Coylure is a liar, and the Horned God's vengeance will strike him down.'

He would have said more, but a heavily jowled man thumped his tankard on a nearby table. 'You there! More ale!'

'Of course.' The servitor hurried away to fetch a jug.

As soon as he was out of earshot, the heavyset man snapped his fingers to demand both women's attention. 'Don't pledge your loyalty on that fool's say-so.'

'Why?' Quenild demanded.

'The priestesses say Princess Idelina's claim to the crown may be in doubt. Princess Alriad was King Fedrin's twin, and the high temple has reason to suspect she was firstborn. If so, she was denied her birthright when King Serken died.'

Quenild hid her irritation at being talked down to as if she was a fool. 'How could that happen?'

The man shifted his chair a little closer. 'The realm feared another war with Mervante. Their law says no woman can rule.'

'That makes no sense,' Ticosa protested. 'Even if the Mervantese refused to acknowledge Princess Alriad as heir, they couldn't ignore Prince Fedrin. Even if he was second-born, Arafaze still had a man to wear the crown.'

The big man shrugged. 'They say the Lightning King struck King Venais down to avenge that lie. Before Venais could beget an heir with Mervantese blood, to betray those who have died to defend Arafaze, in every generation since King Ganirin rode east. Maren of Evarise perished at his side because he negotiated that treacherous betrothal.'

'We have no interest in foolish superstitions.' Quenild had never heard of the Lightning King, but she remembered the taste of soap after a temple sister washed out her mouth, when she and some friends had scared younger girls with tales of the Icicle Witch.

'The Lightning King is a harbinger of—' He fell silent as the scowling servitor returned.

Ticosa lay her hand on top of Quenild's. Their silver wedding bracelets clinked on the table. Quenild lifted her wife's hand and kissed it. 'Let's get everything signed and sealed today.'

Whatever was going on in Velasta, the sooner they left for home, the better. They arranged their ledgers, paper, pens and ink. Tallying a column of figures, Quenild reached for the pasty and broke it in half. She nearly spat out her first bite. The tasteless vegetables were woody or woolly, soured with miserly shavings of hard cheese.

Ticosa stirred the watery bowl of pease. The spoon didn't turn up shredded bacon or dried fruit or anything else to add flavour. 'Ristal won't be impressed if he's been offered this pig swill.'

'The winter brew isn't too bad.' Quenild washed down her half-pasty and pushed the plate across the table.

'At least the rye bread's decent.' Ticosa ate her share of the pease and slid the bowl over to Quenild.

Once they had eaten and copied out their contracts and letters of payment, Ticosa summoned the servitor with a wave of her purse.

He held out a hand. 'A silver star apiece.'

'And a little for yourself.' Ticosa dropped the coins into his palm, along with a few copper pennies.

Quenild stood up, and gave Ticosa a brief kiss. 'I'll see you back at the wharf.'

Outside, it was raining. If it wasn't raining in bloody Velasta, the city was shrouded with fog. Quenild thanked the Goddess she didn't live here year-round. Still, the shallow rivers which flowed from these rumpled hills fed the Dore which would carry them home. The rain had some uses.

She made her way to the Moon God's shrine on Meek Straight. The streets were less crowded than usual, so Quenild walked close to the timber-and-brick shop fronts. Drips from the out-thrust gables above were preferable to splashes of filth from the overflowing gutters when some wagon or coach passed by.

Inside the crescent gate, the infirmary was to the right as usual with the library on the left. The God's sanctum lay straight ahead, with the brothers' accommodations behind it. Quenild joined the people waiting on benches sheltered by a pentise roof on the archive side of the courtyard. Watching those suffering make their way to the door opposite. Quenild silently thanked the Horned God for his blessings of good health for her family.

It wasn't long before her turn came. She gave her name to the young priest at the archive door, and he wrote it on his slate. 'Quenild Ditayan.'

Inside the archive, ranks of shelves separated by tall windows of clear glass held sets of documents sewn together with different coloured ribbons and identified with neatly inked bone tags. As a young priest scrambled up a ladder with some new addition, one of his brethren recorded its location in a ledger. Galleries up above sheltered still more records of contracts, leases, settlements and sacred vows.

Quenild would wager good coin it was usually much quieter in here. Trestle tables had been set up in the central aisle between the polished reading desks where some brothers were still trying to work. Voices rose with queries and clarifications. This was very odd.

An acolyte ushered Quenild to an empty stool in front of a priestly clerk.

'What's your business?' He didn't look up, brisk rather than brusque.

'Trading contracts.' Quenild handed over her copies.

The priest's finger traced each line on both documents as he made certain every word was the same. 'These are in order. Do you want to see if their counterparts have been lodged, or will you call back tomorrow?'

Quenild calculated how long she was prepared to wait in hopes of leaving Velasta as early as possible. 'I can stay for an hour.'

'Very well.' The priest stamped everything as approved, returned one set of documents to her and handed the other set to a hovering acolyte. 'Wait outside.'

Quenild yielded the stool to the next trader. As she headed for the door, stowing her papers in her satchel, an older priest intercepted her.

'Mistress Ditayan? May we speak? I gather you'll be waiting a while.'

He was courteous and amiable, but Quenild wouldn't have bought a sack of wheat from him without checking it was wholesome grain to the bottom. 'Of course, honoured brother.'

'Let's sit.' He escorted her to a bench by the wall. 'Where have you come from?'

Quenild noted other merchants having conversations with affable priests. 'Hurat, good brother.'

'A fine town, so I hear. Tell me, do you trade with the towns between Bastrys and Hurat?'

'We do.' She didn't ask why he wanted to know. Priests serving the Keeper of Secrets never shared the reasons for their questions.

'Do you venture across Lake Chalus and up the Fasil river?'

She shook her head. 'Our barges aren't made for those waters.'

'What about going downstream beyond Hurat?'

'We trade regularly as far as Usenas. We made one trip to the Nilgeh Mire last year.'

'What of the Tane? What goods do you carry upstream from Hurat?'

'We go as far as Mithess.' Quenild explained their dealings with the various towns of the Tane.

Trying to dissemble or conceal would incur the Moon God's displeasure. Besides, these priests would find any lies when they compared notes with their Hurat brethren, no matter how long their messages took to go back and forth. The consequences didn't bear contemplating. No honest merchant could trade if the Horned God refused to endorse their contracts.

While she was wondering what else to say, a young acolyte approached. 'Good day, Mistress Ditayan. I can confirm your contracts' counterparts have been lodged here. You may go about your business.'

The amiable priest rose to his feet. 'The God's blessings on you and yours.'

'Thank you.' Quenild still had no idea what he had hoped to learn.

Outside, the rain had stopped. Thankful for that much, Quenild headed for the wharfs. She passed remnants of city walls built long ago. As Velasta expanded beyond them, their only use was providing dressed stone for masons. King Serken, father to Fedrin and Alriad, had put an end to the pointless expense of building new walls every second or third generation. He decreed folk living beyond the outermost ring of brick and stone had chosen to take their chances if the city was ever attacked.

If that ever happened, Quenild couldn't see how those final walls would help anyone. A map of Velasta looked like a spider's web to her, with roads from every direction cutting through the circles of abandoned fortifications, bringing people and wares to the capital. Any invaders would follow those.

Reaching the river, Quenild had a lengthy walk along the wharves before she saw *The Beech Tree*. Folk who merely watched the tall-masted barges sailing on the Dore said all these vessels looked the same. No one who worked on the river had any trouble telling the boats apart.

'Hello *The Beech Tree*!' she called out.

The sloping cabin door opened onto the little stern deck and Ticosa appeared. 'I'm just lighting the stove.'

'Have you seen Ristal or Yanter?' Quenild followed her wife down the short, broad-runged ladder into the narrow passageway between twin-bunked cabins. She hung her cape and satchel on a peg.

'I sent them out to chase up our deliveries.' Ticosa crouched to tuck wood inside the iron stove between the benches on the cabin's bankside.

The hinged table on the waterside was folded out of the way. There was scant space for four to cook, eat and take their ease between stints managing the tiller and the sails, but no one complained. A barge's business was carrying cargo. The more space for cargo, the more profit for owners and crew.

'How did you get on at the temple?' Quenild sat down and tousled Squirrel's ears. The grey-brindled dog silently nuzzled her hand as his feathered tail thumped the floorboards. Everyone on the river knew a barking barge hound meant intruders somewhere.

Ticosa sat back on her heels. 'I've never known a priestess so eager to gossip.'

'Gossip?' Quenild's hand stung with the memory of a punishing leather strap.

'Apparently, there's rumour Princess Idelina is deathly ill. Some say her unborn child has been lost. Others claim she was never pregnant.'

'A priestess told you that?' Quenild couldn't believe it.

'No, she asked if I'd heard such rumours, making certain I knew every detail,' Ticosa said tartly.

Quenild raised her eyebrows. 'Did this talkative sister care to share the truth?'

'No, but she told me to entreat the Goddess to bless Princess Idelina.' Ticosa paused, thoughtful. 'And we must entrust little Princess Olyshai to the Golden Mother's care, if the poor child is bereaved of both parents. She also mentioned widespread feeling that Princess Alriad should be proclaimed regent in the best interests of the realm.'

'Widespread feeling? That's something everyone agrees?' Quenild saw her wife shared her scepticism.

'Apparently so, not least because Princess Alriad will rear Princess Olyshai with her own sons and daughters, if Princess Idelina dies.' Ticosa shook her head, uneasy. 'What by the stars is going on?'

'I don't know, but Velasta's priests were keen to know every detail of our business for no good reason I could see.' Quenild related her experiences at the shrine, stroking Squirrel.

She wondered if Alory would be able to shed light on any of these puzzles when they got home. He might be one of the Horned God's humblest servants, but the boy was no fool. If he was working in Hurat's shrine library now, that's where news from Velasta would be shelved.

Chapter Five

HURAT

12th of the Blossom Moon

Alory edged along the narrow aisle, careful not to disturb a sheaf of documents jutting from the crammed shelves. He heard the taller of this early morning's unexpected visitors talking to Brother Talaven.

These strangers made him uneasy. He paused, staying hidden. Listening at keyholes had often saved Alory or his siblings a beating from their father. Brother Talaven told him to trust his God-given instincts.

'These rolls record the sworn oaths of every freeholder owing fealty to Margravine Falise of Mithess?'

'Indeed,' Brother Talaven assured the stranger.

Alory heard the old man wheezing. Barely recovered from a vicious winter fever, he shouldn't have been dragged out of bed before first light, but these visitors had presented Brother Archivist Praidel with a letter bearing Earl Padran of Evarise's seal. Then they ordered Brother Praidel out of his own hall, insisting on talking privately with Brother Talaven.

Alory remembered the venerable brother telling him secrecy was a two-edged sword which could do as much harm as good.

'Where's that boy?' The shorter, stockier visitor had a face like a wharf-side brawler and a copyist's ink-stained hands. 'Where are those records?'

These unknown brothers demanded documents that hadn't been touched for years. As Brother Talaven sat by the tables between the rows of shelves, Alory went up and down the ladder to the storage floor above. His black robe was grey with dust and cobwebs.

Brother Talaven coughed. 'Why is the high father in Velasta so interested in the terms of each Hurat noble's fealty to the Arafaze crown?'

Alory closed his eyes and concentrated on listening with the first magic the old man had taught him. The Keeper of Secrets had granted him the ability to hear lies, to safeguard honest people.

'We do not know,' the stocky visitor replied.

Alory heard the lie as clearly as the sour note of a cracked bell. But where was the falsehood? Did these brothers truly not know why Velasta's high priest wanted this information? Or had they lied when they said they were acting for him? Even simple magic wasn't straightforward, as Brother Talaven always pointed out.

Talaven's chuckle turned into another cough. 'Our nobles have never sworn fealty to the Arafaze crown. Their allegiance has been to the Earl of Hurat and King Venais was the last of those.'

Alory heard the old priest's chair shift on the floorboards. He would be waving his age-spotted hands, black sleeves slipping down his skinny forearms. The old man loved sharing obscure facts.

'Then the earldom passes to Queen Idelina.' The sharp-eyed brother was dismissive.

'No, it does not.' Talaven was enjoying himself.

'Explain,' the tall man growled.

Alory's blood ran cold. His father used that tone when he was determined to vent his frustrations and disappointments, using his fists on someone who couldn't fight back.

Oblivious, Talaven was happy to oblige. 'When King Ganirin extended his dominion beyond the Bastrys mountains, he appointed trusted allies to rebuild the devastated towns along the Dore. Those newly-made barons swore him their fealty in keeping with Arafaze custom. King Ganirin also made alliances with those nobles still defending their ancestral lands along the

Tane. Those margraves had long been threatened by Mervante, as well as by raiders from the hill country and the Mire. With the marsh folk and Mervante fighting together, the Tane nobles would have been overrun without Arafaze aid. But the margraves would not yield to the suzerainty of the Arafaze crown. They acclaimed King Ganirin as Earl of Hurat, and agreed treaties of mutual defence when he founded this town.'

'And they will renew those treaties with Queen Idelina,' the tall man said tightly.

'They cannot.' Brother Talaven was irritated now.

Alory couldn't understand why the old priest didn't realise these men were a threat. He gripped the scroll in his hand so tightly the parchment crackled.

'Explain,' the stocky brother snarled.

The old priest cleared his throat. 'Arafaze law grants inheritance rights to the firstborn, from humblest freeholder to the highest in the realm. However, when the Earldom of Hurat was established, the margraves of the Tane insisted local laws took precedence. At that time, as is still the case in Mervante, women could neither inherit for themselves or for their children.'

'This province has seen ruling baronesses and margravines for generations,' the tall man snapped.

'Because each family's terms of succession have been rewritten, case by case. No such changes were ever made for the earldom of Hurat and that male bloodline is now extinct.'

Alory winced at Talaven's satisfaction.

'Queens have ruled Arafaze before now,' the tall man said slowly.

'Indeed,' Talaven agreed, 'while their brothers or cousins inherited the earldom for a generation or two, until a judicious marriage brought the title back to the Crown.'

'Show us proof,' the stocky man demanded.

'There is none here.' For the first time, Talaven sounded uncertain. 'The earldom's archive was taken to Velasta when Earl Eluan's son inherited the crown as King Hakayn, after Queen Chanys died...'

'So this means nothing.' The tall man was relieved.

'I will swear to this truth before the Horned God—' Brother Talaven broke off, coughing.

'Where's the boy?' the stocky man growled. 'If this old fool has told him—'

'He can't swear to any of this. We have get back to Velasta. Any proof in some archive there must be destroyed.'

Booted feet hurried away. The library's heavy door slammed. Alory stepped out from the shelves and saw Brother Talaven claw at his grey-stubbled throat. The old priest was choking. He stared at Alory with a white-rimmed gaze as his frantic heels scraped the floorboards. Alory didn't understand.

Brother Talaven made the sign of the crescent moon with his left hand. Alory focused his mind's eye on the intangible realm. Something long and lithe was strangling the old priest. As he yelped, startled, Alory lost sight of the creature.

He ran up to Brother Talaven, gritted his teeth and looked into the unseen realm again. A cobalt snake as thick as a man's wrist tightened its coils around Talaven's neck. Alory tried to get a grip, to pull the creature off. His fingernails slid uselessly across its scales. He needed a blade but he had no moonlight to draw on.

Brother Talaven flung out a hand. Alory saw the thin bladed knife the old priest used to cut through wax seals. He snatched it off the table and stabbed the snake as hard as he dared. He didn't want to hurt Brother Talaven. Quick as thought, the monster struck at his hand, its fanged mouth gaping.

Alory recoiled, but he had done enough. The monster unwound itself from Brother Talaven's neck, intent on this new prey. Alory braced himself, ready to use the knife again. Talaven sucked in a whooping breath and the nightmare creature spread midnight wings. It soared upwards with a twist of its tail and disappeared in the shadows.

'Brother?' Alory turned to ask Talaven what he should do now.

The old man's eyes rolled back in his head. His withered lips were turning blue.

Alory dropped the knife and felt for the old priest's heartbeat. He yelled as loud as he could. 'Help!'

The hall door flew open. Brother Praidel must have been waiting outside. The wiry librarian didn't waste time with questions. He scooped the stricken old man up like a baby. 'Follow me to the Infirmary.'

Alory was about to do that when he heard a noise overhead. He looked up, but he couldn't see the creature from the unseen realm. Brother Talaven would be furious if he let it get away. And he needed to catch the thing, to prove to his instructors sharing the intangible's secrets that those Velastan brothers had conjured a monster to attack the old priest. Brother Cavore would see them flogged and cast out of the hidden brethren. But Cavore was eighty leagues away on bad roads.

Alory's throat tightened as the heavy door swung closed behind Brother Praidel. As the young priest methodically scanned the shadows above him, movement caught his eye. Scales rasped on wood by the broad-runged ladder leading to the upper floor. A sinuous shadow disappeared through the square hole in the corner of the ceiling.

Alory walked over and climbed up, cautious. There was nothing to see when he stepped away from the ladder, blinking in the dim light filtering through little windows in the eaves.

Wings flapped. The snake flew at his face, straight as an arrow. Alory ducked, his foot slipped, and he fell to his hands and knees. He looked up to see the serpent circling, ready to attack.

Alory dropped onto his belly, rolled onto his back and grabbed at the air as the creature swooped over him. His grip closed on the serpent's tail. He held on as tight as he could, feeling the monster's muscles tense. Alory flung out his arm, snatching his hand back in one swift move. He and his brothers had stung each other's legs with their towels in the public bathhouse. Father had said that's how he'd once killed a marsh snake that had slithered onto the wharf out of a cargo brought up from the Mire.

The winged serpent's spine snapped with the same crack as a whipping towel. Alory threw the monster away. It bounced off a document chest and landed with a thud on the floorboards. A bubbling hiss told him the creature wasn't dead.

Reluctant, he got up and saw the snake's head weaving from side to side. The rest of it lay motionless. One wing trailed useless in the dust. Alory remembered the day he found a dying crow, long before he had sworn himself to the Moon God. Maybe a hawk had savaged the bird, or a cat. Regardless, Alory couldn't leave the poor bird to linger in torment. He'd found a length of firewood fallen from some handcart and smashed the crow's skull, weeping as he asked for the Horned God's understanding.

Alory lifted an iron bound coffer off a nearby shelf. If he couldn't drive the winged snake back into the intangible realm, he had a duty to end its suffering. He dropped the coffer and the crunch of the serpent's head made him want to vomit.

'Who's up there?' A startled voice called out below.

Alory hurried to the corner and called down the ladder. 'I knocked over a chest. I will put everything in order, I promise. Brother Talaven will be furious if I don't.'

Whoever was below paused for a long moment. 'Alory? You had better get down here, lad, as quick as you can.'

'I won't be long.' Alory hurried back to the serpent. He lifted up the coffer. What was he going to do with the mangled corpse? Brother Talaven had told him time and time again, no trace must be left to betray an incursion from the intangible realm to those who had no inkling of any world beyond the one they saw.

Outside, the shrine bell began to toll the measured strokes that announced a death. Alory heard the archive hall's door open and close. Low voices murmured with sorrow and regret.

'Alory?' Brother Praidel's voice was gentle. 'Join us to say goodbye to our beloved brother.'

'I – please – a moment.' Alory's eyes were stinging but he refused to weep.

Blinking and sniffing, he unknotted his black rope belt and dragged his outer robe over his head. Quickly, he stripped off his shirt. As he gathered up the winged serpent's corpse, its limp coils kept slithering out of his hands. It was heavier than he expected too. He persisted, wrapping the dead snake in his shirt and knotting the sleeves around it. He would take the foul thing to Sister Jadewin disguised as a bundle of laundry. She would know what to do.

Before he could do that, he had to get out of the shrine without any other priests seeing what he was up to. Alory walked towards the ladder, praying for the Moon God's help. Kneeling and bracing himself to avoid falling head-first through the hole, he peered cautiously into the hall below.

The other priests had left. Thanking the Dark Father, Alory put his black robe back on. He shoved the bundled shirt beneath it, and knotted his rope belt tight under the stinking bulge. Now he should be able to get down the ladder without dropping the thing.

Alory climbed carefully, holding tight to the wooden rungs. He tried not to gag at his vile burden's stink. The archive was still deserted as he reached the floor. He rested the bundle on the edge of a table and wrapped his arms around the dead snake. Supporting its weight while he used one hand to open the door wasn't easy, but he managed. Alory slipped through to stand on the archive hall steps.

In the shrine yard, townsfolk were asking his brothers who had died. No one was looking his way. He forced himself to walk slowly towards the crescent gate.

Alory was nearly there when someone shouted his name. He didn't look back, dodging around Brother Porter when the portly priest raised a hand to point to whoever had called out. Stepping through the shrine gate, the young priest ran for the temple as fast as he could. Alory had to find Sister Jadewin. She would tell him what to do.

Chapter Six

HURAT

12th of the Blossom Moon

Jadewin swirled the spoon to gather up plenty of honey. Starting the day with a cavalry trooper's brew of copper tea was her least favourite consequence of spending a night with Maixen. There were compensations. His muscular nakedness as he shaved, standing by the washstand, gave her a pleasurably intimate thrill.

She sweetened and drank her tea. Sharing breakfast in his bedchamber rather than eating in the refectory with her sisters was another blessing. Jadewin silently thanked the Goddess and assured her she took none of these boons for granted. She left the table with its crumb-strewn plates and opened the small coffer on the linen press beside the washstand where she kept essentials. Firm strokes with her hairbrush subdued the tousle of last night's love-making.

Maixen wiped his cheeks and chin. 'How's this?'

Jadewin stroked his face. 'Smooth as a dressmaker's flattery.'

He slipped an arm around her waist and kissed her deep and long. 'Will I see you tonight?'

'That depends on the duties waiting for me at the temple.' She hoped so. There hadn't been a whisper of anyone else so much as glimpsing the Icicle Witch. 'Make yourself useful and plait my hair?'

'Of course.' He took the brush and obliged, swift and deft.

'Let's hope for more news from Velasta now the weather's improving.' Jadewin pinned her braids into a neat circlet and emptied the washstand basin into the slop bucket. She wiped it out and poured fresh water from the ewer so she could wash.

'God and Goddess willing.' Getting dressed, Maixen let his exasperation slip.

'From your lips to the sun and the moon.' Jadewin didn't relish another day of dealing with endless visitors to the temple, asking when Queen Idelina would be crowned and how well was her pregnancy proceeding. 'What will you be doing today?'

'Deciding which garrisons deserve new blood and fresh horses, and which must be given them regardless of their captains' inadequacies.' The castellan shook his head.

Jadewin found her chemise and stockings. Warmer weather meant no more layers of flannel petticoats. 'Why are the hill folk such inveterate horse thieves?'

Maixen was always ready to answer her questions about daily life in the province. 'They covet horses for their usefulness when they raid their neighbours' flocks and herds, but they don't breed mounts for themselves. Fodder is scarce in the hills so they prefer to keep what they harvest for their goats and the sheep hardy enough to survive upland winters. Horses die unless they're sheltered in well-built stabling and that costs timber and time. So the hill folk start stealing them after the spring equinox and set the beasts loose to take their chances when the Stag Moon wanes. Downland folk pay a fair price for those that are rounded up. The rest break a leg or freeze to death.' Maixen pulled on his boots. 'With any luck the hill country troublemakers will hold off until they know if Earl Lystro of Coylure or Earl Padran of Evarise will command the new queen's forces. Best to know what breed of dog sits behind a gate before you kick it in.'

'Let's hope so.' Jadewin quickly finished dressing.

Maixen knelt to slip her half-boots onto her feet. 'I'll walk you out.'

Jadewin followed him down the spiral stairs. Several townsfolk were already waiting in the ground floor room, determined to bring their concerns to the castellan's attention.

Maixen acknowledged them, courteous. 'I will be with you shortly.'

As Jadewin took her cape from the peg by the outer door, Senon the steward entered, followed by a gust of fresh air.

'Yes?' Maixen was instantly alert.

'An issue with the delivery from Jedfal.' Senon's face gave nothing away.

'Goddess send you both a good day.' Jadewin knew neither of them would share any details about that, so she left the keep and walked towards the castle gate.

As she passed the sanctuary Brother Delnor, who supervised the castle's infirmary, came out. He acknowledged Jadewin with a nod as he went on his way. His duties included lighting the polished brass lamp above the Golden Mother's altar at dawn. At dusk, he would thank the Sun Goddess for her blessings and carry the day's flame on a taper to the Father of Night's silver lamp. Anyone serving in the garrison, any visitor to the castle, would find a bright reminder of divine vigilance, whatever the hour.

'Good morning, sister.' The sergeant in charge of the night watch saluted as Jadewin passed the guardroom in the tunnel through the rampart.

'The Goddess's blessings on your endeavours.'

Crossing the wooden bridge over the great ditch and going through the town gate, Jadewin walked quickly through the grid of Hurat's newer streets. Mother Finevre had explained how market gardens and animal byres had originally fed the townsfolk inside King Ganirin's fortifications. In the generations since, the growing town needed more homes inside the thick stone walls, protected by the cannons and rampart guns. Now vegetables and animals were raised on the far banks of both rivers.

Few people were out and about so early and nobody sought her counsel. Suppliants were waiting for the crescent gate to open as she crossed the square outside the shrine. Jadewin heard the tolling bell within announce some unfortunate's death overnight. She commended their grieving family to the Goddess's care.

The streets were growing busier. As she reached the high road between the ferries crossing the Dore to the south, and the Tane to the north, heavily laden wagons and carriages trundled over the cobbles in both directions. Beyond the river road, Hurat's older streets curved and crossed in haphazard fashion.

The temple wasn't much further and the gate in the encircling wall stood wide open as always. The Goddess's servants attended births and deaths day and night. Outside, the desperate and destitute waited for the morning's charity of fresh-baked bread and modest portions of ham and cheese.

Going into the yard, Jadewin was surprised to see Alory sitting cross-legged by the temple entrance with a stained linen bundle in his lap.

'Sister.' He scrambled to his feet, ashen-faced.

Before he could say any more, Sister Paske hurried out of the temple. The young priestess was almost as distraught as the boy. 'Thank the Golden Mother you're back. You have a visitor from the high temple.'

'At this hour?' Jadewin raised a hand, seeing Alory opening his mouth to speak. 'One at a time. Sister?'

'She's in Mother Finevre's parlour. Come quickly.' Paske hurried off without waiting to see if Jadewin followed.

'Please—' Alory begged, desperate.

Jadewin glanced quickly into the unseen world, but she couldn't see anything amiss. 'Can it wait?'

'If it must.' Alory sank down to sit on the ground, gathering up his bnundle.

'I'll be as quick as I can,' Jadewin promised.

She followed Paske into the entrance hall. The outer ring of rooms provided every aspect of the Golden Mother's care. On Jadewin's right, the refectory and the kitchen beyond fed anyone who turned up hungry, as well as the sisters who lived within. To her left, the accounting hall recorded financial transactions for the more fortunate and prosperous. That ensured paper and ink were conveniently at hand to record births, deaths and bequests when the Goddess's daughters tended the newborn and the dying brought to the nursing halls on the far side of the circular building. Despite every temple and shrine's best efforts, some unfortunates had no privacy at home for such a life's beginning or end. Others, lacking a family, had no home.

Straight ahead, the passage from the entrance hall led to the glass-roofed inner sanctum with the Sun Goddess's statue. The temple's heart was ringed by the herb garden and overlooked by the inner windows of the priestesses' work rooms and stores. Stairs led to the dormitories above, while Mother Finevre's parlour with its private bedchamber was directly behind the Goddess's statue.

Paske knocked on the parlour door, hesitant.

'Enter,' snapped a Velastan voice.

Jadewin realised Paske was terrified. Who was this visitor from the high temple, asking for her by name and taking over Mother Finevre's parlour? Wary, Jadewin made sure her face showed only amiable goodwill as she went through the door. 'Goddess bless us this day.'

'You may go.' The slender young woman in Mother Finevre's chair dismissed Paske with a flick of her hand. She stared at Jadewin, accusing. 'When I arrived last night, I was told you were absent.'

Jadewin took a seat. She wasn't going to be scolded like an errant schoolgirl by some unknown sister a decade her junior. 'As you were no doubt also told, I spend my nights in the castle when I can be spared.'

The visitor's thin lips tightened with disdain. Her glossy dark hair was drawn back into a tight bun, making her face even more severe. 'Some consider our Goddess is best served with undivided attention.'

So she was a celibate who expected others to make the same choice. Jadewin smiled cheerfully. 'I honour our Blessed Mother by enjoying her gifts of mutual pleasure. Happily, as the Goddess tells us, all preferences have their place under the sun.'

The visitor looked as if she would like to deny that. Jadewin took advantage of her silence to glance into the unseen realm. If this visitor knew anything of the intangible world she was oath-bound to show her presence there at any first meeting, so a fellow initiate might know they shared this secret.

Seeing no one seated behind Mother Finevre's desk, Jadewin clasped her hands in her lap. 'Forgive me, sister, I don't know your name.'

'I am Hasrine Rulleyn.' The newcomer busied herself unfolding some papers and dipping a pen into Mother Finevre's inkstand.

'I am pleased to know you.' Though Jadewin didn't think much of this woman's claims to single-minded devotion to the Goddess if she clung to her noble family name.

Ambitious third or fourth daughters, and those who decided they were unsuited to marriage, often saw serving the Goddess as a path to eminence and influence. Their games of factions and favourites mirrored the manoeuvres of the well-born and wealthy who circled incessantly around Velasta's royal residences. The ruthless used whatever advantage they could claim to advance in either contest. Jadewin was always glad to leave such nonsense behind when her duties to the secret sisterhood took her away from the capital.

Sister Hasrine looked across Mother Finevre's desk. Her pen was poised. 'Where do Baron Lensin of Chalus's loyalties lie?'

'With the Crown.' Jadewin didn't understand the question.

Hasrine's eyes narrowed. 'Does he favour Princess Alriad's appointment as regent?'

The golden gleam of Hasrine's pendant reminded Jadewin the Sun Goddess saw all. Her oaths meant she must tell this unwelcome sister the truth. Thankfully, that wasn't a problem.

'I have no idea.'

Hasrine drummed her fingers on the table. 'What are his debts and obligations?'

'Sister?' Jadewin was taken aback.

'As an auditor, you are familiar with this province's financial affairs?'

Jadewin disliked this stranger's tone. 'And I am sworn to discretion in the Goddess's name. Who gives you the authority to ask such questions?'

The pale young woman took a sheet of paper from the sheaf in front of her and slid it across the desk.

Jadewin took her time reading the brief message. High Mother Elyka instructed her to tell Sister Hasrine whatever she wanted to know. This was unwelcome news. As Sister Elyka serving in a lesser Velastan temple, she had been Jadewin's first mentor in the secret sisterhood.

Learning her sisters who safeguarded the unseen world's mysteries were taking a close interest in who wore Arafaze's crown was unwelcome. So much for their vows to stay out of secular matters. But Jadewin was still oath-bound to obey. She gave Sister Hasrine a brief summary of Baron Lensin of Chalus's income and outgoings.

Hasrine made swift notes, not looking up. 'And Lord Romer of Sharrow? What does he owe, and to whom?'

Jadewin hid her growing unease as she shared what she knew. She didn't pass on Mother Finevre's opinion that Sharrow's unpopular suzerain was as unpredictable as he was devious.

Hasrine studied her notes. 'What about the Margrave of Jedfal?'

'Excuse me. My mouth is as dry as a salt miner's socks.' Jadewin didn't wait for permission, reaching for the water jug and one of the glasses doubtless provided by Paske.

'Does he favour Princess Alriad as regent?' Hasrine demanded. 'Or will he risk the peace and security of the realm by handing the crown to Princess Idelina?'

Jadewin took a drink. 'I have no idea.'

'What sums does he owe the temple in Jedfal town?'

Taking another sip, Jadewin decided that only sharing what she knew for absolute fact would honour her vows to the Goddess. Unfortunately, that was sufficient to expose Jedfal's vulnerabilities.

'Such debts are not unusual towards the end of winter,' she said forcefully. 'Honour obliges Margrave Vauset to empty his strongboxes to ensure his people are fed. They will repay their liege lord by honestly rendering their tithes in due course. By summer's end, after harvest, the temple ledger will show a substantial balance in the Margrave's favour.'

'That's a long way off,' Hasrine remarked, unguarded. 'What of Castellan Maixen? Will he support a regency?'

'I cannot say.' Jadewin decided it was time to ask questions of her own. 'Do you have news of Princess Idelina's pregnancy?'

Sister Hasrine scowled. 'She does not thrive.'

What did that mean? Jadewin wanted to ask Hasrine to repeat herself with one hand on her pendant, to prove she was telling the truth. But that would put her openly at odds with this visitor and that would be a mistake. Jadewin decided to assume she was being dismissed. She stood up. 'I will pray the Golden Mother blesses her and the child.'

Hasrine raised a hand. 'You will not discuss our conversation with anyone within this temple or outside it.'

Jadewin nodded, but she wasn't going to agree. Nothing in High Mother Elyka's note granted Hasrine any authority to give such commands.

'Your brother is Elgis Sernel, I believe.' Hasrine stared at her again. 'Saddle maker in Morin Lane, in the Serriden district?'

'My brothers are sworn to the Moon God and my sisters serve our Golden Mother,' Jadewin said calmly. 'Excuse me. I have duties to attend.'

She left the parlour and walked briskly back to the entrance hall. Once she knew what young Alory wanted, she would tell Mother Finevre about this conversation. Hurat's senior priestess's magical talent might be limited to glimpsing misshapen creatures that slipped through from the unseen realm but Finevre needed to know Velasta's secret sisterhood wasn't supporting Princess Idelina's claim to the crown.

As she went into the yard, Jadewin wondered if Brother Talaven knew the hidden brethren's views on this proposed regency. Young Alory could enquire.

'What can I do for you?' she asked as the boy leapt to his feet.

Chapter Seven

BASTRYS

12th of the Blossom Moon

When they arrived in Bastrys, the sailing barge was directed to a mooring by Baron Zavire's man on the wharf. Reske watched the crew secure the broad vessel with heavy ropes. His battered travelling bag was slung over one shoulder. After ten days on this boat, built for passengers rather than cargo, he was keen to get ashore. He wasn't the only one. The youngest of the trio of priests aboard came up from the cabins below.

'Brother.' Reske offered the lad a friendly nod.

'Good morning.' The muscular youth stuck his hands through his rope belt as he studied the buildings on the Dore's northern bank. He glowered at the Sun Goddess's temple. Reske didn't bother asking why. None of the priests had been inclined to conversation on their journey from the capital. Nor had the two priestesses, both in their middle years, who had been extremely annoyed to find the brothers aboard when they boarded the barge in Velasta.

Reske had been walking along the wharfs, looking for passage down the Dore. He heard the senior priestess berate the barge master. Why had the passenger roster changed since she had reserved her cabin? The barge master explained four passengers had cancelled their plans. He invited the priestess to look elsewhere if she no longer wished to travel on his boat.

Reske had watched the priestesses go aboard, glaring at the three priests. As soon as the Moon God's sons turned their backs, and the women went below deck, Reske strolled over to the barge master and casually claimed the vacant bunk. Anything out of the ordinary was worth a closer look at present.

Right now Reske had work to do before he headed north to Hedvin to find out what was happening there. He had never visited Bastrys before, but the slope of the land meant the town's layout was plain from the riverbank. The steepness of paths and roads here would be brutal on his knees, but it was clear why Baron Zavire's forefather had claimed this place. His fortress dominated the rock-walled gorge which the relentless Dore had cut through these mountains.

The dour, grey castle, high on a crag at the easternmost end of the town, could turn its cannon on any vessel up or down the river. The baron could also control the meagre road following the water eastwards. North of the Dore, Baron Zavire's fiefdom reached to the waters flowing out of Lake Chalus, where the narrow Bastrys road met the highway skirting the mountains and linking Hurat with Arafaze. That highway was the boundary between Baron Zavire's lands and Baron Lebarre's fiefdom to the north, ruled from Hedvin.

The priestesses came up on deck. Reske watched them disembark and walk away. The other priests appeared. The eldest was white-haired and old enough to find climbing the ladder to the deck a trial. The other was around Reske's age and shaven-headed. His pale eyes constantly shifted from one thing to the next.

Once the wheezing priest had recovered, the trio left the boat. From the direction they took, Reske guessed they were going straight to the Bastrys shrine. He left the wharf and followed the most obvious route through the steep streets to the castle. Seeing the two priestesses ahead, he was curious. Where were they headed, if they weren't going to the Golden Mother's temple?

His knees were feeling the strain of the ascent by the time the priestesses reached the broad, cobbled expanse in front of the baron's castle. As far as Reske could tell, this must be the largest stretch of level ground in the town. Tool marks on outcrops of rock showed Bastrys owed a substantial debt of gratitude to whatever long-dead labourers had chipped away the mountainside. A retaining wall overlooking the town stopped the cobbles sliding downhill.

Substantial inns lined the far side of this market place, or parade ground or whatever purpose it served. Two appeared luxurious enough to accommodate wealthy guests who preferred more elbow room than Bastrys castle could offer. With no space to build a separate crown fortress, Baron Zavire was obliged to share his ancestral home with the king's – the queen's – forces. Whichever queen ended up wearing the Arafaze crown. Reske assumed no fresh news about a coronation had arrived while he was on the barge. The wharfs would have been buzzing like a beehive if it had.

The priestesses walked up to the dry ditch that had been cut into bedrock to defend the castle's entrance. After a few words, the sentry crossed the drawbridge to knock on the wicket gate in the main door. After a brief conversation he beckoned the priestesses inside. Now Reske had even more questions.

Hopefully the person he was here to meet might have a few answers. Reske went into the closest tavern and offered the burly tapster a silver star. 'Ale, if you please.'

The man grunted and filled a stoneware tankard from the barrel. Reske glanced idly around. It wasn't long after noon and the place was quiet. A few folk were eating what his nose suggested was savoury pottage. Nobody looked his way.

Reske waved his hand as the man reached into his apron for whatever copper pennies he was owed.

'Could someone take a message to the garrison for me?' Reske had long since perfected the art of friendly conversation. 'I'm hoping to catch up with an old friend.'

If not, he'd find out where the crown garrison drank and be waiting there this evening when the day watch were released from their duties.

'My boy can deliver a note.' The tapster whistled.

A bright-eyed lad around eight or nine years old appeared from a back room. Reske took a leaf of folded paper from his jerkin's inner pocket and held it up between two fingers. He hadn't sealed it. That would suggest it held some secret.

'Will you take this to the crown garrison's gate for me? For a couple of coppers?'

The lad glanced at his father. The tapster nodded. Reske handed the note and the coins to the boy and smiled at the tapster. 'I'll have a bowl of pottage while I'm waiting, if you please.'

The tapster went into the kitchen as the lad hurried off and Reske carried his ale to an empty table. The tapster soon returned. As Reske spooned up the thick mix of pease, root vegetables and shredded ham, he considered how long he was prepared to wait.

Nedre had been sure Elisset was still serving in this garrison. Reske had learned long ago the only certainty in life was change. That went double for those sworn to the crown's service as a courier. Reske had sent a message downstream before he left Velasta, but if she didn't turn up, he'd learn what he could this evening in whatever tavern the garrison favoured, and buy a horse and supplies for the road north tomorrow morning.

Elisset appeared in the tavern doorway as he was wiping the pottage bowl clean with the last of his bread. The tapster's boy pointed to Reske. She tousled his hair and the lad ran off. As she took the stool opposite Reske, the tapster brought her a brimful tankard.

'You haven't changed.' She slid the note across the table to Reske.

'You're looking well.' He pocketed the paper. Not that 'I'm here, R' would mean anything to anyone else.

It would be a stretch to say she hadn't changed. Was it three years or four since he had last seen her? Elisset was as lithe and muscular as Reske remembered, but her hair was brindled with grey. Her deeply tanned face and hands were a legacy of spending spring, summer and autumn carrying the crown's despatches far and wide. Woe betide any bandit who hoped to steal the dark leather case buckled to the back of a courier's saddle. Couriers carried swords, and Reske had seen Elisset wield hers as skilfully on foot as on horseback.

She sipped her ale. 'What brings you here?'

Reske noted her guarded tone. He also saw she wasn't wearing her courier's livery and she had a travel bag. 'My master wants to know which way the wind blows.'

'Let's take some air while the weather stays fine.' Elisset drained her tankard.

'Suits me.' Reske drank his last mouthful of ale and followed her out of the tavern.

Elisset crossed the cobbles to the vantage point by the retaining wall overlooking the town. Clearly she wasn't going to say anything where they might be overheard. Reske couldn't see anyone taking a particular interest in them, but he wasn't going to challenge her caution.

Elisset leaned against the low wall, lowering her bag to the ground. 'Let's hear it. All of it.'

'Earl Lystro of Coylure and Earl Padran of Evarise have been sending envoys to Bastrys and to Hedvin. My master wishes to know what inducements the noble earls might be offering Baron Zavire and Baron Lebarre in return for their support. I asked around to see who I might know serving in either crown garrison, and your name came up. When we're done, I'll go north to Hedvin.'

If Nedre hadn't told him Elisset was here, Reske would have flipped a coin to decide where he went first, trusting in the God and the Goddess's guidance.

She looked thoughtful. 'What's the news from Velasta? Is Princess Idelina any closer to wearing the crown?'

'Not as far as I know,' Reske said frankly. 'Earl Padran of Evarise is issuing decrees in the princess's name, claiming the authority of the crown council. Earl Lystro of Coylure chooses not to challenge him just yet. He's busy making the case to anyone who will listen that a regency is in everyone's best interests. He swears Princess Alriad will hold the crown in trust until Idelina has fully recovered from childbed – or not.'

He made the sign of the crescent moon to avert misfortune. 'The lords and ladies of Velasta mostly say little and agree with whoever's talking to them. Then they go home and do nothing, praying the God or the Goddess sends some resolution that doesn't cause anyone more grief. Earl Debin suspects Evarise or Lystro are planning something to shake this stalemate loose.'

Elisset replied without a trace of humour. 'I'd say the Goddess's daughters will see to that.'

Reske felt a chill that didn't come from the breeze off the river. 'How so?'

Elisset lowered her voice, though there was still no one within earshot. 'Baron Zavire will declare his allegiance to Queen Alriad in the next few days.'

'Queen Alriad?'

Elisset looked grim. 'The Bastrys temple will proclaim her as monarch in the Golden Mother's name. Then we'll see if that pebble starts a landslide to sweep Princess Idelina's claim away.'

'Who – how?'

Elisset understood the questions Reske was trying to ask. 'Baron Zavire fell foul of Velasta's high temple last year, trying to hide the true profits he makes from the river trade. He wanted to pay less in taxes to the crown and to the Goddess. I'm guessing he's done some deal, so the good sisters will overlook his sins, provided he supports Princess Alriad's claim to the crown.'

Before he left the capital, Reske wouldn't have believed her, but he had just seen two priestesses walk into Baron Zavire's fortress.

'This news will get to Velasta in what, thirty days, give or take a few sunsets?' Reske's calculation assumed a messenger could hire or steal the best and freshest horses, and the highway between the Bastrys mountains and Hedvin's forests was in good repair.

Elisset nodded. 'And everyone from highest to humblest along that route will hear what Baron Zavire has done before word reaches Earl Padran.

'Earl Lystro of Coylure wants to see how many voices will support Alriad as queen,' Reske realised. 'Before Earl Padran can shout Baron Zavire down. This way, he can insist Arafaze's people want to see Alriad crowned.'

If Lystro tried this in Velasta, Reske knew no one in court circles would take Princess Alriad's side. No one would risk being the first to throw rocks into this particular pond and get splashed by whatever followed. At worst, there'd be blood on the streets. Earl Lystro could take the blame for that on his own.

Elisset glowered. 'I want to know what the black brothers plan on doing about it.'

'That depends if they know what's going on.' Reske added that to his list of questions. 'Some priests and priestesses travelled here on the same barge as me. The atmosphere between them was poisonous.'

Elisset folded her arms. 'I want no part of this.'

'You're handing back your oath?' Reske asked warily.

Elisset studied his face. 'I swore my oath to King Venais. At his death, my allegiance passed to his heir, Princess Idelina.'

'Will Captain Berake stay true to his vows?'

Elisset gazed over the river towards the sheer cliffs of the gorge. 'That remains to be seen. I'm not staying to find out.'

Reske didn't know the man, but he didn't envy Berake the snare he was caught in. Even when their forces didn't share a castle, a garrison captain's life got very difficult very fast if they fell out with the noble lord or lady who supplied their food and fodder in lieu of taxes to the crown. Keeping his troops fed would only be the start of Berake's problems once Baron Zavire declared Alriad was the rightful queen.

On the other hand, the Keeper of Secrets only knew how Captain Berake expected to escape punishment when – if – Princess Idelina inherited the crown. The man must have sworn his loyalty to King Venais and his heirs before the temple mother here in Bastrys. Her golden pendant's glow would have shown everyone he was sincere. The father of the Bastrys shrine would have called on the Horned God's magic as Berake affirmed his new vows, rendering any previous allegiance null and void. The priest must have declared he heard no hint of a lie. Berake would have been instantly dismissed from the crown's service if that hadn't happened.

'Will the garrison split into factions?'

Elisset shook her head. 'I cannot say.'

Couldn't say, or would not? Reske didn't press the point. Regardless, morale in the Bastrys garrison must be as threadbare as a beggar's breeches. 'May I know where you are going?'

She waited a long moment before answering. 'Hedvin.'

'May I ride with you?'

For the first time, Elisset smiled. 'If you think you can keep up.'

Reske grinned. 'I'll do my best. Do you think Baron Lebarre will keep faith with Princess Idelina?'

'I have every faith in Captain Yedeth who commands the Hedvin garrison.' Elisset shrugged. 'From what I hear of the noble Baron Lebarre, his priority will be continuing to profit from the grain, beef and other goods from the Vale of Hurat crossing his lands on their way to Velasta. Earl Padran of Evarise is better placed to guarantee that, if he's got the whip hand on the crown council.'

Reske knew harvests from the grainlands between the Tane and the Hedvin Gap filled bread baskets as far as the capital. The salt raked from evaporation ponds fed by the brine springs around Hatalys, and the darker crystals hewn from caverns upstream from Mithess, met countless needs across Arafaze. Jedfal's mills produced the realm's most reliable and effective firing powder, reserved for the crown's cannoneers.

The lords and ladies ruling lands along the Dore and the Tane would hardly sit on their hands once these border barons declared themselves. Which claimant to the crown would Hurat's nobility support, to best safeguard their own interests? Would the crown's garrison captains across the province stay loyal to their oaths and to Idelina? Would they yield to necessity like Captain Berake, if the baron or margrave who kept them fed pledged support for Alriad? Hurat's castellan's decision would be crucial.

Reske must get this news to Earl Debin as fast as possible, in a ciphered and thrice-sealed letter, ideally carried by a crown courier. Their brass-riveted cases were sewn from leather boiled in oil, hard enough to foil any knife, and double twists of wire with crimped lead seals were threaded through their buckles. He couldn't do that from here.

'What's our quickest route to Hedvin? Where's the best place to buy a horse?'

Elisset picked up her bag. 'This way.'

Reske followed her towards the river, walking carefully down the steep terraced streets. Sharp-edged cobbles were set at angles into the roadway to help horses and mules hauling carts and carriages uphill. Tripping and falling on those would do his aching knees no good at all.

Eventually they reached the water and Elisset strode along the wharf. 'I know an honest horse trader. She's—'

Commotion ahead drowned out her words. Reske heard shouts of alarm and distress. He forced his way through the gathering crowd. Out on the river, two women in a rowing boat wrestled a dark, bulky shape out of the Dore. As they drifted towards the bank, nearby barge hands used boat hooks to help.

Somebody gasped as they realised the dark shape was a body. The corpse's face and hands were bloodless white against his black robe.

'A priest?' A horrified whisper broke the hush.

One of the boat women shouted to the crowd. 'Does anyone recognise this young brother?'

That was Brother Rendel. No one else seemed to know him. Reske kept his mouth shut as he forced his way back from the water. He'd wager pebbles to pomegranates this death was no accident. Before he had left Velasta, Reske hadn't been able to trace the grey-haired woman or her hirelings who had attacked Brother Haber. But he'd learned several other priests had been attacked. Two had died.

'Did he drown?' a voice asked no one in particular.

Reske didn't think that was likely. He and the young priest had shared a cabin on the journey down river. They had swapped stories of days gone by to avoid discussing the present uncertainty. Rendel had grown up beside Lake Carine. He had been able to swim.

Elisset was waiting by a warehouse door. 'What's happened?'

'Later,' Reske said curtly. 'Where's your horse trader.'

His business was getting answers for his liege lord, not facing awkward questions if the shaven-headed priest saw him in this crowd. Once they were on the road to Hedvin, Reske would see if Elisset could explain what in the blackest night was going on.

Chapter Eight

BASTRYS

13th of the Blossom Moon

'We'll be home in another ten days.' Quenild squeezed Ticosa's hand.

Standing with them on the barge's stern deck, Ristal nudged the tiller to guide *The Beech Tree* into its designated berth. 'More like twelve.'

'After so much rain?' Ticosa countered. 'Bet you a gold mark.'

Ristal grinned, gap-toothed. 'You're on.'

The barge kissed the wharf and Yanter leaped ashore to loop the prow rope around a bollard. The two women secured the stern.

'Don't make a late night of it,' Ticosa advised Ristal. 'We'll cast off at first light.'

Quenild looked across the river to the southern bank and the last looming outcrop of the Bastrys mountains. Dusk was falling fast. 'Yanter, stay with Squirrel while we go and eat.'

'I know,' the lad said, rueful. 'Youngest is last ashore, though—'

'Good evening, ladies. My compliments on your man's boat-handling skills.'

The stranger who had interrupted Yan wore a sable cloak over a silk-embroidered doublet. He could have used his polished boots as a shaving mirror. His precisely shaped beard was slicked to a point with flowery pomade Quenild could smell from ten paces.

'Thank you.' Ticosa curtseyed, despite her boots, divided skirts and thick workaday jerkin.

Quenild watched the man preen, assuming she offered him due deference rather than veiled mockery. 'How may we help you?'

The stranger opened a ledger. Removing a glove that had never seen a day's toil, he licked a soft forefinger to turn the pages. 'You have a cargo of copper tea—'

She listened with astonishment as he detailed every item in their hold.

'— and five jars of pickled evissa berries. An astutely selected cargo for this time of year.'

'Thank you.' Quenild saw three footsoldiers in Bastrys Castle livery watching their conversation. One stood close at hand. One had walked along the wharf to *The Beech Tree*'s prow, to stare at Yanter. The other waited halfway between them.

'We will pay you twelve hundred and eighty gold marks.' The stranger closed his ledger with a self-satisfied snap.

Quenild tucked her hands behind her back so no one could see her clenched fists. 'Thank you for your offer, but our cargo is not for sale.'

She wanted to ask how in the blackest night this crested marsh-cock knew what they were carrying, but this was no time to lose her temper.

'This is not an offer.' The bearded man stopped smiling. 'This is the price you will accept.'

Ticosa was outraged. 'That's barely two thirds of its worth.'

'In Hurat, perhaps.' The marsh-cock shrugged. 'In Bastrys, a cargo is worth what Baron Zavire chooses to pay.'

'We will sell our goods at the place and price of our choosing.' Quenild managed to keep her voice level.

'And we'll be on our way.' Ticosa gestured to Yanter.

The footsoldier by the prow laid his hand on his sword hilt, daring the boy to touch the rope. Ristal glowered at the soldier standing behind the man with the ledger. The barge man's hand went to his belt knife.

'Wait!' Quenild's shout turned heads along the wharf for fifty paces.

'Then we have a deal.' The bearded man was repellently smug. 'I wish you a pleasant evening. We will offload your cargo tomorrow morning.'

'I will need a copy of your ledger entries to register this transaction with the temple,' Ticosa said through gritted teeth. 'And of your terms, to be deposited in the Moon God's keeping.'

The man dismissed that. 'You will have Lord Zavire's seal on a letter of credit.'

'You can whistle—'

Quenild cut Ticosa's fury short. 'Will Hurat's temple honour this letter?'

The bearded man ignored her. 'You should use it here to refill your hold with goods to sell in Hurat. We have much to offer.'

In other words, this paper was worthless outside Bastrys. Quenild bit the inside of her lip so hard she tasted blood. It was that or spit in this midden rat's eye.

'Until tomorrow.' The odious man snapped his fingers at the closest foot soldier. 'See these fair ladies are not disturbed overnight.'

Quenild noted the trooper's studiously blank expression. She watched the man with the ledger stroll along the wharf to the next moored barge. More footsoldiers appeared from behind a warehouse.

Ticosa waved her hands in disbelief. 'We're to hand over our cargo to these bandits, and use their Godless paper to buy goods they've stolen from someone else?'

'Come here, lad.' Quenild summoned Yanter with a jerk of her head.

The four of them went down into the cabin.

'That slick streak of rat shit can stick his offer where the stars don't shine,' Ticosa said, vehement.

'Ristal, go get yourself a meal.' Quenild was sweating despite the evening chill. 'Buy friends you trust a few drinks. Find out what they know about this madness. Be generous. I'll cover the cost.'

'Will do.' The grizzled steersman clearly assumed she would get them out of this trap.

Quenild fervently hoped she'd repay his trust as easily as refilling his purse.

'What do we do when they come to empty our hold in the morning?' Yanter was distraught.

Quenild knew his share of the profits paid his family's rent. 'We choose which arch of that bridge to shoot once we reach it. Stay here and make friends with those watchdogs. Share a couple of bottles of the sunshine stowed behind the ladder and see if that gets them talking.'

'We'll be back as soon as we can,' Ticosa assured the anxious boy, before glancing at her wife. 'Let's visit the shrine for sunset's devotions.'

The mountains across the river cut a saw-edged black line across the reddening sky. Lamps were already lit in the town. The footsoldiers standing guard looked bored.

Ticosa managed a brief smile as the two women walked away from their barge. 'Now we know Yan hasn't been snooping. He had no notion what we keep in there.'

'Let's hope he doesn't get a taste for it.' The potent liquor in the not-too-well-hidden compartment could distract thieves if the barge was broken into. Yes, it was also a test to see if a new crewman could be tempted or trusted. Most of the time though, a glass of the Tane's barley sunshine simply sweetened deals.

She took her wife's hand. 'Let's see what the black brothers have to say.'

They walked through Bastrys in silence and headed up the steep cobbled slope to the Moon God's shrine. The street outside the closed crescent gate was deserted.

Breathless, Ticosa paused for a moment. 'I'd have expected more traders to be making a fuss.'

'I'd have expected at least somebody with a belly ache.' Quenild knocked on the wicket door. No one came. She knocked some more. Eventually a priest with a lamp opened up.

'Why does this shrine allow Lord Zavire to rip up every trader's signed and sealed agreements?' Ticosa demanded. 'Does the shrine father know he's telling merchants what he'll pay and seizing their goods?'

Quenild watched fleeting emotions scud across the brother's face. 'If we reject his offer, will the Horned God's sons defend us?'

'I cannot say.' The black-clad priest tried to shut the door.

Quenild had her booted foot in the gap. 'Cannot or will not?'

The priest hesitated. 'Your safest course is to sell. Don't take his letter of credit though. Demand payment in full in coin and take that to the sisters in Hurat. The temple mother here backs the baron. If you wish to trade with Arafaze in future, sail your barge across Lake Chalus and up the Fasil river. There's a tributary south of Hedvin, a small river called the Ofin, which offers a route to the highway heading west. Your goods can be carried by wagon from there. Now, please, go in the Father's grace.'

He kicked Quenild's foot away. Before she could protest, the priest slammed the door and slid its bolts across for good measure. Quenild thrust her fists into her skirt pockets. It was that, or punch the tarred wood.

Ticosa's fury boiled over. 'Does he seriously think that revolting man will send us a handcart full of coin if we don't accept the baron's letter?'

Quenild shook her head. 'We must find a way out of this storm on our own. Where do you think Ristal will be?'

'Let's start with The Apple Dumpling.' Ticosa started walking.

At least they were heading downhill. They paused when they reached a cross-street and a lone carriage rattled past. As they drew closer to the Dore, the streets and alleyways grew busier. Whoever else might be losing out, innkeepers would turn a profit.

The Apple Dumpling had once been a wealthy merchant's fine house on a broad riverside road with a small courtyard at the front. Nowadays, tantalising scents of grilled meats and baked fish floated out of the ever-open front door.

Reaching the courtyard, Quenild shared a wondering glance with Ticosa. They could hear a single voice inside instead of the usual loud babble of conversation. They went in, alert in case of trouble. Whoever had built this house wouldn't recognise it. Every interior wall that didn't hold up the floor above had been stripped out, to accommodate as many tables and benches as possible. River traders and the folk who worked along the wharves and warehouses came here to eat day and night. Right now, every seat was taken, and men and women lined the walls, two and three deep. No one was interested in food.

An outraged barge man with a Tane accent stood on a table. 'We will not accept this banditry! Let's take our cargoes back home. Bastrys can go hungry and Baron Zavire can face his people's fury!'

A desperate woman challenged him. 'My children can't eat the calamine ores in my hold. If I can't sell them in Velasta, I can't buy them bread.'

A man shouted from the opposite corner. 'At least you can go home to Hurat. If I don't hand over my cargo, they won't let me pass. I'm stuck on the wrong side of Bastrys.'

Arguments flew back and forth. As far as Quenild could tell, roughly one in three of the resentful merchants saw no alternative to submitting. The rest were determined to travel onwards with their goods unplundered, or were ready to turn for home with their cargoes intact.

A weathered trader with sparse hair rose to his feet. 'Surely the Golden Mother will help us.'

'The sisters do nothing,' someone spat. 'The baron backs Princess Alriad and the high temple in Velasta has proclaimed her queen.'

Vehement denials overrode him, though Quenild couldn't hear what was disputed.

'I'll lend my voice to Alriad's cause,' a red-faced woman called out. 'If that's the price of permission to trade as I choose. If someone else wants me to cheer for Idelina, I'll do that as well. What's it to me who wears the crown in Velasta?'

Quenild saw widespread agreement. She and Ticosa didn't give a thought to Arafaze's monarch from one new moon to the next. They trusted the Goddess to safeguard their money when trade was good, and they knew they could go to the sisters for help if hard times struck. They asked the God to witness their private oaths as well as their business dealings, and went to the priests when someone was sick or injured. They trusted the Goddess and the God together would see justice done, if malice ever assailed them. At least, they had until now.

Ticosa nudged her. Quenild followed her gaze and saw Ristal on the other side of the room. He was scanning the crowd, apprehensive. Noticing them, he edged their way, jerking his head towards the door.

Quenild trusted Ristal's instincts. 'Let's get out of here.'

Before Ticosa could agree, commotion erupted outside in the courtyard. A woman screamed, outraged. A man's yell of protest was cut short with sickening swiftness. The baron's footsoldiers forced their way into the room, carrying brutal cudgels. Traders and merchants retreated as far as they could.

A liveried lieutenant advanced with his sword drawn. 'Who incited this riot?'

Those closest shrank from his menacing tone and the gleaming steel. Someone safely hidden by the crowd was bolder.

'There's no riot here unless you bastards start one.'

'This way.' Ristal grabbed Quenild's sleeve. She took tight hold of Ticosa's hand.

Ticosa winced. 'Where are we going?'

'Out through the back,' Ristal growled.

Plenty of others had the same idea. Bruising elbows jostled Quenild as they fought their way through the throng. As they stumbled into the kitchen, fat spilt from a skillet sent up a flare of flame on the range. Cooks and serving maids brandished ladles or long-handled pans. A man in a bloodied apron gripped a cleaver. The people surging past ignored them.

Once they were outside, Ristal paused on the edge of the light spilling from the lamp over the kitchen door. Quenild saw people scatter through the alleys threaded through the riverside streets. She took a deep breath and regretted it, catching the reek of the eating house's garbage. 'Which way, Ris?'

A shout echoed through the night. 'Hold! In Baron Zavire's name!'

Footsoldiers appeared. A burly sergeant went for Ristal. The barge man raised clenched fists as if he was ready to fight. The sergeant rushed forward. Ristal spun sideways, dropping to his hands and knees. The bald sergeant tripped over the kneeling barge man, falling headlong on the trampled earth.

'You there!' A soldier with a raised club tried to grab Quenild.

She sidestepped and swept the liveried woman's grasping hand down and around. Twisting the soldier's arm up behind her back, Quenild used the limb as a lever, forcing the Bastrys woman to bend double. Quenild shoved the back of her neck, driving her face into her rising knee. The woman staggered away, choking on blood streaming from her broken nose.

Ticosa's assailant was already flat on his back, gasping with pain. Ristal snatched up a fallen club and threatened a liveried youth dithering in the shadows. The youngster recoiled. Ristal hurled the club at him anyway.

'Come on!' The steersman darted towards an alley. Quenild and Ticosa followed close behind. As they ran through the concealing darkness, the sounds of brawling faded. No one slowed until they could see the shining river ahead.

Ristal stopped at the corner of a waterside warehouse and snatched a look along the wharf. 'Those toads are still squatting on the bollards.'

'Wait.' Quenild heard the faint shrill of whistles crying out for aid.

A few moments later, liveried men and women ran past the alley's mouth. Helping their fellow soldiers mattered more than guarding moored barges.

'Quick.' Ticosa led the way.

Other traders were coming back to their barges. On the far bank, lanterns hurried to and fro. The night breeze carried urgent voices up and down the river as Ticosa knocked quietly on *The Beech Tree*'s cabin window.

Yanter opened the stern hatch, pale in the light from the neighbouring barge's prow lantern. He kept tight hold of Squirrel's collar. 'It's all right. We're all right.'

'What did you two find out?' Ticosa demanded as they crowded into the cabin.

The boy answered first. 'The baron's soldiers hate that man with the beard. Two left as soon as he was out of sight, saying they were going to sleep in their own beds. I persuaded the last one to go home when I gave him the bottle of sunshine.' He looked anxiously for Quenild's approval.

'Well done.' She smiled to reassure him.

Yanter was still concerned. 'They said they'd be back to empty the hold in the morning.'

'Then we'll be gone before dawn,' Ticosa growled.

'Good to know.' Ristal was torn between relief and apprehension.

'Let's have something to eat and get some sleep. We'll head downstream before the wharf hens wake up.' Quenild hoped the scented, bearded man was so confident he had cowed the merchants that he'd never dream they would defy him. 'If we must, we'll cut our ropes and throw those soldiers in the river.'

Ristal liked that idea. 'Those louts at The Apple Dumpling had no notion how river traders fight.'

Ticosa opened a cupboard, taking out flatbreads, spiced sausage and smoked cheese. 'Not many of them sounded like Bastrys folk.'

Quenild found a selection of pickles. 'These stores will have to last us until we reach Chalus. We can't risk going ashore in Baron Zavire's fiefdom.'

Yan ruffled Squirrel's ears. The dog's attention was fixed on the cheese. 'What do we do when we get home.'

'First we sell our cargo for its true worth.' Quenild tried to sound more confident than she felt.

'Then we report this outrage to the temple and the shrine,' Ticosa said, vehement.

Quenild respected Temple Mother Finevre and Shrine Father Memlin, but she wasn't sure what they could do about any of this.

'What do we do after that?' Ristal demanded.

'Was anyone in The Apple Dumpling talking about sailing Lake Chalus?' Ticosa asked him.

'Then following the Fasil up to Hedvin?' Ristal snorted with derision. 'That fool notion was dreamed up by someone who's never set foot on a boat.'

Yanter raised a hand. 'Why so?'

Quenild realised the lad would only have seen Lake Chalus on a map. 'A boat needs a keel to sail deep, open water. A flat-bottomed barge will heel over as soon as the winds catch its sails.'

'And the Fasil is nothing like the Dore. It's fast water and spiteful, barely navigable,' Ticosa agreed. 'In any case, how many pack mules or wagons would we need to hire to carry even one barge's cargo along the highway? That cost alone would beggar us.'

'Let's discuss our options when we get home.' Quenild unlatched the folding table.

Ticosa set out the food. Yanter found plates, knives, spoons and glasses. Ristal fetched a few bottles of beer. They ate and drank in silence.

Chapter Nine

HURAT

24th of the Blossom Moon

'Her letter said they should arrive today.' Alory scraped up the last of his porridge. 'I'll wait outside.'

The bench where he sat had been pulled close to the table to suit the shorter sisters. As he extricated himself, his face reddened with embarrassment.

Jadewin watched the boy put his empty bowl in the basket for dirty crockery. As he left the refectory, she continued eating, thanking the Golden Mother for the honey and raisins stirred into the oatmeal. Her sisters ate heartily, preparing for a day walking the length and breadth of Hurat.

Sister Hasrine slipped into the space Alory had left. 'Blessings of the new day.'

'And to you.' Jadewin noted the Velastan's breakfast was a beaker of water and a dry heel of yesterday's bread. She helped herself to a soft morning roll and reached for the cherry jam.

'Did you invite that boy to fill his belly?' Hasrine demanded. 'His duties should keep him within the crescent gate.'

'What exactly is your concern?' Jadewin asked mildly as she ate her roll.

Hasrine narrowed her eyes. 'The Moon God's sons have fallen into grave error. Their folly must not influence our sisters.'

'You mean the high shrine in Velasta supports Earl Padran of Evarise and Princess Idelina, rejecting the notion of Princess Alriad as regent.' Jadewin considered taking another roll, but eating merely to provoke Hasrine was an unworthy use of the Mother's bounty. 'Why should we shun our worthy brothers here over a difference of opinion so far away?'

'Princess Idelina still rejects the Golden Mother's care in her pregnancy. What can she be hiding?' Hasrine spoke loudly enough to turn heads at neighbouring tables.

Mother Finevre was sitting directly behind her. 'What has that to do with us?'

The Velastan priestess hadn't noticed. Jadewin hid her amusement in her cup of pale copper tea.

'Good sister.' Finevre twisted around to speak to Hasrine with calm authority. 'We work alongside our brothers to benefit the folk we serve. Our skills and resources complement theirs. Out in the grasslands and grainlands, humble sanctuaries shelter altars to the Goddess and to the God under one roof. As for young Alory, he's been in and out of here since he was a ragged child. Why should he not be welcome?'

'Excuse me, Mother.' Hasrine's lips pressed tight together with annoyance as she stood up.

'Blessings on your day's work.' Finevre sighed as the thin woman walked away. 'I wish she would eat more,' she remarked to no one in particular. 'Hunger as a way of life is as ruinous to the body as it is to the spirit. Shall we take a little air, Jadewin?'

'Gladly.' Jadewin gathered up her cup, bowl and plate, put everything in the scullery basket and followed the old priestess through the temple's entrance hall. Outside, the rain of recent days had cleared, leaving the sky washed pale blue.

'It seems all manner of abstinence is the current fashion in Velasta,' she remarked.

'We must warn our younger sisters how easily fasting can become self-indulgence instead of self-discipline.' Finevre lifted her face to savour the sunshine. 'Hasrine stares into our Mother's light so earnestly, she blinds herself to the world around her.'

Jadewin wasn't overly concerned about that. 'She isn't here to preach denial of the flesh. She's been sent to promote Princess Alriad's cause.'

'What can our sisters in Velasta be thinking?' Finevre was exasperated. 'Princess Idelina is King Venais's heir. That's clear as day.'

'Unless some witness can confirm this story that Princess Alriad was born before Prince Fedrin.' Jadewin still found that hard to believe.

'No priestess attending the birth would agree to such deceit.' Finevre was adamant. 'But Mother Elyka tells me no temple record can be found. Papers get mislaid, of course, but I find such carelessness surprising.'

Jadewin found it suspiciously convenient. 'Is there any news of Princess Idelina's health? And little Princess Olyshai?'

'As far as I know, the child thrives.' Finevre sighed. 'I've heard nothing of Idelina's condition, though Father Memlin tells me the high priest is willing to crown her as queen as soon as the high temple agrees. That must mean she is well enough, surely?'

'Let's hope so.' Jadewin supposed this limited news was better than nothing.

Finevre watched Alory pacing by the open gate. 'If we don't want Hasrine taking an unhelpful interest in that boy, it might be as well if he spent a little less time here.'

'Indeed,' Jadewin agreed, 'but until Brother Cavore or another of Hurat's hidden brethren gets back, he needs someone to instruct him on the lore and perils of the unseen realm. I don't want the lad having nightmares about Brother Talaven's murder and waking up to find a winged serpent in his bed.'

She thrust away the memory of the mangled thing the hysterical boy had unwrapped. Thankfully the temple's furnace burned hot enough to consume the monster.

'Brother Cavore won't return any time soon.' Finevre's brow creased with concern. 'Father Memlin tells me onion-skin fever is spreading through the downlands. Cavore has been told to assist the sanctuary in Streit.'

'Oh dear.' Jadewin grimaced.

Alory raised a hand, turning towards them. 'Sister!'

Jadewin saw two merchant women approach the gate, sensibly dressed for work and travel, though embroidery brightened their skirt hems, and the collars and cuffs of their long-sleeved jerkins.

'The taller woman is Quenild, Prylla's sister,' Mother Finevre murmured. 'Take them to Castellan Maixen. Bring me their news after that.'

'As soon as I can,' Jadewin promised.

She joined Alory. She could see Quenild's resemblance to the lad's mother. Prylla and her younger children came to the temple when her husband's erratic earnings failed to put food on their table.

'Blessings on your safe arrival.' Jadewin greeted both women.

'You're from Velasta, sister?' The shorter woman, Ticosa, was polite but wary.

'I've been in Hurat since the last Ice Moon.' Jadewin hoped that reassured them. 'It's hardly surprising we haven't met, since you've had no need of us, thank the Goddess.'

'Quite so.' Quenild was as reserved as her wife. 'Tell me, Sister, what do you think of recent events in Velasta?'

Jadewin answered, forthright. 'I know any rift between the Moon God's sons and we who serve the Goddess will do nobody any good. As for this quarrel over who wears the crown, mischief flourishes in darkness. Goddess grant the truth will be brought into the light, and soon.'

Ticosa turned to Alory. 'Why are we meeting you here?'

Jadewin answered for him. 'Castellan Maixen wishes to see you. The only letters he gets from Velasta are screeds trying to convince him Princess Alriad was unjustly denied her birthright, or accusing Earl Lystro of Coylure of conspiracy to deny Princess Idelina her rightful inheritance. Neither side offers proof, only rumours and accusations. Alory assures me you will report whatever you have seen and heard honestly. The river traders say the same.'

Quenild narrowed her eyes at her nephew. Alory blushed scarlet.

'Mother Finevre and Shrine Father Memlin share Castellan Maixen's concerns,' Jadewin added. 'We are equally committed to defending the common folk's interests.'

Quenild shrugged, still stony faced. 'Let's go and see the castellan.'

Jadewin led the way. They crossed the high road running between the ferries and walked quickly through the grid of newer streets. Passing through the western gate, they crossed the wooden bridge.

Jadewin greeted the castle's sentries and halfway along the tunnel, she knocked on the guardroom door. 'Sergeant Lund, is the castellan in his audience chamber? Quenild Ditayan and Ticosa Reture have business with him.'

'That's where you'll find him.' The sergeant studied the merchant women, committing their faces to memory before he waved them on. 'Good day to you.'

As they walked into the castle yard, Jadewin saw Quenild and Ticosa covertly looking around. So they'd never been inside these ramparts to attend a quarterly assize. Hopefully that vouched for their honesty and sharp wits rather than skills in hiding shady dealings. The priestess hid her amusement at Alory's airy familiarity as he pointed out the cannon training ground, the workshops, storehouses and barracks.

'Father Memlin trusts me to carry news he gets from Velasta to the castellan,' he explained casually.

Jadewin saw no reason to say Mother Finevre had suggested the shrine father use the boy as his personal messenger.

The soldier on duty at the Castellan's Tower bowed to Jadewin and opened the door. Inside, townsfolk waiting to see Maixen glanced at the merchant women with mild curiosity. Jadewin was relieved to see no one recognised Quenild or Ticosa. The less gossip about their visit the better.

Senon sat at a desk guarding the door to the spiral stair. 'Sister.'

'Is he alone?'

'No, but that won't be an issue.' The steward ushered them up to the floor above. Approaching the audience chamber, Jadewin heard Mistress Zile's voice. Had the chief scrivener, or her smooth-faced deputy Byen, found a significant document in the castle's archive? Something to uphold or disprove Brother Talaven's belief that the Arafaze crown could no longer claim Hurat's loyalty?

She knocked on the door and went in without waiting for a reply. 'Good day, Castellan, Mistress Scrivener.'

Maixen and Mistress Zile sat on opposite sides of the long table. The polished wood was covered with letters. Maixen rose to greet the merchants. 'Thank you for coming, and you are most welcome. Please, what can you tell me about the current mood in Velasta, and what in the blackest night is happening in Bastrys?'

'What other tasks do you have today?' Quenild asked wryly. 'This will take some time.'

'You have my attention for as long as you need it,' Maixen assured her.

Jadewin took a seat at the end of the long table and listened as the women shared what they had learned in Velasta, then told the tale of their journey home. Senon arrived with tall pots of silver tea and two plates of pastries, sweet and savoury. He silently served everyone, then sat beside Jadewin.

'We kept hearing King Venais and Earl Maren of Evarise had been struck down by some night terror called the Lightning King.' Clearly, Ticosa didn't believe in phantasms. 'The superstitious insist this proves Prince Fedrin was second-born, and Alriad should have been crowned queen when their father died.'

'That old nonsense? Shut your mouth, lad, before a fly lands in it.' Maixen advised Alory. 'A glimpse of the Lightning King supposedly predicts misfortune, but the only people I've ever known who claimed they had seen him wanted an excuse for their own bad judgement.'

'As the castellan says, that's a foolish Velastan superstition. Best not repeated.' Jadewin made sure her face showed mild disdain instead of the alarm she truly felt. The last thing she needed was such gossip spawning this manifestation in Hurat.

After the merchants explained the shocking situation in Bastrys, Maixen looked along the table to Jadewin. 'Sister, has anyone brought a letter of credit bearing Baron Zavire's seal to Hurat's temple?'

'We've seen a handful. Mother Finevre has turned them away.' The shrewd old priestess didn't need the Goddess's magic to know those traders weren't telling her the full story.

Jadewin had been interested to see Sister Hasrine's anger. Not because the letters of credit had been rejected. Because the Velastan priestess had known nothing about them.

Unfortunately Jadewin couldn't decide if Hasrine was furious at being left out of her Bastrys sisters' plotting, or if she was enraged by Baron Zavire's trespass on the Goddess's domain.

Alory brushed pastry flakes from his black robe. 'How did you escape with your cargo?'

'We left Baron Zavire and his flunky snoring,' Quenild told him. 'We cast off the next day as soon as I could tell a black thread from white.'

Maixen laughed. 'Who taught you that old trooper's trick?'

Quenild grinned. 'My grandfather. And he said never hesitate when you're threatened, even if the best path ahead isn't clear.'

Maixen nodded, approving. 'When in doubt, gallop.'

Ticosa took up the tale. 'Lots of others were keen to leave Bastrys. By the time someone alerted the garrison, half the boats moored overnight were following us downstream.'

'I don't think the wharf masters were in any hurry to send word to the castle,' Quenild observed.

'Someone did their best to stop us,' Ticosa said grimly. 'They fired the rampart guns and the cannon. Thank the Goddess we were already out of range, but a couple of the stragglers were hit.'

Quenild continued. 'We kept our barges close together until everyone passed safely beyond Baron Zavire's fiefdom. Those who needed to make repairs and tend to their wounded stopped in Chalus.'

'The word along the Dore is the Bastrys Gorge is closed to merchants who won't yield to Baron Zavire's robbery.' Ticosa shook her head.

'People are actually considering this idiotic plan of sailing barges across Lake Chalus and up the river Fasil.' Quenild was dubious.

Jadewin had no idea what they were talking about, but she trusted the women's judgement, if they thought this was a bad idea.

'They won't like what they find if they do,' Maixen gestured towards the letters on the table. 'Baron Lebarre of Hedvin has declared Idelina as queen. Only merchants who acknowledge her unquestioned right to the crown will be permitted to travel his roads. He awaits further instructions from Earl Padran of Evarise, so recent despatches inform me.'

Jadewin considered the hilly forest between Hedvin and Bastrys on the keep's great painted map. 'Do you think Earl Padran will tell Baron Lebarre to attack Baron Zavire?'

'He may not get the chance,' Maixen commented, thoughtful. 'I'm told Baron Lensin of Chalus is on the verge of declaring for Queen Alriad. If I was Earl Lystro of Coylure, I would tell Lensin to attack Hedvin from the east, while Baron Zavire attacks from the west.'

Jadewin's mouth was dry. 'How far and how fast could such warfare spread?'

'There's no way to know.' Mistress Zile slapped the table with a wrinkled, ink-stained hand. 'But there's one way to keep the peace. We tell the nobility here they are not free to swear fealty, no matter whom they believe should wear the Arafaze crown. They remain sworn to the Earls of Hurat.'

Jadewin didn't understand. 'But there is no Earl of Hurat.'

'Can you be certain, good sister?' Mistress Zile's eyes glinted. 'King Ganirin had two wives who bore him eight sons. Then there are his mistresses' children. The old laws on this side of the mountains may have insisted only men could inherit, but those ancient codes made no distinction between those born in or out of wedlock. Seventeen generations have succeeded Ganirin. We have to trace every descending family line to be sure no male heir to the title remains.'

Jadewin pursued her lips. 'You expect Hurat's lords and ladies to sit on their hands while your people scour the archives?'

'I suspect a good many will be glad of an excuse to rebuff both factions.' Mistress Zile peered at Alory like a bird contemplating a tasty morsel. 'You can help, lad. I hear you were Brother Talaven's apprentice in the shrine library.'

The young priest had been explaining the lack of an heir to the earldom to his aunts, low-voiced. He broke off and nodded dutifully.

'That news will soon spread.' Ticosa looked at the castellan, expectant.

'We're counting on it,' Maixen said frankly. 'As long as the townsfolk are gossiping and speculating about long-lost heirs, they won't be choosing sides in this quarrel.'

Quenild had other concerns. 'How are you going to break Baron Zavire's stranglehold on river trade beyond Bastrys?'

'I don't know.' Maixen met her gaze. 'But you have my word I'll do my utmost to find a way. Meantime, bring me whatever fresh news you hear along the wharves. There's no knowing what might be the key.'

'Of course.' Quenild didn't look convinced.

'I don't believe we have anything further to discuss, Castellan.' Mistress Zile rose slowly from her seat. 'I will set Byen searching the archives.'

Senon was already opening the audience chamber's door. He helped the aged scrivener down the spiral stair, and Jadewin followed Quenild and Ticosa out of the tower. Seeing Sister Hasrine greeting passers-by outside the castle sanctuary, the priestess decided asking the merchants not to repeat those rumours of the Lightning King could wait.

She forced a smile as she reached the Velastan. 'Sister, what brings you here today?'

Hasrine smiled back, slyly triumphant. 'Mother Finevre has agreed this sanctuary will benefit from a resident daughter.'

'May the Goddess's light shine upon your service.' Jadewin walked away before Hasrine saw her dismay. Why had Mother Finevre agreed to this? What was the scheming Velastan planning now?

Chapter Ten

HURAT

7th of the Hare Moon

'That accounts for the last of Lord Letarim's grandsons.' Byen crossed out a name on his list, and let the bundle of parchments he had been reading roll themselves up. 'Dead in his bed in his sixty seventh year, with his husband at his side. Sincerely mourned by all who knew and valued him, but not by any heirs.'

'A life well lived.' Across the table, Alory was forcing an obstinate scroll flat with a forearm. He didn't look up, in case he lost his place. The faded script of these ancient documents made his eyes ache.

'How's Lord Ridast?' Byen put his pens in their box.

'Still collecting rents but not remarrying.' With a bevy of adult daughters, Alory guessed this widowed noble had no wish for more children.

'I'm needed upstairs tomorrow. The assizes are nearly here.' Byen used the snuffer on its chain to kill his scrivener's lamp's bright flames. It had four separate wicks and a polished silver shield which could be adjusted to reflect their light onto a page.

'The justiciars will be busy,' Alory commented.

The revelation that King Venais had been the last Earl of Hurat had spread like wildfire in grassland. The startling notion that a long-forgotten heir might be discovered had followed just as fast. Unfortunately, Castellan Maixen had been overly optimistic when he hoped this would distract Hurat's townsfolk. Heated confrontations between factions supporting the rival princesses frequently turned into brawls. The shrine's infirmary treated broken noses, split knuckles and vicious bruises daily. Here in the castle, Brother Delnor was busier too, as footsoldiers returned from nightly patrols through the town in need of bandages or stitching.

Sister Jadewin said the violence was an outlet for fear and anger over Baron Zavire's blockade of the Dore. Aunt Quenild said trade between Hurat's towns as far as Chalus was slowing now. She and Aunt Ticosa had headed upstream on the Tane a few days ago. Alory hoped they returned with better news.

Byen chuckled as he arched his back, diligently easing his shoulders. 'I wonder how many long-lost heirs Mistress Zile has seen today. She said the ink was barely dry on the last lot of supposedly ancient papers endorsing some chancer's claim. Come on, lad, that's enough for today. You have your duties in the sanctuary.'

Alory assessed the yellowing daylight outside the keep. The shallow windows high in the archive walls were at ankle height to anyone walking past. 'I can get to the end of this scroll first.'

'Make sure that's all you do.' Byen stood up. 'I'll see who we can spare to help you tomorrow.'

'Thanks.' Alory tried to concentrate on the scroll instead of the scrivener's retreating footsteps.

He heard the iron-barred door at the top of the stone steps open and close, then Byen locked it behind him. That was fine. Alory had his own key. He reminded himself he had checked every corner and shadowy alcove of this vast stone-vaulted undercroft in the unreal world several times. There really and truly was nothing here except scrolls and ledgers and countless bundles of ribbon-tied parchments. The archive didn't feature in the soldiers' eerie stories he couldn't help overhearing as he helped Brother Delnor in the castle's infirmary.

Resolute, Alory deciphered the last paragraphs of the tattered parchment and found a brief account of Lord Ridast's death. A sudden squall had overturned his boat on a pleasure cruise across Lake Chalus, one fine spring day. Lord Ridast could swim and was rescued, but he suffered inflammation of the lungs which rapidly proved fatal.

Alory crossed him off his list, recalling the laboured wheezing of elderly patients in the shrine's infirmary. How would such ailments be treated without medicines from Velasta's apothecaries? What would cure summer's recurrent fevers? How many folk would die on the other side of the Bastrys mountains for lack of the Nilgeh Mire's potent herbs to soothe toad pox and onion skin fever?

Alory capped his inkwell and put away his pens. Sister Jadewin would tell him to focus on the here and now. Such questions would be answered in the Goddess's and the God's good time. The young priest went through the shoulder and neck stretches Scrivener Byen insisted on every day. Then he lit a candle stub and deftly quenched his oil lamp's flames with licked fingers. Shadows thickened around him as he walked to the archive door. Reaching through the slit side seam in his robe, he found the key in his breeches' pocket.

Once he'd locked up, his quickest route to the sanctuary took him through the keep past the banqueting hall. Aunt Quenild said Hurat's guilds were demanding a feast to celebrate the birth of Princess Idelina's child, whenever that happened. Aunt Ticosa said Maixen was avoiding giving an answer one way or the other.

Jadewin told Alory the castellan had no intention of hosting any feast which might encourage Earl Padran of Evarise to assume Princess Idelina could call on the crown's forces in Hurat, and give Princess Alriad and Earl Lystro of Coylure a reason to list Maixen with their enemies.

Thinking about a feast, Alory realised he was hungry and thirsty. Once he had done his duty in the sanctuary, he would go to the castle kitchen—

Outside the keep, movement caught his eye. In the fading light, Alory couldn't tell if the shadowy figure by the sanctuary door was a man or woman. Regardless, they didn't want to be seen. Glancing this way and that, the furtive stranger slipped inside.

Whoever it was hadn't noticed him. Alory realised his black robes must be lost in the darkness of the keep behind him. He hurried over, soft-footed. Breathing a prayer to the Father of Night, Alory stole a quick look through the sanctuary door.

Sister Hasrine knelt before the Golden Mother's altar. The stranger walked down the aisle between the bench seats to join her. He didn't wear Hurat livery. The Goddess's polished brass lamp was still lit, though Alory saw Hasrine had put the taper and spark maker ready on the Moon God's altar. The interfering priestess persisted in lighting his silver lamp at dusk as often as she could.

Alory ground his teeth. Hasrine had been told these rites were his responsibility. He wanted to rebuke the Velastan, but Jadewin said he mustn't start an argument. She said his most important task was watching Hasrine and reporting whatever the spiteful priestess did.

Was this his chance to learn why she wanted him out of the castle so badly? Alory strained his ears to listen.

'You've made precious little progress,' the Velastan priestess hissed.

'Hardly anyone's heard of the Lightning King this side of the Bastrys mountains,' the stranger protested. 'And your sisters and my former brothers do a cursed good job convincing Hurat folk to shun gossip about phantasms.'

'Do better and do it fast.' Hasrine ordered. 'I want the Lightning King stalking these streets inside ten days.'

'I'll do my best,' the stranger sounded dubious. 'Can't you use some local tale of unquiet dead?'

'Why would a contested crown concern Hurat's ghosts?' Hasrine sneered. 'If you want our continued protection, get this done. Now get out of my sight.'

Alory sprinted away from the door. Halfway to the keep, he halted, turned around and strolled back towards the Sanctuary, fighting to slow his breath. He saw the stranger leave and walk towards the castle gate. The man didn't even glance in Alory's direction.

The young priest hesitated. The stranger must have passed the gatehouse to enter and leave the castle. He could ask the soldiers on duty about him. But that would leave Hasrine on her own in the sanctuary. Alory walked faster. He tried to make his face as unrevealing as the God's icon – until he saw Hasrine lighting the God's silver lamp.

'Sister! I told you I would be here in good time.' Alory didn't hide his anger. Brother Talaven had said that was a good way to conceal anything else he might be thinking.

'I'm so sorry.' The priestess offered the Moon God's icon a graceful curtsey, then crossed to the Golden Mother's altar and extinguished her lamp. 'I mean no disrespect.'

No disrespect to the God maybe, but what about to him? Alory bit back that challenge. He had seen his father goad his mother into a quarrel often enough, so the drunken bully could vent his frustrations on her with his fists. Did Hasrine hope he would storm out of the castle and go back to the shrine of his own accord?

The Velastan priestess walked out of the sanctuary without sparing him a glance. Alory went to kneel before the Moon God's altar. Brother Talaven told him to seek guidance when he didn't know what to do next.

Alory's eyes prickled with tears. He missed Brother Talaven so badly. The old priest had always encouraged his questions, even if the answer was that no one really knew. Why were lifeless things identical in both realms of existence? How did changes in the tangible world manifest in the unreal realm? Did that happen the other way round? If creatures in the intangible realm damaged something, would that be reflected here?

Alory scrubbed his face with his hands. Then he noticed the altar's white drape wasn't falling smoothly to its plinth. Standing up, he went to straighten the linen. He noticed a smudge of oil on the white ceramic jar tucked behind it. Lifting the drape, he reached for the rag in the wooden tray that kept the stone floor pristine. Picking up the oil jar to wipe it clean, Alory was surprised by its weight. He set the jar carefully down and checked the burning lamp. It barely held enough oil to stay lit until midnight.

The young priest looked up at the God's shining icon, wondering what to do. He couldn't pour oil into a lamp that was already burning without most likely making a torch of himself. Letting the silver lamp cool before he refilled it would leave the Sanctuary in darkness. Alory had no doubt Sister Hasrine would discover the divine light had gone out, and blame him for such shameful neglect. She'd insist he was sent back to the shrine in disgrace.

Sister Jadewin needed to know. Also, she might have some idea how to refill the silver lamp before the oil ran out. Alory bowed to the Moon God and left the Sanctuary. He was still hungry but that must wait. He could quench his thirst though. He hurried to the well house and dipped a handful of cold water from the bucket outside the door.

For the second time that evening, movement in the dusk snagged his eye. A slender figure in a pale robe walked to and fro by the practise cannons? He stood very still. As long as he didn't move, Sister Hasrine shouldn't see him with the well house behind him.

A second figure appeared, breeched and booted and wearing a crown livery tunic. Whoever it was staggered forward to lean on the old cannon's barrel. Their head hanging, they seemed utterly exhausted. Alory blinked and the figure was gone. What—?

Drawing a careful breath, the young priest looked into the unreal world. The shifting and shimmering figure stood by the cannon. Sister Hasrine was there as well. But Jadewin had assured him the Velastan had no magic. Hasrine had deliberately concealed her knowledge of the intangible realm. That broke every oath Brother Talaven said the hidden brethren and the secret sisterhood swore to obey.

Now she was summoning a manifestation. Furious, Alory longed to stride forward, to challenge her. He clenched his fists instead. He might know what she was doing, but he had no idea why. He also didn't know how proficient Hasrine might be with magic, and he was painfully aware of his own limited skills.

Alory focused on the phantasm so he could describe every detail to Jadewin. He didn't think this could be the Lightning King, even though Jadewin had refused to describe that supposedly terrifying apparition. As far as Alory could tell, Hasrine was drawing forth someone's memory of a cannoneer.

The treacherous priestess vanished from the unreal realm. Alory hastily returned his gaze to the tangible world. The castle's sounds were deafening. His knees buckled and he landed with a thud on the bench by the well house. He remembered Brother Talaven's lessons and focused on the hard wood under his buttocks, on the chill water dripping from his hand. This was his reality.

As his queasiness faded, he saw Sister Hasrine rounding the keep. She would be going to the room she had claimed, close to the Infirmary. Should he go after her? No. He must dispel the apparition. Then he would find Jadewin, and tell her what he had done. And ask what he could do about the Sanctuary lamp.

Resolute, he walked towards to the cannon. No one was there in the tangible realm. Alory laid a hand on the rusted iron and looked into the unseen world.

The apparition stumbled into him. Its head was a ruin of red flesh and blackened burnt skin. A silent scream showed shattered teeth in its broken jaw. Its arms ended in bloody stumps with shards of bone pale amid seared flesh.

Alory clapped a shaking hand to his mouth to stifle a yell. He knew what this horror was. Old cannons sometimes exploded. Brother Delnor had told him how a catastrophe had killed two recruits last year. One had lingered in the infirmary for a day and a night. Sister Hasrine must have heard someone's recollection of the garrison's loss.

Alory assessed the phantasm as steadily as he could. To his relief, the gruesome figure shivered and dulled. If it could barely sustain itself in the unreal world, he didn't think much of its chances of manifesting in the castle compound. He could make certain it didn't.

A blade of moonlight coalesced in his fist. Alory thrust the luminous blade into the apparition's face, determined to unmake this ghastly vision. The phantasm evaporated like water spilled on a hot griddle. Quickly, he focused on the tangible realm. The phantasm was nowhere to be seen there either.

So far, so good. Alory hurried out of the castle and through Hurat's busy streets. Now the working day was done, the townsfolk were on their way to spend the evening by their own firesides. Others would go drinking with friends, or pay for the temporary embrace of warm flesh.

In the temple's entrance hall, Sister Paske was consoling a woman overwhelmed by grief. Alory rang the brass bell that would summon another sister. He breathed his thanks to the lord of night when Jadewin appeared.

She ushered him to the other side of the hall. 'Have you found Hurat some new earl?'

'Sister Hasrine—' Alory reddened as his empty belly growled.

'Haven't you eaten this evening? Let's find you something in the kitchen.'

'No, wait.' Alory told her about the sanctuary lamp. 'There's worse,' he went on. 'Hasrine has some stranger trying to stir up rumours of the Lightning King, to provoke a manifestation. She tried summoning a phantasm in the castle.'

'She did what?' Jadewin's shout startled the weeping woman and Sister Paske. She ushered Alory out into the temple yard. 'Tell me everything.'

Alory did so. 'He's not one of the men who summoned that winged snake. He might have been sworn to a shrine for a while.'

It was common enough to spend a few years serving the Moon God or the Golden Mother before returning to secular life. Alory had considered that before he decided to become a priest.

Jadewin rubbed the back of her neck. 'Some … are given no choice about surrendering to a temple or shrine. If the hidden brethren or the secret sisterhood discover they can see the unseen world.'

'Oh.' Alory had wondered about that. He'd assumed Brother Talaven would explain in the God's good time.

'Could Sister Hasrine have some inkling of your magic?' Jadewin wondered. 'Perhaps that's why she wants to discredit you.'

'I can't see how,' Alory protested. 'The only magic she could have seen me work was dispelling her phantasm. But I'm sure she didn't.'

'Let's hope so.' Jadewin moved on. 'You were right to do that as soon as you saw it. Hasrine must have heard about that accident you mentioned. As soon as one of the garrison glimpsed it, the tale would be retold. Every time that happened, the phantasm's resemblance to one of the victims would strengthen. It would appear more often and we'd have a task and a half to dispel it.'

'How would that help this Lightning King manifest?' He still didn't understand that.

Jadewin explained. 'If Hurat's townsfolk started looking over their shoulders for some nightmare in the shadows, Hasrine's accomplice, whoever he is, would have better luck stirring up rumours of the Lightning King. And the superstitious claim seeing a ghost is a warning of trouble ahead. I'm sure Hasrine is ready to offer dire predictions unless Princess Alriad claims the crown.'

Alory had more immediate concerns. 'What am I going to do about the sanctuary lamp?'

'Relight the Goddess's flame,' Jadewin said briskly. 'She will gladly lend you her radiance to defeat an unworthy daughter's spite. Let the Horned God's lamp cool and refill it with oil. Relight it, and make very sure you're in the sanctuary before dawn. We want to know who Hasrine brings to witness what she expects to find. Keep your eyes open in the unreal world as well as the tangible realm now, whenever she's around. But try not to let her see you there.'

'Can you be in the sanctuary with me at dawn?' Alory wanted her support if he had to confront Hasrine.

Jadewin grimaced. 'If I can. This changes things. We have to recall our sisters and brothers who can work magic to Hurat. I've already sent word to Cavore, but we'll need everyone here if the Lightning King does manifest.'

'What does he – it,' Alory hastily corrected himself, 'look like?'

'I'm still not going to tell you.' Jadewin startled him with a grin. 'You have a powerful talent for engaging with the unreal world. If you visualise the thing clearly enough, you could make it appear by accident.'

'Oh.' That was a compliment Alory could do without. 'This phantasm, could it really have killed King Venais?'

'No,' Jadewin said firmly. 'No manifestation of the unreal world could possibly control a storm in the tangible realm. The king's hunting party ignored threatening weather and they paid the penalty. Folk have died from folly before, and others will in days to come. The Golden Mother and the Horned God watch over us, but they expect us to look out for ourselves as well.'

She reached into the leather purse threaded onto her rope girdle and handed him a few coins. 'Buy something to eat on your way back.'

'Thank you.' Alory would have preferred the familiar, humble soup and bread served to the indigent each evening, but Jadewin was walking into the temple.

He left through the Goddess's ever-open gate and made his way through Hurat. A food vendor was cooking skewered morsels of spiced meat in the square outside the shrine. Alory handed over Jadewin's coins and ate, trying not to blister his mouth. Looking at the crescent gate, he remembered his simpler life before Brother Talaven had casually asked about his daydreams and nightmares.

There was no going back, as surely as night followed day. There was no unseeing what had been seen, in the tangible world or the unseen realm. Alory tossed the wooden skewers into the brazier and went on his way.

The castle's guards let him pass without questions. Reaching the sanctuary, he found a trio of elderly servants occupied in silent, private devotions. Alory took a seat just inside the door. He could wait for them to undo Hasrine's trickery with the sacred lamps.

Then he would sleep between the altars, to stop the Velastan trying anything else. The sanctuary floor would be no harder than the yard where he'd spent the nights when his father locked him out of the house for trying to defend his mother. It would certainly be warmer.

While he waited, Alory prayed to the Moon God, the Scourge of Liars, and to the Sun Goddess, whose light divined all truth. He and Jadewin needed to know who Sister Hasrine's allies were, and how many there might be.

Chapter Eleven

HEDVIN

10th of the Hare Moon

Finally. At long last, Reske could see Hedvin's walls and southern gate ahead. If he'd had a current crown courier's medallion, if every garrison stable and way-station had fresh horses to swap for their exhausted mounts, he and Elisset could have been halfway to Velasta. But the brass token of his honourable discharge entitled him to a free bed, a meal, and no more.

He was still surprised there wasn't a more direct route from Bastrys. Elisset had assured him they had to follow the meagre river road east almost as far as Chalus. Then they could take a well-worn track through the edge of the Bastrys forest and reach the highway going north-west. After the second time Reske had wasted half a day following what seemed to be a promising short-cut only to find impenetrable trees, he had believed her.

He was grateful Elisset had slowed her horses to a walk, knowing he would have to catch up. They had each purchased two mounts from her friend in Bastrys. Riding the horses on alternate days made sure none was overworked. Setting out with the dawn as the nights grew shorter meant they covered sufficient ground at a decent pace, and the weather had been pleasantly warm.

This final stretch of road was full of slowly moving carts, carriages, pack-animals, saddle-horses and foot-sore travellers.

Seeing the line ahead had ground to a halt, Reske let his horse slow and stop. A few paces behind, its stablemate stood with its leading rein hanging loose.

'What's the delay?' Elisset called out to some lads riding in the back of the cart ahead of them. 'Can you see?'

One of them shrugged. 'Everyone has to state their business at the gate.'

'Is there news from Velasta?' Reske asked as casually as he could.

The youth simply shrugged a second time. 'Not that I've heard.'

They really needed to know if either princess had been crowned while they had been travelling. The riverside road and the highway through the forest had been infuriatingly lacking in anyone who could tell them the latest. Reske was used to travelling between villages where locals loved to gossip with an open-handed stranger stopping at their tavern.

Of course, crown way-stations' dormitories and dining halls would be rife with rumour and verified facts. But crown couriers carried garrison notices from place to place as well as despatches. Captain Berake would be demanding Elisset was returned in irons to Bastrys by now, to answer for her desertion. The way-station clerks who recorded travellers' names and destinations would be watching for her.

So they had stopped at ramshackle traders' halts serving hard-faced men and women who didn't share their business or anything else with strangers. They ate dried meat, dried fruit and travel bread, drinking water tapped from the forest's vines. In between those halts, they found sheltered places out of sight of the road, taking turns to sleep on the blankets strapped behind their saddles. More often than not in the mornings, Elisset commented she had heard Reske grinding his teeth in his sleep.

He drummed impatient fingers on his thigh. News of the succession would have to wait, along with answers to every other question on Reske's lengthening list. He could hear axes ringing in the distance and see freshly-cut stumps among the trees a bowshot from the road. A lot of stumps. Scars in the leaf litter showed teams of horses had hauled the felled timber away. Where to, and why? Children were gathering hacked-off branches and brushwood. Fuel for fires. A lot of fires. Reske considered the pall of smoke hanging over the town. What were Hedvin's artisans working on so intently?

'We'll dine at The Silver Scales this evening.' Beside him Elisset sat relaxed in her saddle.

'I take it you've eaten there before?' Reske asked warily.

She chuckled. 'When someone else is paying. You should have listened when I told you there are no short cuts to the highway.'

'I should have known better than make a wager.' Reske hoped he carried enough coin to settle a stinging bill. He gestured at his creased clothes and his boots dull with dust. 'You're sure they'll let us in, looking like this?'

'If you let them look in your purse. Besides,' Elisset added seriously. 'The Silver Scales is a good place to overhear the wealthy and well-connected share what they know.'

'Good to know.' Reske hadn't only travelled with her because solitary bandits wouldn't take on two riders. Elisset knew her way around Hedvin. She had agreed to help him learn the latest news, in return for a reasonable fee if Captain Yedeth had no use for her in the crown garrison.

She glanced at him. 'So what do we say at the gate?'

'The truth, but only what we must.' He lowered his voice. 'Let's not mention Bastrys if we can avoid it.'

At best, admitting that's where they had come from risked being turned away out of hand. At worst, they could be seized and questioned until a priestess confirmed they weren't Baron Zavire's spies.

The line of people and beasts started moving again, more swiftly now. Reske urged his mount forward. The leading rein tightened as the second horse baulked, but a donkey braying somewhere back along the road got it moving.

Hedvin's twin-towered southern gatehouse was built of cream-coloured masonry, unlike the dour grey of Bastrys. Seasoned footsoldiers in Baron Lebarre's livery flanked the wide arch, apparently relaxed with their halberds sloped. Reske saw their eyes were vigilant. No one passed them without being questioned.

A double line of saw-horses blocked the cobbled road passing under the archway, to slow anyone fool enough to try forcing a way through. They'd regret that folly when these guards caught them. Hedvin was braced for trouble. Reske counted at least twenty soldiers high on the gatehouse and the same number on the bastions jutting out from the walls on either side. Rampart guns were clearly visible, and the dark outlines of cannon on the battlements. Sentries kept watch from the highest turrets.

'You two.' A sergeant snapped impatient fingers.

Elisset manoeuvred her horses ahead of him. Reske's second mount dug in its heels, snorting with alarm at this unknown place. By the time he got the recalcitrant beast moving, Elisset was talking to the sergeant.

'I swore my oath to King Venais. At his death, my allegiance passed to Princess Idelina.' She showed the sergeant her crown courier's medallion, discreetly cupped in her hand. 'I wish to report to the garrison here.'

Baron Lebarre's liegewoman grunted and glanced at Reske. 'Who's he?'

'Reske Masol. He's passing through.'

'I serve Earl Debin of Shirlat. I have his authority to send letters by crown courier, and I hope to find one heading for Velasta here.'

Reske hid his apprehension behind earnest concern. He really hoped the sergeant didn't ask what he was doing for his noble master, so far away from home. The woman hadn't reacted to Elisset's declaration of loyalty, so he could assume Baron Lebarre hadn't unexpectedly turned his coat and accepted Princess Alriad's claim to the crown. If the sergeant questioned Reske further though, and she wasn't satisfied with his answers, he might still end up in a cell. Hopefully, Hedvin's guards wouldn't risk a clash with the crown garrison, so that should protect Elisset. Reske had no such defence.

'You know your way to the garrison?' the sergeant asked Elisset. Seeing the courier nod, the guard waved her on. 'Report to Captain Yedeth.'

Two footsoldiers shifted a couple of sawhorses. Elisset walked her mounts through the archway beneath the portcullis. Reske would have followed, but the sergeant blocked his path.

'Can you pay for your bed and board? How soon will you be on your way?'

Reske gestured at his two horses. 'I'll leave as soon I can sell these and buy a fresh mount to take me to Velasta.'

The sergeant studied him for a moment, then stepped back to let him pass. 'The sunset bell means curfew. Get off the streets. Stay out of trouble.'

To Reske's relief, the horse he was leading decided to behave through the crowded gate. He caught up with Elisset and they rode on at walking pace.

Narrow clapboard houses pressed close on either side. This was where humbler folk lived. As they reached a more prosperous district, they passed workshops and storehouses, three or four storeys high. Brightly painted walls rose straight from the door-sills to weathered, shingled roofs. Hedvin's outer wall and gates might be stone, but this was a town of wooden buildings.

'That went easier than I expected,' Elisset commented after a while.

'Thanks to the God or the Goddess. I'll offer alms to both, to be on the safe side.' Reske wondered if a priest or priestess had been sitting behind one of the closest tower's slit windows. The sergeant's gaze had flickered that way a few times. Divine guidance would certainly help keep troublemakers out. He wondered if the God's servants and the Goddess's were still on good terms in Hedvin.

'I should see if the brothers and sisters hereabouts know of any plans for a coronation or a regency. Can you take my horses to the garrison stables and learn the latest news there? I'll reach the shrine and the temple faster on foot – if you tell me where to find them.'

'Follow your nose to the central marketplace.' Elisset gestured straight ahead. 'You'll find the temple on the road going to the east gate. Go west to find the shrine. If there's a curfew, we had better meet at The Silver Scales a couple of hours before that.'

'That's where?' Reske dismounted.

Elisset took the reins he offered, not bothered by the prospect of leading three horses behind the one she rode. 'In the central market place, next door to the Joiners Guildhall.'

'I'll see you there.' Reske stood for a moment and watched Elisset force a path through the crowded road to reach a side street. She edged her mount's head and forequarters into the first suggestion of a gap. Seeing the rest of the horse would follow, people opted to get out of her way. When they realised she led three more mounts, they kept moving.

Reske started walking, grimacing as he knuckled his back. He hadn't spent so many days in the saddle without a break since he had left the courier service. That had been half a lifetime ago. Right now, he felt every day of it.

An ink-stained man stumbled into him. 'Sorry. I'm sorry. Excuse me.'

By the time Reske regained his balance, the clerk had disappeared. If that's who he was. Reske checked his pockets. He breathed more easily, finding nothing had been stolen. Though the most skilled cutpurse couldn't reach the soft leather belt he wore under his shirt.

Even so, he took his coin purse out of the deep pocket in his breeches beside his balls and tucked it inside his doublet. That stumble might have been an accident, but every pickpocket within five days' travel would be trying their luck in these crowds.

Reske made a swift decision. The sooner he learned what was going on in Hedvin, the sooner he could write his report for Earl Debin. He'd send that by crown courier and follow it back to Velasta as fast as possible. He'd need more money than he carried to do that, so he'd head for the temple first.

Reske walked more quickly, dodging between people, murmuring apologies for treading on someone's heels or jarring an elbow. He caught snatches of conversations.

A tense man made plans with a luxuriantly bearded partner. 'We'll head westwards through the Gap. It'll add days to our journey, but—'

'We'll be safer. The roads won't be so good, but it's summer so the ground should be dry.'

A merchant with a Velastan accent, wearing unobtrusive grey broadcloth, pushed past. She wore no rings or other jewellery but the quality of her cloak and her gown's lace collar showed she was wealthy.

'We had better take enough supplies to see us through. Zavire's next move will be seizing the highway. Bastrys will have a stranglehold on anything passing in or out of the Vale of Hurat.'

The local man with her was staunchly loyal. 'Hedvin's soldiers won't stand for that.'

'And Baron Zavire knows it. How better to provoke Baron Lebarre into the folly of a pitched battle? I want to be well away before we hear Bastrys' forces are marching.'

Reske resisted the urge to stop them and ask how she expected to learn that. Over the heads of the crowd ahead, he could see the buildings on either side of this broad street giving way to a large, open space. The crush eased slightly as carts, carriages and riders turned one way or the other.

Reaching the vast square, Reske could see the ornately carved frontages of the guildhalls overlooking the labyrinth of market stalls. He soon found an outsized wooden hammer and draw knife fixed above an elegant entrance, skilfully carved, painted and gilded. The Joiners Guildhall. A gleaming silver balance hung over the entrance of the eating house next door. Scales a twentieth the size would be used for weighing coin, gems or anything else where size was inverse to value. So that's where he'd be meeting Elisset, though Reske would bet the sign was a tinsmith's work, not silver.

He looked at the crowded market and wondered what folk were talking about there. Seeing a resolute knot of people advance into the road, to force oncoming horses to halt, Reske darted after them, reaching safety as heavy wagons rumbled behind him.

Four women were cutting wheels of cheese at the closest stall. Reske saw one glance up, quick as blinking. A customer held up a silver star. The cheesemonger scored a line on the wheel with her knife and cut him a wedge a third the size Reske would expect for that price. But when the man took the cheese and gave her the coin, she dropped it into her apron pocket, already focused on her next cut. Clearly he wasn't getting any change. Hedvin prices were steep and would doubtless get steeper.

Reske moved on. The noise was deafening. Buyers and sellers bellowed to make themselves heard. No one was idling to gossip. He wasn't going to learn anything here.

He skirted around the edge of the tight-packed stalls, careful not to stray in front of any horses. Halfway along the long side of the market square, he saw what must be the wide road heading for Hedvin's east gate. He waited, impatient, until enough people gathered together to force the carts and carriages to let them cross the cobbles and leave the market.

This road was far less crowded and appreciably quieter. Reske walked past garden squares set back from the thoroughfare, surrounded by spacious homes for the wealthy and well-connected. Premises closer to the road housed tailors, hat-makers and purveyors of fine wines and delicacies.

As he reached the Goddess's temple, Reske didn't like what he saw. The yard inside the tall railings was empty. At the gate, a handful of formidable sisters questioned those hoping for admittance. He stood and assessed the straggling line. Many of the younger women were visibly pregnant, some with other children clutching at their skirts. The sallow weariness of the older women in front of him suggested the end of their child-bearing years had brought different travails. The few men, some young, more of them older, mostly clutched documents or ledgers.

He didn't see any merchants or their clerks. That struck him as odd. With the hectic trade in the marketplace, he would expect the stall-holders would bring their takings here several times a day. Perhaps things were done differently in Hedvin.

Reske saw a priestess hand a suppliant a scrap of paper. Ringing a hand bell, she opened the gate just wide enough to let the woman slip through. Another sister appeared to escort the new arrival inside the temple.

'Excuse me, if you please?' The harassed woman in a plain green gown glared at him blocking her path.

Reske offered his most amiable expression as he gestured over the road. 'Is this usual? For the temple gate to be shut?'

'After two sisters have been murdered?' she snapped. 'Yes.'

'Murdered?' Reske didn't try to hide his shock. 'What happened? Do you think—?'

'I think I'll keep my own counsel,' she said, waspish. 'If you have the wits the Blessed Mother gave a harvest mouse, you'll do the same.'

'Of course. Forgive me.' Reske stepped aside to let her go on her way.

He crossed the road and walked up to the gate, ignoring the line. A pock-marked priestess laid a hand on her sunburst amulet. 'What do you ask of the Goddess today?'

'I have Earl Debin of Shirlat's permission to request funds from the Golden Mother's temples, to be repaid by the nearest sisters who hold a Shirlat strongbox.' Reske carried a letter saying so, wrapped in oiled silk and tucked inside the courier's belt he wore next to his skin. Identifying him by name and with a detailed description, it was endorsed with the earl's personal seal and signature.

The priestess's amulet glowed, dazzling even on this bright, cloudless day. Reske had expected to have his word tested, but not before he even crossed the temple's threshold.

Stony-faced, the priestess fished in a pocket and handed him a slip of paper. 'Enter with the Golden Mother's blessing.'

'Thank you.' Reske wasn't sure she heard him over the clanging handbell. Inside the gate, he read the single word written on the paper. Accounts. He offered it to the priestess approaching him.

She glanced at it and turned around. 'Follow me.'

Going through the temple door, Reske was startled to see a funeral bier in the entrance hall. Two bodies tightly shrouded in white linen lay on a black silk pall embroidered with sprays of yellow flowers. Four sisters sat on stools at the bier's corners with their veiled heads bowed in silent prayer.

'Mother have mercy,' Reske muttered.

'For our sisters? Never doubt it,' his escort said tightly. 'And we will see justice.'

'What happened?'

The priestess didn't answer. She pushed the door to the accounting hall open and ushered him through.

'Please, what—?'

The priestess let the door swing closed between them. He turned and saw priestesses seated at widely spaced desks, in low-voiced conversation with various townsfolk.

Reske walked towards the closest sister with an empty stool in front of her, unbuttoning his doublet. 'Please excuse me. I need to retrieve my master's authority—'

He tugged his shirt free of his breeches and unbuckled the soft leather strap. The priestess waited for him to produce the earl's letter and lay it flat for her to read. When she studied his face, to be certain he was the man described, Reske saw her eyes were bruised from lack of sleep and reddened by weeping.

Handing him the letter, she opened her ledger. 'What coin do you require?'

'Twenty silver marks, if you please, and five gold.' Now Reske had seen Hedvin's prices, he suspected information was going to be expensive.

The priestess wrote the details in her ledger. 'Wait here.'

She rose and went to the door at the side of the hall where common wisdom said stairs led down to every temple's strongroom. Reske gazed idly around. A priestess narrowed suspicious eyes at him and he turned his attention to putting the earl's letter away.

The red-eyed sister returned with a wash-leather pouch of coin. Reske put five silver marks in the purse in his doublet and stowed the rest in his courier's belt, hidden as he rebuttoned his doublet.

'Wait in the entrance hall to be escorted out.' She didn't look up, cleaning her pen nib with a rag.

'Thank you, sister.'

Reske left the accounting hall. As the door closed behind him, another priestess appeared from the corridor to the inner sanctum.

'Follow me.'

Reske followed his new guide to the temple gate and left without a backward glance. He'd wager every coin he carried that none of the priestesses would tell him how their shrouded sisters had died. He'd try his luck with Hedvin's priests.

He headed for the marketplace, wishing he knew his way around Hedvin's byways and back alleys. This might be the straightest route to the shrine, but it wasn't going to be the quickest. The market seemed even louder and busier. Reske went around the outside of the square rather than risk getting lost in the narrow walkways threaded between the stalls.

Sizeable emporiums along the road to the western gate sold boots, shoes and gear for travel. Reske saw a large leather-bound chest loaded into an elegant carriage, its owner's initials emblazoned on the lid in brass nail heads. Lesser traders offered walking sticks and other assistance for the infirm.

Discreet placards fixed beside bell-pulls promised palliatives and comforting tinctures to supplement a priest-physician's treatments.

The crescent gate wasn't far and it stood open. A steady stream of men and women came and went from the shrine. Some of those leaving carried loaves of bread and lumps of meat wrapped in blood-soaked cheesecloth.

Hearing the rhythm of marching feet, Reske glanced back towards the market. Eight halberdiers in Baron Lebarre's livery escorted four men and women into the shrine's courtyard. Each clutched heavy leather bags with brass locks. That must be takings arriving from the marketplace. But safeguarding coin was the Goddess's business, not the God's. So was feeding the hungry.

Three priests appeared in the gateway. Reske stiffened. The brothers escorted a tall woman with long, steel-grey hair held up by a silver comb. She wore a scrivener's robe. Reske looked for her left sleeve. Scriveners rolled back the cuffs of their gowns and the shirt or chemise beneath. Ink washes off skin more easily than out of broadcloth or linen. This woman's sleeves were trimmed with a long fall of lace. Reske couldn't see her hands.

He very much wanted to know what business this woman had in Hedvin. Back in Velasta, she had claimed to be Earl Padran of Evarise's personal representative. She had sent ruffians to beat up Brother Haber, maybe even kill him. But she was clearly on good terms with these priests, judging by their expressions and gestures.

Reske decided not to visit the shrine. He might learn something about the woman, but that had to be set against the risk of her hearing a stranger had been asking questions. A stranger whose description she was bound to demand. The longer she didn't know he existed, the better.

Should he try to follow her? As he pondered that unholy challenge in an unfamiliar town, a carriage pulled up at the crescent gate, blocking his view. When the driver whipped up his horses heading westwards, the three priests stood alone.

Since that answered that question, Reske made his way to The Silver Scales. He would wait there for Elisset, spending whatever it cost to justify holding a table. Once he knew what she had learned at the garrison, he could decide what to do next.

Entering the vestibule, he showed the gold mark in his hand to the smart young man in russet sitting at a clerk's high desk.

'I would like a table for two in a quiet corner.' Reske could sound like a scion of the nobility when it suited him. 'A companion will join me soon. While I wait, I would like food, wine, red for preference, Tiernese if you have it, and some spring water. Also, paper, pen and ink.'

'By all means.' The well-groomed man slid off his stool. 'This way, if you please.'

Reske followed him past tables of various sizes draped with white linen and separated by carved wooden screens offering an illusion of privacy. The servitor led him to a rear corner where his travel-stained appearance would be less easily noticed by patrons who might be offended.

Reske didn't care. He took the chair with its back to the wall, giving him a good view of everyone else. 'Thank you.'

His jug of wine and one of water arrived promptly. Reske tasted both. The wine was indeed from Tierna and the water had no hint of being drawn from a well. His writing materials arrived next and he started drawing. Realising he was grinding his teeth, he forced himself to relax his jaw.

A dish of chicken boiled with gooseberries and white wine arrived with a bowl of spinach in green sorrel sauce. Reske set his sketch aside as a maidservant laid out his plate, napkin, knife and spoon. As she left, he reached for the basket of fine white bread. Eating slowly, he savoured the excellent food.

Elisset appeared as he was mopping up the last of the sauce. She had washed her hands and face, and wore clean, if creased clothes. Her boots were still scuffed and dusty.

'You started without me,' she protested, light-hearted.

'I had to rent this table.' Reske caught a junior servitor's eye and beckoned him over. 'A glass for my friend, and another jug of water.'

'Is the kitchen serving veal today?' Elisset asked the lad hopefully.

'Yes, mistress.' He picked up the water jug.

'Then that's what I'd like, thank you.' She sat and they waited in silence as a maid brought Elisset's napkin, knife and spoon.

The lad came back with a fresh jug of water and another glass goblet. 'More wine?'

'Perhaps later.' Reske hadn't drunk even half of the fragrant Tiernese, alternating each glassful with two of water.

As the servitor retreated, Elisset pointed at the folded sheet of paper Reske had tucked behind the inkwell. 'What's that?'

He handed her the sketch. 'She had some sort of business at Hedvin's shrine today. When I last saw her in Velasta, she claimed to be Earl Padran of Evarise's personal representative.'

Elisset studied the drawing. 'I haven't seen her myself. Was there anything memorable about her?'

That question told Reske she'd heard something that would interest him.

'I believe she has something wrong with her left hand.'

'Assuming this is the woman Captain Yedeth was telling me about, she lost the hand in an accident some years ago. Apparently her stump is unpleasantly memorable, though no one knows what happened.'

Elisset handed back the sketch. 'Her name is Nindera Kyse, and from what the captain says, she absolutely has Earl Padran's confidence. She comes here often, sometimes alone, sometimes with an escort, bringing letters from the earl to Baron Lebarre and taking his replies back to Velasta.'

Now Reske really wanted to find out what the steel-haired woman was doing in Hedvin. 'Baron Lebarre doesn't trust the crown couriers?'

'Earl Padran refuses to use them.' Elisset poured herself some wine. 'Earl Lystro of Coylure and Princess Alriad are shunning them too. Captain Yedeth hasn't received any official despatches since before the equinox. Which makes his life easier,' she added, sardonic.

'The couriers are still riding though?' Reske asked with sudden concern.

Elisset's veal arrived, served in a thick golden broth, with another dish of sorrel-dressed spinach and a basket of bread. Elisset sipped her wine as they waited for the maidservant to leave. She continued as if they hadn't been interrupted.

'They are, and they're carrying a great many letters between the nobles who can claim that privilege.'

'Any interesting whispers on the wind?' No courier ever broke their oath by opening a sealed case, but they listened for gossip in stable yards and at servants' gates.

'Everyone is waiting to see how Princess Idelina, which is to say, how Earl Padran, deals with Baron Zavire choking trade along the Dore. Have you heard about that?'

'Only the bare bones.'

As Elisset explained the full extent of Zavire's offences, Reske was astonished.

'There's been no response from Velasta all this time?'

Elisset shrugged as she cut up her meat. 'Princess Idelina has travelled to the summer palace in the hills above Astyrie, with her daughter and her entire household. That's a long journey on indifferent roads for Earl Padran to get her permission to do whatever he proposes.'

'She's left Lystro of Coylure and Princess Alriad ruling the roost in Velasta?' Reske thought that was ill-advised. Though Idelina's pregnancy couldn't be a cause for concern if she was well enough to make that journey.

'So it seems.' Elisset moved on. 'What else did you learn at the temple and the shrine?'

'The brothers here are treading on the Goddess's hem, and they don't seem to care who knows it.' While Elisset ate, Reske recounted what he had seen and heard. 'Did Captain Yedeth tell you two priestesses have been killed?'

Elisset nodded. 'Their throats were cut two nights ago. The bodies were dumped in the market place fountain to be found by a night patrol.'

Reske would never have imagined such an atrocity. 'The captain's taken you into his confidence then.' He was relieved for Elisset's sake if nothing else.

'He'd be a fool not to.' She drank some water. 'He needs every experienced pair of hands he can muster. Each new moon sees more desertions.'

'To join Baron Zavire?'

'A few, perhaps. Most simply don't want to fight their countrymen.' Elisset grimaced.

'Does Captain Yedeth think that's going to happen?'

'He hopes not, but he wouldn't bet against it. Every day brings more reasons to convince him Baron Zavire will send forces downstream to seize Chalus unless Baron Lensin throws in his lot with Princess Alriad and the Earl of Coylure. If that happens, Hedvin will march.'

Elisset leaned forward and lowered her voice. 'There's more. It's not widely known so far, not outside Velasta, but Captain Yedeth says the black brothers have declared their support for Princess Idelina. Meantime, the high temple's sisters openly back Princess Alriad.'

'Where do the captain's loyalties lie?' Reske had to ask. Earl Debin needed to know.

'With his garrison and with his oath which will compel him to obey, if Baron Lebarre orders him to attack Bastrys forces threatening Chalus. He says he'll answer any questions you have, so you can inform the Earl of Shirlat. There's a bed for you in the fortress tonight, and a fresh horse in the morning.' Elisset reached inside her doublet. 'He gave me these letters which have been waiting for you. A token of his good faith.'

'Thank you.' Reske took the triple-folded and thrice-sealed sheets of paper from her. The date of despatch had been written on each one, above his name and the instructions for whichever courier carried it. Not for the first time, he wondered how many copies languished in other garrisons' baskets, never to be called for, tossed into the guardroom fire after a year.

Cracking the wax on the most recent letter, he dipped the pen in the ink. Earl Debin used the cipher they had agreed on before he left Velasta. Captain Berake would have learned nothing of use to Baron Zavire if he'd opened a copy of this letter in Bastrys. Reske had the key in his head so deciphering the message didn't take long.

'Well?' Elisset finished her meal, wiped her mouth and laid her napkin on the table.

Reske dipped a finger in his wine and rubbed it over the wet ink to blur the writing into illegibility. 'Earl Debin is going to Astyrie, to seek an audience with Princess Idelina.'

He screwed up the paper and shoved it into his breeches pocket. He'd burn that along with the letters as soon he got the chance.

'When you get back to Velasta, send me word if anything's been settled, as soon as you can.' Elisset looked around for a servitor. 'Shall we see what's on offer for dessert?'

'Why not?' Reske said, affable.

Elisset could assume he was going back to Velasta. So could Captain Yedeth, when Reske accepted his offer of a garrison horse in the morning. He had orders to tell no one here he was travelling east to the river Tane. One of those other letters with Reske's name on the outer sheet hid a private message from the Earl of Shirlat to the Margrave of Jedfal.

Chapter Twelve

JEDFAL

19th of the Hare Moon

The river basin was far busier than Quenild had expected. Almost every mooring was occupied by a light, narrow Tane barge like *The Linden Leaf*. Beyond the wharfs, Jedfal's market place was crowded with booths. That was unusual at this season. The unexpected made her uneasy. Still, the bustle boded well for the price they should get for the last of the silver and copper tea they had brought from Hurat.

Ticosa waved, making her way back to their boat. She stepped onto the deck from the wharf and kissed her wife's cheek. 'Edrie was pleased to get her horses back.'

'What did she have to say about trade coming up the Tane of late?' Quenild supposed it was an ill wind that blew no one some good.

Stable owners like Edrie, hiring out teams of horses to haul barges up the Tane's western bank, must be profiting handsomely. That was the only way to make headway against the current. The downlands to the east foiled the winds which swept so steadily across the grasslands and grainlands to drive sailing barges upstream on the broader, slower-flowing Dore.

'She's sent half her beasts westwards.' Ticosa shook her head, incredulous. 'Tane traders are paying hand over fist to hire wagons to haul their goods to new wharfs along the Tresil.

Barges head to the Fasil and unload at Hedvin. Every cargo is tagged with its owner's name, the merchant and the town it's going to, and Baron Lebarre's guarantee. His troopers escort the wagons carrying those wares through the forest and hand them over to carters who deliver the goods across Arafaze. Every handover will be signed and sealed.'

'In the Goddess's name or the God's?' Quenild shook her head. 'I assume this comes at a price?'

'It doesn't come cheap,' Ticosa confirmed. 'Unless prices in Velasta are rising like a groom's interest on his wedding night, we'd barely break even after these added costs.'

'But how else do we sell our wares?' Quenild cudgeled her wits for some alternative.

'Apparently, some barges go down the Fasil to Lake Chalus,' Ticosa observed. 'They follow the shore to the Dore and turn for Bastrys.'

'What's Baron Zavire buying?' No merchant Quenild knew would send a cargo up the Dore without a guaranteed buyer who would pay in coin, not worthless letters of credit.

Ticosa shrugged. 'Cloth. Leather. Foodstuffs. The word on the wharfs is he'll attack Chalus before the Flower Moon is over.'

Quenild hoped that news had reached Castellan Maixen. She still found it hard to imagine one baron sending armed cohorts to attack another noble's fiefdom. She and Ticosa had friends whose children had enlisted in Hurat's garrison. The notion of the ordinary folk of the Dore and the Tane blood shedding each other's blood on the streets and wharfs was too horrible to contemplate.

'Whatever Zavire is planning, his preparations will take time.' Ticosa found a paper pouch of nuts in her pocket and offered them to Quenild. 'There aren't enough boats on the Fasil to handle any great weight of cargo. Edrie says some merchants want to try hauling a loaded barge across the grainlands lashed to a wheeled cradle.'

'Seriously?' Quenild took a couple of nuts. 'After a barge has been bounced over a hundred and more leagues of bad roads, there won't be a water-tight joint in the planking.'

'It'll sink like a stone.' The gleam in Ticosa's eye told Quenild she agreed the idea was a fool's errand.

'Let's see what else we can learn while we're here. And find someone to deliver Sister Jadewin's letters.' She knocked on the cabin door. Yan opened up and handed her both women's satchels.

Ticosa handed him the nuts. 'Stay aboard and stay alert.'

'Always,' the boy assured her.

As they left the barge, Quenild looked beyond the wharfs and jetties and past the market place. The Margrave of Jedfal's ancient castle loomed over the walled town. His noble ancestors had chosen well, when they claimed this land defended by a great loop of the river. Jedfal was the only stronghold on the western bank of the Tane. Whether or not the current margrave's ancestors had intended to dominate the river's trade, they had earned their unquestioned authority up and downstream.

As they walked through the busy market, a familiar voice hailed her from a stall. 'Mistress Ditayan!'

'Nimrin!' Quenild acknowledged him with a friendly wave.

'Who's that with him?' Ticosa asked in an undertone.

'No idea,' Quenild murmured through her teeth.

The stranger offered his hand as soon as they reached Nimrin's striped awning. 'Ret Karynd at your service. I am glad to know you both.'

'As we are pleased to meet you.' The cut of the man's clothing was fashionably Velastan, though his accent must be from some distant province.

'I was telling Master Karynd you trade as far east as Scefet,' Nimrin prompted.

Quenild remembered a pleasant evening drinking beer and barley sunshine as she and Ticosa told him a gruelling tale of Nilgeh mud and biting midges.

'What can you sell me from the Mire?' the stranger asked, intent.

'Alas, we've only brought teas on this trip.' Quenild noted his swiftly concealed frustration.

'We will likely travel to Scefet again soon,' Ticosa said artlessly. 'What might interest you?'

'Assuming we can find a buyer for our teas,' Quenild commented, rueful. 'We need coin for the Mire's markets. Bog-trotters bargain hard, and few trust the Goddess's daughters with their gains.'

'I'm interested in saggats, yellow-racket – dried for preference – pitrel root, myler leaf and ordoven.' The stranger was all business. 'I'll pay you a good sum on account, here and now, in return for your oath that you'll sell only to me. I'll take whatever you bring back from the Mire.'

So he was an apothecary. 'Such an open-ended undertaking could cost you dear,' Quenild observed with a hint of a challenge.

'I will witness your oaths and your seals on this agreement,' an austere voice said behind them.

Both women turned to see a black-robed priest. From the look he exchanged with the stranger, they knew each other.

'Where can we find you?' Ticosa asked the apothecary. 'Once we've sold our teas.'

'Leave word with my clerk at The Brindled Ram. If you're disappointed with the prices offered for your teas,' he added, 'don't sell them cheap. I may buy them too.'

'Till later.' Ticosa favoured the stranger and the priest with her most charming smile.

'Good day to you.' As the two visitors walked away, Quenild saw the Jedfal merchant was satisfied he'd see some silver in return for this introduction. 'Nimrin, where's the best place to eat here these days?'

'The Wheat Sheaf's doing good trade.' His hopeful expression didn't entirely hide his relief.

'Join us for dinner there after the sunset bell,' Ticosa invited.

'That suits me,' Quenild agreed. Then Nimrin could tell them whatever else he knew about those strangers as they ate.

They walked on through the market place.

'What do you make of that?' Quenild discreetly directed her wife's attention to a priestess talking to a man and a woman.

They must be wool merchants, wearing those cloaks with luxurious fleece collars despite the mild weather. Countless sheep roamed the downland pastures east of the Tane. Packhorses carried the massive sacks of wool from the annual clip along the high road between Streit and Aviren which reached the Tane opposite the margrave's castle. Deals were done in Jedfal's market, and ferrymen brought the wool from the warehouses across the river to be loaded onto barges.

'Do you think they might carry a message to the crescent gate in Streit?' Ticosa's hand brushed her cloak. She had Sister Jadewin's letters buttoned in an inside pocket.

Quenild still wanted to know why the priestess wasn't sending those by way of her sisters. 'Let's ask them if they're going that far.'

The priestess walked away. Quenild noted several priests watching. 'Do you see more shrine and temple servants around than usual?'

'I would say so.' Ticosa smiled as the downland merchants looked their way.

'Good day to you,' the woman said cheerfully as the Hurat women approached.

The man raised placating hands. 'If you're looking to buy fleeces, we have no more to sell.'

'Would you care to buy silver tea with your profits?' Ticosa offered.

'Assuming you made a profit.' Quenild realised the two were brother and sister. Their features were similar and they wore marriage bracelets with different designs.

'We have,' the man confirmed with evident satisfaction.

'Through fair commerce,' his sister added quickly. 'Everyone has their living to make.'

'And the Golden Mother sees all,' Ticosa agreed.

The woman blushed. Quenild wondered how recently this pair had been visited by a stern priestess, suggesting a charitable gift would deter the fiery heat of divine displeasure over less-than-fair-dealing which some sisters had noticed when they reconciled their ledgers.

'You're early to market.' Then she saw the man's ill-concealed smirk. 'Or late?'

'We keep some fleeces back each year,' he admitted. 'Wool prices drop fast in the summer.'

'Holding a reserve is good sense,' Quenild agreed. 'Last year's wool must be long gone.

Ticosa nodded. 'If your fleeces keep Jedfal's carders, spinners and looms busy until the new clip arrives, everyone profits.'

Seeing the merchants exchange a glance, Quenild didn't think their wool would be staying in Jedfal. Who had a sudden need for large quantities of cloth? Someone outfitting an army?

'We will certainly buy some silver tea.' The sister took a ledger out of the deep pocket inside her voluminous cloak.

Quenild glanced idly around the marketplace while the women negotiated a price. 'I see no shortage of priests to witness a contract,' she remarked to the brother. 'And plenty of priestesses to record our transaction. Whereabouts do you keep your strongbox?'

The wool merchant shook his head. 'These visitors only serve the merchants they travel with. We must go to the shrine and the temple by the castle.'

Ticosa tapped Quenild's arm. 'Mistress Laveru says they will pass through Streit on their journey home. She can deliver our friend's letter to the crescent gate.'

'I'll take it.' The wool merchant barely glanced at the double folded and twice sealed letter addressed to Brother Cavore as he stowed it in his satchel. 'Now—'

Shouting interrupted him. Two men on the far side of the marketplace stood toe to booted toe, gesturing.

'What's Ranneor done now?' Mistress Laveru wondered.

'You know him?' Ticosa asked.

'To our cost. He's the one wearing yellow.' The wool merchant shook his head. 'He reckons an agreement isn't binding until the ink is dry and the sealing wax has set hard. He'll abandon a deal he's shaken hands on if a better offer comes along.'

Quenild committed the man's face to memory, to make sure they never did business. 'What does he trade in?'

'Leather. Oh!' Mistress Laveru gasped.

The outraged man had punched Ranneor in the gut. The leather merchant staggered, but he was swift to recover. Pinning his assailant's arms in a vicious hug, he tried a headbutt.

The outraged trader squirmed, taking the blow on his cheekbone. Ranneor yelped as he was kneed in the thigh. The two men broke apart and circled slowly, looking for an advantage.

'This has nothing to do with us.' Mistress Laveru tugged at her brother's cloak.

Quenild watched a handful of men and women step forward from the crowd, each with an array of blades on their belts. Two of the newcomers flanked Ranneor. The other three lined up with his opponent.

Were they sell-swords, or bandits? She knew traders who travelled the highways hired guards to defend their wagons and wares from robbers. She suspected some ruffians turned their hands to either venture, depending on which promised more profit. A warning horn sounded high on the castle battlements. People started to move away. Margrave Vauset's soldiers would soon arrive to settle the altercation.

'Let's go to the shrine,' the wool merchant suggested. 'To seal our deal for your tea.'

'An excellent idea.' Ticosa agreed.

They followed Master Laveru to Jedfal's shrine, where grateful donations and Jedfal's prosperity had paid for the finest masons' work. The crescent gate opened onto a broad, paved square which was as crowded as the market.

Quenild remembered Sister Jadewin saying Brother Cavore was travelling in the downlands because onion skin fever was rife. Thankfully she, Ticosa and Yan had sweated through the sickness as children. But other and worse illnesses often followed in its wake.

'You get our deal signed and sealed.' Quenild freed her arm from Ticosa's. 'I'll see if the brothers are in the market for copper tea.'

'I'll meet you back at the boat.' Ticosa's swift agreement told Quenild her wife knew what she was thinking.

The infirmarer would pay a fair price for their tea. They might get a better offer elsewhere, but banking goodwill with the Moon God was always a wise investment, especially in uncertain times.

Quenild crossed the courtyard to the infirmary, where solicitous young priests went from patient to patient in the anteroom, listening to their complaints. They would treat minor injuries and ailments themselves, or summon a more experienced brother.

A grizzled priest with deep-set eyes sat at a desk to note each arrival. 'Yes?'

'I have copper tea for sale,' Quenild said politely. 'I wish to offer it to the God's servants before we look for other buyers.'

'You're from Hurat? Take a seat, daughter.' The priest snapped his fingers at a young acolyte. 'Find Brother Cavore.'

Quenild swallowed a profane exclamation as she stepped aside. She didn't sit beside the coughing strangers. The Moon God wouldn't blame her for that.

The acolyte returned with a shrewd-faced, dark-haired brother. Quenild didn't recognise him. Thanks to the God and the Goddess, she and Ticosa rarely needed a physician.

'You're from Hurat?' His dark eyes were as alert as Squirrel's when the barge hound saw cheese. 'I'm Brother Cavore—'

'I had a letter for you from Sister Jadewin,' Quenild said ruefully. 'I've given it to some wool merchants travelling to Streit. They and my wife are having a contract validated, so we should be able to retrieve it.'

'Let's do that.' The brother walked towards the door.

Outside the crowd parted to let the black-robed priest pass. To Quenild's relief, she saw the wool merchant leaning against the courtyard wall. She raised a hand to get his attention. The priest noticed and walked towards him.

'We need not trouble you to carry that letter,' Quenild explained. 'I found Brother Cavore here.'

'My thanks for your goodwill all the same.' Brother Cavore offered the wool merchant a charming smile.

'It's my pleasure to serve the God and the Goddess.' He found the letter in his satchel and handed it over.

Quenild could see Ticosa and his sister through the archive's open double doors. The women sat on one side of a desk while a priest and a priestess conferred. Quenild couldn't see any tension between the God's servant and the Goddess's as they signed and sealed the necessary documents. Brother Cavore cracked the seals and read Jadewin's letter.

Ticosa and Mistress Laveru came out of the archive. The wool merchant looked as if she'd found half a maggot in her plum. The woman shot a searing look at her brother and hustled him away.

'What sheep shit has she stepped in?' Quenild asked Ticosa.

'Jedfal's shrine and temple are only validating transactions if both parties live and trade east of Chalus.' Ticosa was puzzled.

Quenild was startled. 'Why?'

'Visiting priestesses have been demanding Jedfal's temple honours payments they have agreed in coin, even though none of their contracts carry the God's seal.' Brother Cavore tucked Sister Jadewin's letter inside his black robe. 'Meantime, unknown priests are demanding the crescent moon's seal on letters of credit which they expect temples across the Vale of Hurat to honour. My good brothers and our honoured sisters are having none of it.'

Quenild guessed the wool merchants now realised they were holding paper which might well be worthless.

'What under the stars is going on?' Ticosa demanded.

'That is a very good question.' Brother Cavore didn't offer any answers. 'Jedfal's shrine will buy your unsold tea. Brother Infirmarer will match the best price in the market. We'll get that unloaded today and head downstream tomorrow at first light.'

'Will we?' Quenild raised her eyebrows.

Cavore tried his charming smile on her. Seeing that wasn't working, he grinned. 'If I may beg passage with you to Hurat in the Horned God's service?'

Ticosa opened her satchel. 'Let's get that deal for our tea signed and sealed.'

Quenild didn't follow them into the archive. She found a corner by the shrine gate and studied the townsfolk coming and going. Anyone with enough wits to get out of the rain was clearly uneasy. Like her, they sensed trouble in the air.

She was reminded of late summer voyages on the Dore. The Thunder Moon was well named. A towering storm could be seen tens of leagues away across the flat grainlands. There was no knowing which way the ominous clouds would veer. If they reached the river, brutal winds and hailstones as big as bantam's eggs could shred a barge's sails and snap its mast. Even if the storm took another route, torrential rain could swell the great river's distant tributaries. An unforeseen surge of water might swamp an unlucky boat. Fallen trees swept along by the turbid river could hole the biggest barges.

She fervently hoped Brother Cavore could to help avert whatever disaster was looming.

Chapter Thirteen

HURAT

23rd of the Hare Moon

'Their house is along here.' Alory turned into a side street.

'Good.' Jadewin wanted answers. Brother Cavore's note merely said he was in Hurat and staying with Alory's aunts. The young priest didn't know why he hadn't gone to the shrine.

'Sister,' Alory said suddenly. 'Why is the Golden Mother interested in who makes strong liquor?'

That was unexpected. She had expected the boy to be fretting about Hasrine. The late afternoon was turning to dusk and Alory wasn't in the castle to light the Moon God's lamp. Jadewin reminded herself she had been sent to Hurat to teach him.

'First and foremost, we confirm the liquor is fit to drink. The last huckster I caught experimenting in a Velastan outhouse sold a gullet-scorcher which blinded half the fools who bought it. Knowing who is distilling also means the temples ensure the crown receives the taxes owed.'

She glanced at Alory. 'You and I have additional duties. Intoxication can stir a vestige of magical talent. Pay attention to drunkards coming to the crescent gate with wild stories. Accidental manifestations must be dispelled as soon as possible. At least it's usually easy enough to convince someone who's drunk themselves cross-eyed that they imagined whatever they've seen.'

'I see.' Alory stopped in front of a dark varnished door and rat-tatted the knocker. 'We're here.'

When Mistress Ticosa opened the door, Jadewin offered her the bottle. 'Mother Finevre sends this with her thanks for your hospitality to our brother.'

'Thank you, though we're glad to oblige.' Ticosa took the bottle and read the bone tag tied to its neck. 'From Harles. This is very generous. Please, join us in the parlour.'

Jadewin followed the merchant into the modest house's entrance hall. Alory brought up the rear as they went up the stairs. Cavore sat by a table draped with a lace-edged cloth beneath the parlour window.

'Sister Jadewin. It's good to meet you. Alory.' He greeted the boy with a nod.

Mistress Quenild sat on the other side of the table, with a plate of spiced griddle cakes to hand. 'Can we offer you something to eat? A cup of silver tea?'

'Tea would be most welcome, thank you.' Jadewin wasn't thirsty, but she wouldn't refuse their hospitality.

'Please.' Ticosa ushered her towards a cushioned oak chair beside the hearth. As the merchant went through the door to the kitchen, Jadewin sat. Alory took a stool.

'What's the news from Jedfal?' Jadewin wondered how soon they could leave without causing offence. Cavore would have things to tell her which the merchants must not hear. She must warn him about Sister Hasrine.

Cavore ran a hand through his untidy dark hair. 'Can you tell me the latest from Velasta first?'

Jadewin obliged. 'Mother Finevre has learned Princess Alriad stood willingly before the high temple's priestesses and half the nobility of Velasta. She swore she believes her claim to the Arafaze crown is just. Every sister's sunburst pendant glowed bright in the presence of truth. Princess Idelina refuses to be questioned. She is still in her palace in Astyrie.'

When Mother Finevre had read High Mother Elyka's letter to Hurat's assembled sisters, Jadewin had dug her fingernails into her palms to stop herself slapping Hasrine's smirking face.

Cavore reached for a griddle cake. 'That only means Alriad is telling the truth which she believes. Someone has convinced her she was born first. That doesn't make it true.'

'Quite so,' Jadewin said tartly. 'Temple and shrine have searched for witnesses but found no one who was present at her birth.'

'If only—' Cavore began.

'If ifs and buts were honey and nuts, we'd all save money at weddings.' Ticosa came through the door from the kitchen. She put a tray of tea on the parlour table and started filling delicately painted cups.

Alory spoke up. 'Father Memlin says there was no whisper of deceit over the succession before King Venais died. He says the high priest is trying to trace this lie to its source, but the God only knows how long that might take.'

'Brother Talaven would chase it down.' Cavore accepted a cup of tea. 'The villains who murdered him did more damage than they knew.'

'Brother Talaven was murdered?' On the other side of the table, Quenild was horrified. 'I thought his heart failed him.'

Jadewin glared at Cavore. 'The fatal spasm struck him down after he told two unpleasant men King Venais was the last Earl of Hurat. They were furious, and we believe they threatened the good brother with violence.'

'So I blame them for his death,' Cavore said quickly. 'Though it wouldn't be helpful if that was widely known.'

'You can trust our discretion.' Ticosa brought a steaming cup of tea over to Jadewin and sat in her own chair on the other side of the hearth.

'What's the news from Jedfal and the hill country,' Jadewin prompted Cavore.

'The shrines and temples up and down both rivers, and every smaller sanctuary, follow Hurat's lead.' The priest sipped his tea. 'No brother or sister I've met on my travels wants any part of this quarrel over the Arafaze crown.'

'What about the noble-born?' Jadewin tried to hide her foreboding.

'The lords and ladies of the Tane are in no hurry to make any public declarations. Meantime, they're writing a great many letters, delivered by their own liegemen and women instead of the crown couriers.'

Jadewin caught the glance the merchants exchanged. Everyone believed crown couriers were experts at lifting wax seals with a hot knife and replacing them undetected after a letter had been read. Jadewin didn't doubt Maixen had men and women who could do that. She had perfected such skills herself, and she would wager Cavore had done too.

'What about the barons and baronesses of the Dore?' the priest asked her.

'They're keeping their own counsel for now.' Jadewin read the discreet reports Mother Finevre received from the temples along the river. 'Above all else, it seems they don't want to find themselves opposing Castellan Maixen. No one has any idea which princess's claim he supports.'

Cavore nodded. 'I believe his reputation as a strategist is well-earned. He commanded crown forces on the western borders seven years ago when Arafaze was dragged into the squabbles in the coastal principalities – when the Prince of Inys tried to seize the harbour at Neveyn, and cut off Aderon's access to the ocean.'

Jadewin recalled High Mother Elyka, then Sister Elyka, had been one of the priestesses sent to tend the wounded and keep watch for anything untoward.

'You think there will truly be battles to settle who wears the crown?' Alory's dread warred with disbelief. 'Fighting here in Hurat?'

'If neither princess will yield, someone or something will have to break the deadlock.' Cavore sighed. 'The nobles who support them may be preparing to fight, or they might simply be laying up necessities in case trouble breaks out and cripples trade.'

Ticosa spoke up. 'Arafaze merchants are buying up wool, finished cloth, and leather. They want pots and pans, along with steel and iron for their smithies and farriers. Anyone turning out brass harness fittings can name their price. A muster called to arms would need all these things.'

'And soldiers have to be fed,' Quenild added. 'Freeholders in the grasslands and grainlands are being offered twice and thrice the usual prices for wheat, fodder, salt meat and anything else they still have stored from last autumn's bounty.'

'It's the talk of the wharfs everywhere.' Ticosa sipped her tea. 'Castellan Maixen needs to know.'

'I'll tell him myself.' Cavore got to his feet.

'That's not all.' Quenild looked at Jadewin. 'You know these merchants are travelling with priests and priestesses who try to ram through deals without signed and sealed agreements? It's all very well for Hurat's shrines and temples to refuse to acknowledge anyone beyond the Hedvin Gap, but that makes it impossible for Vale merchants to trade with partners they have trusted for generations.'

'Mother Finevre and Father Memlin are aware of the issues.' Jadewin knew this was a serious concern. Father Memlin had sent a strongly worded protest to the high shrine in Velasta. Mother Finevre had written to High Mother Elyka. Neither had received a reply.

'Thank you for your hospitality, ladies.' Cavore was waiting by the stairs. 'Please excuse us. My young brother and I must attend the castle sanctuary.

'We'll leave you to your evening.' As Jadewin stood up, she saw Quenild looking thoughtfully at her nephew.

After she and Cavore agreed on what they should tell the castellan, they must talk to the boy, and specify what he could tell his aunts. Jadewin decided she should spend the night in Maixen's bed, to learn whatever whispers from Hurat's garrisons he might be willing to share.

'I'll see you out.' Ticosa led them down the stairs and out through the entrance hall.

As she closed the street door, Alory turned to Cavore. 'About the castle sanctuary...'

As they walked through the old quarter, he told Cavore about Sister Hasrine's attempt to sabotage the Moon God's lamp. 'She didn't say a word when she arrived with Brother Delnor the next morning and the silver lamp was burning bright,' he concluded with savage satisfaction.

'Tell him the rest,' Jadewin prompted.

Alory related the renegade priestess's conversation with some unknown ally and her attempt to summon the ghastly phantasm of a dying cannoneer.

'She hasn't tried that again, and there's no hint of anyone seeing the Lightning King,' Jadewin assured the older priest.

'Why does she want a Velastan nightmare stalking Hurat's streets?' Cavore wondered aloud.

Jadewin had given that considerable thought. 'I believe she plans to destroy the horror with as many witnesses as possible. She will claim this is proof the Goddess agrees Princess Aliiad is the rightful queen.'

'The Father of Night will make her pay for that lie.' Cavore asserted as they waited to cross the busy ferry road. 'Do you think she suspects you can see the intangible?' he asked Alory

'I don't think so,' Alory said slowly. 'I've seen no sign of her in the unreal world. Surely that means she hasn't seen me?'

'You still need to be careful around her.' Jadewin warned.

Cavore had other concerns. 'Has anyone come to Hurat's shrine complaining of a new malady? Suffering with sudden sweats, joint pain and headaches?'

'Not as far as I know.' Alory shook his head as they crossed the high road. 'Is this spread by foul water or spoiled food, or contact with the sick?'

'According to travelling priests in the hill country, it's proof of the Moon God's displeasure,' Cavore said acidly. 'Punishing those who deny Princess Idelina's right to the crown her father and brother wore.'

'I take it you never saw anyone with this mysterious ailment?'

Jadewin was surprised when Cavore tilted an equivocal hand.

'As rumour of the sickness spread, I met a few folk convinced they were stricken. They begged for my intercession with the lord of night, confessing that dire portents in Velasta had persuaded them to deny the true queen. Sightings of the Lightning King.'

'Omens which have not happened.' Jadewin was tired of hearing that name. 'We must find the man Hasrine has ordered to raise the phantasm.'

'What did you do for the folk falling sick?' Alory asked Cavore.

'I told them the Horned God knows the secrets of our hearts. He punishes no one for honest error, and never by sending sickness. Summer brings on all manner of agues which my special tonic would relieve, which it did.'

Alory was confused. 'I don't understand—'

'Malaise of the mind can make someone as ill as any disease of the body,' Jadewin explained. 'You must have seen patients laid low with intractable melancholy?'

'I know that,' Alory said, irritated. 'I don't understand what these lying priests hope to achieve.'

'My guess?' Cavore sighed. 'If they can persuade the common people to openly take sides, they believe that will sway their liege lords and ladies.'

They walked on in silence through the largely empty streets of the newer town. Jadewin found herself regretting this loss of Alory's innocence. She'd had time to marvel at the unseen world, to revel in its wonders, before Sister Elyka had shown her the intangible realm's darker potential. It had been longer still before she had learned some who shared her gifts would misuse such knowledge and power.

She momentarily longed for the days when her greatest challenge had been discovering whose unconscious longing, malice, or grief had spawned some incoherent illusion. But her vows of obedience meant accepting the trials the Goddess sent her.

They reached the broad square outside the shrine. Cavore glanced at the crescent gate 'I wonder if we can persuade Father Memlin that Brother Delnor deserves a break from his duties. If I take over as the castle's infirmarer, I can continue your instruction more easily, Alory.' He turned to Jadewin. 'How many of the secret sisterhood can Mother Finevre call on? Do you know where they are at present?'

Jadewin hesitated. She had been taught at the high temple to rarely reveal such things, even to the hidden brethren who shared their knowledge of the unseen realm. But she had Mother Finevre's permission to use her best judgement.

'Five sisters, and we have recalled them, though they're widely scattered across the province. What can you tell me about your hidden brethren?'

The priest grimaced. 'Nine are serving sanctuaries across the Vale of Hurat, none within easy travelling distance. I have no authority to recall them and Father Memlin will need a good reason. Brother Talaven—'

Rats swarmed out of a nearby alley, running across Jadewin's feet. Scores of the foul beasts! No, hundreds! Yelping, she snatched up her skirts, trying to kick the vermin away.

Brother Cavore cursed, trying to stamp on them. Alory was yelling. For an endless moment Jadewin struggled to make sense of the boy's words.

'They're not real! It's an illusion! There's nothing there!'

She summoned all the doubt she could and looked at the ground. She saw one rat pass through another as the creatures' paths crossed. Others merged like shadows on a wall. None of them were squeaking, she realised. There was no rustle of scurrying bodies, no scrabble of claws.

'Cavore!' Alory bellowed. 'Behind you!'

Two men rushed out of the alley. Jadewin saw steel glint in their hands. Cavore spun around as the rats evaporated. The priest thrust the heel of one hand under the closest man's chin. Forcing the attacker's head up and back, he punched the man's knife arm hard with his other fist, just above the elbow. The blade fell from the man's nerveless fingers. Cavore shoved the brute backwards. The man fell and landed hard, gasping for air like a stranded fish.

Jadewin scooped up his knife from the gutter. She saw Alory had a blade in his hand. The second attacker brandished his own dagger to ward off the furious young priest. Blood dripped from a gash on the villain's forearm. He slashed at Alory's face, and the young priest flinched. The wounded attacker fled down the alley into darkness.

'No!' Jadewin saw Alory was about to pursue him.

Cavore stepped into the boy's path. 'Who knows what trap he might lead you to? I can't imagine they are working alone.'

Jadewin knelt beside the fallen man. 'His skull has cracked like an egg.' A dark stain was spreading on the cobbles and blood oozed from the man's ears and nose.

'Are we taking him to the shrine?' Alory asked, uncertain.

Jadewin made a swift decision. 'No. To the castle. If we take him to the crescent gate, his friend who ran may come to have his wound tended. I'd rather he doesn't learn this one's fate too soon. Let him wonder what the scoundrel might tell us.'

Jadewin got to her feet and brushed dust from her robe. 'If we can deliver him to the Infirmary unseen, the castellan can say a patrol found him senseless in some side-street. Let's see if anyone can put a name to him without knowing we have an interest.'

Cavore looked at the dying man. 'I wonder which of them created that illusion of rats.'

Jadewin glanced at the alley. 'Or there was a third.'

'If we take him to the castle, Sister Hasrine will likely hear,' Alory pointed out.

Jadewin quickly assessed this risk. 'If she comes to see who he is, her face might tell us if she knows him.'

If Hasrine recognised this villain, did that mean the Earl of Coylure had paid the pair to risk the Goddess's wrath, or the God's? How much coin could buy such impiety? How would any of their deaths advance Princess Alriad's cause?

Jadewin had so many questions, and little hope of answers. If her treacherous sister didn't know this man, had Padran of Evarise hired these knives in the dark? If so, who did the earl and Princess Idelina want dead?

'Meantime we keep watch for anyone who looks surprised to see us fit and well.' Cavore wedged a boot against the unconscious man's feet and reached down to take his hand. In a smooth, well-practised move, he hauled the casualty up to lie limp over his shoulder.

Jadewin retrieved the unconscious man's blade and tucked both knives into the wide pocket inside her cape. She didn't imagine the weapons could offer any clues, but she wasn't leaving them here for anyone to find.

'Put that away.' She pointed at Alory's dagger. 'When did you start carrying a knife?'

'After I had to fight a winged snake with nothing but bare hands.' Alory's tone dared her to scold him. He slid the narrow blade into a sheath strapped to his forearm.

'This way.' Cavore headed for a side street.

Jadewin was glad the older priest was familiar with Hurat's back lanes. They didn't go wholly unobserved, but no one was going to challenge a servant of the God carrying an unconscious man.

Lund was on duty at the gatehouse. Jadewin silently thanked the Goddess. 'We don't know who this is. We're taking him to the Infirmary. Please send a runner to the castellan and ask him to join us.'

'At once, Sister.' Lund snapped his fingers at a youth sitting by the guardroom fire.

'Yes sergeant.' The boy ran on ahead to the keep.

Jadewin followed Cavore and Alory through the tunnel in the rampart. The castle yard was still bustling despite the late hour. She couldn't see Sister Hasrine in the deepening dusk. That was a blessing of sorts.

They reached the Infirmary to find Brother Delnor dosing a restless patient. Only a handful of beds in the long, pillared hall were occupied, and the other occupants appeared to be fast asleep.

Brother Delnor walked towards them, curious, holding the medicine spoon and glass. Jadewin went to meet him as Alory and Cavore carried the unknown man to a side room.

'We found an unfortunate with a cracked skull lying in the street. I've sent word to the castellan.'

'What does he need?' Brother Delnor was invariably practical.

'Salve and a bandage to staunch the bleeding. I will see to that.' Jadewin swallowed to stop her voice shaking. 'We can only wait to see if he rouses or if the God has decreed his life's end. Brother Cavore will sit with him. You have your other duties.'

'I didn't realise Cavore was back.' Delnor walked toward a table tucked between two pillars. 'Tell Alory I've already attended to the lamps in the sanctuary.'

'Sister Hasrine isn't here?' Jadewin asked as casually as she could.

'I haven't seen her today.' Delnor let slip a hint of relief as he put down the glass and spoon.

'Perhaps she has business at the temple.' Jadewin hoped so. Otherwise she had no idea how to find out what Hasrine had been doing.

Brother Delnor held out a small basket holding dressings and a jar of thick, dark unguent. 'Will this be sufficient?'

'It will. Thank you.' Jadewin took the basket and headed for the side room.

The door stood ajar. A lamp hung above the head of the narrow bed. The only other furniture was a stool and a washstand.

Cavore had laid the unconscious man on the bed. He was examining Alory's knife while the boy told him in an undertone how Brother Talaven had died.

'I won't be caught without a weapon again.' Alory shot a truculent glance at Jadewin.

'How well can you use this?' Cavore asked mildly as he handed back the blade.

'I know enough.' Defensive, Alory blushed as he sheathed it.

Jadewin put the basket on the bed and held her open palm above the senseless man's mouth and nose. He was barely breathing. She gently lifted his head. Blood already stained the sheet.

'Alory, now you see him in better light, is this one of the men who killed Brother Talaven? Or the stranger you saw with Sister Hasrine?'

'Neither.' The young priest shook his head. 'I've never seen him before.'

She supposed that had been too much to hope for. 'If you insist on carrying that blade, there are skilled men and women in the castle who could teach you to fight with a knife. I can ask the castellan for a recommendation.'

'A recommendation for what?' Maixen appeared in the doorway. 'Who's this?'

'We would very much like to know,' Cavore said with feeling.

'And you are?' the castellan asked politely.

Jadewin dressed the man's oozing head-wound with Brother Delnor's salve and a thick bandage as Cavore introduced himself. He told Maixen how they had been attacked and fought off their assailants, without any mention of the rats. After washing her hands clean of blood and ointment, Jadewin took the knives out of her cape pocket.

'They carried these.'

Maixen took the weapons and assessed them. 'Cheap work. Sold by half the traders up and down both rivers. Have you any idea why you were attacked?'

'Possibly to stop me sharing the latest news from Jedfal,' Cavore said tersely.

Jadewin studied Maixen's face as the priest repeated everything he and Alory's aunts had learned. 'You already knew this,' she observed.

'Some, not all. Margrave Vauset of Jedfal writes to me. The noble earls of Padran and Coylure are pressing him to declare allegiance to their chosen princess. They are convinced Hurat's nobility will follow his lead. Enough of them, at least, to make the rest fall into step.'

Maixen passed the attackers' weapons to Senon who had slipped silently through the door. The room was getting crowded. 'I want foot patrols searching for a man with a wounded left forearm. Brother Alory can describe him. Tell the gate guards and ferry captains no one they even suspect of hiding an injury is to leave the town. I want this villain in chains before morning.'

'With the God's favour.' The steward gestured at the knife sheathed on Alory's forearm. 'I can teach you how to use that, my lad.'

Alory mumbled something as he followed Senon out of the room. Jadewin hoped it was thanks.

Maixen contemplated the man on the bed. 'What do you propose to do with him?'

'Honestly, I don't see him rousing before he dies.' Cavore sat on the stool. 'But I will sit vigil in case the God grants him – or us – that grace. If so, perhaps he can give us some answers.'

Jadewin seriously doubted that would happen. 'In the morning, can we ask Mistress Zile to send someone to draw his likeness? The temple and the shrine can show that at their gates and ask if anyone knows him or his family. They will surely want to bury him.'

'Unless he's some outsider sent here to make trouble. Let me know if he wakes.' Maixen left the room, soft-footed.

'I wonder…' Cavore got up to close the door.

'What?' The priest's expression made Jadewin uneasy.

'What trouble might some outsider make for the castellan?' Cavore leaned against the door. 'Perhaps I wasn't this man's target, nor Alory. You often spend nights in the castle. Maybe somebody wanted you dead, and Alory and I just got in their way.'

'Why would someone kill me?' Jadewin fought a shiver.

'Mistress Ticosa told me it's widely known you and the castellan are lovers.' Cavore picked at dried blood outlining his fingernails. 'Killing you would leave him grief-stricken. Weakening Maixen weakens Hurat.'

'What would that achieve?' Jadewin protested.

Cavore sucked his teeth. 'Someone hopes to tip the balance in this province for one princess or the other. The Margrave of Jedfal pledging his loyalty would influence a great many folk. If someone believes the margrave's choice would put him at odds with the castellan? What if Margrave Vauset declared himself while the castellan was deep in mourning? The crown garrisons would be slow to react. Maybe slow enough for the new queen to send her loyalists in to take charge of them.'

If, perhaps and maybe. Honey and nuts. The priestess cast about for another explanation.

'What about the rats? Did our friend here create those illusions, or the other man, the one Alory wounded? At least one of them knows something of the unseen world. Sister Hasrine could be behind this.'

'If so, she likely wants you dead too,' Cavore said bluntly. 'If she and her cabal believe you're their only foe in Hurat who can dispel phantasms. This renegade sister doesn't know me, still less that I am here, and she has no idea of Alory's talents. Either way, you had better stay safe with Brother Delnor tonight. Sit vigil in case this villain wakes up. Alory and I will keep watch for manifestations around the castle.'

Jadewin still wasn't convinced those attackers had wanted to kill her specifically. She sat on the stool even so. 'Very well.'

She could wait until tomorrow to talk to Maixen, to learn what he might be willing to tell her about Margrave Vauset's letters, and anything else significant about Jedfal.

Chapter Fourteen

JEDFAL

11th of the Flower Moon

'Where have you come from, friend?'

The tapster's query was friendly enough, but Reske saw he was being appraised. He didn't flatter himself. This attractive, assured woman in her middle years wasn't interested in taking him to her bed.

'Hedvin.' He picked up the coppers beside his mug of ale.

His journey along the byways across the Vale of Hurat's grainland had taken two-thirds the time he'd spent travelling from Bastrys to Hedvin.

'That's some distance,' the tapster remarked.

Reske shrugged. 'The going was easy enough. Hospitable folk offered me a bed and a meal most nights.'

Whether he stopped in a hamlet of scattered houses, or in a village with a tavern and a forge, the price of accommodation was the same. Freeholders and field labourers alike wanted to know if the rival claims to the crown were resolved. He had been sorry to disappoint them.

These folk had little interest in whose head got stamped on whatever coins came their way. They just wanted no bloodshed. They prayed to the Goddess for rain and sun in due season, to give them good harvests, and asked the Moon God to bless their families with good health. The only reason they ever expected to see Arafaze troops was if Mervantese raiders ventured beyond the Dore.

Reske waited for the tapster to ask for news from Hedvin.

She had more local concerns. 'Did you stop in Vitry?'

'Vitry? Yes?'

Reaching the market town the day before yesterday, Reske had hoped to hire a second mount, to give Captain Yedeth's flagging horse a rest before he delivered the animal to Jedfal's garrison. Returning the weary beast to Hedvin would be the courier sergeant's problem. He soon realised that wasn't going to happen. Vitry was crowded with merchants and muleteers, mostly heading for a town called Decane. That was their next stop on a new trading route using this province's lesser rivers to reach Hedvin. Beyond that, Reske hadn't paid much attention to the merchant's explanations, sitting beside him in an eating house.

'Did you hear of trouble on the roads?' the tapster asked.

Reske shook his head. 'Not as such, though carters and mule trains were banding together. Some were asking if townsfolk could be hired as guards.'

He had been more concerned about the covetous glances at his horse as he rode along Vitry's main street. He slept in the stall he hired for the horse in the stable he eventually found, riding out of Vitry's eastward gate just after dawn.

'What's going on?' he prompted.

'So much trade taking to the roads is drawing hill country bandits across the Tane like flies to ripe fruit. One gang tried to steal a cargo of salt eight days ago. Captain Grezel and his cavalry chased them down.'

'And rounded them up?' Reske guessed that from the tavern owner's satisfaction.

'Eleven of them, can you believe it?' She didn't wait for his answer. 'They were flogged bloody in the market place and left lashed to the whipping post for a day and a night. They're in Mithess by now. They can dig for salt in the mines once their wounds heal. Apart from the youngest few. They were sent to the pillory at Harles. That should warn off their den mates. Anyway, here's your meal.' The tapster moved away as a serving maid who was either her daughter or niece brought Reske a bowl of pottage.

By the time he scraped the bowl clean, Reske had decided to go back to Velasta by way of Decane. Earl Debin would want to know more about this new trade route. Perhaps he could offer his sword and experience for hire. But first he had to request an audience with Margrave Vauset in order to deliver his liege lord's letter. He collected the Hedvin horse from the tavern stable. Now he understood why burly men with quarterstaffs sat on empty barrels inside the yard gate.

It was a short ride to the crown garrison's fortress overlooking the highway. A young cavalry officer hurried out of the wide entrance in the forbidding rampart as Reske dismounted. He had the letter he'd written to Captain Yedeth in his hand, along with his courier service discharge medallion.

'Good day to you, subaltern. I'm surrendering this horse to be returned to the Hedvin garrison with this despatch.'

'Oh.' Whatever the subaltern was expecting, it wasn't this polite request. 'Yes, of course.'

Reske handed over the letter and unbuckled his travelling bag from the back of the saddle. 'I hear you've had a lively time of it lately. That business with the salt?'

The young officer squared his shoulders. 'Lawlessness cannot be tolerated in these uncertain days.'

Reske hid his amusement. The young officer was undoubtedly echoing Captain Grezel, and was clearly eager for another opportunity to draw his sword.

When a young hopeful satisfied a crown fortress's commander that they merited training to lead cavalry or cannoneers, their mothers enjoyed their sewing circles' congratulations while their fathers preened in the local taverns. Arriving in Velasta, fresh-faced subalterns soon learned this honour wasn't what they expected. Their days were filled with cannon drills and schooling horses alongside the raw recruits they might command. An officer had to understand every military discipline, regardless of preference. From dawn till last light, lieutenants and captains instructed them on their duty to the crown, their responsibilities to the cavalry and cannoneers in their charge, and the respect they owed to the nobility and their footsoldiers.

Those subalterns deemed unlikely to disgrace their mentors were sent to one of the garrisons defending the realm. Reske knew cavalry hopefuls often tried to buy their way to a posting in the Vale of Hurat. A Mervantese incursion might be unlikely, but there was every chance of pursuing bandits along the province's highways, or hunting horse thieves and cattle raiders through the downland.

'I have business in Jedfal castle.' Reske passed the tired horse's reins to the youth. 'Please give my compliments to Captain Grezel.'

He guessed the Hedvin mount caught the scent of the stables as its ears pricked with interest. The animal started walking towards the fortress, leaving the subaltern with no other option.

Reske slung his travelling bag over one shoulder. He took two more letters out of his jerkin as he walked towards the town gate. Crimson-liveried guards patrolled the battlements of the forbidding barbican. More stood on each side of the passage through the gateway into the town. If anyone started trouble, Margrave Vauset's loyal footsoldiers would finish it fast. As Reske made his way through the crowded streets to the castle overlooking the river, he noticed frequent, sharp-eyed patrols.

The castle's gatehouse jutted forward from the high curtain wall. Visitors must negotiate a sharply-angled passageway with gates of iron-bounded oak at each end. A horse would manage it easily enough, but Reske wouldn't like to try driving a cart through there. The outer gates stood open flanked by two halberdiers. Reske halted five paces away.

The guard to the right acknowledged him. 'Good day.'

'My master Earl Debin of Shirlat sends word to your liege lord.' Reske held up the letter addressed to the Margrave of Jedfal, as well as the letter which proved his identity to the temples. 'This will vouch for me.'

The guard stuck two fingers in his mouth and whistled. Reske saw a crimson-liveried sergeant appear around the angle of the passage. The guards readied their pole arms as the blunt-featured man arrived.

Reske offered him both documents. 'I have a letter from Earl Debin of Shirlat for Margrave Vauset of Jedfal. I am ordered to deliver it in person.'

The sergeant glanced at that, then read the letter of authority to draw on Shirlat funds. He looked Reske up and down, making certain he matched the description.

'Follow me.' He walked into the barbican.

Reske followed him past the guards at the inner gates and across the castle yard. He saw the margraves of Jedfal had retained their ancient great hall, where their first ancestor to claim these lands would have lived alongside his retainers.

The sergeant went up the hall steps and pushed open the heavy door. Reske followed. Dust motes danced in shafts of sunlight falling through the high, narrow windows to dapple the patterned tiles. The sergeant walked to a small door at the far end. He waited for Reske to catch up, then knocked.

A calm voice replied. 'Enter.'

The sergeant ushered Reske into a modest, wood-panelled room and closed the door behind him.

A white-haired man with age-spotted hands sat in a chair by the empty fireplace. In his prime, he must have been a formidable figure. He would still be taller than most if he were standing, though Reske guessed he would stoop these days. Deep lines on the margrave's face and his bony legs suggested his strength was declining.

His wits still seemed sharp. The margrave had been using a brass-handled magnifying lens to read a letter. His chair was placed to catch the daylight coming through an unexpectedly wide window knocked through the ancient wall. Tables on every side were piled high with papers and books. Reske noted the finely wrought chain mail curtain shielding the fireplace, even though the hearth was empty in this warm weather. Someone was mindful of the danger of stray sparks in a room like this.

'Margrave Vauset.' Reske bowed.

The old man put down his lens. His eyes were faded beneath bristling brows. 'Describe the windows on either side of the door to Shirlat House's rose garden.'

'They're made of panels pieced together from green and gold glass. Each one shows briars and vines twined around a longsword. The one on the right has the Sun at the top. The one on the left has the crescent moon.'

Reske wondered why he'd been asked that question. He wouldn't have been brought to the margrave if the sergeant had the slightest doubt who he was.

'You keep your eyes open. Good.' The old man held up the letter he had been reading. 'Tell me everything you have seen and heard of note on your journey here from Bastrys.'

Fairly certain he recognised Earl Debin's handwriting on the letter the margrave had been reading, Reske did so, as fully as he would have answered his liege lord.

'I left the Hedvin garrison's horse at the crown fortress's gate,' he concluded. 'Then came to seek an audience with you, to deliver my master's letter.'

The margrave held out a hand. 'Fetch me pen and ink. Over there, behind you.'

Reske did as he was asked as the old man cracked the wax seals and unfolded the letter. He waited patiently while the margrave deciphered Earl Debin's message without needing to refer to a key. The writing was too small for Reske to read upside down from where he stood.

The old nobleman refolded the letter. 'Tell me, are you inclined to serve either of these would-be queens?'

Reske had no idea where this conversation might lead, so he opted for honesty. 'Not as things stand. As the God or the Goddess can witness.'

Margrave Vauset leaned back in his chair, steepling his fingers. He studied Reske for a long moment, and then gestured at a chair on the other side of the hearth. 'Please, take a seat.'

The door opened and a grey-haired woman in a dark blue gown brought in a carafe of wine and two fine glass goblets on a tray. A lackey in Jedfal's livery followed, carrying a small table which he set down between the two chairs. The woman poured generous measures of wine and withdrew, closing the door softly once again.

'If you would be so kind. My back pains me.'

Reske handed the margrave his glass of wine and sat in the empty chair. He took a sip and couldn't identify the vintage, so he guessed it was from Hurat. It was very fine.

'I knew King Serken,' the old nobleman remarked. 'Not well, but well enough. I spent several years at his court in Velasta while my own father was still alive. Serken was an honourable man. If Alriad had truly been Queen Misene's first-born child, the girl would have been acknowledged as crown princess from her very first breath. This talk of Serken setting up Fedrin as his heir for fear of Mervantese invaders is hogwash.'

The margrave scowled. 'If Princess Alriad swears she believes she is in the right, some folk can persuade themselves night is day, if it's to their advantage. The temple may have tested her word, but that means nothing without witnesses to settle the question beyond doubt. Besides, shrine and temple alike should remember their vows and stay out of secular matters. Neither the God nor the Goddess approves of meddlers, or so I was always taught.'

The old man gestured in the direction of the encircling river. 'I have decreed Jedfal's ferries will only carry priests and priestesses who serve Hurat's sanctuaries, shrines and temples. Only those who answer to Father Memlin and Mother Finevre. I can't stop newcomers flocking here from who knows where from, making mischief on this side of the Tane, but I can curb their activities in the hill country. I will answer to the God and the Goddess if I must.'

'What mischief are these strangers making?' Reske knew that would be Earl Debin's first question.

The margrave looked at him steadily. 'Priests and priestesses alike threaten my people with the God's wrath or the Goddess's, if I shirk my duty to serve their chosen queen. Specifically, they demand Jedfal's mills supply Earl Padran, or Earl Lystro, with firing powder. Not only am I ordered to supply their chosen queen's forces, I am told I must refuse all requests from her rival's supporters.'

The old nobleman's anger was palpable. Reske sipped his wine.

'If you do not believe Princess Alriad was deprived of her rightful inheritance, does it not follow that you accept Princess Idelina's claim to the crown?'

The margrave emptied his glass. 'I take it no despatches from Velasta have reached you since you left Hedvin?'

'No,' Reske said warily. That sounded ominous. Had Idelina's pregnancy ended in tragedy?

Margrave Vauset grimaced as he leaned forward to put his wineglass on the table. 'Forgive me for breaking this news so bluntly. There is no other way. Princess Idelina has condemned my friend and your liege lord, the Earl of Shirlat, to death for treason.'

The noble waited, patient and in silence, until Reske could ask a coherent question. 'What has he supposedly done?'

'He refused to swear allegiance to Queen Idelina.'

'But she hasn't been crowned,' Reske protested. 'A new monarch is sanctified by the God and the Goddess before any oaths of loyalty are given. How can this be treason?'

'You may well ask. Nevertheless, the decree condemning him has been signed and sealed in Idelina's name as queen. A copy reached me yesterday.' Margrave Vauset gestured at a pile of parchments on the table under the window. 'My sources tell me the earl has been imprisoned, though his death warrant has not yet been countersigned.'

'Surely the justiciars will refuse it.' Reske hoped the archivists in Velasta's court buildings were ransacking their records, searching for precedents for defying the crown.

'Thus far it seems the warrant has not been submitted for their scrutiny. However the earl's children have been disinherited.' The margrave's contempt was icy. 'The Shirlat estates now belong to the crown, according to another newly signed and sealed decree. Do pour yourself more wine if you wish.'

'What in the blackest night is Idelina thinking?' Reske knew of past quarrels where banishment had been the only way to resolve some intractable strife between the monarch and a noble. Even so, it was always accepted an exile's heirs had no part in this breach. Forbearancc ensured those banished lived out their days beyond Arafaze's borders supported by their family's coin – as long as they made no more trouble.

'Who can say?' The margrave shrugged. 'My sources tell me Idelina has barely seen anyone since she withdrew to Astyrie. Meantime Princess Alriad as good as holds court in Velasta, decorating Coylure's mansion like a palace. Though it's rumoured Earl Lystro is travelling to Bastrys.'

The old man shook his head. 'I don't know what he expects to find there. Jedfal's mills haven't sent Zavire of Bastrys any firing powder since this pestilential uncertainty began. Lebarre of Hedvin's had none from us either, and neither baron will.'

'That's good to know, my lord, but may I have an answer?' Reske's stomach hollowed. 'Do you accept or dispute Princess Idelina's claim to the crown?'

'I will not swear allegiance to Princess Idelina, even though she is King Venais's rightful heir.' The margrave gestured towards a hefty tome resting on a lectern by the window. 'The ancient laws of the Tane make it clear I am free to offer my fealty to the Arafaze crown or to withhold it as I see fit. You may read the details for yourself, if you wish.'

'If you please.' Reske got hastily to his feet. 'Thank you, my lord.'

He needed time to think through the shocking news of his master's imprisonment, quite apart from anything else. He walked over to the lectern. At the third attempt, he managed to make sense of the page laid open for him to read.

'So you are bound by treaties made with the earls of Hurat, but since a woman cannot inherit that ancient honour, you are under no obligation to swear loyalty to an Arafaze queen.' Reske didn't find this any easier to believe spoken aloud, but it was written right there under his hand.

He turned to see the margrave watching him. The old man's face was inscrutable.

'Correct, and I choose to withhold my oath. No monarch has the right to condemn anyone to death, from highest to humblest. The Sun Goddess and the Moon God together grant life and only they can sanction execution. That penalty is only for those who shed innocent blood, not for some imagined crime.'

Reske drummed his fingers on the ancient book. 'Would you accept Idelina as queen if this death warrant was withdrawn? If Earl Debin went into exile, provided his heirs were restored?'

'No.' Margrave Vauset was adamant. 'Condemning the Earl of Shirlat is an outrage against law and custom, as well as against shrine and temple. If Idelina can do this, she cannot be trusted with the least authority over my people.'

Reske went back to his chair by the hearth. He poured more wine and drank it down. 'What are you going to do?'

'As far as Arafaze is concerned, I will do nothing.' The old man paused, stern-faced. 'The princesses and their earls can make what they wish of my refusal to answer their letters. Let them come and challenge me face to face if they dare. You should know every noble who rules along the Tane has agreed to stand as one. None of us will swear fealty to either princess, no matter who grabs the crown in Velasta.'

'I will tell Earl Debin...' Reske wondered how, by all that was holy, he was going to reach his liege lord. 'Do you know where he is being held?'

'No, but he sent me this.' Margrave Vauset held out the letter he had been reading when Reske arrived. 'He has no wish to see you imprisoned alongside him, or equally unjustly condemned.'

Reluctantly, Reske read the few, brief paragraphs. He recognised Earl Debin's hand writing and some turns of phrase. The message wasn't ciphered, so either the earl trusted whoever had carried it without question, or he didn't care who else might read these words. Reaching the familiar flourish of the signature, Reske looked up.

'So I am to serve you until such time as my lord is released and restored to his rightful honours. Until then, we cannot assume I can return to Velasta in safety.' Reske resisted the urge for another glass of wine. Right now, it would be far too easy to start drinking and not stop.

'Let's see what we can do to bring about that day.' Margrave Vauset's faded eyes glinted. 'You can take a message from me to Castellan Maixen in Hurat. You must carry it in your head. I'm not committing this to paper. I want you to tell him three things.'

The old man held up a pale, withered forefinger. 'First, he should know I will not supply firing powder to anyone whom I suspect intends to impose their chosen allegiance on others by force of arms.'

'I'm glad to hear it.' Reske didn't hide his relief.

'However...' The old margrave raised a second finger. 'These priests and priestesses whom no one has invited here are keen to learn which merchants trade with the Teijent Dagh. You know of them? They live far beyond the hill country, and deal in the sulphur my powder mills require. Other strangers with fat purses have appeared at the saltpetre mines beyond the Motar's headwaters. Apparently they're willing to pay triple the price I have agreed.'

Reske felt a chill. 'Because if you won't sell firing powder to people you don't trust, someone in Coylure's faction, or Evarise's will try to make their own.'

'Most likely both noble lords will attempt it,' Margrave Vauset said curtly. 'The process is no secret.'

True, but Reske knew the skills to make the lethal stuff safely were rare. Occasionally, elsewhere in Arafaze, an ambitious noble spent the silver to build a powder mill, hoping to earn that coin back in gold. Such enterprises came and went with varying tallies of death and destruction. Reske wasn't aware of anyone trying in recent years.

Why would they? Jedfal had been a constant source of reliable firing powder for five generations. Every cannon master agreed on Jedfal powder's excellent qualities, due to the saltpetre mined along the edge of the high plateau. Making firing powder without it involved some revolting alchemy with dung heaps which gave inferior results.

Reske set that aside. 'You said I'm to tell Castellan Maixen three things.'

'I did.' The margrave paused. 'Remind him I was present when he stood before Father Memlin and Mother Finevre in front of Hurat's town gate. Before he set foot in the castle, Maixen made the castellan's declaration which has not been altered since King Ganirin's day. He swore to hold Hurat castle and to defend the town in service to Earl Venais of Hurat. His vows made no mention of the Arafaze crown. Moreover, Maixen repudiated any and all previous fealties. The God's magic and the Goddess's witnessed and endorsed every word. He is bound by that declaration.'

'So no one holding a castle or fortress across the Vale of Hurat owes allegiance to Velasta now.' Reske could hardly believe it.

'No,' the margrave said sharply. 'The laws in that book only apply to the nobility of the Tane, and the oaths sworn by Hurat's castellan are unique. The barons and baronesses along the Dore hold their lands under entirely different treaties with the Arafaze crown.'

'Meaning?' Between weariness from his long journey and the effort of trying to make sense of all this, Reske's head was aching.

The margrave explained, precise and merciless. 'Castellan Maixen has no right to commit the town and castle of Hurat to either would-be queen's cause. If he does so, those of us entrusted with safeguarding the lands of the Tane will relieve him of the position he has so clearly betrayed. On the other hand, as long as he remains true to his oaths, in the name of the diviner of truth and the scourge of lies, he can trust us to come to Hurat's aid, if the nobles of the Dore unite behind either princess. If they reach an agreement, they will surely attempt to seize Hurat's castle as well as the town for their queen. We of the Tane cannot allow that. At present, they are divided, busy watching each other and suspicious. I recommend Castellan Maixen does all he can to ensure that mistrust persists.'

The prospect of bloodshed in the Vale of Hurat was getting closer. Reske recalled Elisset's words over their expensive meal in Hedvin.

"Baron Zavire will send forces downstream to seize Chalus sooner or later, unless Baron Lensin throws in his lot with Princess Alriad and the Earl of Coylure. If that happens, Hedvin will march."

Zavire of Bastrys and Lebarre of Hedvin might be preparing to do battle with each other, but they could just as easily march on Hurat. They would undoubtedly do so if there was any chance the Tane nobles opposed to their chosen queen might seize the town and the castle. Unless they were already fighting for dominion over the nobility of the Dore.

Reske wondered what news might have arrived from Chalus by the time he delivered the margrave's message to the castellan in Hurat.

Chapter Fifteen

CHALUS

11th of the Flower Moon

Alory had spent the summer before he swore to serve the Moon God working on his aunts' barges. He'd travelled up the Tane as far as Reole. Since then, he'd gone downstream on the Dore to Masecal and upstream as far as Crespil. Whenever Brother Talaven heard about an unfamiliar book in a town's shrine, he insisted Mistress Zile's scriveners make a copy for Hurat's library.

Alory remembered telling the old priest he wanted to travel the length of the Dore, from the Bastrys Gorge to the new towns growing around the castles on the edges of the Mire. He wanted to see the headwaters of the Tane, far beyond Hatalys. Watching the Chalus wharfs ahead getting closer, he recalled Brother Talaven's advice. Be wary what you wish for, in case the God gives it to you.

If the Moon God did ever send him beyond the Bastrys mountains, Alory hoped he'd travel in a better boat than this washtub. Though the young priest allowed *The Tansy Flower*'s broad beam and stubby masts were sufficient for endlessly plodding from town to town between Hurat and Chalus and back again. Every time they moored up, Master Tanwar handed over sacking-wrapped parcels, tightly-roped baskets and painstakingly written letters before filling the capacious hold with more of the same.

Thankfully Alory and Cavore had Father Memlin's orders to save them from this tedious task. They visited each town's shrine to gather news. Alory wondered what they would learn in Chalus.

'That's interesting.' Sitting beside him on the hatch to the hold in the prow, Brother Cavore pointed to the great river's southern bank. 'See how many merchants are setting up camp over there? They're twenty days too early for the Solstice feast and fair. The first harvests are more than a month away, and most crops won't be gathered in before two full moons have come and gone.'

Alory considered the sprawl of tents and wagons around countless cooking fires. He knew the highway from distant Gernet reached the river over there. Countless wagonloads trundled south for hundreds of leagues to sell grain from Baron Lensin's harvests to the Mervantese. They came back with luxuries and rarities to be sold in Chalus's markets.

Sospirin sent grain to Mervante as well. Aunt Ticosa said the Mervantese paid in sacks of sugar, honouring a deal made with Sospirin's nobility generations ago. She said Baroness Gossen guarded her dominance over the sugar trade across Arafaze like a mountain bear guards her territory. The young priest pictured the painted map the castellan had shown him in the castle's long room. That furthest fiefdom from Hurat was a long way south of the Dore.

'What do they want? Whoever they are.'

Cavore sucked his teeth, thinking about that. 'To be the first to hear whatever news King Tadiri of Mervante will pay handsomely for.'

He might have said more, but *The Tansy Flower* reached the confluence where Lake Chalus emptied into the Dore. Master Tanwar shouted instructions to his sons as the washtub lurched violently in the turbid currents. To distract himself, Alory studied the landing stages on the far side of the foaming waters.

'Those are Tane barges moored on the Bastrys bank!' He'd agreed with Aunt Quenild that the notion of hauling boats overland from Jedfal and sailing them down the Fasil was ridiculous. But the barges were there.

'And those are Bastrys crown cavalry pennants on the warehouses,' Cavore said grimly.

Alory saw coloured strips of cloth fluttering from the gable ends of the buildings. 'Bastrys troops cannot cross the Fasil without permission from Hurat's castellan.'

Cavore hung on tighter to the hatch. 'Should not and cannot are very different things. Let's hope Baron Lensin of Chalus continues to see the wisdom of not committing to either princess's cause.'

Priests along the Dore had told them the townsfolk had heard Baron Zavire and Earl Lystro of Coylure were mustering an army in Bastrys. Most prayed their own baron or baroness would watch and wait to see which princess won the crown. Then negotiations over renewing their fealty could begin.

A few optimists hoped for an unexpected claimant to the Earldom of Hurat might be found. The hunt for a long-lost heir was still turning every archive upside down. Unfortunately, Alory knew Mistress Zile had concluded no heir still drew breath. She had sworn him to secrecy about that.

The Tansy Flower hit a swirl of water with a shocking jolt. Cavore muttered a prayer.

Alory grinned. 'You can swim, surely?'

'Barely,' Cavore said through clenched teeth. 'I grew up about as far from open water as you can get in Arafaze. Our village was three days ride from the nearest town. I was six years old before I saw the markets there, and twelve before my father took me on an autumn swine drive to Velasta.'

'Dad!' One of the barge-master's sons pointed at the crowded wharf.

Tanwar heaved on the tiller as his other son hauled on a rope to angle the sail. The ungainly craft surged into a space vacated by a departing vessel.

'Here before noon as promised, good brothers,' he called out to the priests.

Once the older son had finished securing the barge to the wharf, Cavore picked up his travelling bag. As they stepped off the boat, he shook Master Tanwar's leathery hand. 'Our thanks, and the Horned God's blessings on your endeavours.'

'Thank you.' Alory still felt presumptuous speaking for the Moon God. His own bag was new and stiff compared to Cavore's soft one, creased and patched after untold journeys.

Ahead, sweating labourers carried bales, barrels and crates to and fro. They shoved and hauled handcarts across the brick paving. Traders and travellers returned to their vessels with provisions or satchels of records. Alory wondered how many were heading for Bastrys. Castellan Maixen would want to know, but he had no idea how to find out.

Cavore walked cautiously across the floating wharf and Alory followed. Chalus folk and visitors alike yielded to the authority of priestly black robes. They left the riverside and passed through one of the gates piercing the city's crumbling walls. These defences had originally been built from pale stone, which reminded Alory of home, but attempts to patch the worst neglect had used ruddy bricks and lime mortar. He was reminded of crusted sores he had treated on beggars in Hurat's infirmary.

Inside the walls, Chalus was a sprawling town. Buildings of brick and ochre tile claimed any slight rise in the land. Aunt Quenild said winter floods were a fact of life hereabouts. She hadn't mentioned the trees that lined every street with unexpected elegance and offered welcome shade.

'Where are we going?'

'To the old castle.' Cavore pointed north. 'The crown garrison holds it these days, with cannon to guard the river crossing. Their new fortress is east of the old city gate.'

'Where does the baron live?'

'A league to the north. His grandfather built a new mansion outside the town after Chalus had an outbreak of twilight distemper.'

'Is that common here?' Alory tried to hide his alarm. The virulent sickness killed three or four out of any ten sufferers. They struggled to breathe until they recovered or their faces, hands and feet turned the ghastly blue heralding their death before dawn or dusk.

'Not this side of Bastrys for a generation,' Cavore assured him.

They reached a broad square where statues of the Goddess and the God faced each other across the immaculate paving. More trees shaded benches for waiting supplicants and a fountain could quench their thirst.

On the far side of the square, men and women went in and out of the circular yard around the temple. But the crescent gate was closed and the shrine's windows were shuttered. Alory stopped so suddenly that an incautious housewife walked into his back.

She was mortified. 'Brother, forgive me.'

Alory was equally embarrassed. 'No, I was at fault.'

'No harm done,' Cavore gestured towards the shrine with his most charming smile. 'What's amiss?'

'It's not for me to say.' Flustered, the woman hurried off with her skirts fluttering around her ankles.

'Shall we ask the good sister?' Alory saw a priestess walking swiftly towards them.

Cavore smiled as the woman arrived. Alory wondered if his face ever ached by the end of the day.

'Good day to you, sister This is Brother Alory and I am Cavore. We serve Hurat's shrine.'

The priestess wasn't smiling back. 'Good day.'

'Is Sister Perris within?' Cavore asked hopefully.

'No, alas.'

'Sister Sengave?'

'I'm sorry, no.'

Alory didn't think she was remotely sorry. She wasn't inviting them into the temple, and she hadn't shared her name.

'Can Mother Hasperre see us?' Cavore persisted

'It is possible she's still on the road.'

'What do you mean?'

'She spoke of visiting the sanctuary at Cormir for meditation and reflection.'

Alory noticed the nameless sister holding Cavore's gaze. Aunt Quenild said someone looking you straight in the eye didn't want you looking elsewhere. A moment later, he laid a hand on the older priest's arm. 'It doesn't matter, brother. Remember, the boat to take us downstream will be waiting to cast off.'

'Of course.' Cavore ducked his head politely to the obstructive sister. 'We should be going. Wishing to greet old friends is self-indulgence.'

They walked briskly away.

'Well?' Cavore demanded as soon as they were out of earshot.

'I saw four sisters in the temple yard, in the intangible realm.' Alory still couldn't quite believe it.

Cavore was startled. 'What made you look there?'

'That first sister reminded me of Sister Hasrine.' Alory still felt uncomfortable doubting a priestess, even though he had been right.

'The Keeper of Secrets blesses you with good instincts.' Cavore grimaced. 'Though the sisters will have seen you too.'

'Have I done something stupid?' Alory's stomach hollowed.

'I hope not. They know you have magical talent, but they have no reason to suspect I might.' Cavore crossed the road to a quiet side street.

Alory realised they weren't retracing their route to the waterfront. 'Where are we going?'

'Still to the old castle. The sanctuary is the obvious place to find our brothers, if they've shut up the shrine. Once someone explains why, I'll ask the cannon captain to send a despatch to Mother Finevre by fast courier. Jadewin will tell the castellan what he needs to know.'

'Are there any brothers adept with magic here?' Alory wondered. 'Or any of the sisters you know?'

'Alas not,' Cavore said grimly.

They walked on in silence. Townsfolk went about their own business. When he saw the old castle ahead, Alory realised they weren't far from the river Fasil. Those watch towers would have a good view of Lake Chalus. Sentries would also see travellers coming along the highway from Arafaze to the landing stages on the Bastrys bank.

'This castle was built so long ago that its walls were a curtain of stone to shelter archers.' Cavore gestured as they got closer. 'Earth and timber turned them into solid ramparts. The towers were reduced and filled with rubble to make solid platforms for cannon.'

'What happens if the Mervantese attack?' Or Baron Zavire and Earl Lystro of Coylure, though Alory didn't say that aloud, in case some passer-by overheard.

'The townsfolk will grab a seat on any boat that floats and hope the Dore carries them out of danger. The crown cavalry will ride out from their fortress beyond the eastern gate while the cannon here are turned towards the Dore.'

Alory didn't think much of that plan. Not everyone could escape downstream. The old and infirm and women burdened with children wouldn't be able to flee. Aunt Quenild would have plenty to say about that. He wondered what she and Ticosa might be learning of use to themselves and of interest to the castellan. They had headed downstream to Usenas while he and Cavore travelled here.

Walking into the castle wall's shadow, Alory saw cannon barrels jutting from the squat towers' embrasures. The outermost iron-studded door was firmly closed, but someone patrolling the battlements had seen them approach. The wicket door swung open, and a white-haired priest with a hooked nose stepped out.

'Ragat!' Relieved, Cavore greeted him. 'May I introduce Alory, one of Hurat's acolytes. Alory, Brother Ragat is the Chalus shrine's librarian. He taught me more about life along the Dore and the Tane than anyone else. I spent half a year here when I was first sent to serve Hurat.'

Alory wanted to ask why the white-haired brother wasn't still in his library. He settled for shaking his hand. 'I am pleased to meet you.'

Cavore didn't waste any more time. 'What's going on?'

The priest shook his head. 'Not here.'

He led them through the wicket gate. They emerged from the long arch of the gatehouse into a castle yard crammed with wooden buildings and a startling number of priests and priestesses.

'Cav!' A sister hurried over.

'Perris.' Cavore's hug for her was more than friendly greeting. 'Is Mother Hasperre really travelling?'

'Not by choice,' the priestess said acidly.

Brother Ragat clapped his hands. 'You can talk later. Cavore, with me.'

Sister Perris raised her hands in surrender and walked away. Brother Ragat strode towards the tall keep. He led Cavore and Alory into the sanctuary on the first floor.

Glorious stained-glass windows above the altars showed the Keeper of Secrets in a hooded robe of midnight blue rather than black. He held the crescent moon as a sickle. The Sun Goddess was a dazzling beauty, swathed in the yellow of spring flowers as she cradled a sheaf of golden wheat in her arms. The sanctuary was huge. Half the garrison could kneel in prayer here, if someone shifted the book chests stacked three high and four ranks deep.

'What is happening?' Cavore demanded.

'Have a seat.' Brother Ragat took three stools from a stack by the door. 'Our troubles started when six sisters arrived from Velasta. They worked hard and made themselves agreeable, though they were adamant Princess Alriad is the rightful heir.'

Cavore sat down. 'But—'

Ragat raised a hand. 'Mother Hasperre reminded her sisters they serve the Goddess alone. Soon, whispers in corners started, doubting the good mother's grasp on the temple's obligations. Irregularities were found in ledgers and records.'

'No one found that suspicious?' Cavore protested.

'Of course,' Ragat retorted, 'but nobody could prove malice. Believe me, Perris and Sengave searched high and low. Then Sister Daryon suggested Mother Hasperre should take time for rest and reflection.'

'Sister Daryon?' Cavore was appalled.

Ragat nodded. 'However these incomers convinced her, they used her like a stick to steal bread from a windowsill. The next day, an unsigned letter was laid at the Golden Mother's feet in the Sanctum. It called for Mother Hasperre to relinquish her duties until she recovered her strength.'

'Insisting a shrine father or temple mother steps down requires the votes of two out of every three brothers or sisters. How did the decision go against her?' Cavore glowered. 'Why has Mother Finevre not been told?'

'There was no vote. Mother Hasperre is proud.' Brother Ragat looked hastily at the Golden Mother. 'I mean no insult. She was humiliated to think her sisters believed she had failed them. She retreated to Cormir of her own free will to seek the Goddess's guidance.'

Alory interrupted. 'But why are you here? And those sisters outside? With all this?' He waved at the stacked book chests.

'You don't know?' The white-haired priest was taken aback. 'Father Memlin didn't send you here?'

'No.' Cavore waited, expectant.

Ragat sighed. 'We have had our own troubles. Two brothers from Velasta came to consult our archive. At least, they claimed to be our brothers, and they claimed to be from the capital. Since we had no cause to doubt them, no one tested the truth of their words.' His embarrassment turned to anger. 'I caught them cutting pages from our parchment rolls. One turned his blade on me.' His right hand drifted to his opposite shoulder.

'After they fled, whoever they were, we foiled two attempts to start fires in our archive with alchemical concoctions. There was no knowing who had done that, with so many people going in and out of the shrine every day. Father Cradis ordered me to bring our most valuable books and records here.'

From the number of chests, Alory guessed Ragat had decided nine volumes out of every ten were priceless. Brother Talaven would have done the same.

'What parchments were mutilated?' Cavore demanded.

'The original settlement between Chalus and King Ganirin,' Ragat said gravely 'If Baron Lensin doesn't hold a copy, the terms of his ancestor's fealty to the Arafaze crown are lost.'

'Convenient for some.' Cavore grimaced. 'Do you know if he intends to declare for one princess or the other?'

'Not as long as his waterfront stewards are collecting mooring fees and dues on goods destined for Hedvin by way of Lake Chalus, or heading up the Dore to Bastrys,' Ragat said wryly. 'Chalus is profiting handsomely. Besides, the noble baron knows full well that backing Princess Alriad will prompt a wrathful response from Baron Lebarre. That will give Baron Zavire an excuse to send Bastrys forces across the river to attack Hedvin. Whoever wins that fight, Chalus will lose. So Baron Lensin sits tight and keeps his own counsel.'

Cavore sucked his teeth. 'How much longer can he do that?'

Ragat's confidence faded. 'I know we're warned not to indulge the foolish in their superstitions. I know the God's light, or the Goddess's, reveals folly or connivance behind visitations and apparitions, in ninety-nine times out of a hundred…'

'Go on,' Cavore prompted with foreboding.

'The Lightning King has been seen. It circled our shrine at dawn and dusk. Too many townsfolk have seen the phantasm for us to convince them it isn't real. People began seeking treatment or asking to get a record sealed at this sanctuary, not at the crescent gate. Soon most folk were shunning the shrine. Father Cradis decided we should all come here. It wouldn't have been my choice,' Ragat said frankly, 'but I am bound by my vows.'

The white-haired priest sighed. 'Those Velastan sisters have the whip hand in the temple. They say those fires in our archive were the Lightning King's doing. They say his appearance reflects the Moon God's displeasure with the high father and our brothers in Velasta, for supporting Idelina's false claim to a crown her father should never have worn.'

'Have sightings of the Lightning King stopped?' asked Alory.

'No. Why do you ask?' Ragat was puzzled.

Cavore didn't let Alory answer. 'Do you know what Baron Lensin makes of these apparitions?'

Ragat shook his head. 'Though he has sent his personal servant to ask me several times what lore our library holds on such visitations. I suspect he is uneasy.'

No one spoke. The routine sounds of the garrison drifted through the open doorway.

Ragat's forehead wrinkled. 'If Father Memlin didn't send you, why are you here?'

'An unseasonal outbreak of onion skin fever is spreading up and down the Tane,' Cavore said readily. 'We want to know if the contagion is being carried along the Dore.'

That was perfectly true. They asked that question at every stop on their journey. Alory wondered if would he ever meet an unfamiliar priest or priestess in future without searching their words for some hidden motive.

'That would inconvenience those interfering sisters from Velasta,' Ragat said venomously.

'True enough.' Cavore rose from his stool. 'Well, you have your duties, brother, and we have ours.'

Ragat got to his feet. 'Indeed.'

Alory held his tongue as he followed them out of the keep and down the steps. Brother Talaven said silence was a valuable tool in its own right. He wiped his sweating palms against his robe. Gathering information for Castellan Maixen was one thing, but if the Lightning King was manifesting in Chalus, he and Cavore had a duty to destroy the vile phantasm. At least, they had to try. He guessed he'd find out if they could when night fell.

Chapter Sixteen

USENAS

The 11th Day of the Flower Moon

Walking through the Usenas pleasure gardens to meet Ticosa at their favourite tea house, Quenild wondered how Alory was faring. Given the choice, she would rather have gone upstream. Who better than a merchant to sift tittle-tattle from the Chalus wharfs for hints of trouble, to warn Castellan Maixen?

But the same was true in Usenas, and the tall priest Brother Cavore had visited here recently, so he had no excuse to return to ask the same questions. Besides, she and Ticosa would make a profit on this trip. With trade beyond Bastrys still impossible, Arafaze merchants weren't the only folk paying premium prices for the Nilgeh Mire's roots and herbs

The pleasure gardens were crowded and scent from the flowers beneath the trees filled the balmy evening. As she walked, Quenild indulged herself with fond memories of her father. She had first visited Usenas as his apprentice, enjoying the acrobats and musicians and the purveyors of fine food and drink. Later, as mistress of her own barge, she had learned other sensual delights could be purchased in discreet tents tucked behind the dance pavilions.

Like so many others, the prosperous town nestled in a broad loop of the Dore, on the northern bank. Barges riding the river downstream offloaded their cargoes on the waterfront looking westward. Vessels coming up from Nilgeh Mire moored at jetties on the eastern side. They had an easy journey, thanks to the constant winds blowing over the countless leagues of grassland and marsh further east. As her father often said, a fool in his nightshirt could catch a breeze to carry him from Scefet to Usenas.

Travelling further upstream to Hurat was a different matter. A barge heavy with cargo had to wait for the winds from the grasslands to veer into the narrow quarter between the forested heights on the southern Sharrow bank and the downland to the north. Then a barge's tall sails could defy the Dore's sluggish current and carry them upstream. Fortunately, such winds were frequent and generally reliable.

Quenild skirted a small crowd applauding a well-trained dog's antics and tossing coppers into its master's cap on the ground. She ignored a bevy of winsome young women in translucent Mervantese gowns, along with their escort of handsome youths, shirtless beneath unbuttoned jerkins. The hard-faced woman following a few paces behind them didn't bother offering her company for the night.

Ticosa had claimed a table for two beside a wide window in the tea house. They shared a brief kiss. Quenild was glad to sit. It had been a long day and her feet were aching.

'There are a lot of bog-trotters about,' she observed. Marsh dwellers were easy to pick out, with their golden hair and dark brown eyes.

'You should see the eastern moorings.' Ticosa summoned a serving lad. 'Silver tea and spice cakes, please.'

'What are they selling?' Quenild had overheard several traders asking for intoxicant herbs which flourished in the Mire. Those toiling in the hill country's mines would empty their pockets to pay for temporary oblivion.

'Nothing of interest.' Ticosa shook her head.

'I've seen plenty of Velastans.' Quenild scowled. 'Prices for dyestuffs are up, thanks to them.'

'I doubt that.' Ticosa leaned forward and lowered her voice. 'Marsh folk won't take their letters of credit.'

Quenild raised her eyebrows. 'Nobody told them bog-trotters insist on full payment in silver?'

'Don't call them that. They don't like it.' Ticosa waited as the servitor arrived with their pot of tea, the jug of hot water, and a plate of cakes topped with candied fruits. She paid the boy and filled their cups. 'The marsh folk are here to buy salt, saltpetre, and scrap metals. Iron, brass, steel or bronze, even lead.'

'Since when have they started smithing?' Quenild took a careful sip. The silver tea wasn't the best this far downstream, but it was scalding hot. At least the cakes, made with freshly ground spices, were delicious.

'They're selling the metals to traders from the Teijent Dagh.' Ticosa refreshed the pot with hot water. 'Who have no interest in talking to the Velastans either.'

'What do the bog – the marsh folk want from the Dagh Isel?' As well as spices, the horse-riding traders from the remote grasslands brought mineral pigments for enamels and paints, gem stones and ivory for jewellers, and the coloured hardwoods that furniture makers prized for inlays.

Ticosa bit into a cake. 'The Teijent sell sulphur. If the marsh folk have saltpetre, they only need charcoal...'

Quenild wasn't convinced. 'Firing powder must be kept bone dry. Good luck doing that in the Mire. Besides—'

Ticosa stiffened like a cat catching sight of a mouse. Quenild looked around to see two bog-trotters walk into the tea house, wearing leather breeches and sturdy jerkins like anyone else working the wharfs. No one would give them a second glance without their golden hair.

'I saw that pair talking to the captains of *The Lilac Bough* and *The Oak Apple*.' Ticosa raised her cup to hide her mouth.

Quenild knew both those barges regularly traded as far as Scefet. The garnets and gold Master Thiol's wife wore at Midwinter had helped persuade her to make their own journey to the Mire. That didn't mean she trusted bog-trotters. The back of her neck prickled as the two men approached their table.

The taller one spoke with barely a trace of a swamp accent. 'Do I have the honour of addressing Mistress Reture of Hurat?'

'You do.' Ticosa inclined her head gracefully. 'And you are...?'

'May we sit?'

'By all means.'

The second marsh man quickly fetched two unused chairs from a neighbouring table. The first waved a servitor away.

Quenild's father had told her marsh folk never ate or drank with outsiders, though he didn't know why.

Ticosa plucked the candied redberry from the top of a cake and ate it, waiting for the marsh man to speak first.

His grin acknowledged her tactic. 'You have a sound reputation in Scefet, Mistress Reture, for honesty and integrity.'

'I aim for fair dealing with everyone.'

'We have something you may wish to obtain.'

'Alas, we have all but concluded our business here. Our funds are largely committed.'

Quenild recognised Ticosa's regretful expression from the opening of countless negotiations.

'Information,' the marsh man said bluntly. 'You seek news from Nilgeh.'

Quenild wondered where he had heard that. Ticosa would have been as discreet as she was.

Ticosa met the stranger's gaze. 'Before I agree to buy anything, I must be sure of the quality as well as the price.'

'Let us give you something on account, to prove our good faith.'

Now the marsh man's silence challenged Ticosa. Quenild saw her own thoughts mirrored in her wife's eyes. Hearing the man out would cost nothing, and perhaps…?

'Go on,' Ticosa prompted.

'Many merchants from Mervante have visited Avelsir this past month. Some travel onwards, and not to trade.'

Ticosa put her elbows on the table, resting her chin on her interlaced fingers. 'Where are they going?'

Quenild saw the marsh man's companion watching for anyone coming close enough to overhear. The fluent man spoke quickly and quietly.

'West of Scefet, on the bank of the Dore, as your people call the Mother River, these Mervantese are taking a little-used pass through the mountains you call the Sharrow Heights. They are travelling to Sharrow to negotiate with Lord Romer.'

Quenild had never heard of any such route. The Goddess alone knew what savage animals prowled those forsaken hills. The miners and loggers who lived out there had a brutal reputation. Thankfully she and Ticosa didn't deal in the ores ferried down the foaming white waters of the Mezin. Or was it the Methin? Quenild could never remember the name of the tributary flowing into the Dore opposite Usenas.

'You must have been misinformed.' Ticosa shook her head. 'A Mervantese merchant with business in Sharrow would follow the highway north from Gernet.'

The marsh man spread his hands. 'A Mervantese merchant with no wish to meet Hurat's patrols would take a different route.'

He had a point, Quenild conceded. No one travelling to or from Gernet could predict when or where they might encounter the castellan's cavalry. Maixen made it widely known that he varied his troopers' routes as well as the intervals between their forays.

Ticosa angled her head. 'Why tell us this?'

The marsh man seemed surprised. 'The Mervantese have long been your people's foes.'

'Forgive me, I didn't make myself clear,' Ticosa apologised. 'Why are *you* telling *me*?'

The marsh man glanced at his silent companion, who gave the slightest of nods.

The speaker leaned closer. 'Mervantese are no friends to my people. They play us false too often. If fresh sparks start a blaze between your realms, that threatens us. We wish to assist Hurat's commander, and we believe you have his trust.'

Quenild really wanted to know how and where they got their information.

Ticosa pursed her lips. 'What could the Mervantese offer Lord Romer of Sharrow?'

The hitherto silent man had an accent as thick as mud. 'To learn, you must pay.'

'How much?' Quenild asked.

The first man answered her. 'Come to Scefet when Hurat's commander wishes to purchase the chance of peace. Then we will set a price.'

The two of them stood and walked off.

Ticosa pursed her lips as she cut the last spice cake in half. She gave Quenild the piece with the candied cherry. 'How, by all that's holy, do they know we have dealings with the castellan?'

'I wish I knew.' Quenild drank her cooling tea. It had lost its remaining fragrance. 'If they're so keen to sell us information to keep the peace, they must be expecting war. Unless they're out to trick Maixen into fighting the Mervantese while they can profit by selling to both sides.'

'Or they don't want to be blamed when the weasel king tries something underhand.' Ticosa countered. 'Tadiri must be wondering how far he could push north while everyone in Arafaze is watching the princesses fight for the crown.'

'Talking of underhand.' Quenild ate her morsel of cake. 'Father said if I ever made a deal with anyone answering to Lord Romer of Sharrow, I should check my fingers after shaking hands, to make sure they hadn't stolen my rings.'

'Let's discuss this back on the barge. Yan and Ristal deserve some time ashore.' Ticosa stood up.

Outside the tea house, coloured lanterns shone like jewels among the pleasure garden's trees. Music drifted from the larger pavilions and Quenild stifled some regret. She would have enjoyed an evening dancing, if her feet weren't so tired.

Ticosa gestured at the topmost lanterns swaying in the breeze. 'The winds look to be veering. We should be able to head upstream tomorrow.'

Quenild was still considering what they had been told. 'If there is a route through those heights to Sharrow, Castellan Maixen needs to know. Unless this is a ploy to turn his attention towards the Mirc while Baron Zavire and Earl Lystro attack Chalus.'

Ticosa shook her head. 'I don't think so. Those two sounded genuine to me.'

'I don't know what to think these days,' Quenild said wearily.

She wondered if Alory was learning anything useful in Chalus. If fighting broke out there, she could only pray Brother Cavore kept their nephew safe.

Chapter Seventeen

CHALUS

11th Day of the Flower Moon

Distant chimes on the evening breeze signalled the Sun Goddess's watch over the day passing to the Moon God's night vigil. On the waterfront Alory gazed at the swirling waters. After some discussion, he had spent the rest of the day going from barge to barge, to share Father Memlin's decree that shrines along the Dore could validate traders' contracts provided payments were guaranteed by a temple or sanctuary answering to Mother Finevre.

Once he'd done that, he asked how he could cross to the opposite bank, to inform any merchants from Sospirin. His youth, and being able to honestly say he had never visited Chalus before, prompted a good many traders to share their opinions of those camped across the river.

Most folk distrusted the Mervantese on principle. The southerners didn't worship the Moon God and the Sun Goddess. They swore by some strange and formless deity. Evidently little trade was being done at present, and the visitors were asking a lot of questions. The charitable didn't find that surprising. Everyone in Chalus was wondering who would wear the Arafaze crown.

Now the working day was over and barge stern lamps were being lit. River traders set stools on the floating jetties and took their ease with a mug of beer. Savoury scents reminded

Alory of the excellent noon meal they had shared with Brother Ragat.

Heading back to *The Tansy Flower*, he found Brother Cavore chatting to Master Tanwar's eldest son. 'Are we going to the castle for supper?' They had left their bags there after all.

'Why not?' Cavore seemed to be gazing upstream, but Alory saw his eyes slip sideways.

Sneaking a look in that direction, he glimpsed a pale robe of undyed wool. Of course, the Goddess's daughters might be here to tend somebody in need. Except Alory had spotted priestesses on the wharfs three times, and one was a sister from the quartet he had seen in the intangible world.

The two priests walked away from the river. Chalus's streets were largely deserted. Alory swallowed to quell any tremor in his voice.

'If we see this manifestation, if we destroy it, what's to stop the Velastan sisters recreating it as soon as we're gone?'

Cavore wasn't worried. 'Creating a substantial phantasm is no small feat. Once we have dispelled it, the Velastan sisters will have to devote significant time and effort to remake their apparition. The more nights the thing goes unseen, the harder that will become. Dread fades fast. While they're preoccupied, Perris and the other priestesses can rally their sisters and restore Mother Hasperre to authority over their temple.'

Alory decided not to ask what they were going to do if they didn't see the Lightning King tonight. He didn't want Cavore to think he was afraid to face the challenge. Since that was partly true, he asked the Moon God to forgive his cowardice.

Cavore had other concerns. 'What have you learned this afternoon? What do Chalus folk want to hear from Velasta?'

'One in three want the high divines to proclaim someone is queen, so life can get back to normal. Of the rest, half reckon they were foully deceived when King Venais was crowned. They won't hear a word against Princess Alriad. The rest are just as convinced Princess Idelina is being denied her birthright.'

Cavore sighed. 'The optimistic are confident something will reveal the truth, and the generous-minded want to believe the royal ladies' grief at their bereavement somehow caused a misunderstanding. The pessimistic foresee endless arguments and posturing, no matter whose claim to the crown is upheld.'

Alory had heard the same. 'And no one wants to see fighting, but everyone is afraid they will.'

They walked on in silence. When they reached the square with the fountain and the statues of the God and the Goddess, Alory saw huddled figures on the benches beneath the trees passing bottles from hand to hand. The temple gate was firmly shut.

'These Velastan sisters don't shelter or feed the destitute?' He was outraged.

'Charity can be found at the castle. I wonder where those bottles came from.' Cavore paused, thoughtful. 'Giving these unfortunates hard liquor, knowing they can't resist such temptation, would help them believe in the phantasm. That would help sustain the manifestation.'

How hard was it *not* to crack the seal on a bottle and *not* to drink until you drowned your wits? Alory reminded himself Brother Talaven said it wasn't their place to judge the hungry and homeless. Only the Horned God knew the flawed choices and missteps which had brought them low.

'What do we do now?'

'Let's take a walk around the shrine. With luck, the Velastan sisters will want to scare these vagrants before they're too drunk to see the phantasm. They can't roam the city spreading fear if they're snoring in a stupor.'

Cavore walked around the edge of the square, staying close to the shuttered shop fronts. Alory followed close behind him. At least someone had lit the silvery steel lamp hanging over the silent shrine's crescent gate. Though its glow emphasised the wrongness of the dark windows and the barred door for Alory.

They approached a narrow alley beside the shrine's enclosing wall. Cavore reached back to draw Alory forward. 'Do you see it?'

Erratic ripples of light coalesced in the darkness. The phantasm shimmered, growing more distinct. Alory stepped forward, clenching his fists. Now Cavore's firm hand restrained him.

A man – no – a figure stood in the alley's entrance. He – no – it had deathly pale skin and steel grey hair. It held a bundle of lightning bolts in its left hand. The jagged fragments of light were painfully bright.

Alory had expected to be scared. To his surprise, he was mostly puzzled. For a moment the Lightning King was broad-shouldered and as tall as the shrine door. In the next blink of an eye, the thing was whip thin, barely the height of a schoolboy. It shuddered and grew larger again, with eyes of cold, white flame. Its beard crackled with blue-white sparks. Before Alory took another breath, it was clean shaven.

'Drunks don't have the most coherent imaginations,' Cavore observed.

Nevertheless the manifestation grew clearer. The phantasm wore armour now, even if that shifted between chain mail and a carapace of steel plate. Settling on a breastplate over a hauberk, the Lightning King strode into the square. Bare-headed with a shock of silver hair and a bristling beard, it tossed those blinding-bright shafts from one hand to the other.

The vagrants scrambled for the far side of the fountain, dragging their blankets and sad bundles, whimpering with terror.

'Why don't they run?' Alory couldn't help whispering.

'Where to? They have nowhere to go. Come on, and hide your face.' Cavore raised his hood.

Alory did the same. As they walked forward, fresh commotion stirred among the destitute.

'Good.' A spear of silver light appeared in Cavore's hand. 'We want them swearing the Father of Night's servants have slain the Lightning King.'

Alory summoned every vestige of his faith. The Moon God's power was real and true. This phantom was a filthy lie. He gripped the sword of his own gleaming magic. The apparition turned to face them and bared its teeth in a silent snarl. Plucking a lightning bolt from its bundle, it drew back its arm.

'It has no voice.' Cavore shook his head, contemptuous. 'These sisters have nowhere near the skills I expected.'

The phantasm hurled its weapon. The tall priest didn't flinch as the jagged shaft of light came nowhere close. It skittered across the paving and shattered into uncounted sparks. Alory saw no hint of a scorch mark on the stone.

The phantasm flung another bolt. That spiralled into the starry night sky and evaporated. Cavore hurled his silver spear at the apparition, straight and true. The bright tip sank deep into its breast plate, and the lightning bolts in its hand were snuffed like candles.

Cavore strode forward, holding another silver spear. 'Get behind it.'

As soon as Alory moved, the phantasm's lightning bolts reappeared. The apparition hurled a deadly shaft at his head. This time its aim was true. Alory swept his moonlight blade upwards in pure instinct. He hit the bolt and the lightning disappeared.

Cavore gripped his spear in both hands, jabbing and thrusting at the monster. Every time the priest's weapon struck home, a shadowy stain spread across the phantasm's gleaming form. But it held a sword now. For every blow he landed, Cavore had to parry two.

Alory circled the phantasm to attack from the rear. The thing looked ominously solid. He gritted his teeth. Holding his sword's hilt low and level in two hands, he drew the moon blade back. This worthless eruption of spite had no place in the world of the living and loving. The Moon God's power would force it back to the intangible realm.

He put all his weight into a savage strike at the phantasm's hamstrings. The magical blade bit deep and the thing collapsed to its knees. Alory hacked at its neck. The phantasm began shifting between its earlier forms. Cavore thrust his spear's blazing tip into its face and the phantasm exploded. Alory staggered backwards, dazzled.

'Are you hurt?' Cavore gasped.

'No,' Alory gasped, knuckling his eyes. He heard cheering. Between the bright smears across his vision, he saw the beggars and vagrants creep out from behind the fountain.

Cavore turned his back on the ecstatic crowd, the fountain, and the temple, pulling his hood further forward. 'We must leave before anyone sees our faces.'

Alory saw a slice of lamplight come and go as the temple door opened and closed. He counted six pale robes in the shadows beyond the trees. 'The Velastan priestesses are watching us.'

'Forget them,' Cavore ordered. 'The Moon God's magic destroyed the Lightning King. That's all that matters.'

The tall priest hurried along the narrow alley where the manifestation had first appeared. Alory snatched a glance at the treacherous sisters. What were the sisters saying to the beggars surrounding them? Could the Velastans twist what had just happened to somehow bolster their lies?

'Alory!' Cavore stopped and beckoned. 'Come on!'

He did as he was told. Well-mortared brickwork rose high on either side, windowless and austere. Alory realised this alley must run right around the Chalus shrine's sacred precinct, meeting other paths.

Cavore pointed to a gap between two buildings outlined against the night sky. 'We can cut through there to head for the castle.' He broke off. 'Who's there?'

Alory saw movement in the shadows. Two men stepped forward to bar their way. They wore black, but they didn't look like priests.

'How may we serve you?' Cavore asked.

Alory wondered if the pair had seen the Lightning King's destruction. He wondered why they were looking so intently at him. He shifted his gaze to the intangible realm, but saw nothing there. A hand buffeted his arm. Alory recoiled, then realised Cavore had grabbed him. He looked back into the real world.

One of the men had a knife. It was longer than the blade sheathed on Alory's thigh. Cavore had told him not to wear that on his forearm. Alory had decided that wasn't the same as forbidding him to keep it. He'd unpicked the side seam of his robe so he could slide his hand through to grab the hilt.

'You can go.' The man with the knife gestured to Cavore. 'We only want the boy.'

'Piss on that,' the other one hissed. 'We take them both.'

Cavore coughed and staggered. Alory saw a small crossbow in the foul-mouthed man's hands.

Cavore pressed a hand to his chest. 'Run!'

'No!' Alory's fingers found his knife. He tried to pull it out. The pommel snagged on cloth.

The first man walked towards him. 'Come with us and we'll send help for your friend.'

Alory didn't need magic to know that was a lie. He still couldn't see them clearly, but he recognised the man's voice. These were the forsworn priests who had killed Brother Talaven.

The crossbow man laughed, callous. He fired again and Cavore slumped to his knees. Alory panicked. He didn't know what to do. He couldn't even get his knife out.

Flames ripped through the darkness. A fire bird soared over Alory's head, twice the size of the fish eagles that flew over Hurat. Golden sparks trailed from its wings. Its crest was scarlet flames and its eyes were pinpoints of white light. Heat like an open furnace seared Alory's face.

The fire bird circled and Alory tasted a scent like hot metal. It attacked, tearing the killers' faces with golden talons. Its head darted forward and its murderous beak snapped. The crossbow man shrieked and staggered backwards, clutching the bloodied stump of his wrist. His severed hand fell to the cobbles still holding his weapon.

The knife man hacked at the bird. His vicious blade struck between its neck and one fiery wing. The steel passed straight through the creature. The knife man gaped at the pitted and mangled metal in his hand. Then the fire bird's blazing wings enveloped his head and shoulders. Alory heard his last muffled scream. He retched at the stink of burned hair and scorched flesh.

'Run!' Cavore rasped.

Alory could see the crossbow bolt stuck in his chest. The other was deep in his belly 'Let me—'

'No.' Blood spilled dark over Cavore's fingers. 'Run!'

Alory saw the crossbow man stumble towards them, pressing his bleeding stump to his chest. The killer snatched up his dead comrade's warped blade. The fire bird vanished, and Alory saw murder in the man's eyes. The young priest's nerve broke and he ran. Not back to the square with the trees and the fountain. He fled into the alleyway Cavore had pointed towards. Alory didn't know where he was going. All that mattered was getting away.

He ran and he ran, until eventually, exhausted, he slowed. Unshed tears burned his eyes and throat, but Alory had long since learned not to weep. If his father saw a hint of tears, he'd threaten to give whoever he was tormenting something to really cry over. He always made good on that promise.

Passers-by were staring. No one expected to see a priest running through the streets like a scalded cat. Alory hunched his shoulders, pulling his hood forward to avoid anyone's gaze. He glanced from side to side. As soon as he saw an empty street, he turned into it. Throwing back his hood and looking up, he searched the stars to get his bearings.

He wanted to go home. Home to Hurat and the temple. Even if he could find Chalus's castle, he sure as shit didn't know who he could trust. Anyone wearing priestly black might be out to cut his throat. Any priestess could be a Velastan abusing her magic to create foul deceits.

He resolutely thrust those fears aside. He had to get back to Hurat. Forcing himself to concentrate, Alory worked out the way to the waterfront. Reaching the warehouses by the river, he pulled off his black robe and tossed it behind a heap of broken crates. In the next street, he saw an amiably intoxicated man being ushered out of a tavern. Doing his best to feign a Chalus accent, Alory traded his useless knife for the barge man's leather jerkin.

He didn't care who got the better deal. What mattered was the man was so drunk he wouldn't recall what had happened next morning, when he wondered why he had come home in his shirtsleeves, and acquired an unknown blade. Alory had years enough of assessing his father's drunkenness to be certain.

He walked slowly along the moorings where the barges were shut up tight. Alory expected that. Finding a nook between some empty barrels, he settled down to wait for first light. He would trade his labour for passage home. No one would question his skills. Sitting in the darkness, hugging his knees and shivering, he finally wept anguished tears for Brother Cavore.

Chapter Eighteen

HURAT

20th Day of the Flower Moon

Reske didn't mind waiting outside while a castle guard took the letter bearing Margrave Vauset's seal to whoever had authority to grant him entry. He studied the fortifications. Reske was impressed, and he had seen plenty of supposedly impregnable fortresses.

If some enterprising enemy got close enough to launch a direct assault, this high-walled redoubt would protect the castle's main entrance from cannon fire. Attackers had no hope of breaching those massive ramparts without finding a weak point. And while the redoubt itself might protect the attackers from the castle's cannon on the battlements above Reske's head, their backs would be exposed to a ruinous onslaught from the town wall, just beyond the massive ditch he had crossed.

Hurat town could defy a siege indefinitely, supplied with food and other essentials by boat. Could an assault across either river succeed? Reske very much doubted that. He had noted the cannon and rampart guns on the towers that overlooked Hurat's ferries. Anyone hoping take advantage of those breaches in the town's encircling wall would soon think again.

Of course, the castle must have a few lesser gates. Dumb animals dug burrows with more than one way in and out. But a smaller gate would be harder to take. Attackers passing through one by one would be picked off. Add to that, enemy forces would have to capture town and castle at the same time. Otherwise loyal troops still holding one or the other would bombard their foes from the battlements opposite.

The guard returned. 'The castellan will see you. Please follow me.'

'By all means.' Reske noted a portcullis's iron teeth as he passed under the arch into the tunnel cutting through the rampart. He picked out holes in the curved ceiling overhead and saw the fangs of a second iron gate at the far end. Would Hurat's defenders pour boiling water or embers mixed with burning hot sand onto the heads of those caught in this lethal trap?

A woman in Hurat livery appeared ahead of the guard, coming through a door halfway along the tunnel. She carried her halberd past them without a word. Passing the door, Reske noted the large guardroom. Maybe soldiers would be waiting to slaughter anyone who survived the murderous water or sand. As far as he could see, the only guaranteed outcome for anyone attacking this castle would be an unholy number of dead and injured.

Blinking as he emerged into bright sunlight. Reske followed the guard towards the great keep, wondering how such mayhem could be avoided.

The Hurat guard opened a door into a tall tower. He led Reske up a spiral staircase and ushered him into a long, high-ceilinged room that must surely stretch to the keep's next tower. Sunlight falling through the tall windows shone on miniature copies of castles and other defences in polished glass cases. Years ago in Velasta his instructors had used similar models to explain the vagaries of different towns to junior couriers.

Close by the door, a lean, bald-headed man sat at a desk piled high with letters. Reske saw he had been sketching a complex array of rampart guns defending a spearpoint bastion.

A second man stood with his back to them, studying a vast map painted on the room's far wall. He turned, and Reske saw he held Margrave Vauset's letter. So this was Castellan Maixen. A calm-faced man of middling build and plainly dressed. His dark hair showed a little grey, though he was surely a few years younger than Reske. Anyone not paying attention might underestimate him. Reske decided that would be a grave mistake. The castellan didn't miss a detail as he studied this unexpected messenger.

'I gather the Margrave of Jedfal has sent you with vital news. Let's hear it.'

Reske clasped his hands behind his back. 'He told me this message was for your ears alone.'

'That's for me to decide.' Maixen's tone hardened. 'You may leave and return to Jedfal to tell your master that, if you wish. Master Senon is this castle's chief steward and my most trusted aide.'

'Margrave Vauset is not my master.' Reske replied, forthright. 'I serve Earl Debin of Shirlat.'

The castellan was surprised. 'The Earl of Shirlat? Do you know—?'

'Yes, and I have no idea how my lord angered Princess Idelina so excessively. He sent me to gather news from Bastrys and Hedvin. When he realised returning to Velasta might put me in danger, he ordered me to Jedfal.'

Rustling papers hinted at some reaction from the bald man at the desk. Reske kept his eyes on the castellan.

'As far as I know, no warrant for Earl Debin's execution has been signed. I'm told he is confined under guard in Velasta.' Maixen studied him for a long moment. 'It seems you have plenty to tell us. Start with whatever Margrave Vauset isn't willing to write down.'

Reske repeated the old margrave's words, though he softened the tone where he could. He need not have bothered. Maixen wasn't offended.

'Of course, you already knew this,' Reske concluded, seeing discreet amusement in the castellan's eyes.

'Some of it,' Maixen agreed. 'Certainly that I'm no longer oath-bound. I took those vows and I pay attention to what I'm saying. I've been waiting to see who else realises, now it's certain there will be no more earls of Hurat.'

'You're sure?' Reske asked before he could stop himself.

Maixen nodded. 'Scrivener Mistress Zile has traced every possible bloodline descending from King Ganirin to a dead end. I still can't decide if I'm disappointed or relieved.'

'Only the God knows if that would have solved our problems or added more unholy complications to this mess.' The steward Senon fetched a couple of chairs and set them by his desk.

'Please, sit.' Maixen took a chair. 'We haven't mentioned my unexpected freedom and I must ask you to do the same. This province's garrison captains have sworn fealty to the Arafaze crown, as well as obedience to me. I want to avoid forcing them to decide which oath they must break for as long as I can. I imagine Margrave Vauset has similar reasons for his discretion.'

'Undoubtedly,' Reske agreed.

Maixen leaned forward. 'Tell me about Bastrys and Hedvin.'

Reske repeated everything he had shared with the margrave, though surely, this must be old news? As he talked, the steward Senon left the room. When the bald man returned, Maixen was sharing his most recent information.

'My sources tell me Padran of Evarise is on his way to Hedvin. Baron Lebarre is mustering an army there. You can also tell Margrave Vauset that Chalus scouts reported a substantial force of cavalry and footsoldiers arriving in Bastrys six days ago. They marched under Lystro of Coylure's banner.'

The castellan sorted through a stack of papers on the steward's desk. He handed Reske a letter. 'I received this from Baroness Karlin of Evesk. That's the next town upstream on the Dore. How would you advise her?'

First the models, now this test. Reske felt more and more like a novice courier. He read the letter quickly, grateful someone had taught this noble lady to write a neat script. He thought for a moment, then answered the castellan.

'She's right when she says if Lystro of Coylure wants to seize Hurat, he won't waste firing powder and footsoldiers' lives conquering the towns along the Dore one by one. She's also correct when she says his army won't be fit to attack this castle or Hurat town if they come downstream on the river. They'll be battered by every crown garrison they pass, even if the noble barons and baronesses refuse to join the fight.'

Cannon pointing south to deter a Mervantese attack would be equally well placed to bombard troop barges surging downstream. Reske wondered how easy it might be to blockade the river with rafts of boats chained together. He'd mention that later.

Reading the letter again, he considered what might be unwritten between the lines. This unknown baroness believed Coylure's forces would march along the highway to attack Evesk. Her town offered a stronghold where his forces could regroup behind high walls, while the earl and his commanders planned their assault on Hurat.

'She says Evesk will defy any and all assailants as long as the Sun Goddess blesses them. However, she warns you she will surrender to save her people from being starved or slaughtered.'

Reske looked at Maixen. 'She's afraid she'll be betrayed. She thinks Evesk's gates will be opened by a traitor or a coward. I can imagine plenty of her people would bow their heads and swear fealty to either princess as queen to save their homes from being ransacked after a siege.'

'We hear such murmurs here.' Senon scowled.

'We are ready to act on any hint of unrest in Hurat becoming more than talk,' Maixen assured Reske. 'So many would have to be involved in a plot to betray us, we are certain to hear of it.'

Reske hoped he was right. He continued.

'The baroness has no faith in her noble neighbours along the Dore. Lystro of Coylure could only besiege Evesk if his army could travel the highway unopposed and as long as he was confident he was safe from attack from behind. This would mean the crown garrisons in each town were penned up by the ruling lord or lady's sworn troops.'

'That's assuming those crown garrisons would march against either earl's army.' Maixen was bleakly realistic. 'They wear a different livery, but we speak the same language. Hurat's garrisons stand ready to fight the Mervantese, not friends and neighbours. The captains and their officers are posted here from across Arafaze, but footsoldiers are recruited in this province. I can't risk sending orders that might be disobeyed.'

If that happened, Reske could see the castellan's options would rapidly narrow from bad to catastrophic. To reassert his authority, Maixen would have to order Hurat's garrison to march on a garrison that defied him. He might face mutiny from his own officers or mass desertion from the ranks. Even if Hurat's forces obeyed, they would leave the safety of these fortifications. They would be open to attack from all sides. Was that what one of the rival earls hoped for?

Reske shifted his chair to see the great painted map. 'Lystro of Coylure's not your only threat. Padran of Evarise could attack Evesk for the self-same reasons, and he might find it easier to take the baroness's town. His army won't face much opposition if he heads for Hurat across the grasslands. He'll take a route around the headwaters of those two rivers flowing into the Dore.'

'The Tresil and the Arne,' Senon told him.

Reske waved that away. 'No commander will risk a crossing when he might be attacked with half his forces on each bank. That means Evarise's forces will have already covered three quarters of the journey to Evesk. If it was me, I'd try to take the crown garrison first. Then I could turn the fortress's cannon on the town's undefended side.'

Maixen looked thoughtful. 'What do you suppose Baroness Karlin's fate will be if Earl Padran takes her captive?'

'Given how Princess Idelina has treated Earl Debin?' Reske tried to swallow his anger. 'I imagine she'll be offered the choice of swearing fealty or being condemned for treason and seeing her children disinherited.'

'Unless the Earl of Evarise attacks Jedfal first,' Senon interrupted. 'If he takes the powder mills, Padran will gain a massive advantage over everyone.'

'So speaks a cannoneer,' Maixen commented.

Reske's blood ran cold. Boats on the river could supply Hurat's besieged townsfolk with all the food they could eat, but the castle could only hold out as long as the castellan had firing powder, cannon balls and shot for the rampart guns.

Maixen walked towards the map. Reske and Senon followed. The castellan folded his arms, thinking aloud.

'Both earls will want to conclude their campaigns before the autumn rains arrive, and soldiers and horses get bogged down in mud. If they still believe victory is within reach by the equinox, they might risk staying into the early days of the Stag Moon. I can't believe they'll persist once the Frost Moon arrives with winter's hardships. Is there any way we can hold out until then?'

The door from the tower stair opened behind them. Maixen ignored it. 'We need to send scouts to watch for Padran of Evarise preparing to march from Hedvin. We need a relay of riders to bring us word by the most direct route. An army won't want to cross those rivers, but a single man on a horse could swim them and save days of travel.'

'Maixen. When you have concluded your business with this visitor, we must speak.'

Startled, Reske turned to see a dark-haired priestess in her middle years standing by the door.

'They're back?' Maixen's relief vanished as he saw the priestess's stricken face. 'What's happened?'

The priestess knotted her hands at her waist. 'Alory is back. Brother Cavore is dead.'

'What? How?' Maixen demanded.

'That is a matter for the shrine and the temple.' Fleeting emotion in the priestess's eyes came and went before Reske could decide what it was.

'Jadewin,' the castellan protested. 'You told me yourself the Moon God's sons have taken up Princess Idelina's cause. If your Velastan sisters are so determined to crown Princess Alriad that they have killed a priest—'

'Cavore's death is no concern of yours.' The priestess's stony face gave nothing away.

Maixen was shocked. He rallied fast. 'I have to talk to Alory. I must know what he's learned upriver.'

'I will let you know when he is able to see you.' The priestess's bloodless lips pressed tight together. 'I also came to tell you Mistress Quenild and Mistress Ticosa have returned from Usenas. It will be safest if no one knows they bring news from the Mire. I will escort you to their home.'

Reske wanted to know who this priestess was, Velastan by her accent, and telling the castellan what to do.

'Won't their neighbours be curious to see Hurat's castellan knock on their door?' Senon objected. 'Coylure and Evarise are sure to have spies in Hurat town.'

Looking intently at the priestess, Maixen shook his head. 'They're merchants. Spread the word in a few taverns that I'm enquiring about provisions for sale in the markets downstream.

Everyone knows we've started filling the castle's stores with the first harvests.'

Senon didn't like this, but Reske could see the castellan had made up his mind.

'After you, sister.' Maixen gestured and the priestess Jadewin turned for the door.

The castellan followed, then the steward, and Reske fell into step from ingrained habit. Outside, Senon strode off to deal to one or other of the tasks Maixen had given him. Reske followed the castellan and the priestess, staying a few paces behind. If Maixen didn't want him coming along, he could say so.

As they walked out through the long arch in the castle's rampart, Reske noticed the priestess tuck her sunburst pendant inside her robe. Anyone in need of the Goddess's advice or a blessing had better look elsewhere.

They walked quickly through Hurat. Curious glances slid over Reske. Good. His unremarkable grey clothing was close enough to the castle's livery the townsfolk most likely assumed he was the castellan's attendant.

When they reached a modest street in what must be one of the town's oldest quarters, an attractive woman with dark eyes red-rimmed from weeping opened the door to the priestess's knock. The householder blew her nose on a crumpled handkerchief. 'Forgive me. You are welcome to our home, Castellan.'

She led them upstairs and into the kitchen at the back of the house. A stockier woman with a no-nonsense expression swung a kettle on its hook over glowing coals. Reske saw no sign she had been shedding tears.

'Can I offer you tea, Castellan? Please, sit.' She gestured at a well-scrubbed wooden table.

'Thank you.' Maixen pulled out a chair and sat. 'Copper tea if you have it, for preference.'

'Of course.' The stocky woman busied herself with tea canisters and cups.

Reske noticed her hands were shaking. He stayed standing by the door as a good lackey should.

Maixen didn't waste any time. 'Sister Jadewin says you have news from the Mire?'

'Unwelcome news.' The pretty woman filled two tea pots with hot water. 'Excuse me, but who are you?' she asked Reske bluntly.

Maixen replied. 'A trusted ally who has brought valuable news. Reske, sit down. These ladies are Quenild and Ticosa.'

'I am honoured.' He bowed briefly and took a seat.

The stocky woman, Quenild, looked sceptical, but she put a cup in front of him. 'Silver tea, or copper?'

'Copper, if you please.' Reske had no real preference, but it couldn't hurt to align himself with the castellan.

Mistress Ticosa filled everyone's cups. She poured silver tea for the priestess without asking. 'So..."

Reske listened with growing concern as the two women told their tale. When they finished, Sister Jadewin spoke for the first time since leaving the castle.

'What does Lord Romer of Sharrow hope to gain from conspiring with the Mervantese?'

'To be Baron of Sharrow,' Maixen said grimly. 'He has always envied and resented Masecal and Usenas. So did his father by all accounts. Romer also wants the coin to build himself a magnificent residence.'

'He should blame his ancestors for claiming such a useless stretch of waterfront.' Mistress Quenild topped up both tea pots. 'Barges don't moor in Sharrow because it's on the wrong side of the bend. It's past the mouth of the Olion as well. No one's going to forego the benefit of riding that current downstream. Barges sailing back to Hurat steer for the slacker water under the northern bank.'

'Tadiri of Mervante can't make Lord Romer a baron,' Sister Jadewin protested. 'Such elevation can only come from the Arafaze crown.'

Maixen nodded. 'So we should assume he's offered to help whichever princess will do that.'

'Or whoever has outbid the other,' Sister Jadewin suggested. 'Lord Romer lives in lavish style, so he is perpetually short of funds.'

Reske raised a hand. 'If he is receiving envoys from Mervante, does that mean Princess Alriad or Princess Idelina has made an alliance with King Tadiri?'

'Surely not.' Mistress Quenild was appalled.

'King Venais agreed to a marriage alliance with his daughter.' Sister Jadewin was more willing to consider the possibility. 'Hostility to Mervante doesn't run nearly so high in Velasta. It's been generations since the towns along the Dore were attacked. Folk have got used to buying cotton and sugar and other treats from Mervantese merchants.'

Mistress Quenild leaned back and folded her arms. 'We'll likely get a lot of these answers, and without anyone knowing we're asking, if we pay the Mire folk. They'll know if the Mervantese have made an alliance with one princess or the other.'

Maixen looked dubious. 'Can we be sure we'll learn the truth?'

Mistress Ticosa was affronted. 'Mire folk drive a hard bargain, but they are honest traders.'

Mistress Quenild supported her wife. 'I'd rather rely on information that's bought and paid for instead of gossip and rumour. My father always said anything you're offered for free is most likely worthless.'

Heavy boots ran up the stairs from the entrance hall. A tall, wide-shouldered priest appeared in the kitchen doorway. A moment later, Reske realised he was younger than he might seem. The youth would be barely halfway through an apprenticeship if he wasn't sworn to the God.

Sister Jadewin sprang to her feet, shocked. 'What are you doing here?'

The hollow-eyed boy didn't answer her. He hugged the merchant women and found himself a cup on the dresser. He poured hot copper tea and drank it down without taking a breath.

Reske recalled the priestess's words at the castle. Alory was back, and a black brother called Cavore was dead. That explained the boy's distant gaze.

Reske knew the brutal horror of friends dying. He remembered going over events time and again, searching for some path not taken that could have led to a different outcome. He had known young officers throw themselves from a garrison's rampart to escape the torment of guilt piled on grief. He didn't need Sister Jadewin's glare warning him not to ask the lad about the other priest's death.

The boy Alory put his cup on the table. 'Mother Finevre told me you would be coming here, Castellan. You want the news from Chalus? Townsfolk along the Dore don't care who wears Arafaze's crown. They just want that settled before the princesses' earls start fighting like feral dogs out to steal each other's prey.'

'Did you hear any news of the Mervantese?' Maixen asked urgently. 'Any word of Baroness Gossen in Sospirin?'

'The baroness is keeping her own counsel as far as anyone knows. No one trusts the Mervantese, no matter how hard they're trying to make friends.'

As the young priest shared what he had seen and heard, Reske grew increasingly suspicious of the supposed traders camped on the Dore's southern bank.

The boy faltered to a halt. 'Then Brother Cavore—'

'We know what happened,' Sister Jadewin interrupted. 'The Moon God will see his murderers punished.'

'May his vengeance be swift and merciless,' Mistress Ticosa added, vehement.

Reske realised the merchant women must have visited the temple earlier, to let the sister know they had returned.

'Such justice is no concern of the castellan's,' the priestess said quickly.

'Sister Jadewin.' Quenild stood up and began to collect the tea cups. 'I would never presume to pry into the affairs of the temple or the shrine, but I would never have imagined a priest would be murdered on a Chalus street. Is Alory in danger?'

'I have no way to know.' The priestess drew out her sunburst pendant. 'I swear I will do everything in my power to keep Alory safe, and to see that Brother Cavore's killers face the judgement of the Goddess and the God.'

The gold glowed bright and warm in her hand as the Mother of Life showed them the priestess was telling the truth. As always, Reske found that reminder of unseen, unknowable power intimidating.

'Thank you, sister.' Mistress Quenild dutifully ducked her head. 'We'll be heading to the Mire soon, one way or another. We can take Alory, to keep him out of harm's way.'

'I will bear that in mind, and thank you.' Sister Jadewin rose to her feet. 'Let Mother Finevre know when you'll be travelling downstream.'

Reske saw Maixen could take a hint. The castellan stood up, and so did he.

'We'll send word to castle and temple.' Mistress Quenild looked at Maixen. 'Let us know what you're willing to pay and we'll get you the best value we can.'

'What's happening downstream?' Curiosity momentarily distracted the young priest from his wretchedness.

'We'll tell you later.' Mistress Ticosa reached across the table to take his hand. 'Do you think you could eat something?'

Reske saw the boy's lip quiver at that small kindness.

Sister Jadewin intervened, apologetic. 'In any case, Alory, I need you to come with me.'

'I'll see you out.' Quenild ushered the four of them down the stairs. She shut the house's door with a solid thud.

Maixen turned to Sister Jadewin. 'Are you coming to the castle?'

The priestess shook her head. 'We must attend to other matters.'

'Are you going to tell me how Cavore died?' Maixen challenged her. 'Don't expect me to believe his murder has nothing to do with divisions in Velasta between the high shrine and the high temple. Stars above, someone tried to cut his throat on Hurat's streets, and yours, and the boy's. There must be some connection.'

'Mother Finevre and Father Memlin are striving to keep the peace across the Vale of Hurat.' Sister Jadewin said, expressionless. 'The Goddess and the God will ensure justice for Brother Cavore. Alory, come with me.'

The priestess walked away before Maixen could say anything more. The tall young priest followed, wiping away tears with his black sleeve. The castellan stared after them, fighting to subdue his fury and frustration. Reske waited.

Eventually Maixen drew a deep, resolute breath. 'You'll have plenty to tell Margrave Vauset when you get back to Jedfal. I'd very much welcome his opinion on this.'

'There's something you should know.' Reske braced himself. 'Black brothers have been murdered elsewhere, as well as some good sisters.'

To his relief, Maixen was too startled to be angry when Reske told him what he knew.

'So that's something else Jadewin is keeping from me,' the castellan said grimly.

'Only if she knows about these deaths herself,' Reske pointed out.

'It doesn't look as if I'm going to get a chance to ask.' Maixen shook his head.

'You said the three of them were attacked here in Hurat? Her and the boy, and this dead priest?' Reske prompted.

Maixen explained what had happened. 'The man they brought to the castle infirmary died before dawn. The patrol we sent out that same night tripped over a fresh corpse with a gash in one forearm. Someone had cut his throat barely three streets from the attack.'

He sighed. 'Jadewin confirmed the second dead man was the attacker young Alory had sliced, but no one came forward to identify either one, even after I offered a reward. They've been buried nameless, known only to the Moon God. Senon pays some of the town's ne'er-do-wells to keep him apprised of Hurat's back-alley dealings. None of them knows who they were.'

Reske was frustrated. Once again, he'd get nowhere making enquiries in a town where he had no contacts of his own.

The castellan started walking briskly. 'Let's see what Senon makes of this.'

When they reached the castle, Maixen led the way to a different tower, climbing the spiral stair to an audience chamber. Senon was sitting at a long, polished table. Reske noted he was sketching wagons and carts.

The steward looked up. 'What's the news from the Mire?'

'Later.' Maixen walked over to the crown courier case on the table. 'When did this arrive?'

'Less than an hour ago.' Senon offered Maixen the leather roll of tools to free the buckles. 'Evarise insignia on the seals.'

'Is he waiting for a reply?' Maixen found pincers to cut the wires.

'No. He's already gone. He said he had orders to return at once and I didn't see anything to be gained by detaining him. The sooner he left, the less he could see to report.' Senon held the case steady so the castellan could pull the soft lead discs apart.

'He wasn't alone,' the steward added. 'Six troopers in Evarise livery stayed with their horses outside the gate. Sergeant Lund had fodder and water taken out to them. He told me they had come from Hedvin.'

The messenger might have brought a crown courier's case, but that didn't mean he held a service medallion. Reske wished he'd had a chance to talk to the man.

'Doubtless they've been warning freeholders and village elders along their route that their safest course is swearing allegiance to Idelina.' Maixen took a letter from the case and snapped the wax seals.

Reske saw his own impatience reflected on Senon's face as Maixen took his time reading the letter. The castellan refolded it, looking thoughtful.

'We are advised that Princess Idelina's ambassador will arrive in Hurat on or around the fifth day of the Thunder Moon. This letter calls her Queen Idelina, obviously. I suppose we should be thankful whoever this is didn't invite himself for the Solstice.'

'Why is he coming here?' Senon asked the obvious question half a breath before Reske.

'Apparently this noble gentleman will bring joyous news to resolve the current unpleasantness without further strife.' Maixen's sarcasm was withering. 'We're told to make ready to welcome him, together with the honoured lords and ladies of Hurat's nobility. They have been sent royal invitations to meet this ambassador here at their earliest convenience.'

Reske spoke up before Senon could vent his wrath. 'She's sending an ambassador? Not an envoy.' A monarch sent an envoy to those who owed their allegiance. An ambassador spoke for the crown in negotiations beyond Arafaze's borders.

'That's interesting, isn't it?' Maixen agreed. 'Do you suppose Princess Idelina or Earl Padran, or possibly both, are willing to concede the Vale of the Tane's nobility are under no obligation to swear fealty to Arafaze? They must know it's open to question by now.'

Senon cracked his knuckles. 'More notice would have been welcome.'

'Do the best you can.' Maixen tossed the letter onto the table. 'Make sure everyone under my command knows I will not recognise either royal princess as monarch until they have been blessed with divine approval by both the high shrine and the high temple.'

'Some will still say you're as good as acknowledging Idelina as queen by hosting her ambassador,' Senon warned.

Maixen didn't take offence. 'Remind the townsfolk I swore my loyalty as Hurat's castellan to the Earls of Hurat alone.'

'How many people know there are no more earls to be had?' Reske recalled how viciously court rivalries played out in Velasta, even if blood was rarely shed, and only behind closed doors.

'You need to be careful,' he warned the castellan. 'That's a double-edged blade. If you have no allegiance to bind you, you don't have a suzerain to defend you. If Coylure or Padran contrives to take Hurat, unlikely as that must be, Arafaze's new queen will find it very convenient to have you to blame for the province's tardiness to acknowledge her. Any garrison captains who followed your orders can be excused as staying true to their oaths of obedience. You could even be blamed for leading the nobility of the Tane astray.'

Maixen's grim expression acknowledged these possibilities. 'I wonder if I will be formally condemned like the Earl of Shirlat, or simply beheaded on the nearest block of firewood? But let's ford that stream when we find it. Senon, send word to Mother Finevre and Father Memlin. Tell them about this gathering and ask for the Goddess's help and the God's to keep everybody honest. Idelina's ambassador most of all.'

He paused for a moment. 'Please send my compliments to Mistress Quenild and Mistress Ticosa, and tell them to learn whatever the Mire folk have to tell them. I have every confidence they'll agree a fair price, but I'll pay whatever I must. If they need to take silver coin with them, tell them to come and see Captain Stava. Give him this.'

The castellan reached for paper and pen and wrote a swift note. Waving the paper to and fro to dry the ink, he looked at Reske. 'Do you need to write anything down, to make a full report to Margrave Vauset?'

'No.' Reske would have welcomed more than one night's sleep before he took to the road or a river boat again, but that was past praying for. 'Is there anything else I should tell him?'

Maixen folded the note and handed it to Senon. The steward left as the castellan answered Reske. 'I'd like to be certain Margrave Vauset has received his invitation to meet this ambassador. It would be awkward if it turns out the messengers riding from Hedvin to the lords and ladies of the Tane have met with some accident or delay.'

'You think that's likely?'

Maixen walked over to a window and stared out. 'If I wanted to take Hurat's castle and town without firing a shot? I'd gather the nobility of the Dore here, along with the town's guild worthies and justiciars. I'd tell them why their current castellan has no right to hold office. I'd allow them time to panic, then offer Queen Idelina's champion to bolster these defences with a sizeable army. I'd swear Hurat's crown garrisons would be added to their own town's strength. That champion would have to be someone experienced in battle, able to lead the Vale of Hurat's forces to defeat Lystro of Coylure, Zavire of Bastrys and anyone else fool enough to join them.'

He glanced at Reske. 'Baron Lensin of Chalus and Baroness Karlin of Evesk would take that deal. Every other landed noble in between would surely do the same. Can you honestly see the nobility of the Tane marching into battle against them? Margrave Vauset is well-respected, but his allies have minds of their own. Don't you think they would come to terms, especially if they continued to enjoy their illusion of independence?'

Reske abandoned the idea of setting out for Jedfal next morning. 'Where can I get a horse? And something to eat before I leave?'

Chapter Nineteen

HURAT

The 20th Day of the Flower Moon

Jadewin didn't need to look over her shoulder to know that Alory was scowling. He finally spoke when they reached the broad road that linked Hurat's ferries.

'I don't want to go to the Nilgeh Mire.'

'I don't want to send you there,' she replied, forthright, 'but let's keep every route open until the Goddess or the God shows us the best way forward.'

'Oh.' Expecting an argument she wasn't offering, Alory fell silent for a moment. 'Are we going to the temple or the shrine?'

'Neither.' Jadewin turned north towards the Tane. 'Do you remember Cavore and I agreed to recall our brothers and sisters who understand the unseen to Hurat? They're in the Tane Ferry Fever Hall.'

'Really?' Alory was apprehensive.

'Don't worry.' Jadewin chose to misunderstand his concern. 'The fever hall is empty. There's no danger of contagion.'

'That's alright then.' Alory lengthened his stride. Jadewin was forced to break into a trot several times to keep up with him.

As they reached the Tane, the ferry was approaching the broad, shallow steps set into the bank. A smooth ramp ran down to the water for wagons. Towers on both sides housed the treadmills that wound the chains hidden beneath the dark waters to haul the ferries from bank to bank.

Jadewin's pale robe and Alory's priestly black ensured they walked straight onto the vessel. They had their pick of seats on the coveted benches on the raised decks on either side. They waited while pack animals and wagons were driven into the belly of the broad, flat-bottomed boat. Jadewin watched the beasts shuffling their hooves and wagging their ears to convey their displeasure. The ferry's gate closed behind them. A horn call from the Hurat side was answered by the Tane's tower.

The vessel began its short journey as the treadmills turned and Hurat's criminals paid another measure of painful, sweat-soaked penance. Disembarking on the Tane bank, Jadewin led Alory past the travellers' hostels where those who arrived after sunset could stay the night and stable their horses. The fever hall was a prudent distance away.

'Have you ever served here?'

Alory shook his head. 'No. Should I?'

Jadewin shrugged. 'It can be instructive. Fever dreams can prompt uncommon manifestations.'

'I'm sure Brother Talaven intended—' Alory broke off, looking wretched.

'I'm sure.' Jadewin smiled at the boy.

Inwardly, she scolded herself. She had only been making conversation to silence her own worries. She was barely acquainted with her Hurat sisters who shared the gift of sight into the unreal. She had counted on meeting the shrine's hidden brethren with Cavore at her side. But what was done was done, and she and Alory must go on.

The fever hall had no outward facing windows, but Jadewin knew what the layout would be. Above the communal rooms at ground level, four floors offered individual accommodation reached by staircases which could be guarded. Travellers showing symptoms which could signify some virulent ailment were denied passage on the ferry until a priest concluded they were no threat to Hurat. Anyone travelling with somebody who was detained, even if they appeared to be in the best of health, must wait for five days until they were permitted to cross.

They walked through the open gate into the empty courtyard.

Alory read the signs above the doors around them. 'Where do we go?'

Jadewin' mouth was uncomfortably dry. 'The dining hall.'

As Alory opened the door, she saw a cluster of priestesses and priests studying a map unrolled across a table. Some wore cloaks and boots dusty and creased from travel. Others had been here long enough to bathe and change their robes. Jadewin counted quickly. All five of her sisters had arrived, but only four priests. Cavore had spoken of nine brothers who knew the secrets of the intangible realm.

A priest stepped away from the table. 'Where is Brother Cavore?'

'Brother Belid.' Alory's voice broke. 'He was murdered in Chalus.'

This wasn't remotely how Jadewin wanted to share that news. She only hoped the Moon God knew better. She sat on the closest bench to let the brothers' disbelief and distress run their course. Once silence fell, Alory looked at her for guidance.

She addressed the priest standing beside the table. 'Brother Belid. When will the rest of your brethren arrive.'

'I very much fear they won't.' He rubbed a hand over the beard that didn't hide toad pox scars on his cheeks. 'Something is gravely amiss. I buried one of our absent brothers myself. Please, how did Cavore die?'

The priests and priestesses abandoned the map to take seats at different tables. Jadewin nodded at Alory. 'Tell them.'

The first time he told this awful tale in the safety of Mother Finevre's parlour, still filthy from his journey, he had choked on his sobs. Now Alory was coldly furious with the Velastan sisters who were so foully misusing their magic in Chalus. He couldn't say whether or not Cavore's killers were truly sworn to the Moon God, but he was viciously pleased they had died.

As he stumbled over his words describing the fearsome fire bird, Jadewin saw her sisters were as astonished as she had been. She noted the brothers were not.

Alory dragged the back of his hand across his eyes. 'I worked my way back to Hurat as a barge hand. I went to the temple instead of the shrine, because no one's tried to kill me there.'

The silence was absolute. Jadewin watched her sisters look out through the sunlit windows, seeking the Goddess's guidance. The brothers closed their eyes and communed with the Moon God.

Brother Belid spoke first. Mother Finevre said he was a stern man but fair, and she thought it likely Hurat's hidden brethren would choose him to lead them, now Talaven and Cavore were both dead. Much Jadewin's own age, Belid served the Horned God primarily as a bane of liars. Between invitations to sit at some noble's assizes at solstice and equinox, he travelled to any sanctuary whose priest needed help mediating a dispute.

'Who is killing us?' he demanded. 'And why? I have asked our hidden brethren in the high temple what they know, but I've had no answer.'

Sister Meida cleared her throat. 'Too many of our sisters and brothers in Velasta have forsaken their oaths to take sides in this quarrel over the crown.'

Mother Finevre said the plump sister had a tendency to state the obvious. She also said Meida wielded magic more effectively than anyone she had ever met.

Jadewin stood up to get everyone's attention. 'This may or may not be related, but a treacherous sister from Velasta called Hasrine is in Hurat, conspiring with strangers who can reach into the unseen world.'

She told them about the man Hasrine had met in the castle's sanctuary, and about the Velastan's campaign to discredit Alory. He told everyone about the phantom rats and the attackers who had followed.

Sister Deyadir rose from the table where she sat with the other priestesses. Tall and lean, she paced to and fro, making Jadewin think of a stork. 'We have to stop this intolerable abuse of the unseen world.'

A rotund brother with a face like a creased cushion nodded. 'Meantime, any further manifestations may lead us to the culprits.'

'Excuse me.' Jadewin interrupted before Deyadir could reply. 'Hurat faces other threats besides the forces mustered in Hedvin and Bastrys.' She told them the news from the Mire.

'Two of us should go to Sharrow,' Sister Meida declared. 'To remind Lord Romer the Moon God knows his secrets, and the Sun Goddess can insist he settles his debts.'

Belid shook his head. 'Too risky, if he's plotting treachery.'

Sister Meida was outraged. 'He would not dare to raise a blade against a servant of the Goddess or the God.'

'What about sending out footsoldiers who had been told to hunt down imposters profaning stolen robes?' The rotund brother challenged her. 'That we were spies who must be killed before Hurat is betrayed?'

'Or they could just make your deaths look like an accident,' the priest sitting beside him observed.

Seeing he had lost the two leading fingers of his right hand. Jadewin knew he must be Brother Augol. Mother Finevre had mentioned he'd suffered a mishap with firing powder and a rampart gun after three decades of faultless service to the crown. Apparently, his talent for magic had emerged as he recovered. Jadewin suspected he had successfully concealed his sight of the intangible for years.

'Before any of us leave Hurat for whatever reason, we must deal with this Sister Hasrine,' Brother Belid said firmly.

Jadewin realised the newly-returned priestesses were looking at her. 'Mother Finevre is ready to expel her from our temple, and to bar her from every temple and sanctuary answering to Hurat. But she doubts a sister prepared to misuse her magic so foully will respect her authority.'

'Then we put her on a barge heading upstream to Bastrys,' Brother Augol said robustly. 'She can join her traitorous sisters there.'

'She'll jump ashore the instant she gets the chance.' Sister Deyadir shook her head. 'And spread the Goddess only knows what lies.'

'Not if we dose her senseless,' the rotund priest countered cheerfully. 'She will need an escort though, to make sure she doesn't wake before we're rid of her.'

Jadewin saw such ruthlessness startled her sisters, but none of them objected.

'We are getting ahead of ourselves.' Brother Belid slapped the table. 'Does anyone know where Hasrine is now?'

'She could be anywhere in the town. She serves the Goddess as diligently as any temple mother could wish.' Jadewin hated to admit it. 'Sisters, you should go and let Mother Finevre know you've arrived. Ask if Hasrine has been sent on some errand or if she's in the temple. Send word to me at the castle. I'll look for her there.'

'Take the boy,' Brother Belid ordered. 'He can find us at the shrine once we know where the renegade is. Then we can decide how to trap her.'

Brother Augol raised his maimed hand, addressing Jadewin. 'May I come with you, sister? I have friends among the cannoneers who may have seen her ally inside the castle.'

'Yes, do that.' Brother Belid agreed. 'Alory, you come with me.'

'If Hasrine is at the temple, we'll make sure she doesn't leave,' Deyadir said, resolute.

Jadewin wanted to ask how the tall priestess proposed to do that without their other sisters intervening. She wanted to ask how the priests proposed to load the Velastan woman senseless onto a barge without river traders gawking. But her sisters and the black brothers were ready to leave.

She led them out of the fever hall. If people waiting for the ferry were surprised to see this gathering of priests and priestesses, no one approached them. As the chained boat crossed the Tane to Hurat, Jadewin silently sought the Goddess's guidance. She would never have imagined she and her sisters would conspire against one of their own, but what else could they do? She found no answers before they left the ferry and everyone went their separate ways.

When Jadewin and Augol arrived at the castle, she paused at the guardroom door. 'Sergeant Lund, have you seen Sister Hasrine today?'

'I believe she's helping Brother Delnor in the Infirmary.'

Jadewin silently blessed the Goddess. 'Thank you.'

'Good to see you, brother.' Lund greeted Augol as an old friend.

'You too.' The maimed priest replied.

As they crossed the castle yard, he pointed towards a gathering by the disused cannon. 'The castellan's striving for peace, but he has the sense to prepare for war. I see familiar faces. Shall I see what I can learn before we go to the infirmary?'

'By all means. I'll make sure nothing's amiss in the sanctuary.' Jadewin hoped the Goddess would answer her there.

Instead she saw Sister Hasrine kneeling in front of the altars. Startled, Jadewin stepped back from the doorway.

Hasrine stood and turned around. 'Sister?'

Jadewin could only trust the Goddess's wisdom, in bringing them together. 'Mother Finevre wants to see you.'

Hasrine ducked her head with every appearance of humility. 'I am the Goddess's servant.'

'I will walk with you.' Jadewin said placidly. Once the Velastan was inside the temple, she, Deyadir, Meida and the others would have to keep her there, until Mother Finevre approved the black brothers' plan.

'You've convinced the old woman to expel me from Hurat, have you?' Hasrine sneered. 'I had no idea Finevre was so beloved as well as respected. It was far easier to undermine Mother Hasperre.'

Jadewin felt a chill. 'So you are conspiring with those treacherous sisters in Chalus.'

Hasrine's face hardened. 'What has your wharf rat been saying? We hoped he had drowned.'

'Haven't your fellow oath breakers told you their assiduously crafted deceit has been destroyed? Regardless, you're right. Mother Finevre is going to expel you. Report your failure to High Mother Elyka in Velasta.'

'You may have won that battle in Chalus, but we will win this war.' Hasrine was unrepentant. 'Queen Alriad will give the secret sisterhood free rein. A few portents here and there will convince the people that only we can protect them from the unseen and unknown. Once they see the black brothers fail time and again, they will acknowledge the Goddess's superiority over the God.'

Jadewin steeled herself. 'We who serve Hurat's temple and shrine will not allow such abuse of the sacred mysteries we guard—'

'You think you can stop us?' scoffed Hasrine. 'After Princess Idelina's envoy is struck down by the divine revenger who slew King Venais?'

Splinters of light coalesced between them to form a nightmare figure made of razor-edged knives. Opening her mind's eye, Jadewin saw the Lightning King was even more fearsome in the unseen world. She fought against doubt and despair. How could she possibly destroy this terrifying manifestation before Hasrine brought it wholly into the tangible realm?

Something else shimmered in the sanctuary. A shifting shadow. Jadewin glimpsed a short, hunched figure. Something in the unreal world was drawn to Hasrine's hate-filled thoughts like a blowfly to carrion.

The figure grew more clearly defined. Paralysed with horror, Jadewin recognised the semblance of an age-withered woman. All these months, ever since she and Alory had driven the Icicle Witch from the tangible world, the monster must have been searching for a way to return. In her hurry to manifest her malice, Hasrine had ripped through the veil that separated real from unreal. The Icicle Witch had found the tear.

The apparition hissed and reached for the Velastan with black-taloned hands. Jadewin saw the Lightning King shimmer and fade as Hasrine recoiled from the unexpected phantasm. The witch was no longer the manifestation Jadewin and Alory had seen. Some time in Hurat's past, this legend must have spoken of an imperious woman with dark hair piled high and studded with jewelled pins. This phantasm wore a high-collared black dress and diamond bracelets glittered around its wrists. Its ashen face was cruelty personified. It licked dark lips with a pointed black tongue.

Hasrine lost her footing on the altar steps. She fell hard as the monster loomed over her. Jadewin felt the Icicle Witch's presence in the tangible world strengthen as its clawed hands reached for Hasrine. The priestess drew up her knees like a terrified child, hiding her face in her arms.

The Lightning King blazed with furious light. It lashed out, ripping through the black-gowned phantasm's forearm. The glittering thing's blades rippled like feathers. The blow barely left a smear of radiance on the Hurat apparition's sleeve.

The Witch's talons tore a gash deep across the Lightning King's belly. It shook its hand, scattering iridescent shreds. The Velastan's phantasm retaliated, landing blow after blow. Its blades didn't leave a mark. As the Witch clawed at the Lightning King's face, it began to fade. A moment later, with shocking abruptness, the last vestiges of silver light vanished. The Witch shrieked with savage triumph.

The sanctuary door slammed behind Jadewin. She spun around, fearing some new threat. Brother Augol stood there, his eyes wide in horror. Hasrine screamed. Jadewin saw the

Icicle Witch had one clawed fist tangled in the Velastan's hair. Standing between the altars, the phantasm forced the renegade priestess's head back with calculated cruelty. Its fangs glittered in the lamplight and it raised its other taloned hand high.

Jadewin knew Hasrine's terror would allow the monster to kill her. Once this foul creature shed living blood, its tie to the tangible world would be unbreakable. It would pass between the two realms with increasing ease. This disaster would be her fault.

'No!' Jadewin would not allow it.

'No?' The Icicle Witch stared at her, incredulous. 'You forbid me?'

Jadewin had never heard a phantasm speak. She clenched her fists. 'You have no place here.'

'You summoned me.' The Icicle Witch tore its hand free of Hasrine's hair and dropped the sobbing Velastan between the altars. The phantasm stalked towards Jadewin, 'You want me to kill her.'

Jadewin's certainty wavered. Did she truly wish Hasrine was dead, deep in her innermost thoughts? Could she deny she wanted Cavore's murder avenged, as well Brother Talaven's death?

The monster bared its fangs, triumphant. Jadewin fumbled for her sunburst pendant. She gripped it tight and the golden rays stabbed her fingers. She welcomed the pain. That was reality.

'The Goddess alone grants life. The God alone has the right to take it.'

This monster was a simulacrum. It merely echoed the spite and resentment that spawned it. It was nothing more than a reflection of bitter dreams of vengeance that would never occur. Jadewin pictured the phantasm she had destroyed with Alory.

'If I summoned you, I can banish you.'

The creature halted and hissed. For a moment, Jadewin saw the haggard old crone. The apparition flickered between those two forms, like some distorted shadow cast by a candle in a breeze. Jadewin gripped her pendant tighter. Faint light rose from the bloodied gold. Feeble radiance drifted towards the Witch and its outline blurred like smoke from a smouldering fire.

'Kill her!' Hasrine screamed. 'I will serve you!'

The phantasm laughed, instantly restored to the semblance which had terrified the Velastan. It stalked towards Jadewin. She stepped sideways, edging between the benches. If Brother Augol could get behind the thing—

Hasrine scrambled to her feet and ran for the Sanctuary door. Augol blocked the Velastan's path. Hasrine tried to dodge around him. Augol grabbed her sleeve. His maimed hand couldn't hold her. Hasrine tore herself free so violently that she lost her balance and fell. Her head hit a bench with a sickening thud. She lay still.

Was she dead? No, Jadewin would not allow it. She would not permit an accident to give this monster a foothold. As she flung furious denial at the Icicle Witch, her pendant blazed. Incandescence consumed the apparition. Only the soft light of the Goddess's lamp shone from the altar now.

'I— She—' Jadewin couldn't stop shaking.

Augol knelt and carefully straightened Hasrine's limbs. 'She's alive, if that's what you're asking. Her skull and her neck are intact as far as I can tell.'

'We – we must take her to the Infirmary.'

'Open the door.' The priest lifted Hasrine as easily as a child.

He carried her out of the sanctuary and Jadewin followed, knotting her hands in a prayerful clasp to hide the smears of blood on the front of her robe. Thank the Goddess, none of the soldiers in the castle yard spared them more than a passing glance. By the God's grace, Brother Delnor was alone in the Infirmary, with his few patients sound asleep.

'What under the stars has happened?' he asked Augol, appalled.

'The sister fell. She hit her head. This way.' Jadewin went straight to the side room where their unknown attacker had died. As soon as Augol laid Hasrine on the bed, Jadewin hustled him out, pulling the door closed behind her.

'Tell the others what's happened. Bring your brother who wanted to keep her senseless. Alory must find a barge to take her upstream before she recovers her wits.'

'We can't send her to her allies in Bastrys now she's seen what you can do.' Augol shook his head.

Before Jadewin could ask what he suggested, Brother Delnor joined them.

'Let me see my patient.'

To Jadewin's relief, as the priest-physician examined the unconscious woman, she realised he was annoyed with Hasrine.

'Trying to do a day's work for the Goddess on a crust of dry bread and cold water morning, noon and night will make anyone unsteady on their feet. She'll have some nasty bruises and a viciously sore head, but I see no reason why she shouldn't wake with her wits intact.'

'I'll sit with her until she does.' Jadewin managed to reach the stool before her knees gave way.

'What have you done to your hand?' Brother Delnor didn't wait for her answer. 'I'll dress that with some styptic.'

'I'll tell our brothers and sisters what's happened.' Augol left before Jadewin could say anything to stop him.

She sat on the stool and stared at the blood oozing between her fingers. Hasrine didn't stir as the Infirmarer returned and cleaned her cut hand. The wounds stung viciously as he applied a dark, pungent paste. Jadewin didn't mind. Pain was reality.

When the bleeding stopped, he bandaged her hand. 'Keep this dry and I'll look at it tomorrow.' Delnor glanced at Hasrine. 'Call me as soon as she wakes.'

'I will,' Jadewin assured him.

She closed her eyes for a moment. She was exhausted. The others could decide what to do with Hasrine. As soon as Augol or somebody who understood the unreal world arrived to sit with the traitorous Velastan, she would find somewhere to sleep. A bed in the Infirmary, not in Maixen's—

Delnor had left the side room's door ajar. Jadewin heard a faint hiss in the shadows outside. She opened her eyes. For a heart-stopping instant, she glimpsed the Icicle Witch. The phantasm bared its fangs and vanished.

Chapter Twenty

HURAT

4th day of the Thunder Moon

Keeping this fractious horse in hand demanded every skill Reske had learned. The animal hadn't enjoyed the ferry across the Tane, and it liked Hurat's narrow, crowded streets even less. He realised why he had seen hardly any horses, saddled or harnessed, when he had been here before.

Add the burden of the sultry summer heat, even though it was barely mid-morning, and he could hardly blame the beast for its bad temper. Reske had a lurking headache, though that was only partly due to the oppressive weather. Tense with apprehension, he hadn't slept well on his journey from Jedfal. Only the God and the Goddess knew what might happen in the next few days.

Crossing the wooden bridge over the town's defensive ditch, he saw a jostling crowd between the outer redoubt and the castle entrance. Men and women with an array of liveries and insignia were trying to make themselves heard. As Reske rode closer, their shouts and protests became deafening.

A line of footsoldiers with levelled halberds stopped anyone trying to enter the castle. Sergeant Lund stood a few paces in front of this barrier, listening to a woman making sharp gestures. Reske placed her as an upper servant in a wealthy household.

In front of him, a man and a woman abruptly turned their anger on each other, yelling abuse. Reske's horse shied away and reared up, fighting his hold on the reins. As its flailing front hooves scattered those closest, their warning shouts panicked the horse even more. Reske leaned forward, gripping with hands and knees. He had to stay in the saddle. If the stupid animal bolted through the crowd, there'd be chaos and injuries.

A moment later, his horse stood sweating and trembling on four feet. A burly man in Hurat grey had firm hold of its bridle. Not a soldier but a stable hand, Reske realised. The footsoldier with the man was impressed. She was also wary of getting any closer. She reminded Reske of Elisset in her younger days.

'Sergeant Lund's compliments,' she called out. 'Are you here to see the castellan?'

'I am.' Relieved, Reske dismounted. 'Thank you.'

The groom led the trembling horse away 'Come on, sweetheart, let's get you somewhere nice and quiet.'

'Make way!' The young footsoldier turned around, holding her halbard angled across her body. She didn't wait for anyone to start moving, and her brisk pace didn't slow when the wooden handle smacked hard into the unwary

Reske walked close behind. He followed the young woman's lead in ignoring outraged questions. Who was he? Why was he allowed into the castle?

The front line of the crowd was a prudent distance from the footsoldiers guarding the entrance. Reske saw Senon in the shadows beyond the portcullis. He spoke to one of the guards. The line flexed and a halberdier tapped Lund's shoulder.

'Step back.' The sergeant dismissed the protesting woman and beckoned to Reske. A guard let him pass into the tunnel. The crowd surged forward to follow. The young woman with the halberd spun around to block the gap in the line.

Underneath the portcullis, Senon said something. Reske couldn't hear him over the uproar. Lund ushered them through the tunnel to the comparative quiet by the guardroom door.

'It seems every noble guest expected from Evesk to Ailur will arrive within the hour.' The sergeant didn't seem concerned. 'Their household stewards have come ahead to inspect their lieges' accommodation and make sure everything is suitably prepared. They're also demanding their lieges' personal guards are admitted to the castle.'

'They're early.' Senon glanced at Reske. 'We expected the first of them tomorrow.'

'The ambassador has also arrived.' Lund's face gave nothing away. 'It seems he rode across the grasslands to meet a light barge waiting for him on the Tane below Stannar. He brings twenty footsoldiers, his personal servants and a scrivener.'

That explained why Reske hadn't seen any sign of the ambassador or his retinue on Tane highway these past six days. Then he realised who the sergeant hadn't mentioned. "What about Baron Lensin of Chalus? And whoever rules Gostesh?'

Reske couldn't remember that baron's name, but he knew Gostesh was the closest town to Chalus downstream on the Dore. If Chalus fell, that was the next place Earl Lystro would threaten.

Lund was unperturbed. 'They should arrive tomorrow as planned.'

Reske wondered how the sergeant stayed so calm. The commotion outside the castle was getting steadily louder. It wouldn't be long before some fool lashed out. He was relieved to see Senon respond, decisive.

'Give me until the next chimes, then let the servants in. Only the servants, and if any of them carry swords, they must surrender them. If they argue, send them away. Their liege lord or lady's footsoldiers must go to the cavalry riding school to sleep in the barracks there. Hurat's castle can and will accommodate the nobility of both rivers with their personal servants, but our space is limited. Any noble who doesn't like this is welcome to explain to the castellan why they need a personal guard inside these walls.'

'Very good.' Lund headed back to the halberdiers.

Senon glanced into the guardroom. Two young men and a young woman sat on stools, expectant.

'Jorin.' Senon pointed at her. 'You heard that? Good. Get to the cavalry stables and tell Captain Iralo to expect guests. He is to make it clear to our own that no one is to be drawn into any quarrel. Even if that means taking a punch without fighting back. Stay there for the rest of the day, count heads, and sift through the gossip around the water trough. Bring me any hints of their lieges' thoughts at sunset.'

As Jorin stood up, the steward pointed at the youth beside her.

'Torad, my compliments to Mistress Berve, and I want a trusted servant escorting each group of visitors here, to make sure they have all they need and to report anything we should know.'

'Master Steward.' The boy got to his feet.

Senon looked at the last of the three. 'Geil, we'll be with the castellan in his audience chamber if I'm needed.'

Out in the castle yard, Reske and the steward walked quickly to the keep. Up in the castellan's audience chamber, Maixen sat at the polished table with his doublet unbuttoned, reading the last page of a lengthy document. Reske and Senon exchanged a glance and waited for him to finish.

The castellan put the paper down. 'I have a report from Captain Oref in Sospirin. Baroness Gossen receives a great many letters but she's sending none of her own. Not officially or by covert messengers, as far as Oref can tell. She is definitely not coming to meet this ambassador.'

'Is that good news?' Reske asked.

'As far as it goes.' Maixen clearly had reservations. 'I have no issue with Baroness Gossen staying close to home to safeguard Sospirin's interests. If she declares for Princess Idelina, or if Earl Lystro even suspects she's sympathetic, he can't leave even a potential foe on his flank while he attacks Chalus. He'll march against Sospirin first, or more likely, send Zavire of Bastrys to lay siege, and Hurat can't help her. Sospirin is on the wrong side of the Dore and much too far away.'

Reske considered that. A siege would be bad news for Baroness Gossen and the townsfolk of Sospirin, but Lystro of Coylure splitting his forces would favour Hurat. Could Earl Lystro be persuaded to suspect the baroness of favouring Princess Idelina? Though he would have to know Maixen a good deal better before he suggested that.

'On the other hand, the baroness may have agreed terms with the earl,' Senon pointed out. 'She may support Princess Alriad, even if she won't declare herself.'

'Right now, as long as she's not making trouble, that's good enough for me. When can we expect the margrave?' Maixen asked Reske.

'Some time after noon today. You were right. Margrave Vauset's invitation to this gathering didn't arrive until the first day of the solstice holiday. Margrave Satrel of Stannar's turned up on the festival's last day. The Tane nobility would have been hard pressed to get here by tomorrow, or even the day after, if those letters had been the first they heard of this. Even coming by boat.'

Reske could have travelled downstream to Hurat on a barge, but he and the Margrave of Jedfal had agreed he should ride on ahead, several days before Margrave Vauset took to the river. Someone needed to scout out anything likely to delay the Tane nobility still further. Someone hopefully unknown to the spies of the not-so-noble rival earls.

'Castellan,' Senon interrupted. 'Princess Idelina's ambassador has arrived a day early, along with the noble lords and ladies of Evesk, Crespil, Donin and Ailur.'

Maixen was startled. 'All of them? Have they travelled here together?'

Senon hesitated. 'I'm not sure. The ambassador came down the Tane on a light barge with his entourage. I don't know if the others kept each other company along the Dore highway.'

'It's the obvious thing to do,' Maixen said with misgiving. 'Baron Ferrar of Ailur would travel to Donin, and Bernet would offer him hospitality before they travelled on together. They'd stop at Crespil where Baron Pagel would make them welcome. They'd share a carriage as far as Evesk, and invite Baroness Karlin to join them.'

Reske realised he knew something that might be relevant. 'Baron Ferrar of Ailur is much of an age with Princess Idelina. Only a few years older, anyway. I don't recall him spending much time in court circles after his father died, but when he was a child he spent half of each year in Velasta with his mother. The dowager baroness and Queen Sefriya were friends. I'm not saying Idelina and Ferrar were playmates, but they're certainly well acquainted.'

'You think Baron Ferrar will declare for her?' Senon asked.

Maixen spoke before Reske could answer. 'If Lystro of Coylure believes he will, that might explain why Lensin of Chalus and Esclin of Gostesh were slower to set off on their journeys here.'

'You think they're negotiating with Earl Lystro?' Reske had been wondering what Princess Alriad's husband would do when he heard Princess Idelina's ambassador was coming to Hurat. Holding all these people in his thoughts, and assessing their potential alliances, would be a cursed sight easier without his current headache.

'If I were in his boots, it wouldn't be much of a negotiation,' Maixen said frankly. 'I'd offer a simple choice. Join forces with Coylure and Bastrys to uphold Alriad as queen, or be trampled into the bloody mud as Coylure's army advances on Ailur to punish Baron Ferrar. Earl Lystro can hardly leave Chalus and Gostesh undecided behind him, any more than he can ignore Sospirin.'

'But we don't know any of this for certain,' Senon pointed out.

'No.' Maixen scowled at the heaps of paper on the table. 'We know precious little for certain.'

Someone knocked on the audience chamber door.

Maixen raised his voice. 'Enter.'

Geil, the third of the young soldiers from the guardroom came in. 'Castellan. Master Steward. Princess Idelina's ambassador, the Earl of Ripat, he has—'

'Ripat has an earl?' Maixen interrupted, looking at Reske. 'When I was last in Velasta, Ripat was a reclusive baroness's fiefdom.'

'She died during the last Ice Moon in her eighty-third year, peacefully by the Goddess's grace. She was succeeded by her grandson.' Reske recalled Earl Debin didn't think much of the new liege lord of Ripat. 'His name's Firio. He was a friend of Maren of Evarise, as well as one of King Venais's close confidantes.'

'Not close enough to be caught in the same lightning strike,' Maixen observed. 'My apologies, Geil. Go on.'

'He has summoned the nobles who've reached Hurat today to the crown tower's audience chamber. Their servants have barely had time to complain about their rooms and now they're demanding hot water and refreshments. Their noble lords and lady are expected at any moment.'

Maixen's face gave nothing away. 'Very well, Geil, thank you.'

Senon jerked his head at the door. The young soldier left.

The castellan leaned back in his chair. 'He wants them to agree to some proposal before the Tane nobility arrive. He thinks that will leave the margraves and margravine with no choice but to fall into step.'

Senon pursed his lips. 'Clearly, he doesn't know Margrave Vauset.'

Maixen stretched to ease stiff shoulders. 'See to your duties as steward. Let me know as soon as Idelina's ambassador has gathered the Dore nobles together.'

'You'll put a stop to this?' Reske was surprised to see Maixen shake his head.

'Not before Baron Firio sets out his wares. I want to know what we're dealing with. When Senon sends word, I will welcome the noble lord to Hurat and apologise profusely for interrupting their gathering.'

'Make sure you do so before they can come to any agreement.' Senon headed for the stairs.

'What shall I do?' Reske asked.

'Come with me and stand by the door like any good lackey.' Maixen drew a steadying breath. 'Once we know Ripat's clever scheme, go straight to the wharfs. Tell Margrave Vauset what's going on as soon as he arrives. Forewarned is forearmed.'

'Can we send word to that priestess, Sister Jadewin?' Reske said quickly. 'If she can get here in time, would she be willing to listen at the door? This ambassador won't lie to her face, but he might try some untruths if he doesn't know she's outside.'

'We can send a message to Mother Finevre, but I haven't seen Jadewin in days.' Caught off guard, Maixen's face was bleak. The moment passed. 'Don't worry. She's safe. She's looking after one of her sisters who tripped on the sanctuary steps. The fall knocked the poor woman senseless. When Sister Hasrine is fit to travel, the black brothers will take her back to Velasta.'

'She's from Velasta?' That made Reske uneasy. 'You're sure this was an accident?'

'I was until now.' Maixen sighed. 'But Jadewin will say it's the Goddess's concern, not ours.'

Reske wished he could go through the papers piled high on the table. 'Is there any news of Earl Debin?'

'He is still confined to his house under guard, but his family are allowed to visit him. That's as much as I can tell you.' Maixen stood and walked over to a window to watch the comings and goings in the castle yard below. 'As for the rest, see for yourself.'

Reske saw that letters and dispatches relating to each fiefdom in the Vale of Hurat were stacked together. Other heaps held news of Earl Lystro and Earl Padran, with the most recent reports uppermost. He pulled out a chair and started reading.

When Senon's return startled him, Reske realised he had no idea how long the steward had been gone. He put the letter in his hand back on the correct pile. Senon waited by the open door.

Still standing by the window, Maixen buttoned his doublet's collar. 'What have you heard? Have any alliances been made?'

'Far from it.' Senon shook his head 'Every Hurat noble's retinue is looking sideways at Ripat's entourage. None of the nobles themselves talked to each other when they walked to the crown tower. Silver tea and pastries have just been sent up.'

'Let's see what this ambassador has to offer.' Maixen led the way down the spiral stair.

Reske followed a few paces behind, as a good lackey should. They walked along a wide corridor separated from a great hall by wooden partitions. Several were folded back and Reske saw servants polishing long tables.

'Be generous with the wine tonight,' Maixen told Senon. 'Let's see if that loosens some tongues.'

'I'll let the cellar steward know.' Senon opened the door to the waiting room in the next tower.

Reske followed them. Attendants in various liveries sat on chairs around the wall, studiously not looking at each other. A man in what must be Ripat livery guarded the door to the spiral stair. Maixen's pace didn't slow. Ripat's sentry hesitated then stepped aside. Reaching the audience chamber on the floor above, the castellan walked in without knocking.

The room had several clusters of comfortable seats and a long table for sizeable meetings. A man expensively dressed in black lounged in a chair beside the fireplace. His pointed beard and moustache were precisely trimmed and waxed. Reske put him at much the same age as the late king, so half Maixen's age or thereabouts. This must be the late Baroness of Ripat's grandson.

A man and a woman shared a plumply cushioned sofa. Both were perhaps ten years younger than Maixen. His doublet and her gown were well-tailored, though not ostentatious, and the lace at her modest neckline was of the finest quality. She must be Karlin of Evesk, the only baroness ruling along the Dore. An elderly man and one young enough to be his grandson flanked the sofa on matching chairs.

Reske recognised the youngest man sitting beside the baroness as Baron Ferrar of Ailur. He would have to wait to put names to the two who had taken the chairs. Plates of dainty cakes on side tables were untouched and elegant tea glasses stood empty beside silver pots with steaming spouts.

'Castellan.' A tall woman in a scrivener's robe rose from her seat at the long table. 'This is an informal gathering. You need not take time away from your duties.'

Reske pressed his back to the wall by the door. He'd have recognised her anywhere. Once again, her left hand was hidden by the fall of lace from her cuff.

'Not so informal, since you are taking notes,' Maixen observed with measured politeness.

She could hardly deny it, with paper, pens and ink on the table in front of her chair.

'Castellan, you are welcome.' The ambassador's smile verged on a smirk. 'As I have been explaining, I bring the best possible news. King Tadiri of Mervante can no longer threaten this province. You need only swear allegiance to the new Earl of Hurat to guarantee Velasta's aid against any threat.'

'I wasn't aware King Tadiri had threatened anyone,' Maixen said mildly. 'But if Velasta's archivists have found an heir of King Ganirin's bloodline, the Keeper of Secrets has truly blessed us.'

Reske watched the nobles busy themselves choosing cakes or pouring silver tea.

The ambassador sat up straight. 'Queen Idelina has decreed her son Prince Talem will be acclaimed as the Earl of Hurat. I am here as his proxy to receive the oaths of fealty which are his rightful due.' His stare was a barely veiled challenge. 'Your own first of all.'

Maixen looked back unblinking. 'It is indeed splendid news that Princess Idelina has been safely delivered of a healthy son. We will gladly celebrate that. But the baby prince cannot inherit that title. Mistress Zile, our scrivener, is clear on that point. The ancient laws of the Tane and the Dore do not allow inheritance through a mother's blood.'

The ambassador brushed that aside. 'This isn't a question of inheritance. According to those musty parchments detailing tiresome and outdated laws, the suzerains of the Vale of Hurat chose to acclaim King Ganirin as earl. What they did once before, their descendants may do again, and trust in the protection of Arafaze's armies against Mervante.'

He gazed around the room. 'This new settlement acclaiming Prince Talem will unite the people of Hurat with Arafaze. Henceforth, the earldom will pass down his bloodline through both sons and daughters.'

'May I read this proposed settlement?' Maixen asked mildly. 'Mistress Zile can examine its provisions—'

'You have no say in acclaiming Hurat's new liege lord.' The ambassador wasn't smiling now. 'As I have just explained, your oaths are void. If you wish to continue to serve the Arafaze crown as castellan here, I suggest you prove your worth by staying within the bounds of your duties. For the moment, your presence is not required.'

Maixen ignored the ambassador's dismissive gesture and bowed to the barons and the baroness. 'You are most welcome to Hurat. Please let Master Steward Senon know if you require anything. If Senon cannot be found, my door is always open. Our honoured neighbours of the Tane will arrive this afternoon.'

He walked unhurried to the spiral stair. Senon and Reske followed. No one spoke until they were in the castellan's audience chamber and Senon had closed the door.

Maixen grimaced. 'The Tane's margraves and margravine will find that notion as appealing as a bowl of maggots. A babe in arms can hardly lead Arafaze's armies to defend Hurat, though I suppose Earl Padran of Evarise would serve as his proxy. Senon, my compliments to Mistress Zile, and ask her for any precedent that'll hole this proposal below the waterline.'

'I'll see to it,' Senon assured him and left.

'We have to speak with Sister Jadewin,' Reske told Maixen urgently. 'And that boy, Alory, he needs to hear this too. The ambassador's scrivener is nothing of the sort. Well, she might be a scrivener, but she answers to Earl Padran first and foremost. That's not all. She's been involved in attacks on the God's servants in Velasta. I know that for certain. She may be involved in deaths elsewhere, of priests and priestesses. Her name is Nindera Kyse

A woman in castle livery opened the chamber door. 'Baroness Karlin of Evesk.'

'My lady.' Maixen bowed as the noblewoman entered. 'It's always a pleasure to see you. Is your husband well, and your children?'

'Yes,' she said briskly, 'and my bed here is well-aired, my chamber is comfortable, and my maids' needs have been met, so let's dispense with trivialities.'

The baroness wasn't a tall woman, and while her face was amiable, no one would call her a beauty. Reske decided anyone overlooking her on that basis was a fool.

'I told my noble neighbours and that impertinent whelp I needed some air. That will also give them an excuse not to make any decisions without me.' She took a seat by the hearth and settled her tawny silk skirts. 'I take it you would like to know what Idelina's lackey had to say before you joined us? I won't bore you with his assurances of Idelina's fitness to rule and the many favours we can expect from her.'

The baroness wrinkled her nose with disdain. 'The noble Earl of Ripat hasn't brought any written proposal. Bernet of Donin had already asked for one. Idelina's lackey says it's for us to decide on the terms of the fealty we will swear. That scrivener will draw up copies of our agreement and he will take those to Velasta, bearing the seals of every Hurat barony and margravate, endorsed by Mother Finevre and Father Memlin. He will present this new settlement for our province to the high shrine and the high temple.'

'And to the court in Velasta, telling everyone and the cats and dogs in the streets that this spontaneous declaration of loyalty has come from the nobles who rule beyond Bastrys.' Maixen shook his head. 'Who's to say different?'

'Who's to say those documents will arrive in Velasta with the wording we've agreed above our signatures and seals?' The baroness wasn't amused. 'Young Ripat must think we're mutton-headed. But I don't suppose he knows much of anything about the Vale of Hurat, any more than Idelina. She's never shown any interest in this province. Neither has Alriad. Come to that, neither of them has ever shown any interest in governance. They simply want the crown.'

The baroness paused for a moment. 'If Idelina expects her aunt will meekly accept this, the silly girl is sorely mistaken. For a start, Alriad will demand proof from each and every one of us that our signature and seal on the document is genuine, most likely insisting that is sworn in the presence of the high temple sisters who support her. At least that will tell us if the agreement has been altered in any way. Those nobles at court who support Idelina will make a lot of noise, but Alriad won't care. Far from it. While everyone else is arguing, she will expect Earl Lystro to devise some counter to this ploy.'

Maixen was still standing out of respect for the baroness's rank. 'Do you think your noble neighbours of the Dore will agree to this?'

'As the Golden Mother is my witness, I have no idea,' Baroness Karlin said wearily. 'But you know as well as I do, someone is already carrying word upstream to Bastrys. Idelina's proposal will not be well received there. Earl Lystro and Baron Zavire may even be provoked to attack Chalus.'

The baroness rose to her feet.

'Do you know of any threat from Mervante?' Maixen asked quickly. 'My patrols south of the Dore have seen no sign of King Tadiri's scouts.'

'I have received hints rather than threats.' Baroness Karlin pursed her lips. 'In letters from Lord Sharrow of Romer, and from Baroness Gossen of Sospirin. We can assume they have written to my noble neighbours.'

'Thank you.' Maixen bowed. 'I will see you at dinner, baroness.'

'Until then. Oh, one thing further.' She turned to Reske. 'I believe you serve Earl Debin of Shirlat?'

'That's correct.' He knotted his hands behind his back.

'No harm has come to him,' the baroness said. 'I am told Idelina has realised treating a blameless man so harshly was a serious error. Alriad's faction constantly remind court circles of the earl's long friendship with King Serken. Unfortunately Idelina cannot work out how to rescind her decree without humiliation. Perhaps she hopes if she ignores the problem, it will somehow evaporate. Opinions are divided. If I learn more, I will send you word.'

'Thank you, my lady.' Reske bowed and opened the door to the stair for the baroness. He stood in silence with the castellan until the door leaving the tower below closed behind her as well.

'You have plenty to tell Margrave Vauset.' Maixen found pen and paper on the long table and started writing. 'And you're right. Jadewin needs to know what's going on, especially if you suspect that woman with the ambassador. I'll ask Senon to see what he can find out about her. Lund will tell you how to find the temple. It's not too far from the Tane waterside. If Jadewin's not there, give this to Mother Finevre.'

Maixen reached for a second sheet of paper. 'If Alory's there, give him this. I want to know when he expects Quenild and Ticosa. If you can't find him, ask around the wharfs, as casually as you can. See how long most river traders reckon a trip by barge to the Mire and back should take. The marsh folk can tell us if the Mervantese are truly a threat.'

The castellan folded the notes. Walking to the mantel shelf, he lit a taper with a spark maker. Shielding the flame with his hand, he took it back to the table and found a stick of sealing wax. Dripping red clots onto the letters, he pressed his ring bearing Hurat's seal down hard.

He grimaced, frustrated. 'Until the nobility of the Tane arrive, I can't think of anything else to do.'

Reske knew exactly how Maixen felt. They had far too many questions and nowhere near enough answers.

Chapter Twenty-One

SCEFET

4th day of the Thunder Moon

Quenild stood on *The Beech Tree*'s stern deck and counted seven other vessels moored on this western side of the river. The ground was just about solid enough to call itself a bank. When she and Ticosa had made their first journey to the Mire, she had seen five times as many barges. Had this trip been a mistake? Yesterday, she and Ticosa found a scant handful of traders in the market place. None of the marsh folk could – or would – tell them why Scefet was deserted. Every sound outside the barge last night had woken her. Seeing dawn's light through the shutters, she had given up hope of sleep and left Ticosa curled up like a cat in the lower bunk.

The cabin door opened. Ristal stood blinking in the strengthening daylight. 'You're up early.'

'You were early to bed last night,' Quenild observed. 'Couldn't you and Yan find any amusement?'

Ristal joined her on the stern deck. 'We were warned off. Told to eat up our supper and drink light, then tuck ourselves into bed and make our own entertainment.'

'Who said that?' Quenild's misgivings deepened.

'A patrol from the garrison came into the tavern.' Ristal nodded towards the castle dominating what passed for high ground overlooking the marsh. 'The sergeant said the bog-trotters' feuds flare up in this hot weather. That means knives on the streets and blood in the gutters and a hasty blade won't know a local from a stranger caught up in some mayhem. Best to steer well clear.'

Quenild wouldn't argue with that. 'Did he say what these feuds are about?'

Ristal shook his head. 'Yanter asked and he told the lad to keep his nose out of it. Said Hurat's girls won't be impressed if he goes home with his nostrils slit. He wasn't joking.'

Quenild's stomach hollowed. The mutilations she had glimpsed on their previous visit had been an unpleasant surprise. Evidently marsh folk with cropped ears, slit noses, or hands missing the top joint of one or more fingers didn't venture up river.

'Don't call the locals bog-trotters, Ris, not even on the barge. Tell Yan to watch his mouth too. We don't want to cause offence if someone overhears.'

'Not much risk of that hereabouts.' Ristal gestured at the near-deserted river bank. 'What are the prospects for trade?'

That was as close as he would come to asking outright why they were here. Quenild decided the barge man deserved as much of the truth as she dared tell him. 'Ticosa struck up a conversation with a Scefet man when we were in Usenas. He said he could make a journey here worth our while. We'll give him a day to find us, then I'll vote for heading home.'

Ristal pursed his lips. 'From your mouth to the Goddess's ear. Unless that's him?'

Quenild saw two men in a flat-bottomed boat being poled across the weedy water by a third. At least, she thought they were men. All three wore the hooded capes that were common around here. She couldn't make out faces at this distance. She needed her wife's sharper eyes.

'See if Ticosa's awake, please.' She watched the punt approaching as Ristal went below.

Her wife appeared a few moments later, dressed for the day and eating a round of travel bread spread with jam. She swallowed, clearly recognising the approaching marsh men. 'They're not wasting any time.'

'Is Yan out of his nest yet?' Quenild realised she hadn't had breakfast.

'He is,' Ticosa confirmed. 'He can take Squirrel out to stretch his legs.'

Quenild understood. Whatever their visitors wished to discuss, the fewer people involved, the better. 'Ris can go with him. They can keep each other out of trouble.'

The flat-bottomed punt drew alongside *The Beech Tree*. The boatman drove his pole deep into the mud, pinning the shallow vessel against the barge. The two seated men made no attempt to stand. Now Quenild recognised them from the tea house.

'Good day to you, Mistress Ditayan. Mistress Reture. Please come with us, so we may show you what we have to trade.'

'The trade we discussed in Usenas?' Ticosa queried, cautious. 'Are we still your preferred partners in this venture?'

'At present, you are the only partners we wish for.' The other man's accent was thicker than ever.

Quenild wasn't remotely reassured. 'Please come aboard, and we can talk in comfort.'

Ticosa was already unrolling their rope and plank ladder. With *The Beech Tree* largely empty of cargo, the barge was riding inconveniently high in the water to be easily boarded.

'That does not suit us.' The first man pointed across the wide river where the eastern bank frayed into a maze of narrow channels and muddy islets. 'You must come with us to see what we offer. Delay is nobody's friend.'

Hearing his urgency, Quenild looked at Ticosa, who gave her an infinitesimal nod. 'One moment.'

Quenild went into the cabin where Yanter was eating travel bread and jam. Ristal stood by the table, tense.

'Make me some breakfast, Yan.' Quenild closed the curtains. Reaching above her head, she twisted a piece of decorative wooden moulding covering the joins in the varnished ceiling. She pressed another, releasing a hidden catch. A panel dropped on concealed hinges.

'I thought I knew all this boat's secrets.' Ristal was startled.

'What's life without a few surprises.' Quenild tried to keep her tone light as she took out the leather wallet Ticosa had hidden there and closed the panel. 'We're going to meet some more of these Mire folk. You two stay on the boat.'

She noticed the dog watching Yan's every move with the bread knife and jam spoon. 'You can take Squirrel ashore for a pee. Don't go far though. If we're not back by sunset, go to the garrison and tell the guard you have to see Captain Walsint. Don't take no for an answer. Give him this.'

She handed Ristal the wallet. Quenild could see he had a bushel basket of questions. She wished she had some answers. Yan was simply dumbfounded. She took the bread and jam from the boy's hand and managed a bracing tone. 'Hope for the best, plan for the worst. Chances are we'll be back before noon.'

Goddess be gracious and grant it, she prayed silently. If not, she hoped Castellan Maixen's vengeance would see the marsh's streams running red. Cramming the food into her mouth, she swapped her boat shoes for bankside boots. Grabbing Ticosa's boots, she went up to the deck.

Ticosa was holding two hooded capes with ties at the neck, sewn from stiff, dark green cloth. 'Our friends have given us these.'

'Better to go unnoticed.' The first man's smile was strained.

'As long as you don't expect us to go barefoot.' Quenild handed her wife her boots and took the cape.

The man's expression lightened. 'Decide for yourselves when you are tired of sodden stockings.' Like all the marsh dwellers hereabouts, he wore a tunic and breeches cut short at the knee and no shoes of any kind.

'Let's go.' Quenild put on the cape. It wasn't dyed, she realised, but woven from coarse, dark green fibre. It would be hard-wearing and most likely waterproof and the hood would ward off the sun's heat as well as rain. She wondered why the Mire folk didn't offer this cloth in trade.

They climbed carefully down to the punt and sat on the central thwart beside her, facing forwards, opposite the marsh men. Both women raised their hoods without waiting to be told. The smiling man's companion looked a little less grim.

The boatman freed his pole with a deft twist and drove the flat-bottomed boat across the sluggish, pungent water towards the marsh. Quenild tried to match what lay ahead with the map she had studied in their warehouse at home.

According to that, Scefet's castle lay north of the point where the Dore divided into two main channels. One headed east, and Quenild's map showed those waters dividing into a braided stream which flowed past Julach and its castle, built to watch over the marshland's northern boundary.

The waters flowing south from Scefet divided and criss-crossed before curving around to run eastwards. The new town and garrison of Avelsir marked the edge of the Mire in the south. The land beyond rose up, returning to grassland. In between these two branches of the Dore, the great river's waters unravelled into the vast marsh. If any river emerged, that was far beyond Hurat's interest.

On their map, the Nilgeh Mire appeared to be perfectly navigable. The reality was very different. Quenild tried not to grip the thwart as the boatman headed for what she thought was solid ground, thick with wizened bog plants. The punt nudged the bog plants aside. Quenild looked back to see them floating back together, leaving no sign of their passage.

The boatman's pole drove them through twisting channels fringed with tall reeds. Here and there, they passed thickets of unfamiliar, yellowing trees. Twice they reached substantial stretches of open water. Marsh folk in oval boats made from withy frames covered with the dense, dark green cloth darted past, steering with leaf-shaped paddles. Quenild lost all sense of her bearings. Sitting so low on the water, it was impossible to see what lay beyond the vegetation surrounding them. She didn't like this in the least.

Ticosa pointed to men and women busy around a half-built dwelling where some quirk of the Mire offered solid footing. 'I had imagined your houses were wood and brick like our own,' she commented to their escorts.

Quenild wondered where the marsh folk got those substantial timbers. The builders were filling gaps in the frame with panels woven from split withies. A gang of children stuffed something like straw between the new wall's inner and outer skins. Further along, the woven wood disappeared beneath a thick layer of what looked like mud. Surely that daub must be something more? Mud would wash away in the first autumn rain.

The unsmiling man laughed. 'Brick is heavy. House would sink. The marsh reclaims.'

Quenild managed an expression of amiable interest. Inwardly she wondered how badly she and Ticosa might have miscalculated. Ristal would do as she'd asked, if they didn't return, but how could any Scefet garrison patrol hope to find them?

The silent boatman poled past men and women emptying fish traps. They barely spared the punt an incurious glance. Not much further on, the punt headed along a narrow channel flanked by trees whose branches met overhead. Ahead, a muddy slope supported a wooden landing stage. A substantial round building beyond was thatched with thick bundles of sedge. This was closer to a permanent island than anything Quenild had seen so far.

'We arrive.' The accented man jumped onto the landing stage as the boatman secured the punt with his pole.

The smiling man offered Ticosa his hand. She graciously accepted his assistance, though they were hardly unused to getting on and off boats. Quenild took the accented man's hand as well, as she stepped out of the punt. This was no time to slip and fall.

The marsh men led them into the doorless, sedge-thatched building. Forty or more people stood in the inadequate light coming through narrow unglazed windows. Quenild could only see a handful of faces and she knew none of them. Most of the Mire folk kept their hoods raised.

In the centre of the round building, a modest fire burned in a stone-lined trough. Spit rests and cooking pots were stacked to one side. Four stools had been set in an arc around the hearth.

'Please.' The smiling man gestured.

'Thank you.' Ticosa took the closest seat, offering her brightest smile to the silent gathering.

Quenild did her best to look relaxed as she sat beside her wife.

'You are welcome to this meeting place, Mistress Ditayan, Mistress Reture.' The strongly accented man threw back his hood as he took the furthest stool. 'I am Enge of the Speckled Divers.'

The smiling man did the same. 'I am Omel of the Scarlet Fishers.'

'We are honoured to be here.' Ticosa lowered her own hood. 'The castellan of Hurat values peace above all else. We travelled to Scefet with his blessing, and he has agreed to pay fair recompense for the knowledge you wish to sell. We will carry your words straight to him and share them with no one else.'

Uncovering her head, Quenild waited, impassive, as murmurs ran around the room. She guessed those who understood Arafaze's tongue were translating for the ones who didn't. Now everyone knew Castellan Maixen knew she and Ticosa had come to Scefet. Anyone who remembered Hurat's last reprisals for Mire treachery should think twice before drowning them in a bog. Hopefully.

'Let us speak plainly.' Enge rested his hands on his thighs. 'Who wears the Arafaze crown is none of our concern. We fear this quarrel will intrude on our peace because the tyrant of Mervante seeks to profit from the uncertainty.'

Palpable hostility among the hooded gathering made the back of Quenild's neck prickle as Enge continued.

'He sent spies to solicit an alliance with both sides in this quarrel. Alriad and her husband of Coylure believe a Mervantese army will pass along the edge of our marsh and pass unseen through the high ground to muster at Sharrow. This army will attack Hurat from the east when their own armies advance down the Dore.'

Enge pronounced these names with care. Renewed murmuring made Quenild think the Mire folk called these places something else entirely.

Ticosa matched his directness. 'What does the Weasel of Mervante expect from Alriad and Coylure in return?'

Stifled amusement suggested the Mire folk hadn't heard this name for the southern king.

'A wife for his son.' Omel clearly disapproved. 'Coylure has three daughters to barter. The tyrant's spawn can have his pick.'

'And what bargain has the tyrant struck with Idelina and Evarise?' Ticosa enquired.

Enge answered. 'They believe Mervante's army will strike across the mother river, which is to say, across the Dore, at the watersmeet on this side of the Gate of Stone. Near the place you call Bastrys. Once the tyrant's forces have defeated Princess Alriad's army, they will menace those who dwell along the Dore.'

'Then Earl Padran turns up to save everyone's necks and the Mervantese unaccountably melt away.' Quenild could see where that was going. Any Velastan, especially any rich Velastan, would always seize the chance to have someone else do a job's heavy lifting.

'Yes, but that is not all.' Enge sighed heavily. 'It grieves me, but some among us have made their own alliance with King Tadiri. As soon as the Mervantese move down the Dore from Bastrys, these traitors will attack the castles at Scefet, Julach and Avelsir. Hurat's castellan will be forced to choose between sending aid to those towns along the Dore which he has vowed to defend, or keeping faith with the garrisons sworn to him here. Either way he will be disgraced. If he divides his forces, he may even be defeated to both east and west.'

'What is the weasel king's price for seeing Idelina claim the crown?' Ticosa enquired.

'He planned to marry his daughter to your dead king. He will give the girl to Padran of Evarise.' Enge folded his arms. 'You have questions?'

Ticosa's brow furrowed. 'Padran of Evarise's children will sit close to the Arafaze throne, but they're unlikely to wear the crown as long as Idelina's children thrive. Tadiri of Mervante's son would be a consort, not a king, even if he weds Alriad's eldest daughter. I would expect a man as cunning as the weasel king to want a far more substantial return from an alliance with either princess.'

'That does not concern us,' Enge said dourly. 'Both would-be queens have traded our peace away. If Princess Alriad prevails, the traitorous vermin among us believe they will be handed the keys to Hurat's castles. They dream of controlling trade between Arafaze, Mervante and the Mire. Those who believe Princess Idelina is their friend have been promised Mervante's army will seize those castles and throw down their towers.'

Omel continued, wrathful. 'Whereas in truth, Idelina and Alriad have both agreed to give the castles to the tyrant of Mervante. These traitors will gain nothing for themselves, at incalculable cost to the rest of us.'

'King Tadiri would profit hugely from a stranglehold on the Mire's resources.' Now Ticosa was satisfied. 'That tips the balance far enough for him to get involved.'

Muted anger stirred the gathering.

'Excuse me,' Quenild said cautiously. 'How does Mervante's army propose to move up from the south without being seen and pursued by Hurat's cavalry patrols? Whether they're heading for Sharrow or Chalus.'

Omel's expression grew even more fearsome. 'Those who have betrayed us to Princess Alriad have promised to guide the tyrant's armies to Sharrow through hidden paths and secret channels. Those who have betrayed us to Princess Idelina believe Tadiri of Mervante's assurances that the grainlands south of the Dore are vast enough to hide his forces.'

'Then they're fools.' Quenild couldn't help herself. 'On both sides.'

'But we are not,' Enge interrupted offended whispers growing louder around the room.

'That's as clear as day. Can you see a route out of this—' Ticosa hesitated. 'Out of this quicksand?'

Quenild fervently hoped that wasn't an insult. Bog and swamp were such everyday words of disparagement in Hurat, it was hard to find alternatives.

Omel said something in his own tongue that prompted a few reluctant laughs.

Enge continued without much humour. 'I am glad you recognise we are experts at finding safe paths through uncertain ground. Can you convince Hurat's castellan of this?'

'The price for our help will be high,' Omel added. 'But we believe you will agree it is fair.'

Ticosa looked interested, but didn't answer. Quenild knew she would never commit herself so early in a negotiation.

Enge leaned forward, elbows on his knees. 'The question is not which alliance Mervante's tyrant intends to honour. We believe he will send his forces as far north as Gernet and no further. You know Gernet?'

'In general terms.' Quenild wondered how he had seen her uncertainty. She knew Gernet was the southernmost town founded by King Ganirin and garrisoned by Hurat. It guarded the fork in the highway coming north from Mervante. From there, one road headed for Sharrow along the eastern side of the heights. The other road would eventually reach Sospirin and then Chalus. Beyond that, she had no interest in a place so far from any river.

Ticosa understood. 'King Tadiri will have to defeat the Hurat forces there, and take the town for his own, for Mervante to control the Mire.'

'Quite so,' Enge confirmed. 'Once the tyrant holds Gernet, we believe he will bide his time. When he sees which army of Arafaze moves first, King Tadiri will order an advance either to Sharrow, or to Bastrys. Whether Princess Idelina's cause prevails, or Princess Alriad's, Tadiri will claim Mervantese aid was vital for their victory. Therein lies opportunity, for Hurat and for ourselves.'

Ticosa raised her finely shaped brows, inviting him to go on. He obliged with a glint in his eyes.

'We can frustrate Mervante when we know which way the wind blows. If the tyrant sends his forces to Sharrow, we will kill their guides and lead them astray to drown. We will taint the water they drink and harry weaklings and stragglers who succumb to sickness and flux. We will drop herbs and roots into their cooking pots unseen. Some will be unable to sleep before they die of exhaustion. Others will sleep for days and nights, tormented by dreams of monsters. When they wake, they will not know what is real or illusion. Hurat's castellan need not fear any attack from the east as Princess Alriad's army advances from the west.'

Omel grinned just as viciously. 'If the Mervantese march westwards, we will cut the throats of those of our own who plan to attack the castles which fetter the Mire. The castellan will have no need to divide Hurat's forces. He will be free to crush King Tadiri's army before the Mervantese can reach Chalus. Princess Idelina's commander will have to fight Princess Alriad's army without reinforcements.'

Enge nodded. 'We will pour water to draw good fortune and hope to see Earl Lystro and Earl Padran both slain.'

Quenild hid her shock at such ruthlessness. She and Ticosa needed to discuss this unsuspected side of the Mire folk and soon. Right now though, they had to get back to Hurat as fast as they could, to warn Maixen about the weasel king's duplicity.

She hoped they had enough coin on the barge to pay this reckoning. She didn't want to have to beg for more from the sisters in Scefet's sanctuary, with or without the garrison captain's backing. Castellan Maixen's brief letter in the leather wallet hidden away was unhelpfully imprecise, and there was no guarantee Captain Walsint would recognise the castellan's writing. She also wondered uneasily if silver was the only payment the marsh folk would demand.

Ticosa clasped her hands in her lap. 'Your information will be of the highest value to Castellan Maixen. Let us agree a price for what we have learned today, and for your help to come.'

Omel's sudden chuckle startled both women. Enge said something in his own tongue that made all the marsh folk laugh. Quenild could hear the mockery in their amusement, even derision. She saw Ticosa blush, equally at a loss.

Anywhere else, Quenild would have walked out. Never mind this dank building had no door to slam behind her. But she would have nowhere to go. Ten paces in any direction would see her up to her knees in muddy water. That would give the bog-trotters a really good laugh.

Ticosa cleared her throat. 'Excuse me. If you have no more to tell us, shall we agree a price? That's why we came here, putting our trust in you.'

Quenild hoped Enge and Omel heard the edge in her wife's words. She breathed a little easier as Omel twisted around on his stool, subduing the noise with outspread hands.

'Forgive us.' Enge seemed genuinely contrite. 'Let us talk plainly. We do not want Hurat's silver. We want the keys to our fetters. Tell the castellan he must turn over the castles Arafaze built to confine our waters. That is our price for help against his enemies.'

Quenild sat frozen with shock. Castellan Maixen could not have foreseen such a demand when he gave them his authority to act in Hurat's best interests. Did she and Ticosa truly have the right to bind him with an agreement of this magnitude? She wished they could discuss what to do for the best, but there was plainly no chance of that.

'Once we are free to govern our own affairs, we will welcome honest merchants to the Mire,' Omel assured them.

'If Hurat refuses,' Enge continued calmly, 'those of us who seek only peace will leave these waters. We will go east into morasses where neither Hurat nor Mervantese can follow. These battles may unfold without us. We will return after the crabs and worms have stripped the dead to their bones and these waters run clean once more.'

Sharp voices around the gathering agreed.

Omel looked at Ticosa sitting motionless on her stool. 'We speak the truth. If you wish, we will go to Scefet's castle and swear it before the servants of your Goddess and your God.'

'We don't doubt you, but please forgive us. Only Hurat's castellan can agree to these terms,' Ticosa managed to reply calmly and courteously. 'May we please be returned to our boat?'

Her wife was right. There was nothing more to be said. Quenild reached for Ticosa's hand as they both got to their feet. They followed Omel out of the round building and onto the landing stage where the boatman had waited.

As they stepped into the punt, Quenild saw the marsh folk were leaving. She soon lost sight of their green capes among the shifting foliage. She wondered who would be taking this news to the different factions among the marsh folk. Doubtless King Tadiri of Mervante had his spies here as well. Would she and Ticosa reach Hurat to offer Maixen this bargain before Tadiri heard what was on the table?

The ferryman poled away. A few minutes later and the women were surrounded by reeds and trees with no idea how to find the landing stage. The only sounds were the soft patter of drips from the pole and birds singing cheerily without a care in the world.

This time Ticosa's hand found hers. Neither woman spoke. Quenild knew she and Ticosa were thinking the same. The ferryman's silence was no guarantee he didn't understand their tongue. They would compare notes when they were safe on the barge.

As so often, the journey back felt much shorter. The rope ladder still hung down the side of *The Beech Tree*. Ordinarily Quenild would chide Ristal for leaving it, but not today. Yanter sprang up through the hatch as soon as the punt stopped beside the barge. He must have been watching through the cabin window.

As Ticosa stood up, the boatman snapped his fingers and made a tugging gesture at his throat. Quenild pulled the ties loose and let the coarse green cape slip from her shoulders into the bottom of the punt.

Ticosa did the same. She called out to Yan. 'We told you we wouldn't be long.'

'Well?' Yan asked anxiously as they climbed aboard the barge

Once the Mire man had poled away, Quenild answered him. 'We're going home.'

'Beloved.' Ticosa looked thoughtful. 'We need to think about that.'

Quenild stared at her wife. What else were they going to do? The castellan had to hear what they had learned as soon as possible. She was only sorry Maixen hadn't known about this sooner. If he needed to cut short any negotiations underway in Hurat, throwing Princess Idelina's treachery in her ambassador's face would be very effective.

Chapter Twenty-Two

HURAT

5th day of the Thunder Moon

Reske was impressed by the accommodation Hurat castle offered honoured guests. Three long ranges had been built at the far end of the extensive area enclosed by the ramparts. Each building offered separate, luxurious suites of rooms for groups of different sizes. Ground-floor reception rooms had generous bedchambers above them, with servants' quarters above those. With a trusted attendant outside their door, guests could relax, safe from interruption.

Reske had arrived just after dawn to play this role. He sat on the bench beside the entrance to the central range's largest set of rooms. Three men and a woman sat outside other widely separated doors into the other buildings.

A pleasure garden planted in the open-sided square bounded by the accommodation ranges was meticulously tended, fragrant with herbs and colourful flowers in the height of summer. Gravelled paths offered guests gentle exercise, or leafy bowers for confidential or flirtatious conversations. This early in the day though, the garden was deserted.

The rest of the castle was wide awake. Servants brought water and firewood to each set of rooms shortly after first light. Reske watched the constant activity between here and the keep. Seeing the castellan approaching, he stood and waited, as a good lackey should.

Maixen greeted him, speaking quietly even though the other sentries were a good distance away. 'Have the Dore nobility been talking among themselves?'

'So far, they have stayed in their own apartments. Their servants have been out and about, fetching food and drink. They could have passed notes to each other.' Reske would wager good money they had done exactly that.

'Have you seen anyone from the ambassador's retinue?'

'No.' On balance, Reske was relieved Nindera Kyse hadn't appeared. If she had, he would have wanted to follow her, but a good lackey couldn't leave the Margrave of Jedfal's door unattended.

'May I see him?' Maixen glanced at the window.

'Let's ask.' Reske knocked softly in the rhythm Margrave Antrem of Reole had taught him the evening before.

The youthful nobleman opened the door. 'Castellan, you are welcome. Lewein, take over the watch.'

One of the Jedfal entourage came down the stairs to take Reske's place outside the door. Margrave Antrem led them into a ground floor reception room. Reske was startled to see Margrave Vauset lying on a daybed, stripped to his shirt and under linen with his fleshless legs bare.

The surprise wasn't the old man's infirmity but that he and Maixen were allowed to see it so plainly. When Reske had met the barges from Jedfal on the Tane waterfront yesterday, Margrave Vauset had been brought ashore in a carrying chair. Hopefully not too many people had seen his face was grey and creased with pain.

The margrave's retinue brought him straight to these rooms. Reske had taken his request to dine privately to Senon, and Maixen offered Margrave's Vauset's apologies for his tiredness to the nobles gathered in the keep's great hall. Reske had seen Princess Idelina's ambassador smirking. The alleged scrivener Nindera Kyse's face had been unreadable.

The old man's colour was much better this morning. He relaxed against the soft cushions, sipping from a silver goblet. A young woman in an apothecary's gown took pungent steaming cloths from a metal dish in the hearth and laid them carefully on the old man's knees and ankles.

Maixen did his best to hide his own surprise. 'Good morning, Margrave. I came to ask when you intend to call on the ambassador. So my steward can provide refreshments.'

'Tea and pastries will not be necessary. Once Mistress Ziska's ministrations enable me to walk to the keep and climb a spiral stair, I will let you know.' Margrave Vauset managed a wry smile. 'Please invite the honoured lords and ladies ruling the fiefdoms along the Dore to join us at this meeting. I see no reason to waste anyone's time. You will also be present, in your capacity as castellan.'

That was an order, not a request. Reske wondered what the old man was planning.

Maixen nodded. 'Also, the barons of Chalus and of Gostesh have reached Hurat and are on their way to the castle.'

'Good.' The margrave took a sip from his goblet. 'We can allow them a little time to recover from their journey before we gather in the Crown Tower.'

'Is there anything further I can do for you?' Maixen asked.

'My compliments to Scrivener Mistress Zile.' The old man answered with a glint in his faded eyes. 'I want her most accomplished underling to record this meeting in the clearest possible hand. The rest of her people need to be ready to make fair copies as soon as our business is concluded.'

Maixen grinned. 'As you command, Margrave.'

'My thanks, Castellan.' Vauset of Jedfal raised his hand as Antrem of Reole opened the door to the hallway. 'Reske, one moment. I've had word that Earl Debin has travelled to his residence in Shirlat. That's to say, he's been taken there under guard. But there's no reason to think he has been mistreated.'

Reske bowed briefly. 'Thank you, my lord.'

The Margrave of Reole ushered them out onto the gravelled path that circled the pleasure garden. 'I will send word when we're ready.'

Reske waited until the Jedfal servant guarding the door went back inside. 'Have you had any answer from the temple or the shrine?' he asked Maixen. 'Will we have a priestess and a priest here today?'

'No word so far.' Maixen couldn't hide his frustration. 'I'll see you later.'

As the castellan walked away, Reske hoped the Moon God was paying attention, and not just so he could pick apart Idelina's ambassador's truths or lies. Reske wanted to be sure Sister Jadewin and Brother Alory were safe, not knifed in some back alley on that grey-haired scrivener's orders.

He sat on the bench and surveyed the other doors. Every one stayed firmly closed. Reske leaned back against the wall, folded his arms and stretched out his booted feet. A good lackey took any opportunity to rest.

He studied the nearest bower through his eyelashes. He hadn't imagined that stealthy movement. Somebody had sneaked into the lush shelter of the malden vine trained around the wooden bench and the lattice arch above it.

Reske waited, patient as a cat. Eventually his stillness convinced whoever was there he must be asleep. Taking an incautious step, a skinny, pinch-faced girl revealed herself, trying to see the door to the guest quarters to Reske's right. She withdrew hastily, frightened by something or realising the risk she had taken. Reske thought she was being too hard on herself. She had crept almost the full length of the pleasure garden before he noticed her. He saw no sign any other sentry knew she was there.

Reske knew the girl's allegiance, if not her name. He had committed the faces of every visiting lord and lady's attendants to memory. In Princess Idelina's ambassador's retinue, she was the lowest of the low, at everyone's beck and call to deal with soiled linen and other unpleasantness.

Somebody everyone overlooked made a good spy. He guessed the girl had been sent to see who was discussing the ambassador's proposal. Well, she wouldn't have much to report.

A short while later, Senon escorted two parties of new arrivals to their accommodation. As they approached the pleasure garden, Reske sprang to his feet with the other sentries. These must be the barons of Chalus and Gostesh. He didn't know if the older man or the balding one was Baron Lensin of Chalus. Both nobles appeared tired and tense.

The Margrave of Vauset's door opened. Margrave Antrem of Reole handed Reske a sealed note. 'Please take this to Margravine Falise.'

'At once, my lord.' Reske cut through the pleasure garden.

The two barons' arrival seemed to have stirred the other nobles to action. Servants criss-crossed the garden, carrying messages. Reske tried to keep track of who went where as he delivered Margrave Antrem's note. When he returned to the bench by Margrave Vauset's door, he saw no sign of the Ripat spy in the bower. She must have made her escape while everyone was distracted.

The door opened and Margrave Vauset of Jedfal emerged, elegantly dressed in purple with lace at his cuffs and throat. The nobility of the Tane joined him a few moments later. More doors opened. Baroness Karlin appeared with a rustle of azure silk. The barons of Donin, Ailur and Crespil appeared, quickly followed by Chalus and Gostesh.

Margrave Vauset walked to the keep at a measured pace, using a silver-handled cane. Following with the other attendants, Reske listened as the Tane nobility and the barons of the Dore compared the trials of parenthood, discussed the merits of rival inks to address the problem of fading records in an archive, and shared tales of hunting in the hill country and across the more open grainlands.

As they approached the Crown Tower, Nindera Kyse, still in her scrivener guise, opened the door. 'Good day,' she said graciously. 'My lord, the Earl of Ripat—'

She broke off as everyone heard a voice behind her. The woman stepped away from the door.

'Shall we?' Margrave Vauset led the way inside and up the spiral stair without a glance into the ground floor waiting room, where Mistress Nindera was arguing with Byen. Reske took a seat alongside the other attendants.

'I am here to record this meeting.' Byen held up his scrivener's box.

Maixen came through the keep door on the far side of the waiting room. 'At my order.'

Nindera rounded on the castellan. Reske saw the anger in her eyes. He wondered if she was going to challenge Maixen's right to join this gathering. Byen took the opportunity to step around her and slip deftly through the door to the stair.

'After you.' Maixen looked blandly at the steel-haired woman.

Nindera stared at him for a moment. Hearing loud surprise from the ambassador in the chamber above, she hurried up the staircase. Maixen followed her. Reske followed him and slipped into the audience chamber, silently closing the door.

Reske stood with his back to the wall. He wanted to watch as many faces as possible. Princess Idelina's ambassador sat at the head of the long, polished table. Mistress Nindera took the seat beside him. She had already set out her writing materials. Her left hand was still hidden by the lace at her cuff.

Taking a chair at the foot of the table, Byen opened his scrivener's box and took out paper, pens and ink. Maixen sat beside him.

'Castellan,' Firio of Ripat snapped. 'I see no need to keep you from—'

'Let us not waste time. We have heard Princess Idelina's proposal.' The Margrave of Jedfal lowered himself into an upright chair halfway between them. The Margraves of Reole and Stannar sat on his right.

The Margravine of Mithess took the chair to his left. She was puzzled. 'Where are Baroness Silyan of Usenas, and Baron Presjin of Masecal?'

Sitting opposite, Baroness Karlin was equally concerned. 'Our esteemed friends who rule fiefdoms between here and the Mire have as much right to share in this decision.'

'Baroness Gossen of Sospirin isn't here either.' Margrave Antrem of Reole made a fair pretence of only just realising that.

Reske studied the barons of Donin, Ailur and Gostesh. Their expressions gave nothing away. The barons of Chalus and Crespil looked uneasy, but not guilty, as far as he could tell.

'Who is or is not here is of no consequence,' Firio of Ripat snapped. 'Decisions will be made by those who are present in the interests of all. Princess Alriad's forces are poised to attack your province. Queen Idelina is your true defender. Swear fealty to your new earl, Prince Talem, and Arafaze's armies can march to your aid.'

'Will we need aid?' Margrave Vauset countered. 'If we don't antagonise Princess Alriad, or more immediately, Earl Lystro of Coylure, by pledging ourselves to a babe in arms?'

'We cannot speak for those who are not present,' Antrem of Reole insisted. 'We cannot commit their vassals to battle.'

As the lords and ladies around the table murmured agreement, Nindera leaned close to Firio, talking to him in an undertone. He leaned back in his chair, looking sulky.

Mistress Nindera addressed the gathering. Reske had seen gambling den guard dogs with friendlier eyes. 'The Earl of Hurat—'

'There is no Earl of Hurat.' Margrave Vauset shook his head. 'No monarch can create an earl. The ancient laws of Hurat clearly state this rank is awarded by acclamation. Arafaze law says the same. The right to confer that honour rests with the landed nobility, not with the crown.'

The old man looked calmly at Idelina's ambassador. 'Tell us where and when such acclamation honoured you. Otherwise, you remain Baron Firio of Ripat as far as I am concerned.'

'Laws change when circumstances alter. That is no longer how these things are done.' The Velastan lord glared at him. 'I find your lack of respect for your queen's authority distasteful.'

'Respect is earned, not demanded,' Margrave Vauset observed. 'So the Moon God's servants and the Golden Mother's daughters teach us anyway.'

Baron Firio slapped the table with both hands. 'Queen Idelina and her children are the lawful and natural heirs to King Venais—'

'I find Earl Debin of Shirlat's condemnation more than distasteful.' Margrave Vauset's calm was chilling.

Baron Firio's eyes narrowed. 'There is more to his treachery than you will have heard.'

'Enlighten us, please,' Antrem of Reole invited.

'A margrave does not command an earl,' Baron Firio snapped.

'I believe that was a request,' Baroness Karlin said mildly.

Glances between the Dore nobles should be warning the ambassador he was making no friends here. Reske also noted Nindera, his supposed scrivener, wasn't writing anything down.

Byen's pen scratched softly in the silence. Firio glanced at Mistress Sile's deputy, clearly reminded that his words were being recorded. Reske wished Sister Jadewin or young Alory was here, or better yet, listening outside the door. He wanted any specific accusation against the Earl of Shirlat tested by a priestess's magic, and a priest's.

Firio of Ripat shook his head. 'Shirlat's fate is none of your concern.'

Reske realised he was grinding his teeth. He forced himself to stop before someone heard the sound.

'Then let us address the Vale of Hurat's specific concerns,' Baron Ferrar of Ailur suggested. 'Lord Firio, you spoke yesterday of the threat from Mervante. Believe me, we live with the knowledge that King Tadiri covets the grainlands south of the Dore, as his forefathers have done for generations. We had hoped to see lasting peace following King Venais's marriage, but that prospect died with him. Even so, there is no sign of any Mervantese advance.'

'The army that threatens our calm is mustered under Lystro of Coylure's banner in Bastrys.' Baroness Karlin's tone was severe.

'That's the closest army to threaten us, but not the only one,' Baron Lensin interjected. 'Earl Padran of Evarise has gathered a substantial force in Hedvin.'

Margrave Vauset looked steadily at Baron Firio. 'If this rivalry for Arafaze's crown leads to open battle in the Vale of Hurat, surely that will provoke the Mervantese to seek whatever advantage they can.'

'Earl Padran of Evarise seeks only to protect Hurat and its people,' Lord Firio tried to sound reasonable, but rising colour on his cheekbones betrayed his anger.

'Thank you, but we are well able to defend ourselves,' the Margrave of Jedfal assured him. 'Our foremost duty is to ensure peace and prosperity for those who swear fealty to us. Accordingly, I believe our safest course is to take no part in this quarrel over the Arafaze crown.'

He looked at Firio, unblinking. 'Once the question of the succession has been resolved, and your realm's new queen has been crowned with the blessing of the high shrine and the high temple, we can discuss a new settlement between Hurat and Arafaze. Meantime, we will swear an oath witnessed by Hurat's shrine father and temple mother not to send any resources to aid either Earl Padran of Evarise or Earl Lystro of Coylure in battle. We will send signed and sealed assurances of our commitment to peace to Princess Idelina and Princess Alriad, as well as to Velasta's high shrine and high temple.'

Reske wondered if Baron Firio saw the trap the old margrave was setting. If either Padran of Evarise or Lystro of Coylure advanced to seize grain, horses, firing powder or any other necessities for war, ignoring the Vale of Hurat's neutrality would dishonour his would-be queen's cause in the eyes of undecided Arafaze nobles.

'I believe our business is concluded.' Margrave Antrem of Reole stood and offered the Margrave of Jedfal his arm, to help the old man up from his chair. The other assembled nobles rose to their feet.

'No.' Firio of Ripat snapped. 'I will not have this. Queen Idelina's son Prince Talem is the new Earl of Hurat. You will swear fealty to him. We will celebrate this new settlement at this evening's banquet in the great hall. You may have this afternoon to come to your senses.'

The lords and ladies of the Dore and the Tane were walking towards the stair. No one was listening.

'If you do not—' Firio of Ripat broke off as Mistress Nindera gripped his forearm. Even from the far side of the room, Reske saw her fingernails dig deep. Firio gaped at her.

Maixen and Byen, eyes lowered, were studiously collecting Byen's neatly written pages, pens and inks.

As the nobility passed Reske to leave the tower, Karlin of Evesk exchanged meaningful glances with the barons of Crespil and Donin. Lensin of Chalus was stony faced and Esclin of Gostesh looked terrified. Moving stiffly with the support of his silver-topped cane, the Margrave of Jedfal was the last to leave, escorted by Antrem of Reole.

Byen finished packing his scrivener's box.

'Leave us!' Baron Firio snarled.

Reske lowered his head as the castellan and the scrivener walked towards him. Turning quickly and closing the door, he followed Maixen and Byen to the ground floor. At the bottom of the stair, Byen took his written record from Maixen and hurried through the waiting room's inner door, presumably to report to Mistress Zile in some other part of the keep.

Senon was speaking to the servants following their liege lords and ladies out into the castle yard. 'I will see to it. Yes, cakes and tea. Some wine? Of course. You are welcome.'

Maixen wasn't leaving, so Reske stayed where he was. Looking out through the open door, he saw the nobles walking towards the pleasure garden in twos and threes. Those from the Tane were deep in conversation with those from the towns along the Dore. He wondered if the humiliated ambassador and his supposed scrivener were watching from the windows above.

As the last servant left, Senon closed the tower's outer door and the one to the spiral stair. The door to the keep's corridor was already shut.

'Castellan,' he said quietly. 'You wanted to know more about Mistress Nindera. I can only tell you she scares the shit out of everyone in Baron Firio's retinue. The few willing to speak insist she's a priestess, even though she never wears a sister's robes. No one knows how she lost her left hand, but by all accounts, her stump is a gruesome sight.'

'Maixen.' Reske wasn't going to let this lie. 'If she has ever served the Goddess, we must tell Sister Jadewin, and warn Brother Alory.'

Chapter Twenty-Three

HURAT

5th day of the Thunder Moon

'Excuse me. May I pass?' Jadewin tried to make herself heard. Hurat's town gate was crowded with men and women avidly speculating about the gathering at the castle.

Word had spread fast yesterday that Princess Idelina had sent an envoy to Hurat. The news had sprung up in so many places there was no hope of stifling it or tracing a single source. Seeing the Tane's nobility pass through Hurat had stirred the gossips into a frenzy.

Jadewin was forced to raise her voice. 'Excuse me!"

A man spun around with a belligerent sneer. Seeing the priestess's pale robe, he stepped hastily aside with a mumbled apology.

'Thank you.' Jadewin walked serenely past him.

Close behind her, Alory was apprehensive. 'Do you think this ambassador has really brought the castellan an ultimatum?' he asked in an undertone

Jadewin considered the knot of men and women ahead, who had ventured across the bridge, to loiter avidly watching the castle's entrance. She replied calmly and clearly so they could hear.

'Whatever this visitor from Velasta may have said, on anybody's behalf, speculation is pointless. We must wait for an official announcement.'

Alory persisted. 'I heard five different theories about what this Velastan wants before we left the temple.'

'So did I. For the most part, those guesses contradicted each other.' Jadewin spared him a backward glance. 'I will trust what the castellan and his steward have to tell us in the Goddess's and the God's good time.'

Alory grunted, dissatisfied, but to Jadewin's relief, he fell silent. She reminded herself a blessing could be found in most twists and turns of events. With the townsfolk's attention on the castle, rumours of phantasms on Hurat streets had melted away. Good. The last thing they needed was some terrifying manifestation causing fresh panic.

Unless that was why Maixen had summoned them. Even with the help of Sister Deyadir, Brother Belid and the others, they hadn't been able to find Sister Hasrine's accomplice. Sister Meida wanted to assume the renegade had run away. Jadewin couldn't believe that, especially since the man had no way to know what had befallen Hasrine.

Jadewin had no idea where the hidden brethren had taken the Velastan priestess after Brother Delnor released her, still unconscious, into their care. Her fingernails dug into her palms. She must not dwell on her confrontation with the treacherous priestess. Mother Finevre believed that encounter was why the Icicle Witch was able to find Jadewin so easily now. She saw the terrifying apparition so often, watching her... waiting...

Jadewin snatched the swiftest glimpse she could into the intangible world. The Icicle Witch wasn't there.

Alory caught her arm as she stumbled. 'Sister?'

'Thank you.' Jadewin forced a short laugh. 'That'll teach me to watch my step on these cobbles.'

The Icicle Witch wasn't there, but she had seen the fire bird. It wasn't always in Alory's company, but more often than not the phantasm was somewhere close to the boy. He hadn't said anything about it, so she wasn't sure if he knew it was there or not. Jadewin wished she knew how Cavore had enlisted the apparition as the boy's defender. Brother Belid simply said she should leave the matter to Hurat's hidden brethren. Brother Augol said the same. The fire bird was staying in the unreal world for now, but that was scant reassurance.

The halberdiers let them pass through the tunnel unquestioned. Sergeant Lund stepped out of the guard room. 'Castellan's compliments, good sister, and please join him in his audience chamber.'

'Thank you.' Jadewin managed another smile. Her cheeks were starting to ache.

They reached the keep where the young footsoldier Jorin opened the door to the castellan's waiting room. Jadewin hoped Maixen would realise her heightened colour and rapid breathing came from hurrying. This had nothing to do with having to face him again after ignoring his messages so completely.

Alory followed her up the stair. Jadewin heard a man's voice behind the young priest, loud and anxious.

'We have concerns to discuss with the castellan.'

A woman spoke too. 'It is a matter of urgency.'

Jadewin heard their footsteps following Alory. As she went into the audience chamber, Maixen walked towards her with his hand outstretched. The Earl of Shirlat's man Reske was there and his expression was startlingly grim.

Jadewin raised a warning forefinger 'One moment.'

Alory was barely through the door when a richly-dressed man pushed past him. A noble lady followed close behind.

'We will wait below.' Jadewin turned to leave.

'Please stay,' the noble lady said quickly. 'Then there can be no doubt we are sharing the truth under the Goddess's gaze and the God's.'

'If the castellan agrees.' Jadewin clasped her hands at her waist. Though she could see Alory would have to be dragged out of here by his feet if Maixen ordered them to leave.

'Stay, please.' The castellan bowed to the nobles. 'Baroness Karlin. Baron Lensin.'

Baron Lensin's expression reminded Jadewin of girls at Velasta's temple school who had done something spectacularly ill-judged but who had nevertheless come to own up and face the consequences.

She took a seat at the nearest end of the long table and laid a hand on her sunburst pendant. Alory perched on the edge of the chair beside her. Shirlat's man Reske retreated to stand beside the closest window.

Baroness Karlin adjusted her jewelled rings. 'Castellan, the noble barons of Ailur, Crespil and I have agreed we will not swear fealty to Princess Idelina, regardless of her blood claim to the Arafaze crown.'

'While I am no longer convinced that swearing fealty to Princess Alriad serves this province's best interests,' Lensin of Chalus said tightly. 'Nor are the noble lords of Gostesh or Donin.'

Jadewin's pendant glowed, warm and reassuring beneath her hand. Out of the corner of her eye, she saw Reske staring at the divine light, awed.

'What we say must not leave this room, Castellan.' Baroness Karlin was deadly serious. 'Baron Pagel of Crespil tells us that this Earl, which is to say Baron Firio of Ripat, has been writing to him long before he came here as Idelina's ambassador. Pagel has shared Earl Padran of Evarise's plans with us. As soon as Hurat's nobles swear fealty to Idelina's son—'

'Excuse me?' Jadewin couldn't help interrupting. 'The princess's baby has been born?'

'So it seems,' Baroness Karlin said tartly. 'A boy she has called Talem, and she wishes him to be acknowledged as the new Earl of Hurat. We do not know any more than that, not even precisely when he was born. We must assume Idelina came safely through her ordeal and the child thrives, with the blessings of the Goddess and the God. But we know full well how suddenly illness can strike newborns and their mothers. This is merely one more reason why we're unwilling to declare for Idelina.'

Curious, Alory opened his mouth. Jadewin nudged him quiet with an elbow, though she wanted answers too. Had Idelina's pregnancy been more advanced than they had guessed, when her husband died? Had the baby been born in due season, or had it arrived perilously early? She would have to find out later. Baroness Karlin was speaking to Maixen again.

'As far as Padran of Evarise is concerned, once Hurat's support for Idelina is secured, he will appoint Lord Firio as commander of the crown forces here. Firio of Ripat is to attack Bastrys from the east when Earl Padran strikes southwards from Hedvin. Apparently, Earl Lystro of Coylure's forces will be crushed in an overwhelming victory.'

'That's quite an assumption.' Maixen didn't seem too concerned.

'Not if Baroness Gossen sends Sospirin's forces north to fight,' Lensin of Chalus growled. 'That will tip the scales.'

Maixen wasn't amused now. 'Baroness Gossen has sworn allegiance to Princess Idelina?'

'As good as, so Baron Pagel has been told.' Baroness Karlin scowled. 'In return for sole control of the sugar trade from Mervante. Apparently King Tadiri has agreed to grant her this favour.'

'So Idelina has come to terms with the weasel king.' Maixen shook his head.

'So Earl Padran would have us believe, which is curious.' Baron Lensin of Chalus wiped sweating palms on his breeches. 'Because Earl Lystro has been writing to me that if I help him ensure Princess Alriad is crowned, he promises me Chalus will become the sole gateway for trade between Arafaze and the Vale of Hurat. I will collect all taxes and dues instead of the new crown castellan. Add to that, I will enjoy sole control of trade in sugar from Mervante. Apparently King Tadiri looks forward to dealing with me.'

'This morning we assumed there was no threat from Mervante. If that isn't true...' Baroness Karlin was pale. 'Declaring ourselves neutral will leave us unprotected. The Vale of Hurat cannot fight off King Tadiri's armies without Arafaze support, whoever might be queen. But it's clear we cannot trust either queen.'

Maixen's grin didn't only startle Jadewin. 'Princess Idelina's faction must be confident in the peace they've agreed with King Tadiri if they plan on installing Lord Firio as castellan. He has no military experience, has he, Reske?'

Over by the window, Shirlat's man shook his head. Not for the first time, Jadewin wondered why he was here.

'Do you know who Princess Alriad plans to put in my place?' Maixen went on.

Baron Lensin looked sick. 'The first of your captains who proves truly loyal by proclaiming her queen. Earl Lystro is sending messengers to tell every garrison across the province they no longer owe you obedience. However, he insists they are still bound by their oaths of loyalty to the Arafaze crown.'

'That couldn't stay hidden in the dark for ever.' Maixen was unconcerned. 'With luck, I won't be pursued if I leave quietly. I could go north and east through the downlands, to see if the fabled cities of the Teijent are everything travellers' tales say. Or I could ride west beyond Arafaze. Maybe someone has discovered the far shore of the ocean.'

'You – you cannot,' Lensin of Chalus stammered with undisguised horror.

Baroness Karlin looked at the castellan more closely. 'You won't do any such thing.'

'No, I won't,' Maixen admitted.

Jadewin's pendant glowed softly and she breathed a little more easily.

'It is true King Venais's death releases me from fealty to him,' Maixen said briskly, 'but I swore to uphold the rule of law and to see justice done without fear or favour. I made that vow to all who look to Hurat to defend them, alongside their liege lords and ladies. I don't believe those particular oaths only bind me as long as an Earl of Hurat still draws breath.'

Jadewin's pendant flared bright as the noonday sun. Alory wiped his cuff across his eyes. Reske frowned as if he was trying to solve some riddle.

'Then what are we going to do about the threat from Mervante?' Lensin of Chalus demanded. 'I don't trust Lystro of Coylure or Padran of Evarise as far as I could spit.'

'None of us do,' Baroness Karlin said heavily. 'But if your garrison captains are sworn to the crown, castellan—?'

Commotion erupted in the room underneath them. Doors slammed. Outside the window, shouts shattered the castle's calm. Alory, the baroness, and Jadewin were on their feet when Senon threw open the door.

'The Margrave of Jedfal has been attacked. He is gravely wounded.'

Maixen was already pushing past the steward. 'Has Brother Delnor—?'

Jadewin didn't hear anything more as the castellan and Senon hurried down the spiral stair. Baroness Karlin and Lensin of Chalus looked at each other, aghast.

Alory hurried after Maixen. Jadewin followed. Outside, servants and soldiers were running towards the pleasure garden at the far end of the castle. Jadewin hitched up her robe and ran too. As she drew closer to the garden, she saw a gaggle of people clustered around a leafy bower. Halberdiers from Hurat's garrison blocked the garden's gravel paths, challenging servants in different liveries. Demands and protests clashed. Fear and anger echoed back from the accommodation buildings.

'Stop!' Maixen's shout cut through the uproar. 'You! Identify yourself!'

Everyone stood still and silent as the castellan stabbed the air with an unerring finger. Jadewin saw him point at an unremarkable man in drab brown clothing. The man turned as if he thought Maixen was pointing at someone behind him.

'That's him,' Alory shouted. 'He was talking to Hasrine.'

Whoever the stranger was, his shock made it clear he recognised the young priest. He saw footsoldiers moving to seize him and grabbed the nearest lackey, throwing him bodily into a maidservant. They fell together, blocking the footsoldiers' path. The stranger was already running away.

'How does he think he can escape?' Alory was baffled.

The fugitive fled towards the keep with footsoldiers in pursuit. A handful of others raced for the castle entrance, to make sure the portcullis was dropped. Most people stood where they were, uncertain what to do for the best, asking each other questions none of them could answer.

Jadewin ran after the stranger. 'Alory! With me!'

If this would-be killer had been working for Hasrine, they had to be the ones to capture him. The villain must answer to the temple and to the shrine for his abuses of magic. She caught sight of Brother Delnor and a handful of infirmary servants hurrying towards the pleasure garden. She ran on. Alory was somewhere to her left. She didn't waste time looking.

The man in brown disappeared behind the keep. If he kept on running, he would reach the garrison's practise grounds on the far side. If he stopped... Belatedly, Jadewin wondered what weapon had wounded the margrave. What might the fugitive use against her? A knife? A sword? She didn't imagine the stranger would hesitate because she served the Goddess. His priest's robe hadn't saved Cavore. But there were footsoldiers between the villain and her. She kept on running.

As she rounded the keep's corner tower, a phantasm shimmered into being ahead. Twice as tall as a man, it was a monster from some fearsome fable. The long-bodied, scaly beast reared up on crooked hind legs. Its bird-like feet were tipped with murderous talons which dug up the cobbles. Its outspread arms unfurled into leathery wings akin to some giant bat. Lashing a spiked tail, it lowered its head to hiss at its pursuers, showing a mouth full of dagger-sharp fangs.

The footsoldiers stumbled backwards, choking on their terror. Several tripped and fell. Jadewin clasped her sunburst pendant. Dismissing this horror would be ten times as hard now so many had seen it. She had to do so regardless, as fast as she could. Before the apparition could kill and gain a solid foothold in the tangible realm.

Her hand shook. If she looked into the unreal world, the Icicle Witch would surely be waiting. How could that nightmare not be drawn to this manifestation? What if she made some misstep that allowed the witch to step through the veil between the intangible and tangible realms? Radiance shone briefly through Jadewin's fingers and faded away.

Where was the man in brown? If she could find him and fight him, at whatever risk to herself, he should lose his hold on the phantasm. Her heart pounded, but the man was nowhere to be seen.

The monster lunged for the nearest footsoldier. Before it reached him, bright light seared Jadewin's eyes. The fire bird fell from the skies and sank gleaming talons into the snarling phantasm's neck. Flames fell from the apparition's burning wings like shed feathers. Inside a breath, the clawed horror was consumed by a white-hot blaze.

The footsoldiers gasped and coughed. The smoke already drifting away on the breeze, Jadewin watched the fire bird soar upwards to hover high above the castle yard. A bright spark against the cloudless sky, it sought fresh prey.

The fire bird stooped, diving impossibly fast. The crowd around the practise cannon scattered. Unerring, the fire bird struck the man in brown. The impact knocked him flat on his back. Shifting from foot to foot on its victim's chest, the fire bird spread blazing wings. The killer's drab clothing burst into flames. The fire bird opened its beak to peck out his eyes.

Alory ran past Jadewin. 'Leave him!'

The fire bird squawked at the young priest, raising a crest of golden sparks. In the next breath, it disappeared. Jadewin thanked the Goddess, as she ran after Alory.

The fugitive rolled over and over to snuff out his burning clothes. Clad in blackened rags, he struggled to his feet. The man was gruesomely injured. Skin had been seared from his face and limbs to leave raw flesh visible. Alory reached him and knocked him to the ground with a jaw-breaking punch. Castle guards surged past the priest to pin the captive down. The man cursed them in hoarse whispers, spitting and struggling.

'Pray for the God of Night's mercy, you bastard,' rasped Alory.

Someone had thought to bring rope. Jadewin watched as the man was trussed with no concern for his appalling wounds.

'Where to?' a voice demanded.

'The infirmary,' Jadewin shouted before anyone else could answer. 'If he's to live to answer for his crimes, Brother Delnor must tend to his burns.'

The footsoldiers obeyed her without asking questions. Jadewin thanked the Goddess for the authority of her pale robe as Maixen's men dragged the villain away. The stink of scorched cloth, seared flesh and burned hair made her nauseous.

Alory joined her. Jadewin drew a shaking breath. She didn't want to be too hard on the boy but he must be told—

'It's been with me since Chalus,' he said bluntly. 'Brother Belid says it was Brother Cavore's companion. He says it means me no harm, and since we know we have murderous enemies, he ordered me not to even try to dispel it.'

The young priest looked back towards the pleasure garden. 'What's happened to the margrave?'

Jadewin waited for her racing heart to slow to something approaching calm. 'Let's find out.'

Chapter Twenty-Four

HURAT

5th Day of the Thunder Moon

Alory walked ahead of Jadewin, sweating in the heat. The pleasure garden was deserted. He saw deep gouges in the gravel paths and the pretty flowers had been trampled underfoot. Every door to the guest accommodation was closed with a Hurat footsoldier guarding each one.

'Has the margrave been taken to the Infirmary?' Jadewin asked the man at the Jedfal contingent's door.

'Good sister.' The soldier ducked his head nervously. 'The castellan has ordered everyone to the great hall.'

Why couldn't people just answer the question they were asked? Who was 'everyone' anyway? Alory swallowed his anger as Jadewin replied to the guard.

'Thank you. We will go at once.'

He followed her towards the keep, but as soon as they were out of the guard's hearing, he laid a hand on the priestess's hurrying shoulder.

'I should go to the infirmary. Brother Delnor needs someone who knows what that forsworn priest can do. He might lose control of his magic, don't you think, if those burns are as painful as they look?'

If the margrave died, that would be a crime and a tragedy, but as Brother Talaven always reminded Alory, dead was gone. The living were in danger now.

Jadewin hesitated, but shook her head. 'We have to stand witness to whatever's said in the great hall. Debates behind closed doors are done with, and the castellan will need us both to show everyone who is telling the truth, and who lies. We'll go to the infirmary as soon as we can, I promise.'

She walked quickly away. Alory was tempted to go and help Brother Delnor regardless, but thinking over what Baroness Karlin had said, he decided Jadewin was probably right.

When they reached the keep, the tiled corridor outside the hammer-beamed great hall was choked with servants. Footsoldiers were closing the wooden partitions that separated the hall from the corridor, leaving a single doorway in and out. Maids tried to keep glassware, cutlery and crockery from sliding off their trays. Lackeys wrapped their arms around baskets of fresh candles for the wall sconces and the ornate table stands. Alory realised they'd been preparing for the evening's banquet.

The noise was deafening. Jadewin didn't shout but her voice was penetrating. 'By your leave!'

People hastily got out of her way. Alory stayed close behind her. As they went into the hall, he saw the high table was draped with pristine linen, but the chairs were empty. The only people he could see were castle stewards huddled around Master Senon at the other end of the long room. Where was everyone?

A door hidden in the oak panelling behind the high table opened. The barons of the Dore entered, led by Baroness Karlin. The margraves of the Tane followed with Margravine Falise the last to appear. The castle stewards hurried away through their own concealed doors at the opposite end of the hall.

As they left, Alory saw a familiar face. The Earl of Shirlat's man Reske was standing against the outer wall, beneath the last window by the stewards' doors. Hadn't he been serving Margrave Vauset? He'd done a rotten job of keeping the old man safe.

The noble lords and ladies were choosing their seats at the high table. Castle servants appeared with trays of silver goblets and tall, lidded jugs. Hurat footsoldiers marched into the hall from the corridor and lined the walls.

Jadewin walked to one of the lower tables and sat on the bench. Alory sat beside her. Everyone at the high table was watching them, so he did his best to look self-assured. He was the Moon God's representative here.

The door behind the high table opened again, and a man with a fussy beard came into the hall. A stern-faced woman in a scrivener's gown followed. The man went straight to the seat of honour at the head of the table even though no goblet or jug had been placed there. The scrivener sat beside him. The nobles at the table stirred. Most didn't try to hide their displeasure.

Alory wasn't surprised they were annoyed. That was Castellan Maixen's chair. Hearing faint murmurs from the footsoldiers, he stole a sideways glance at Jadewin. Her face was as expressionless as the sanctuary's icon of the Golden Mother.

Maixen came in from the corridor. Behind him, Senon shut the door on shouted questions from people gathered out there. The castellan's eyes widened a little when he saw the stranger in his seat, but he showed no other reaction. Alory sat up, squaring his shoulders. He must remember everything he witnessed here. Brother Belid would expect a full account. So would Father Memlin.

Maixen stood in front of the high table. 'My lords and ladies of the Tane and of the Dore. Our honoured guest of Ripat.' His glance barely acknowledged the man who had taken his seat. 'I have grievous news. The Margrave of Jedfal is dead. He has been murdered.'

The assembled nobles turned to each other in distress and outrage. Someone swallowed a sob of futile protest. Alory didn't see who that was. He watched the man who had taken the seat of honour. So this was Princess Idelina's ambassador. Who was that woman with him? Alory had seen her momentary grim satisfaction when Maixen said the margrave was dead. The man with the fussy beard leaned over, raising his soft hand to hide whatever he whispered. The woman's eyes narrowed in swift calculation. Alory wouldn't trust her to tell him if the sun was shining.

The noble lords and ladies fell silent, turning their attention to the castellan as Maixen continued.

'We have captured the killer and he is held under close guard in the infirmary. By the Moon God's grace, he will live to answer for his crime. However, Brother Delnor tells me he could not travel as far as Jedfal without grave risk of him dying on the journey. I propose we see justice done here in Hurat, under the gaze of the God who knows all guilty secrets and the Goddess who brings every evil deed into the cleansing light.'

'Very well!' Idelina's ambassador rapped his knuckles on the table. 'Bring this villain before me! At once!'

Maixen ignored him. 'The heir to Jedfal is duty-bound to pass judgement, but it will be days before this dreadful news reaches Lady Montaise – excuse me, Margravine Montaise – and longer still before she can join us. I propose—'

'I ordered you to bring the murderer here!' The ambassador's outrage echoed around the hall. 'In Queen Idelina's name, I will—'

'You will do nothing.' A solidly-built nobleman rounded on the man. 'You are an uninvited guest, and I suggest you shut your mouth. You have no authority and no jurisdiction in Hurat, wherever you choose to sit.'

'Margrave Satrel of Stannar,' Jadewin murmured to Alory as the angry man glared at the head of the table.

'I am the rightful queen's representative,' the ambassador shot back. 'I will—'

'Castellan.' Baroness Karlin raised a hand. 'How was our honoured friend killed?'

Maixen answered her, unemotional. 'Margrave Vauset was sitting in the pleasure garden, so that anyone who wished to speak to him could do so. The murderer crept up unseen behind the bower with a long, narrow-bladed knife. Perhaps Lord Vauset heard something to alert him. He moved but could not avoid the strike entirely. He was able to raise the alarm, but Brother Delnor could not save him. The blade had pierced his lung.'

Everyone around the high table was appalled, even Idelina's ambassador. Margrave Satrel stood up as Baroness Karlin sat.

'Nothing will lessen Margravine Montaise's distress at her father's murder,' the nobleman said grimly, 'but we should see what this villain has to say for himself in case he dies before she arrives. We can call on the wisdom of the God and the Goddess to at least separate truth from lies.'

He gestured towards Jadewin and Alory. The young priest couldn't help stiffening with apprehension.

'That is by far the wisest course.' The Velastan lord with the stupid beard looked smugly at Maixen.

The castellan didn't react. He stood with his hands clasped behind his back, as the nobles at the high table discussed this, low-voiced.

Alory whispered to Jadewin. 'What are we going we tell them? We know this man is Sister Hasrine's ally. Since she supports Princess Alriad's cause—'

'Surely Brother Talaven taught you better than that.' Jadewin didn't take her eyes off the high table. 'Whatever we might suspect, you and I can only test the truth or lies in somebody's words, no more and no less.'

'What if he summons a phantasm into the middle of everyone?' Alory had the hollow satisfaction of seeing Jadewin turn pale.

'Pray to the Good Goddess and the Mighty God that he doesn't.' Jadewin quietly identified a slender woman in her middle years getting to her feet. 'That's Margravine Falise of Mithess.'

'Castellan Maixen.' The margravine's slight bow acknowledged him as her equal. 'We agree this killer should be questioned as soon as possible, in case this vile murder is merely one element of some wider conspiracy.'

She glanced at Princess Idelina's ambassador with cold contempt and barely hidden suspicion before addressing the castellan again. 'However, if he is so gravely ill, he should not be moved. Please ask Brother Delnor to allow us into the Infirmary.'

Alory thought Princess Idelina's ambassador was going to challenge the margravine, but the grey-haired woman laid a quelling hand on his forearm.

'By all means.' Maixen gestured to Senon.

The master steward disappeared through the door to the corridor. Alory saw Shirlat's man Reske follow him. The crowd out there was silent, but the young priest knew this news would be flying around Hurat's streets well before the debate in the hall had ended. Word would be carried up and down both rivers before night fell.

No one in the great hall spoke. Castle stewards appeared with silver baskets of freshly baked butter biscuits, plates and napkins. Baroness Karlin poured herself a goblet of wine. The other nobles reached for the untouched jugs. No one offered the ambassador any refreshments. The woman beside him had to get up to fill a goblet and to fetch him some biscuits. The man ignored those treats, though he sipped his wine.

The warm scent of baking made Alory's stomach rumble. He had been thirsty before they had come to the castle, but nobody beckoned to him and Jadewin so they could help themselves.

The nobles talked quietly. Maixen stood as motionless and seemingly as unconcerned as a statue. Eventually, Senon came back with Brother Delnor. The Infirmarer was wiping his hands on a damp cloth. Blood and nameless stains smeared the white linen apron tied over his priest's robe.

'Three of you and the castellan, no more.' Brother Delnor looked at the high table and then at Jadewin and Alory. 'Together with the good sister and my young brother. You will leave as soon as I say, whether or not you have got your answers.'

'Very well.' The ambassador planted his hands on the arms of the castellan's chair, about to stand.

Baroness Karlin spoke to Brother Delnor. 'We assumed as much. I will come with Margrave Antrem on behalf of those ruling along the Dore and the Tane.' She turned to the ambassador for the first time. 'You may join us in order to carry a full account back to Velasta. Tell the crown council everything, and make the same report to the high temple and the high shrine.'

Whenever Alory had heard that tone from his aunts, he knew he wouldn't want to know the consequences if he disobeyed. So he didn't.

The bearded man scowled at being addressed like a lackey, but before he could find a suitably cutting retort, Brother Delnor spoke. 'Very well. Please come with me.'

Jadewin was on her feet. She moved quickly to leave close behind the Infirmarer. Baroness Karlin and the margrave followed. Alory was still watching Princess Idelina's ambassador. He was whispering to his companion with vehement gestures. She shook her head. Alory saw her shove the baron's elbow, forcing him to his feet while she stayed seated. Alory wondered which of those two strangers really had the whip hand,

The ambassador hurried out of the hall. Now Alory followed, doing his best to stay as blank-faced as the God's silver mask. The ambassador glanced over his shoulder several times as they crossed the castle yard. Something about Alory seemed to unsettle him. Good.

Brother Delnor was waiting at the Infirmary door. 'This way.'

The prisoner lay in the side aisle. Other beds had been moved away and castle guards stood some distance off. The Earl of Shirlat's man Reske was with them. Alory wondered why he was still hanging around, but decided that didn't matter just now.

A rope had been tied across the murderer's thighs to make sure he couldn't get up and leave. Assuming he could walk. The prisoner's hands, his arms and his chest were swathed in bandages. The bulk under the light coverlet draped over his belly and legs showed he'd suffered burns as far as his feet. His face was covered with dressings apart from his eyes and mouth. Brother Delnor's salve was pungent.

Margrave Antrem was startled. 'What in the blinding light happened to him?'

'Depending on who you ask, either the Goddess sent a divine servant to scorch him with her outrage,' Maixen said neutrally. 'Or he was carrying an incendiary to set the castle's powder store alight. It seems he used it on himself when he saw he would be caught.'

Alory found it hard to believe that anyone who'd seen the monstrous apparition would accept that explanation. Or seen his fire bird come to that. He glanced sideways at Jadewin. Her face was serene. Then Alory realised everyone was looking at them both, and he hoped his unguarded expression hadn't given anything away.

He stood tall. He was the God's servant, present to hear if this man told any lies. He focused his mind's eye on the icon in the castle's sanctuary and silently recited the litany Brother Talaven had taught him, to open himself to the God's magic.

'What is your name, villain?' Princess Idelina's ambassador snapped his fingers to demand the prisoner's attention. 'Whom do you serve?'

The prisoner lay still and silent with his eyes closed.

'He is fit to answer questions,' Brother Delnor observed. 'Or not to answer, if that's his choice.'

'Were you sent to murder Margrave Vauset, or merely to kill any Tane noble you could?' Margrave Antrem asked.

The prisoner didn't reply.

'You!' Idelina's ambassador pointed at the closest guard. 'Use your fists to loosen his tongue or he can lose some teeth!'

The guard looked at Maixen. The castellan shook his head.

'You don't want him to answer? Are you afraid of what he will say?' The ambassador sneered. 'I hear Margrave Vauset refused to acknowledge your authority as the crown's castellan. Perhaps you have taken your revenge for that insult. A killer could get into a castle if its commander tells the guards to let him pass.'

Maixen studied the man in the bed and folded his arms.

'We might just as well accuse you, Baron Firio,' Baroness Karlin retorted. 'Margrave Vauset was never going to accept Idelina's baby son as his liege lord. A foolish man might think his cause could prevail if resolute opposition was removed.'

'How dare you?' The man with the stupid beard was furious. 'I swear before the Goddess who sees all, and the God who knows the secrets of every head and heart. I am innocent of any involvement in this murder. I had no knowledge of this foul deed's planning and I played no part in its undertaking.'

The golden glow of Jadewin's pendant showed the Goddess's magic attested to the truth of the Ripat lord's words. Alory stood as still as he could, fervently wishing he had a silver mask to hide behind. He nodded once to confirm the Father of Night absolved the ambassador of falsehood.

Baron Firio smirked. 'Clearly, this man is in Earl Lystro of Coylure's pay. He knew I was coming here with the rightful queen's proposal, so you could honourably renew your ties with Arafaze and safeguard your sons' and daughters' futures under the crown's protection. How better to sow dissent between us than by murdering your revered elder? Margrave Vauset would have come to agree we are natural allies. Honour his wisdom by defying his murderer. Reject Princess Alriad's false claims once and for all.'

'You may guess at the Earl of Coylure's involvement, but that is not proof.' Baroness Karlin looked at the man on the bed, frustrated. 'If he will not speak, his words cannot be tested by the God or the Goddess.'

'We can see him hanged from the castle's ramparts regardless,' growled Margrave Antrem. 'He cannot deny his guilt. Whatever his motives, he was pursued as he fled from his crime. His fate is assured, unless Margravine Montaise chooses to be merciful. She might if he tells us who he is and why he was here. If the Goddess's magic and the God's attest to his honesty.'

The prisoner still said nothing.

Margrave Antrem shook his head. 'His silence condemns him as surely as any lie.'

'Can we be certain of that?' Baroness Karlin was troubled. 'He wasn't caught red-handed. Did anyone actually see him behind the bower, where the knife was found? Did anybody see him strike the fatal blow?'

'Go and find out.' Maixen pointed at a soldier who promptly left the infirmary.

Baron Firio snapped his fingers with sudden inspiration. 'He can be pressed for an answer.'

Everyone stared at him, appalled.

'That penalty for silence has not been imposed in Hurat for three generations,' Baroness Karlin protested.

'When was a margrave last murdered?' the ambassador countered. 'Doesn't Margravine Montaise deserve to know who ordered her father's death?'

Alory's mouth was dry. Was this burned and bandaged man really going to be laid out on a stone floor under a board that reached from his neck to his knees? Would he and Jadewin have to watch as heavier and heavier weights were stacked on top, to compel the prisoner to speak?

He waited for Jadewin to forbid this torture in the merciful Goddess's name. They both knew this man could reach into the unseen realm. Who could guess what dire manifestation might spring from his fear and pain? But the priestess stayed silent.

'There are good reasons why we no longer permit this barbarity,' Brother Delnor said forcefully. 'Anyone under such duress will say whatever they think their tormentors want to hear, whether or not a priest or priestess is there to witness it.'

'Let us see if divine grace can achieve more than brutality,' Margrave Antrem suggested. 'While this man waits for the Margravine of Jedfal to arrive, he can reflect on his crime as he heals. Perhaps she will be merciful if he makes a full and uncoerced confession.'

'How likely is that?' the man with the silly beard scoffed. 'I am here to take office as Hurat's castellan—'

'Try it and see—' A growl from the shadows where the footsoldiers stood subsided as Maixen looked their way.

The bearded man persisted. 'Guards, take this prisoner to the cells and have him pressed.'

Nobody moved.

'Pack your bags and go back to Hedvin, Firio.' Baroness Karlin was coldly furious. 'Tell Padran of Evarise we reject Idelina's proposal. We won't be bullied or bribed by Alriad either. No oath or allegiance compels us to support either princess. We refuse to be dragged into quarrels that are none of our making.'

'We will tell Lystro of Coylure the same.' Margrave Antrem was adamant. 'Withdraw your forces to Arafaze lands. Try to fight your battles on Hurat soil and you will face the forces of the Dore and the Tane united against you.'

Baron Firio stared at them in disbelief. 'You dolts. You think—'

The prisoner's cry of pain took everyone by surprise.

'What is it?' Brother Delnor leaned over the bed, stooping to hear whatever the man tried to say.

The prisoner threw a loop of his bandages over Brother Delnor's head. Crossing his hands, he pulled it tight. Brother Delnor recoiled instinctively. That would have dragged the prisoner out of his bed, but the rope across the man's thighs held him down. The Infirmarer clawed at the strangling bandage. The nearest guard rushed up to seize the prisoner's hands. Blood blossomed on the white dressings. Another guard reached the bed, drawing back his fist to punch the prisoner's face.

'No! That's what he wants.' Alory reached the bedside and shoved the guard away. 'He wants you to kill him.'

He made a blade of his extended fingers and thrust it hard into the killer's side, as he had been taught. Patients brought to the crescent gate were sometimes maddened by pain or intoxicants. Sometimes they attacked the brothers trying to help them.

The prisoner flinched as Alory struck the nerves where his ribs met. The bandage slackened enough for Brother Delnor to draw an agonised breath. Shirlat's man Reske sliced through the linen with his dagger.

The two guards grabbed the prisoner's hands, wrenching his arms apart. They dropped him back onto the bed where the man lay limp and still. Blood seeped through his bandages around wrists and forearms. His eyes were closed once again.

Brother Delnor leaned over him undeterred. 'He lives, by the Dark God's grace. Tie his hands to the bed frame.'

'We will leave you to…' Baroness Karlin looked horrified. So did Margrave Antrem. The two nobles walked quickly towards the Infirmary door.

Baron Firio hurried after them. 'Do not turn your backs on me! You will obey your rightful queen!'

Alory waited for Jadewin to tell him what they should do. She spoke to Brother Delnor instead.

'Can you move him to a side room? That will be easier to guard.'

Brother Delnor was rubbing his throat. He gestured and four guards picked up the bed. Jadewin followed them to the room where the unknown man who had attacked them had died. Alory followed her. The prisoner didn't stir.

'Watch the main door as well,' Maixen ordered the Hurat guards. 'Don't let anyone enter unless Brother Infirmarer agrees.'

As the soldiers walked away, the castellan looked into the side room. 'Baron Firio would never have suggested pressing this killer for an answer if there was any chance his confession could implicate Padran of Evarise or Princess Idelina.'

He glanced at Shirlat's man Reske. 'And it makes no sense for Lystro of Coylure and Princess Alriad to send someone to kill the Margrave of Jedfal, especially not before the Tane nobility had rejected Idelina's ambassador. Earl Lystro is no fool and a blind dog could see Margrave Vauset would refuse to follow orders from a popinjay like Firio. He wouldn't accept a newborn child as suzerain either. Lystro would see this offered him an excellent opportunity to court Margrave Vauset on Alriad's behalf.'

'So who killed the old man and why?' Reske demanded. 'How can we find out?'

Alory clasped his hands behind his back. He didn't understand why Jadewin didn't say something. They knew this killer had been conspiring with Sister Hasrine. They knew the treacherous sister had come here to advance Princess Alriad's cause. Surely they could tell the castellan the Velastan woman was ultimately responsible for the margrave's murder without revealing the secrets of magic?

Reske scowled. 'I don't believe either princess will respect Hurat's neutrality.'

'Nor do I,' the castellan agreed. 'But we're safe until word of Baron Firio's failure reaches Bastrys and Hedvin. After that, the Earls of Coylure and Evarise will have to wait for instructions from their royal liege ladies, or at least they'll wait long enough to appear to be consulting them. But they will attack sooner or later. It's all very well for Margrave Antrem and Baroness Karlin to tell them to fight their battles elsewhere, but any war in Arafaze will still need resources Hurat can supply.'

Maixen's eyes were calculating. 'We can expect some further delay while Coylure waits for Evarise to make the first move, and Evarise does the same. Both will be wary of their true enemy attacking from behind if they advance against us too hastily.'

'Why wait? Why not attack?' Alory demanded. 'These princesses and their earls are bullies. They don't care who they hurt, so they can get their own way. You stop a bully by hitting them harder and hitting first. Prove you can hurt them more than they can hurt you.'

'I wish it was that simple.' Maixen ran hooked fingers through his hair. 'Hurat has no army until the Dore nobles and the Tane lords and ladies go back to their fiefdoms to muster as many battalions of footsoldiers as they can. Even then, we cannot go on the attack. If we strip the towns of the Dore of the forces we would need to attack Padran of Evarise, Lystro of Coylure will advance downriver, seize Chalus first and the rest one by one. The same is true for the towns of the Tane. If we take their defenders to march against Earl Lystro,

Earl Padran will see his chance to seize Jedfal and its powder mills.'

'Then how are you going to win?' Alory demanded.

The castellan shook his head. 'I'm not planning to win. I aim not to lose. The best we can hope for is to force whichever earl takes the initiative to a costly standstill. If we can convince them both that the lives and time they will spend trying to break Hurat risks costing them victory over their true enemy, with the God's grace, they will retreat.'

'I see.' Alory wondered if that was possible.

'Do you?' Maixen demanded, grim. 'Padran and Evarise can squander ten or more lives for every casualty Hurat can't replace and they'll surely plunder as they advance. Before they retreat, they'll torch our harvests, houses and anything else that will burn, to destroy resources their rival might steal.'

The castellan turned sudden anger on Jadewin. 'Why won't you tell me what really happened? Tell me honestly how that man suffered such burns. You know what my soldiers truly saw. Explain that to me! No, don't bother. I know what you will say. That is the Goddess's business.'

He stalked off, not waiting for her reply. Shirlat's man Reske followed and Alory watched them leave the infirmary.

'What are we going to do now?' He wasn't sure if he was asking Jadewin or himself.

The priestess scrubbed her face with her hands. 'You and I must stay here. We have to guard this man, in case he summons some manifestation. We need answers from him. We have to know who in Velasta's temple is ready to use magic so recklessly. If we cannot stop them, every secret we have sworn to protect will be exposed. Only chaos can follow.'

On the verge of tears, she pulled the stool close to the bed and sat. The prisoner lay still with his eyes closed, but Alory noted the regular rise and fall of his chest. The murderer hadn't suffered scorching to his nose and windpipe which so often killed those caught in a fire.

Jadewin leaned close to the killer, speaking quietly. 'I suggest you tell us how many of the secret sisterhood have been suborned. Tell us what you know of the hidden brethren betraying their vows. Then I will grant you an easy death. You know that's more than you deserve for your sins against the Goddess and the God.'

The man's eyes snapped open. He was terrified.

'I will give you this night to come to your senses. If not, you will learn what horrors I can draw from the unseen world. Nobody else will see them torment you. No one will come to save you. There will be no escape.'

Jadewin's tone made Alory's blood run cold. 'I should … the altar lamps...'

He didn't go to the sanctuary. Leaving the castle, he prayed fervently to the Keeper of Secrets that he would find Brother Belid at the shrine.

Chapter Twenty-Five

HURAT

The 14th Day of the Thunder Moon

Reske leaned against the wall, sat on a stool in the shadows at the far end of the infirmary. He heard Alory snoring on the bed closest to the side room. That boy never had any trouble falling asleep. He didn't stir through the day's comings and goings, and he'd wake refreshed when the sunset bell rang, ready to take over the vigil at the prisoner's bedside. Reske tried not to be envious. The Father of Night must have his reasons for giving the lad that gift.

Reske waited. Sister Jadewin would go to tend the altar lamps at sunset. Then she'd go to sleep in the narrow room she had claimed close by the infirmary. Well, she'd try to sleep. He didn't think she was getting any more rest than he was. Frustration kept him awake long after the castle fell silent each night. When he did finally get to sleep, he'd wake with his jaw aching from grinding his teeth in dreams he didn't recall.

For the past nine days, Reske had pursued every slightest hint, the faintest scent, inside the castle and across Hurat town, which might lead him to answers. Every possibility had faded into nothingness. There was nothing else for it now. He had to persuade Alory to let him question the prisoner. The man still lingered despite his dreadful burns, but one way or another, he'd be dead within days, taking whatever he knew to his grave. Reske and Maixen would never know who had ordered Margrave Vauset's murder, or why.

The faint glow of Jadewin's lamp outlined the side room's closed door. She refused to let anyone talk to the man. She wasn't speaking to him either. She wasn't asking the Goddess to release him from his pain and distress. Granted, he had no family or friends by his deathbed for the priestess to reassure. Even so, Reske found her silence odd.

Still, until he heard her ask the Moon God to receive the man's discarded body in the earth's gentle embrace, to reclaim the gifts the Sun Goddess had granted him in life, Reske could still hope he might get some answers.

Unfamiliar voices approached the infirmary. He sat up straight. Jadewin opened the side room door and looked towards the entrance. Alory was still snoring.

Reske stood and moved closer, cautious and quiet. He stopped in the shadow of a pillar as Maixen and Brother Delnor approached the side room with a woman ten years or so older than either of them. Her kinship with Margrave Vauset was plain to see, even in the lanterns' dim light. Her face was drawn with weariness and grief.

The castellan introduced her to the priestess. 'Sister Jadewin, we have the honour to welcome Margravine Montaise of Jedfal.'

Jadewin bowed her head. 'I am sorry to meet you in such circumstances, my lady.'

The margravine had no interest in courtesies. 'Has he told you who sent him to kill my father?'

'He hasn't said a word since he was brought here.' Jadewin's face reflected her regret.

Maixen grimaced, disappointed. Reske knew how he felt.

'I wish to see him regardless,' the margravine said tightly.

'This way.' Brother Delnor went ahead into the small room.

Jadewin followed as Maixen deferred to Margravine Montaise. That left the castellan standing in the open doorway. Reske joined him and snatched a look around the door post. Brother Delnor was examining the prisoner as closely as he could without touching the salve-stained bandages.

The priest-physician took a pace back from the bed. 'He lives, though only the Father of Night knows how. I cannot tell if he can hear you.'

Brother Delnor had done everything he could to keep the man's extensive burns from festering but Reske could smell their rot from the threshold.

The margravine didn't seem to notice. She stared at the bandaged man. 'Why were you willing to kill my father when you had so little hope of escape?'

Maixen cleared his throat. 'You have the right to order him hanged, my lady. Since he has not defended himself, we can only assume he is guilty.'

Reske saw Jadewin duck her head and clasp her hands in prayer. What was she hoping for? Why had she insisted she and Alory must keep this unbroken, exhausting vigil alone? Why had Hurat's temple mother and shrine father agreed?

'If you want to waste rope on a noose for a dying man.' Margravine Montaise sighed. 'Very well. Let Hurat's townsfolk see what passes for justice. Hang him as the sun rises. I will thank the noble barons and baroness for staying to honour his memory, then my kinsfolk and I will take my father's body home to be buried. His monument should be raised among those whose loyalty he repaid lifelong.'

Her voice broke somewhere between grief and anger. 'Where is his body?'

Reske winced at the margravine's pain.

'The God and the Goddess watch over your father's remains,' Brother Delnor assured her. 'I will take you to our sanctuary.'

Reske stepped quickly backwards. Maixen gave Jadewin a bitter look as he retreated from the door. The margravine left without a glance at either of them. Brother Delnor walked beside her, not saying a word. Alory was still fast asleep.

Maixen turned to follow the margravine. Reske reached out to stop him, lifting a finger to his lips. Maixen raised questioning brows. Reske took hold of the castellan's shoulders and turned him around. Jadewin sat on the stool with her back to them, speaking quietly to the prisoner. 'Is there anyone who should know of your death? I swear I won't share any name you give me, not your own, nor whoever you wish to be told. I will send word to the nearest temple under the Goddess's seal of secrecy.'

The glow of her sunburst pendant proved she was sincere. Would this persuade the prisoner to talk at long last? Reske tensed as the bandaged man opened his crusted eyes.

The prisoner forced sticky lips apart and whispered. 'Water, for the love of the Golden Mother.'

Jadewin reached for the jug and cup on a small table. She half-filled the cup and raised the man's head with a gentle hand. 'Sip slowly.'

The prisoner drank greedily before coughing and spluttering.

Jadewin took the water away. 'You'll choke yourself.'

'You should let me.' The prisoner's laugh was a derisive rasp. 'Fool. You have the Goddess's gift, but you won't support the queen who will free us to use it. You didn't even summon a monster to scare me.'

Jadewin's fingers tightened around the cup. Reske heard the earthenware crack. 'We are sworn never to reveal our magic, or to use it to serve secular power. We subdue the unseen and the intangible as the Goddess and the God command.'

'While your hidden brothers are slaughtered.' The prisoner forced out the words between painful, shallow breaths. 'What will you do when that lad is cornered? When his throat is cut? They will kill you too, you know.'

The prisoner's voice grew fainter. 'They told Idelina the Lightning King had killed her husband and brother. They showed her monsters can be real. They promised to protect her and her children by killing anyone who could summon such horrors from the unreal world.'

He closed his eyes. 'They told me murdering my brothers would buy me my life. I ran to the Goddess's true daughters instead. They hid me in return for my service.'

'Your service to Sister Hasrine?' Jadewin's voice shook.

'Queen Alriad knows the truth, and the secret sisterhood will see her crowned. She will protect us. But I swear,' the prisoner gasped, 'I did not kill the old man.'

Jadewin's pendant glowed bright as the noonday sun.

'What is he talking about?' Maixen demanded.

The cup shattered in Jadewin's hand. Shards clattered to the floor as she sprang to her feet. 'You left!'

Alory spoke up behind Reske and Maixen. 'He told no lies. I can swear to that.'

Reske's heart was pounding. He hadn't realised the boy had woken up. Jadewin wasn't the only one whose weariness blunted their awareness.

'What is he saying?' Maixen demanded again.

Jadewin lifted her chin. 'He didn't murder Margrave Vauset. He cannot be hanged.'

'He said priests are being murdered,' Maixen snapped. 'Is that what happened to Brother Cavore?'

Jadewin shook her head, refusing to answer despite the regret Reske saw plain on her face.

The faint chimes of the castle bell floated through the tense silence. Jadewin took a step towards the door. 'I must tend to the Sanctuary lamps. Alory, stay with the prisoner.'

'Brother Delnor can see to the lamps.' Maixen shot the young priest a fulminating glance. 'What was he saying? What are you keeping from me?'

'Wait.' Reske had been about to suggest they send for Mother Finevre. Whatever was going on, whatever this talk of monsters and murder might signify, magic was temple business. But he heard voices approaching the infirmary a second time. Different voices.

'Why was I not informed when Jedfal's new margravine arrived?' Baron Firio strode though the doorway, petulant. 'I should have been present when she questioned the villain.'

Every day, Reske knew Maixen hoped Firio of Ripat's impatience would get the better of him while they waited for Margravine Montaise to retrieve her father's body. The castellan had offered the ambassador horses from Hurat's stables and a cavalry escort back to Hedvin. Baron Firio brusquely declined to leave. He was convinced he would hear Princess Alriad condemned by a murderer's testimony.

Reske was in less of a hurry to see him leave. Once Firio told Earl Padran that Hurat had rejected Idelina's baby son as their new earl, the castellan would be counting days not months before one or other of the two Arafaze armies marched. Whichever earl moved first, wherever those forces were headed, Maixen would face hard choices, and none of his options were good.

Baron Firio snapped his fingers at Maixen. 'Margravine Montaise has said the man must hang? I will offer him a pardon if he will talk. He's in there, isn't he? Step aside!'

Maixen didn't move. Alory filled the side room's doorway. Firio of Ripat stared at them, outraged.

'You have no authority to offer clemency.'

Reske was impressed the castellan could sound so calm. He waited for Maixen to explain how the God and the Goddess had exonerated the man.

'Let me pass!' Firio spat.

'My lord.' Mistress Nindera called out as she hurried into the infirmary. 'You should be persuading Margravine Montaise that Prince Talem is the rightful Earl of Hurat.'

She stopped short and stared at Alory. For an instant, Reske saw fear on her face, swiftly followed by hatred. He looked back to see what the young priest made of that. Instead, he saw the prisoner jerk with shock as he heard the woman's voice. The dying man's eyes snapped open. He lay rigid as his breath came faster and harsher, catching in his throat.

Baron Firio was still determined to reach him. 'Queen Idelina appointed me to serve as Hurat's new castellan. I have her signature and seal to prove it.' He snapped his fingers at his scrivener. 'Fetch the royal decree!'

Mistress Nindera turned and strode out of the infirmary.

Firio of Ripat folded his arms as he looked at Maixen and Alory, repellently smug. 'You will see.'

Reske couldn't understand how the Velastan noble could still believe Maixen would yield to him. Right now, that didn't matter. Skirting empty beds, Reske went after Mistress Nindera. Whether the woman was a scrivener, a priestess, or neither one, she was up to something. Reske hadn't been able to unravel her scheming in Velasta or in Hedvin. He wasn't going to miss his chance here.

Outside, dusk was deepening. Lights shone in windows as he followed her past workshops, storehouses and barracks along the inside face of the ramparts. Reske expected Nindera would head for the keep and the crown tower. Instead, he realised with some surprise, she was heading for the castle's kitchen. The high-ceilinged building with its three massive hearths stood between the keep and the well house in case a fire got out of hand.

There weren't enough people out and about in the castle compound for Reske to lose himself among them. The best he could do was stay far enough back to hope he'd be hard to recognise in the dim light. He was ready to head for the nearest doorway if the woman checked to see if anyone was following.

She didn't. Mistress Nindera also walked straight past the kitchen. She approached the long hall where the castle's servants were fed. She rounded the gable end, heading for the yard behind the hall where servants released from their duties could relax, alone or with others.

Reske had spent several days stopping by the yard, drawing servants from different noble entourages into apparently casual conversation. None of them knew anything about Margrave Vauset's murder. Clearly, he'd been asking the wrong people. Mistress Nindera summoned someone with her uninjured hand and retreated into the shadow of the rampart.

Reske crouched low behind a log store, thankful his sight had grown accustomed to the dusk. He easily identified the pinch-faced maid answering Nindera's summons. Evidently he had been wrong about the underfed waif as well. The servant girl stood with her hands on her hips. From her defiant gestures, she was challenging Mistress Nindera, maybe even refusing her orders.

Nindera grabbed the girl's elbow. Head and shoulders taller, she slammed her maimed forearm into the maidservant's face, knocking her off her feet. Nindera dropped into a crouch, leaning over her victim. Reske had no hope of hearing what she said, but when Nindera stood up and strode away, her satisfaction was unmistakeable.

The skinny girl lay motionless on the ground. Reske waited in the shadow of the log store. He watched Mistress Nindera reach the castle sanctuary, where Margrave Vauset's sealed coffin rested on a bier between the altars. People gathered every morning and late into the evening to share memories of the old margrave. Plenty of witnesses would be able to honestly swear Mistress Nindera had been nowhere near whatever she had just told that girl to do.

The maidservant sat up, rubbing her cheek. She got to her feet and carefully flexed the arm Nindera had grabbed.

She started walking with a purpose. She wasn't heading for the sanctuary though. Reske followed, keeping his distance. He waited in the shadow of the well house when she went into the kitchen. The girl came out carrying a tray with a loaf of bread wedged between covered bowls. She walked towards the keep, careful not to let the dishes slip or spill. Reske closed the gap between them a little.

The maidservant didn't go into the keep. Reske realised she was going to the infirmary. That convinced him she was up to no good, but he had no proof. Whatever she was doing, he had to catch her in the act. Then he could shake whatever she knew about Mistress Nindera out of the wretch.

The pinch-faced girl went into the infirmary. Reske ran after her. Crossing the threshold, he kicked the door shut behind him. She wouldn't escape that way.

He saw the laden tray on an empty bed. Where was the girl? Reske couldn't see her anywhere. Alory came out of the side room, leaving the door ajar. The young priest's eyes brightened as he saw the food. Walking over to the bed, he reached for the loaf and lifted a bowl's lid, releasing a puff of steam. Behind him, lamplight gleamed on steel as the girl stepped out of the pillar's shadow, sliding a long, narrow knife out of a hidden pocket.

'Alory!' Reske had assumed the prisoner knew some secret Mistress Nindera couldn't risk him sharing. But the girl was intent on the priest.

Brilliant light filled the dark room. A bird made of living flame appeared in between the maid and the boy. Its ear-splitting shriek obliterated her screams as she fell backwards, hitting the floor hard.

Alory staggered forward, thrusting out his hands to save himself. The bed lurched sideways, wooden feet screeching on the tiles.

On the floor, the bird flapped its wings, hopping around the screaming girl's head. Reske could smell her hair singing as she raised her arms to save her face. The bird's hooked beak ripped flesh from her forearm. Tossing its head back, beak gaping wide, it swallowed the raw morsel. Blood gushed from the wound and dripped onto the waif's face.

'No!' Alory bellowed.

The bird's fiery head turned to squawk a protest.

'Leave her be,' Alory told it forcefully.

Still squawking, though not as loudly, the bird sprang into the air. It flew up to perch on the top of the side room door.

Reske smelled wood scorching as the creature peered down at the bleeding, shivering girl.

In the merciless blazing light, he could see her shrivelled hair and blistered skin. By some divine grace though, she wasn't badly burned. Reske ripped the blanket off the closest bed and tore the sheet beneath free. He watched the fiery bird warily as he approached the sobbing would-be killer. What under the sun, moon and stars was that thing? It cocked its head and gazed back with piercing, hawk-like eyes. How could it be alive?

Whatever it was, the creature didn't move. Still keeping half an eye on it, Reske knelt and wrapped the thick swathe of linen around the whey-faced girl's horrible wound.

'She had a knife.' He looked up at Alory. 'Can you see it?'

'I – no. I don't know—' The lad stared at the girl with wide, white-rimmed eyes.

'Fetch Brother Delnor,' Reske ordered. 'Now!'

'No!' Jadewin hurried up. 'Let me.'

Reske hadn't even realised the priestess was there, sitting in the shadows just as he had done earlier.

Jadewin knelt on the other side of the girl. 'Let me see.'

Reske let her take hold of the bloody sheet. Seeing the long knife's hilt under a nearby bed, he picked it up.

'Alory!' Examining the girl's wound, Jadewin's sleeves and robe were already gruesomely stained. 'Bandages! Quickly!'

'We have to tell the castellan.' Alory didn't move. 'You know he can keep a secret.'

'Tell him what?' Reske demanded.

'We need to ask Mother Finevre.' Jadewin was answering the boy. 'She can tell us what Father Memlin knows. We have to be careful.'

Reske raised his voice. 'About what?'

'Why can't we tell him?' Furious, Alory challenged the priestess. 'The secret sisters of the high temple have broken their vows by telling Princess Alriad about the unseen realm. Someone has shown Princess Idelina monsters are real, so she agreed they can kill the hidden brethren. Why are we bound by oaths our enemies don't honour?'

Jadewin shook her head. 'Two wrongs don't make a right.'

Reske felt she was trying to convince herself.

'The God and the Goddess help those who help themselves.' Alory was relentless. 'We serve them so we can help others. We have to help the castellan. He'll be fighting with one hand tied behind his back if his enemies summon phantasms on a battlefield. We know they're willing to misuse magic. We cannot keep these secrets any longer!'

The young priest was shouting. Reske bellowed louder.

'For the love of night and day, will you tell me what's going on!'

Trying to wipe her face on her shoulder, Jadewin blinked away tears. 'I wish it was that simple.'

The infirmary door slammed shut. Reske hadn't even heard it open. He turned his head to see Maixen stare at the shining bird, astonished. It flapped its wings with a metallic rattle and squawked, cheerfully enquiring. Now it looked like a gatepost ornament crafted from brass. When had that happened? How had it happened? Though Reske was relieved to realise this transformation lessened the danger of the entire infirmary going up in flames. Hopefully.

'What is that thing?' the castellan demanded.

'Never mind.' Jadewin had the blood-soaked linen clamped tight around the girl's wounded arm again. The waif whimpered. A moment more, and she lay limp and unconscious. 'Alory, fetch Brother Delnor.'

Maixen plucked the long knife out of Reske's hand. 'Where did you get this?'

'It's hers.' He stood up. 'I thought she was here to kill the prisoner, but she tried to murder the good brother.'

The bird screeched and Maixen glanced warily at the uncanny creature. 'That blade is from the same workshop, likely forged by the same hand.'

Reske nodded. 'Agreed.'

'What are you talking about?' Jadewin demanded.

Maixen studied the knife. 'This is twin to the blade that killed the margrave.'

'She'll be the only one who can explain that.' Alory came out of the side room. 'He's dead.'

'Lord Firio's scrivener, Mistress Nindera, sent her to kill you.' Reske realised the young priest had managed to stay out of the girl's blood. 'Run and tell Sergeant Lund not to let her leave the castle. Not under any circumstances. Tell him to chain her up if he must.'

'Go!' Maixen barked. 'Now!'

To Reske's intense relief, the eerie metallic bird vanished as the infirmary door closed behind the young priest.

'What has this to do with Mistress Nindera?' Maixen demanded. 'Jadewin, for the love of all that's holy, will you please tell me what's going on?'

'I suppose I must.' Still kneeling to staunch the girl's bleeding with gory hands, Jadewin sighed. 'As far as I can and still keep faith with my vows. But first, find me some bandages for this wound!'

Chapter Twenty-Six

CHALUS

The 9th Day of the Hay Moon

The castle sanctuary was still cluttered with book chests. Outside, cannon fire thundered. At the start of this bombardment, every shot had set Alory's heart racing. Now he barely noticed.

'You were up early,' Jadewin closed the door behind her. 'Have you had breakfast?'

Alory wondered if she had slept at all, if she'd been awake to hear him leave the floor above, where Hurat's priests and priestesses shared rooms. 'I went to the gatehouse. I wanted to look across the river before anyone over there was out and about.'

'Are you sure no one saw you?'

'Yes.' Alory tried to curb his impatience. He didn't need reminding that malevolent sisters and mysterious murderers could be lurking in Chalus, and too many of both knew his face.

'We can't take unnecessary chances,' Jadewin reminded him regardless. 'Well? Have Baron Zavire's scouts been driven out of the landing on the Bastrys side?'

'Yes, and those cannon are wrecking the warehouses and stables, so they can't sneak back. What's the news from the Dore waterfront?' Alory knew Jadewin spoke to the garrison commander first thing every morning.

'Rampart guns have been set on the old walls.' The priestess ticked the town's preparations off on her fingers. 'Troop barges trying to land on those wharfs will face a hailstorm of small shot. Chalus will be taken within a day or two even so. The volunteers are under strict orders not to waste powder, shot or their own lives in some futile stand. The camps on the southern bank have been cleared. Merchants or spies, everyone there was told to make themselves scarce or be counted as Hurat's enemy.'

'Is there any word from Hurat?' Alory wanted to know if his aunts had come home.

'Yes.' Jadewin was relieved. 'A courier arrived before dawn. He must have ridden his poor horse half to death. Maixen's letter says Mistress Quenild and Mistress Ticosa have sent sworn proof that Mervante is plotting treachery. The Mire folk have agreed an alliance with Hurat.'

'They sent proof?' Alory didn't like the sound of that. 'They didn't bring it themselves?'

Jadewin leafed through the maps spread out on top of the book chests. 'It's time to go. We must catch Earl Lystro and his army while they're still on the highway.'

'I know.' Alory bit back the urge to remind her he had been there when they had devised this plan with Castellan Maixen and the Earl of Shirlat's man.

Perhaps she was trying to reassure herself. Alory had gone over the details time and again, to be certain nothing had been overlooked. He had just used a ribbon to follow the rivers and roads on these maps, to measure their journey against Brother Ragat's scale rule.

The door opened and a breeze scattered his scraps of paper covered with calculations. Sister Perrin looked as close to happy as anyone Alory had seen in Chalus.

'Mother Hasperre has returned from Cormir. She's taking charge of sending the elderly and the children to Gostesh and Ailur, by boat and by road. Goddess be thanked, no one needs persuading to leave. Father Cradis has unshuttered the town shrine. Our brothers are ready to treat the wounded when the town is attacked.'

'The Goddess and the God watch over them,' Jadewin said, heartfelt.

'And over us all.' Perrin paused, expectant. When neither of them spoke, she shrugged and left the sanctuary.

'Let's go.' Alory opened the chest where he'd stowed the silver mask Brother Ragat had given him. He put it on and followed Jadewin out of the keep. Strictly speaking, he hadn't come close to earning the right to wear the mask, but Brother Belid assured him the God would understand. Alory tried not to dwell on what might follow if the Father of Night thought differently.

Crossing the courtyard, a few strides took him to Jadewin's side. 'Tell me we're travelling by water. My arse – I mean, my arms and legs are still aching.'

After spending twelve days in a saddle to get here, he had decided that was his first and last journey on a horse. When this was over, if he couldn't get back to Hurat on the river, he'd walk.

'We'll take a small boat up river to the lake and sail across to the western shore. After that, we go on foot.' Jadewin hurried onward.

The castle yard was thronged with footsoldiers, river traders and townsfolk. The paths between the buildings were lined with crates and barrels. Like the crown fortress to the east, the old castle was braced for the coming attack.

Alory's four brothers stood by the gatehouse, talking quietly with Jadewin's secret sisters.

'There are no good choices.' Brother Augol scowled. 'We can only seek out the least ruinous path.'

Sister Meida nodded grimly. 'The path to the greater good.'

Brother Belid raised a hand to greet them. Alory silently thanked the Keeper of Wisdom that the older priest had agreed to try halting the rival earls before they advanced any further into Hurat. Bold as this plan was, it was surely their best hope of saving countless lives.

'Lead the way, good brother,' Belid prompted.

'Oh, right.' Alory should have realised he would go first, wearing a priest's black robe and the God's silver mask. The others had picked out well-worn clothes from the charitable donations to Chalus's shrine and temple. Any Bastrys scout watching through a spyglass should see townsfolk fleeing the imminent attack.

They left the castle and walked northwards along the west-facing waterfront. Alory began to enjoy how swiftly people gave way to the God's masked servant. Though he hadn't realised how much it would limit his vision. With the black robe's hood muffling his ears, he hoped he didn't miss hearing something vital.

Along the riverside, Chalus boatmen were chaining floating walkways together. The ungainly rafts drifted away from the bank, tethered by a single rope. Cut loose, they would clutter the waterway. Bastrys boats wouldn't find an easy landing beyond the range of the old castle's cannon.

'Alory. With me.' Brother Belid led him into a gap between two deserted buildings, out of sight of the waterfront.

Alory stripped off his black robe and the silver mask. As he wiped sweat from his face with his shirtsleeve, Belid handed him a battered barge man's leather jerkin and stuffed the mask and black robe into the drawstring bag which had held it. They rejoined the others and they hadn't gone much further when Alory saw a solitary vessel sailing towards them.

It was shorter and narrower than the barges he was used to, with steeper sides and a taller mast. A lad about his own age was catching the wind in a triangular sail. An older man with a family resemblance sat in the stern and managed the tiller.

As the boat reached the wharf, Alory saw two crown garrison scouts were stowing canvas bags beneath the seats lining the bulwarks of the hollow hull. They wore leather breeches, long boots and long-sleeved jerkins, and their curly black hair was braided close to their heads.

'Quick as you can,' the man at the tiller called out. 'It's going to be a long day.'

The boat master wasn't wrong. By the time the evening sun slid behind the forest on the shoreline ahead, Alory was desperate to feel solid ground under his feet. He was even ready to consider this journey might have been better by horse.

Sailing Lake Chalus was nothing like travelling by barge. Not even in the spring, when the Tane flowed wild and white with snow melt from the hill country. The lake boat had surged and darted this way and that, pursuing the gusting wind. The passengers had to stay alert for the crewman's shout to duck, before the sail's heavy boom swept across their heads. It was exhausting.

Evidently the boatmen knew where they could land among the dense trees on the shore. The man at the tiller turned the prow into a shallow inlet. A few boatlengths more, and gravel grated under the hull. The leather-clad scouts jumped over the rails, splashed ashore, and disappeared into the trees. The boatmen anchored the vessel.

Alory saw uncertainty on several faces. He knew how his brothers and sisters felt. This plan had seemed far more plausible when he and Jadewin had proposed it in Hurat castle's sanctuary.

Brother Augol cleared his throat. 'I'm taking my boots off. I don't fancy hiking to the highway with damp feet.'

'Good idea.' Sister Deyadir reached down to untie her own laces.

'Definitely.' Brother Belid began handing out the sailcloth bags that had been stowed under the seats.

When the scouts returned, the priests and priestesses climbed out of the boat, holding their burdens high as they waded through the shallows.

As soon as Alory got his socks and boots back on, he hurried to find privacy for a piss. When he returned, the others were eating rye bread, soft cheese and drinking small beer in the fading light. No one had wanted food while they were bouncing from wave to wave on the lake.

'Are we spending the night here?' Sister Deyadir asked through a mouthful.

'No.' The taller scout reappeared. 'We have dark lanterns. We should cover as much distance as we can before we sleep.'

'One moment, if you please.' Brother Belid clapped his hands.

Alory hurried to stand beside Brother Augol. Brother Halev and Brother Reblane as Sister Meida led the priestesses in their litany.

'Father of Night, we who serve the sun commend those who have earned your grace, and those who should seek your forgiveness, to your divine care through the darkness. We entrust the fates of all to your unfathomable wisdom until the dawn.'

Alory recited the answering prayer with his brothers.

'Mother of Light, we who serve the mysteries of darkness thank you for the blessings of your divine radiance, shared with the deserving and undeserving alike. We hope all will awaken to a true understanding of your bounty.'

The familiar rite felt very odd with everyone in workaday clothes and no altar. Still, Alory felt more at ease once they were done. The others seemed less tense as well.

The shorter scout handed out small candle lanterns with slatted metal sides instead of translucent horn panes. 'Talk only when you must. Voices carry through the trees and there's no knowing who might hear you. We're in Baron Zavire's fiefdom now.'

The tall scout led the way. Alory was somewhere in the middle of the file following the narrow path. A deer must have made this, he decided. A small deer. He concentrated on not tripping over tree roots in the dim, constantly shifting lamplight.

One step at a time. That's what Brother Talaven said, whether they were deciphering an ancient scroll or tackling some facet of the mysteries of magic. He'd worry about whatever challenges lay ahead when he met them. Their first task was reaching the highway without sprained or broken ankles. One step after another.

It was many, many steps before they stopped. No one said more than a few words as the scouts shared out dried meat and dried fruit. Brother Augol found a nearby spring and Alory helped him fill water skins the shorter scout provided. Finding a grassy bank, he slackened his bootlaces and pillowed his head on his drawstring sack, thanking the Father of Night for bringing them safely this…

Dawn and birdsong woke him. Sitting up, Alory retied his laces. The scouts were shaking his brothers and sisters awake. The shorter scout handed them slices of dense nut-bread and the taller one offered a bulging skin of fresh water from the stream. They were as comfortably at home in this wilderness as Alory was on Hurat's streets.

They recited their respective morning prayers and continued their journey through the trees. Thick summer foliage made it hard to see ahead, even in the daylight. Alory couldn't keep track of the taller scout's comings and goings. The shorter scout only reappeared when someone called for a halt to relieve themselves or to drink some water.

Noon came and they stopped briefly to eat more dried fruit and nut-bread. They walked on, only speaking when necessary. They were committed to this plan, so there was nothing to discuss.

The daylight filtering through the leafy branches was yellowing when Alory saw the tall scout hurry towards them, making urgent gestures to get off the path. Alory retreated behind a grey-barked tree. His heart pounded as the shorter scout arrived with a dark stain on one sleeve and what looked like blood on their other hand. The two briefly conferred, then beckoned the apprehensive priests and priestesses forward.

'Lystro's army is closer than we expected,' the tall scout told Belid. 'They're making camp for the night, none too far away.'

Alory realised some part of him hadn't entirely believed they would reach this point.

'How close can you get us without risk to yourselves?' Brother Belid asked quietly.

'Close enough.' The short scout was confident.

'Then it's time…?' Brother Augol hefted his canvas bag.

Alory struggled back into the disguise he had worn as they'd walked through Chalus. The robe was a tight fit over his leather jerkin, but it was the largest one the Chalus shrine could offer.

Dubious, Sister Meida shook out her black robe, loose enough to go over her townswoman's clothes. 'If they are so hostile to priests…'

'I'd rather wear this than dress up as a camp follower.' Deyadir smoothed the black cloth over her skirts. 'I think I can remember how to walk like a man. Just be careful not to trip and fall over. We don't need someone wondering why a priest is wearing petticoats.'

The short scout spoke up. 'Earl Lystro and the renegades from Velasta's high temple may treat your brothers like dirt, but these soldiers offer the God's servants proper respect.'

Alory saw the sisters' reluctance as they put on their masks. His stomach felt hollow and not for fear of the God's displeasure. He hadn't known what wearing a mask felt like when he'd come up with this plan. Could the sisters play their parts if they couldn't hear or see properly? But the God and the Goddess must know they could not risk being recognised.

Brother Belid was already masked. 'Let us do the talking.'

'Our treacherous sisters should think twice before taking on this number of unknown brothers,' Jadewin added.

Alory wondered who she was trying to convince. And what had happened to Sister Hasrine after she had attacked Jadewin in Hurat's castle sanctuary? All Jadewin and Brother Augol would tell him was she had lost, and she was gone.

Hooded and masked, they started walking, two by two on a wider path. Brother Belid and Sister Deyadir took the lead. The scouts disappeared into the trees. Alory fervently hoped they would be able to do their part. But he couldn't worry about that now.

A short distance further on, Alory heard voices and hammering and clattering. He could only see what lay straight ahead, but that was enough to show they had reached the outermost edge of Earl Lystro's camp. Soldiers gathered firewood or hauled leather buckets of water from some stream. Further on, sailcloth shelters were strung between the trees and rings of stones had been built to confine cook fires. A sweating gang was digging a latrine trench. This was what the castellan and the Earl of Shirlat's man had told them to expect.

He caught sight of a few black-clad brothers and several pale-robed sisters. None of them approached this unexpected delegation of masked priests, though Alory saw one priestess hurry off. Hopefully to alert her leader. They were relying on that.

Brother Belid and Sister Deyadir followed the priestess. In a clearing ahead, Alory saw supply wagons and cooking fires surround a cluster of superior tents made from scarlet sailcloth. Men and women sat eating close to a picket line where saddled and bridled horses waited. Those messengers were ready to carry the Earl of Coylure's orders wherever he cared to send them. Just as Reske and Maixen had said.

Two sentries guarded the biggest tent. The wide door flap was drawn aside and held out of the way. Alory could see trestle tables and stools inside. The priestess they were following walked straight past the guards. Brother Belid's stride didn't falter as he and Sister Deyadir did the same. Alory's breath sounded louder than ever inside his mask.

The sentries weren't prepared to challenge twelve masked servants of the Moon God. Inside the tent, Brother Augol quickly unhooked the rope that held the door flap open. Oil lamps on the tables glowed in the gloom as Augol wound the rope around the cleats that would keep the entrance closed. Carpets underfoot muted the scent of crushed grass.

Alory saw this tent had a second room beyond the space where they stood. A man some way into his later years sat behind a table strewn with maps and lists. He looked apprehensive as well as startled by their arrival. Good. Hurat's priests and priestesses were counting on Earl Lystro's guilty conscience.

Chapter Twenty-Seven

THE ARAFAZE HIGHWAY

9th Day of the Hay Moon

The priestess they had followed joined six renegade sisters standing behind the earl. Jadewin only recognised one of them. Mother Elyka. This was more than she had dared hope for. It also meant carrying their plan through to success would be a far greater and more perilous challenge.

A few days' stubble indicated Earl Lystro of Coylure preferred to shave his head instead of vainly trying to conceal a receding hairline. He could still boast a full beard, barely streaked with grey. His dark blue livery coat had a gold satin collar and cuffs.

An unknown priestess was outraged. 'How dare you—'

'Earl Lystro, we have come to warn you.' Brother Belid addressed the nobleman sternly, ignoring everyone else. 'In the Moon God's name. Whatever the rights and wrongs of your wife's quarrel with her niece, you have no cause to wage war beyond Bastrys. The Arafaze crown has no claim to suzerainty in the Vale of Hurat.'

'Who are you?' the same priestess demanded. 'Show your face!'

Brother Belid spared her a glance. 'I serve the Scourge of Lies, as you should serve the Diviner of Truth. Open yourself to her grace, sister. Let her light vouch for my words.'

His resonant voice was reaching well beyond the tent's sailcloth walls. Jadewin heard the bustle outside slow and fall silent. Her apprehension grew.

The belligerent priestess's hand drifted towards her pendant. She clenched her fist instead. 'The sons of night have broken faith with the crown by supporting the usurper Idelina—'

'Whoever says that in Velasta does not speak for us,' Belid told Earl Lystro. 'We have sworn no such allegiance. Nor will those serving any shrine or temple across Hurat. Just as we will not be bribed or threatened into bowing our heads to Princess Alriad.'

He challenged the oldest of the women standing behind the earl. 'Prove our good faith, Mother Elyka. In the Sun Goddess's name!'

The Velastan high priestess stared at him, startled. Her face hardened. 'Where is Hasrine?'

The priestess doing all the talking flapped her hands as if she was trying to scare away crows. 'Be gone. All of you! Leave!'

'Or we'll be murdered like Brother Cavore? Like Brother Thendre? Like Brother Mohlan? Like Brother Edace? Stand in the sight of the Goddess,' Belid roared with sudden fury. 'Swear you knew nothing of these deaths!'

His silver mask turned from one priestess to the next. 'You knew our brothers, your brothers, were being hunted and killed. You never breathed a word of warning. Instead you sought to profit from this evil. You only sheltered those who begged for your help if they agreed to assist your unholy scheme.'

Mother Elyka's face was as pale as milk. The priestess beside her trembled. Jadewin could barely draw breath behind her mask. How had her sisters come to this?

Brother Belid stepped forward and Earl Lystro recoiled in his chair.

'My lord of Coylure,' the priest said earnestly, 'if Mother Elyka will not put our words to the Goddess's test, if these other sisters refuse to declare their own truths, can you be certain they are giving you good counsel?'

Jadewin saw a crease deepen between Earl Lystro's brows as Brother Belid continued.

'We know you have agreed terms with King Tadiri of Mervante. We know you expect him to send men to Sharrow, to threaten Hurat so the castellan dare not send forces westward to help Chalus. You have agreed the weasel king's son will wed whichever of your daughters you can persuade to submit to such a match, once his forces have helped you subdue us.'

The earl was clearly appalled to realise the extent of the priest's knowledge. Belid shook his head.

'You cannot know King Tadiri has also agreed an alliance with Princess Idelina. In return for his aid, Earl Padran promised to wed the weasel king's daughter who had been betrothed to King Venais. In truth though, Mervante's armies will not march until their king can see whose victory is assured. He seeks only to claim a share of the spoils without spilling Mervantese blood.'

'Mother Elyka.' Earl Lystro slammed his fist on the table. 'Show me the truth in these claims!'

'Our magic will not serve you.' Elyka hissed with fury. 'These intruders doubtless believe what they say, but that is no proof they have not been told lies.'

Jadewin was glad the silver mask hid her satisfaction. As she and Alory had hoped, the priestess dared not call on the Goddess's grace for fear of Brother Belid repeating his accusations against her. The light of her own sunburst pendant would reveal her guilt.

The priest shook his head, regretful. 'My lord, you expect Mervante forces to pass along the western edge of the Mire before taking passes through the Sharrow Heights to attack Hurat. You believe you have allies among the marsh folk who will seize the castles at Avelsir, Scefet and Julach to give the Mervantese army safe passage. Believe me, far more of the marsh folk oppose this scheme than support it. If by some chance King Tadiri honours your alliance, his soldiers will be netted and drowned, skewered with snake spears.'

Earl Lystro ran a hand over his beard. 'How do you know this?'

Once again, Jadewin was certain Brother Belid's uncompromising words reached well beyond the tent.

'We serve the Keeper of Wisdom. Our sisters in Hurat serve the All-seeing Light. Shrine and temple may be divided in Velasta but we who serve the people of the Dore and the Tane honour the God and the Goddess as equals.' The priest folded his arms, now speaking friend to friend. 'Advance, my lord, and the Dore will run red with blood long before you reach Hurat. Beyond that, you have no hope of conquering the towns of the Tane. When King Tadiri of Mervante reads the tally of your dead, he won't send his forces to die alongside your own. Are you truly prepared to waste so many lives on this futile venture? Will such slaughter bolster support for your wife's cause in Arafaze?'

Earl Lystro studied the maps on his table. He glanced at the masked figures standing silently behind Brother Belid. 'Have you sent envoys to Padran to inform him of Mervante's double-dealing?'

Mother Elyka stepped forward, shoving the earl's shoulder. 'You know our magic will undo all resistance.'

Jadewin braced herself. The renegade high priestess had just confirmed the dying man's confession. These women had forsworn their oaths to the secret sisterhood and revealed the unseen realm to the Earl of Coylure and Princess Alriad. Behind their silver masks and the concealing black robes, Hurat's other priestesses stirred. Jadewin could sense her true sisters' contempt for Mother Elyka and her acolytes like heat from an unseen furnace.

Elyka slapped the table in front of Earl Lystro. 'You have seen this for yourself. The people will see the Goddess bless your royal wife with your victory.'

As the high priestess glanced at the other renegades, Jadewin looked into the unreal world. The tent was the same as it was in tangible reality. Only two of the renegade sisters were there with her. The manifestation they were trying to summon was barely indistinct mist, and Jadewin could already tell it wasn't the Lightning King. This was some sort of four-legged beast. A big one.

Jadewin kept watch for the Icicle Witch. She had confessed her fears to her sisters, telling them what had happened when she confronted Hasrine. Sister Deyadir asserted the Goddess had sent Hurat's ancient phantasm to defeat the Lightning King. Sister Meida was confident the apparition would be no match for the true priestesses' combined strength. Jadewin prayed they were right.

The pale shape between the renegades swirled and thickened like wood smoke. Jadewin reminded herself that Mother Finevre believed the Icicle Witch was bound to Hurat town.

The apparition would be unable to sense the veil thinning over such a great distance. Then the wretched fire bird turned up. That forced her to set aside her fears.

Alory's protector hovered on wings of brilliant flame, turning its head this way and that to study the coalescing apparition. The nebulous shape flashed into completeness and Jadewin was impressed despite herself.

The treacherous sisters had summoned a unicorn. Standing in front of the earl's map table, the apparition was taller and broader than the biggest horse she had ever seen. The fearsome creature swept its head from side to side. Its lethal spiral horn was translucent white and edged with an amethyst glow. Its eyes were darkly purple, vivid against its ivory hide.

The fire bird darted towards it, but the renegade sisters disappeared and the phantom stepped into the tangible realm. The fire bird followed. Biting her tongue on an exasperated curse, Jadewin returned her gaze to the real world.

Her sisters from Hurat stood motionless. They had been astonished when Alory had shown them the fire bird, when Brother Augol had explained the hidden brethren summoned such creatures to defend them against more dangerous monsters. Now Jadewin and her sisters must make certain none of the priests' perilous magic got loose. And they had agreed twelve masked priests would be far more intimidating when Brother Belid confronted the earl.

The unicorn was intent on skewering the fire bird. The blazing phantasm circled erratically around the unicorn's head. Its hooked beak gaped as it tried to peck at its ears or its mane. A moment later and the fire bird miscalculated. It flew too close and the gleaming horn stabbed clean through one flaming wing. The smaller phantasm vanished in a shower of burning fragments. Earl Lystro sprang to his feet, frantic to brush sparks and embers from his papers and his clothing, until he realised they were an illusion.

Mother Elyka laughed, harsh with triumph. 'Is that the best you can do?'

The unicorn stared at Alory. Jadewin swallowed, dry-mouthed as the monster stamped its cloven hooves. Could she and her sisters send this creature back to the intangible realm, before it drove that murderous horn through the boy's chest?

As Brother Belid and Alory retreated to stand with their silent brothers, she flexed her hand, hidden by her long black sleeve. She would reach through the neck of this black robe for her pendant if she must, even though using the Goddess's magic would unmask her as a priestess. Their original plan would unravel, but if this apparition broke free of the renegade sisters' control, they would have far greater problems than that.

Lystro of Coylure was watching the unicorn warily as he resumed his seat. Jadewin realised he had seen the beast before. He was apprehensive, not shocked.

Mother Elyka berated him. 'How can you doubt your cause is just? The Goddess sends you this emissary of truth and purity! The towns of the Dore will throw open their gates when they see this herald your advance. Hurat's people will beg the Golden Mother's forgiveness when this manifestation of her divine power endorses Queen Alriad's right to the crown.'

'Not when they see the Keeper of Secrets manifest his displeasure at such misuse of perilous magic.' Brother Belid stepped forward and his brothers came with him.

Silver radiance glowed in front of the unicorn. In the blink of an eye, the light shone so bright that everyone had to look away. It faded as swiftly and Jadewin saw what Hurat's hidden brothers had wrought while they had been standing in silent communion.

The priests had agreed they would summon a griffin. Brother Belid had described the monster, but Jadewin found its appearance infinitely more unnerving. This apparition wasn't as tall in the shoulder as the unicorn, but that didn't matter. It was unmistakeably a predator. Above the tufted tail, it had the solid, tawny body and taloned paws of a lion from the northern hill country. Its chest and shoulders were covered in dark golden feathers, banded with black. So were the great wings folded against its flanks. Its fearsome eagle's head looked around the tent as its pointed ears twitched irritably.

'There is more than one guardian of justice and bringer of divine retribution.' Brother Belid sounded almost apologetic.

The griffin fixed its gaze on the earl. Lystro's eyes widened with fear. The unicorn lowered its head and levelled its long horn at this foe. The griffin swiped at the translucent spiral with a massive forepaw. As the unicorn shied away, the griffin's talons gouged scars in the central pole's varnished wood. The scarlet sailcloth shuddered overhead.

A voice outside the tent shouted, startled. Someone responded, concerned. Jadewin resolutely ignored the voices. She must not risk the distraction of trying to make sense of half-heard words.

One of the renegade sisters couldn't match her resolve. As the woman gasped, Jadewin saw the unicorn retreat right through the table strewn with maps. This apparition had no more substance than mist. She realised only Mother Elyka and those two priestesses had the strength and the skill to sustain the phantasm. The other renegades cowering against the tent's back wall had no more magical talent than Mother Finevre. Jadewin's fears lessened a little.

The griffin reared up on its hind legs, flapping its massive wings. Maps and letters flew everywhere.

The unicorn menaced the griffin with its horn. It didn't move forward though, stamping its cloven hooves noiselessly on the carpet covering the grass.

Anxious voices outside grew louder. As the griffin dropped back onto four paws, Jadewin was forced to wonder how much longer the presence of twelve black-robed and masked priests could stop the earl's captains from entering the tent.

One of the priestesses who had summoned the unicorn sank to her knees, raising her hands in surrender. Jadewin could hardly blame her. Her own head was ringing, and the Goddess only knew what Lystro's guards outside the tent could be thinking. Right now, she heard stunned silence beyond the sailcloth walls. That could not last.

'As you see, my lord,' Brother Belid explained to the ashen-faced earl. 'Our argument carries far more weight than theirs. Bring magic into this fight and you will lose.'

Jadewin summoned all her resolve and focus. She had to believe Hurat's priestesses could unmake this unicorn. Even so, she was glad the mask would hide any doubt on her face, just as she couldn't see if any of her sisters were uncertain.

Mother Elyka was still on her feet. She gestured, and the Lightning King appeared. The nightmare figure of razor-edged blades was so tall its head slashed the sailcloth roof. Outside, cries of alarm rang through the trees. Inside the tent, the line of black robed figures wavered.

'Kill them,' Mother Elyka spat.

The horror took a step towards them. The griffin sprang. The Lightning King raised a lacerating arm, but the monstrosity was too slow. The griffin's taloned paw ripped deep into its chest. Every one of the blades that made the nightmare was outlined in burning gold.

The Lightning King exploded. Lethal splinters of light shot in all directions, ripping through the sailcloth walls. Jadewin heard screams of pain outside. Inside the tent, Mother Elyka collapsed. Blood from wounds to her chest and belly darkened her pale robe. Lystro of Coylure clutched a deep gash in his shoulder. The cowering renegades had suffered cuts to their arms, hands and backs.

Jadewin didn't care about them. Who had been hurt from Hurat? No one, she realised a moment later. The strength of their faith had protected them.

'My – my lord?' Outside, some soldier far braver than most tugged vainly at the weighted flap that covered the tent's entrance. The rope Brother Augol had wound around the cleats held, but someone else was tearing a rip in the sailcloth wider.

'Alory!' Brother Belid gestured. The young priest moved to block the view of whoever stood outside, trying to look into the tent.

'Be gone,' Alory ordered with cold authority bolstered by his height, broad shoulders and the God's implacable silver mask. 'Lest the Lord of Vengeance decides to chastise you too.'

Jadewin saw Deyadir and her sisters were unmaking the fading unicorn. Before she could gather her wits to help, the apparition vanished so completely that no one would ever know it had been there.

Augol was on his knees beside Mother Elyka. He ripped open her robe to staunch the worst bleeding with dressings and salves from his belt pouch. Brother Belid had a knife in his hand. He cut the earl's coat away to assess his wound. Brother Halev and Brother Reblane tended the wounded priestesses. The brothers had come prepared.

The griffin was still solidly present. It stretched its head towards the wounded earl. Its feathered ears pricked with interest as the nobleman leaned as far back as he could without toppling his chair.

'None of that,' Brother Belid chided the phantasm. 'You can't have him. Not yet.'

The griffin shook its wings with a squawk of annoyance and disappeared. Empty of apparitions, the tent seemed ten times bigger. As her sisters shared her relief with muted gasps and murmurs behind their masks, Jadewin let go a breath she hadn't realised she was holding. She also realised a crowd was gathering outside, trying to see through the rips in the sailcloth. Jadewin clapped her hands to get her sisters' attention and gestured towards Alory. Quick to understand, Hurat's priestesses in their borrowed guises moved to stand in front of the worst rents in the tent's walls. Looking through the shredded scarlet, Jadewin saw the closest footsoldiers hastily retreat before the Moon God turned his displeasure on them.

She glanced over her shoulder, frustrated. She wanted to tell the priests that they must leave, but her voice would instantly give her away.

The priests were still busy. Brother Belid used Lystro's hand to press a wadded-up shirt sleeve against his wound. Walking around the table, the priest picked up a black and gold feather off the carpet. He laid it in front of the trembling earl.

'This keepsake can remind you why the secret magic of the God and the Goddess is only known to a few for good reason. Tell no one, other than your wife, what you have seen today. The God's winged messenger has your scent now. It will know where to find you to punish any lack of discretion. If needs must, we can send it to pursue your wife as well.'

The earl stared at the feather, transfixed. Jadewin took care not to stir the Goddess's magic as she wondered how much truth there might be in Brother Belid's warning.

'She will live, if you nurse her diligently.' Augol finishing dressing Mother Elyka's wounds and glared at the other cowering renegades. 'Take her to the high temple in Velasta. Whether she lives or dies, tell whoever else bears the most guilt for your impiety exactly what happened here today. Warn your forsworn sisters to stay out of Hurat's affairs or face the justified wrath of our shrine alongside our true sisters' temple.'

Mother Elyka didn't stir. Jadewin wondered what else was in Brother Augol's salves besides herbs to slow bleeding.

Alory cleared his throat. 'I think we had better leave.'

'Let's go.' Brother Belid cut the rope securing the entrance with a single slash of his knife.

Alory threw back the heavy door flap and walked out. Black-robed and silver-masked, Hurat's priests and priestesses followed, going straight to the messengers' horse line. Just as Shirlat's man Reske had assured them, no one dared to object as each of the Moon God's servants claimed a steed.

Jadewin watched Alory mount what she fervently prayed was a docile horse. Urging her own chosen ride towards the highway, she stayed as close to the boy as she could. They cantered through Earl Lystro's camp, past gaping, astonished faces. Uncertain shouts pursued them, offering assistance or begging for news. Jadewin saw Alory clutching desperate handfuls of mane along with his reins.

They reached the highway and Brother Belid kicked his mount into a gallop. The other horses took up the challenge. Jadewin rode as close to Alory as she dared, ready to pull up at once if the boy fell off. She wasn't entirely sure how far they had ridden before they turned off the highway and halted on a stretch of open grass. As Jadewin dismounted, Alory more or less tumbled out of his saddle. Brother Belid helped the young priest to his feet. The two leather-clad scouts appeared to gather up the black robes and masks the priests and priestesses were stripping off.

Sister Deyadir made sure her pendant was still hidden beneath her everyday clothes. 'Did anyone see how many outside the tent were wounded?'

'Enough to give them plenty to worry about.' Brother Augol was unrepentant. 'And young Alory declaring the God was chastising Earl Lystro should be good for a fair few desertions.'

'Why did you say that, Alory?' Brother Belid was curious rather than critical.

'What's done is done.' Sister Meida interrupted before the young priest could answer, smoothing her skirts. 'We must leave.'

'Everything's ready,' the tall scout assured her.

The shorter scout was pulling aside a screen skilfully woven from cut branches, still green with leaves. Master Steward Senon's instructions had been carried out to the letter, sent ahead by fast courier before the priests and priestesses set out from Hurat. A neat, open carriage with its hood folded back stood beside a farm wagon stacked with bales of straw. Beside them, a battered coach had been some minor noble's pride ten or more years ago. Two more scouts were harnessing fresh horses in each set of shafts.

Brother Halev laughed as he and Brother Reblane climbed into the back of the farm wagon. 'Do you think Coylure's men will chase after those mysterious servants of the Moon God, or leave well alone?'

'Who knows?' Brother Belid joined Sister Deyadir on the seat behind the farm wagon's two horses. 'Who cares?'

Alory wasn't amused. 'Have we stopped Earl Lystro's advance?'

'Only the Goddess and the God can know that right now.' Brother Augol climbed up to the coach's driving seat, confident as he took up the reins despite his maimed hand. 'We will find out in their good time.'

Sister Meida paused before joining her sisters inside the coach. 'We've done all we can. Let us pray for the castellan's success.'

As the others echoed her words, Jadewin shared Alory's apprehension. If Maixen and Reske's half of this bold plan failed, everything they had done here today would achieve nothing.

Well, perhaps not entirely. Earl Lystro of Coylure would hopefully cut ties with Mother Elyka and her promises of magic, even if he refused to give up this war. She did her best to shake off the dread that plagued her so often these days. Sister Meida was right. What was done was done. The other drivers were guiding their vehicles onto the highway. The four scouts had divided the stolen horses between themselves, ready to ride off and lay a false trail leading who knew where. Jadewin checked over the light carriage and its single horse. The luggage Senon had promised her was stowed in the back.

Alory joined her. 'Is there anything I can do?'

'Get comfortable. We have a long journey ahead of us.' Jadewin climbed into the driving seat and waited for Alory to settle himself beside her.

She snatched a quick glimpse into the intangible realm. There was no sign of the fire bird, though she caught sight of Alory for an instant. She hoped the young priest didn't see her relief at his apparition's absence. Truth be told, Jadewin wouldn't be sorry if the unicorn's horn had dispelled it entirely.

Encouraging their horse to walk on, she wondered how to turn Alory's thoughts in a different direction. 'Would you like to learn how to drive?'

He stared at her. 'Could I?'

'I don't see why not.' She paused to get the carriage safely over the ruts at the edge of the highway. 'We'll have plenty of time. It's a long way to Velasta.'

Chapter Twenty-Eight

JEDFAL

10th Day of the Hay Moon

Reske didn't understand how Maixen could sit calmly reading the morning's reports in the castellan's oppressively stuffy tent. How could he ignore the shouts and conversations outside, and the never-ending strike of tools on metal or wood?

'There's nothing from Shirlat.' The castellan continued reading.

Reske wished he could believe that guaranteed Earl Debin was still confined within his estate's boundaries, unharmed. Whoever believed no news was good news was a God-cursed idiot.

'I'm going to get some air.' This heat wouldn't lessen until well into the Harvest Moon. That couldn't come soon enough.

Maixen laid his papers on the table. 'Padran of Evarise will send an envoy in the next day or so.'

Reske rounded on him. 'You're sure of that? Shouldn't we consider our options? How long do we wait? The priests and priestesses should have confronted Earl Lystro by now.'

'And we'll hear how they fared soon enough. Until then, we sit on our hands and do nothing hasty,' Maixen retorted. 'Whatever's happened, whatever Earl Lystro decides to do once he knows he cannot trust Mervante, Earl Padran won't get any word of that before us.'

'What if it's bad news?' Reske started pacing across the ridiculous width of matting. Someone, years ago, had decided the dignity of Hurat's castellan would be disastrously undermined unless he travelled with a tent big enough to host a solstice dance. 'What if they haven't stopped Coylure's advance?'

Were Sister Jadewin, Brother Alory and the other priestesses and priests now Earl Lystro of Coylure's prisoners? Had they been hauled off in chains to Velasta, to face whatever blasphemous retribution the high priestess decreed, doubtless in Princess Alriad's name? Were they lying dead in the dust of the hoof-pocked highway while Earl Lystro's army advanced to attack Chalus?

'No plan accounts for every contingency,' Maixen said firmly. 'Trying to predict and forestall every potential bad outcome is how battles and wars are lost. A good commander thinks on their feet and deals with whatever situation they face.'

He sighed, surprising Reske. 'If they have failed? We should see our side of this plan through regardless. We've already made Earl Padran pay the highest possible price for every league his army has crossed in the past ten days. We can think of other ways to harass him that shouldn't risk too many lives. With luck, word of this will distract Earl Lystro. That might offer us some unforeseen opportunity.'

'Right.' Reske couldn't stand the airless tent any longer. He walked out into the bright morning light.

Over towards the river, Jedfal's barbican guarded the margravine's domain. The town's gates were solidly bolted and barred. Close at hand, the crown fortress loomed over the highway. Reske watched a broad-shouldered carter manoeuvre a covered wagon around the redoubt defending the entrance. She was bringing more wounded to the priest-physicians at the fortress infirmary. Another cart paid no heed to the deep ruts in the road. The blanket-shrouded bodies stacked in the back were beyond feeling anything.

He saw Senon talking to the lieutenant who kept a scrupulous record of the dead, and walked over to join them. 'How many for the charnel barges today?'

He had learned the Tane forces buried their dead where they fell. Maixen sent those killed in Hurat's service, or from a town along the Dore, home. When Reske had questioned that, given the summer heat, Maixen said their families deserved a grave they could visit. Later, Senon told Reske the dead weren't struck off Hurat's muster roll until they had been buried. Delay gave their dependents a few more days' pay. So the dead went downstream in coffins made by Jedfal's skilled joiners, lined and sealed with wax, and paid for by the castellan.

'Fourteen,' Senon replied, dour. 'Let's hope they're the last.'

'From your lips to the Moon God's ears,' the lieutenant agreed before walking away.

'Any news of the rearguard?' Reske asked quietly.

'The last to leave Vitry should be here by noon.' The master steward gazed westward over the grainland.

Like Reske, he was looking for a distant plume of dust raised by galloping horses' hooves. Once the castellan's army had reached Jedfal, Captain Grezel's grimy and ragged patrols soon confirmed Padran of Evarise hadn't wasted a day. As soon as he learned Firio of Ripat's proposal had been rejected, the earl had ordered his forces to march.

The castellan had assured Margravine Montaise that the Arafaze army would not reach Jedfal unopposed. Not that Maixen had any intention of meeting Evarise forces in pitched battle. Reske knew that for certain. Hurat forces led by hand-picked lieutenants and sergeants had been sent to Vitry. The margravine had wondered if that risked provoking the advancing Arafaze army. Maixen told her he very much hoped so. Soon enough, Captain Grezel's scouts confirmed the earl had been tempted by the prospect of winning a swift and decisive victory.

Reske knew Hurat's troops had been ordered to inflict as many casualties as they could when Vitry was attacked. At the first hint of an enemy withdrawal to regroup, they were to retreat steadily and stubbornly towards Jedfal. Maixen assured Reske that Earl Padran would not commit his forces to a siege of a mere market town. The earls' orders to pursue their foe, intent on revenge, should also ensure his forces didn't sack and loot Vitry. That retreat had begun three agonising days ago.

'I've had word Earl Padran's scouts collected the reports and maps left in the Vitry command post,' Senon remarked.

Reske had given up wondering how many people kept Senon informed. 'Let's hope he takes the castellan's bait.'

Maixen had explained Earl Padran had to believe he had the whip hand if he was going to accept Hurat's castellan's invitation to meet and negotiate.

'What's the tally of Evarise dead?' Reske asked.

'Substantial.' Senon didn't hide his satisfaction.

'Your wagons worked well then.' Reske knew he should be pleased by the cold arithmetic of battle. He still couldn't help sympathising with those Evarise horsemen riding unawares past covered carts seemingly abandoned in Hurat's retreat.

Those sailcloth sides hid racks of hackbuts, similar to rampart guns but smaller. Linked by slow-burning match cord lit by volunteers lying hidden beneath the wagons, the weapons fired a storm of small shot in a single, murderous volley. In theory those brave volunteers would be able to flee amid the mayhem of lead scything through men and horses. Reske didn't ask how many had actually escaped.

'Grezel's scouts say Evarise's men won't go near an unattended wagon. Their entire advance ground to a halt twice yesterday after the scouts left a farm cart in their path.' The steward stiffened and shaded his eyes with a hand. 'There. A herald.'

Reske picked out the distant horse trotting along the road. The rider carried a flag, fluttering not furled. 'I'll tell the castellan.'

Inside the sprawling tent, Maixen was already shoving lists and reports into leather cases. 'At least this folly will be put to good use for once.'

Footsoldiers were carrying away clothes chests and dismantling the castellan's travelling bed and washstand. The folding table and chairs were taken away and Reske hurried to lend a hand as the coarse matting was covered with an elegant carpet. A solid, polished table appeared from somewhere with cushioned chairs.

They had barely got everything straight when Senon arrived with a sealed letter for Maixen. 'From Earl Padran.'

The castellan read it quickly. 'The earl will arrive under a flag of truce some time after noon today, accompanied by Firio of Ripat, his scrivener and an advisor. They will be escorted by ten troopers.'

'Reaching us on the heels of the rearguard from Vitry,' Reske observed. 'Hoping to find us in disarray.'

'No doubt.' Maixen chewed his lip. 'Do you suppose we'll recognise this scrivener?'

'I imagine so.' Reske still found Nindera Kyse's escape from Hurat infuriating, even though they discovered she had fled the castle immediately after she'd sent the pinch-faced girl to kill Alory.

The castellan glanced at Senon. 'Tell Margravine Montaise the earl's expected, with my compliments.'

'I'll do that,' Reske volunteered.

After he had delivered the castellan's message, he found a bathhouse in Jedfal town. A few silver coins bought him a clean shirt and the services of a nearby laundress to brush his doublet and breeches while he bathed and shaved. The bathhouse keeper's lad polished his boots. When he got back to the castellan's tent, Maixen was freshly groomed, wearing a new livery with pristine linen. Senon had even trimmed the castellan's hair.

Preparations continued. By the time trumpets announced Earl Padran of Evarise's arrival, Maixen sat at the head of the polished table contemplating gilded plates of dainties fit for a Velastan banquet. Reske sat two places to his right with an open scrivener's box.

Reske rose as Senon escorted Earl Padran, Baron Firio and Nindera Kyse into the tent, followed by a plainly dressed lad carrying a writing case. So Mistress Nindera was the earl's advisor. Reske looked at the paper in front of him rather than risk meeting her eyes. Sister Jadewin had assured him priestesses couldn't read minds, but he wasn't taking any chances.

Senon accepted the visitors' cloaks. 'May I offer you wine to wash away the dust of the road?'

'Spring water, if you please.' Dark-haired, dark-eyed, and blunt featured, the Earl of Evarise took the seat at the far end of the table, warily assessing this reception.

The nobleman wore serviceable breeches and boots and a well-tailored maroon doublet with no insignia or adornment.

Reske knew he hadn't got that muscular build dancing at courtly gatherings, and he had warned the castellan Earl Padran was not a man to underestimate, despite his comparative youth.

Baron Firio took the chair to the earl's right. Mistress Nindera sat on Padran's left. The scrivener picked a chair halfway along the table and opened his writing case. Evidently he didn't warrant an introduction. Senon poured fresh water from a silver jug into four fine glass goblets for the visitors. Reske sat and picked up his pen.

'Castellan.' Earl Padran took a fruit tartlet from the platter Senon offered. 'I understand you wish to discuss coming to terms, to avoid further bloodshed.'

His confidence told Reske the earl had indeed read those half-burned reports scattered around Vitry. Maixen had taken great care writing them, to indicate Hurat had suffered heavy losses.

'I'm glad to hear it,' the castellan said earnestly. 'Shall we summon a priestess and a priest, so we may be assured of each other's good faith?'

Earl Padran's face hardened. 'I see no reason to bring shrine or temple into the crown's affairs. Those who serve the God and the Goddess should restrict themselves to the care of the sick and destitute, mindful of their vows.'

'Their assistance in administering justice is surely crucial?' Maixen queried.

Earl Padran studied the sweet pastry he had selected. 'The magic of temple and shrine has its uses, but over-reliance hands too much influence to priests and most particularly to priestesses.'

'Princess Alriad does not think so,' Maixen observed. 'I hear she will allow the priestesses who support her to use far more of their enchantments.'

Reske stared at the few words he had written on the paper in front of him. Finding out if Padran of Evarise knew what the renegade priestesses had promised Earl Lystro and Princess Alriad was crucial.

Earl Padran was puzzled. 'What further enchantments?'

'The high temple's claims are baseless rumour,' Mistress Nindera said swiftly. 'Exaggeration to sway the gullible and credulous.'

'Really?' Maixen stared at her. 'When so many witnesses swear they have seen this Lightning King?'

'Castellan, I had no idea you shared the common folk's superstitions,' Firio of Ripat sneered.

Earl Padran cut him short. 'Let's have no more of this nonsense.'

Reske didn't need the glow of a priestess's amulet to convince him the earl had no idea of magic's terrifying potential. That was good news and also inconvenient. Jadewin and Alory had made him and Maixen swear, before the Goddess and the God, that they would not reveal the truth of the unseen world to anyone who didn't know about it. The castellan would need other arguments to convince Earl Padran of Evarise to cut his losses and go home.

'Let's speak plainly, my lord.' Maixen took a sip of water. 'A new monarch will reign in Velasta sooner or later, but who wears the Arafaze crown is of no interest to us in the Vale of Hurat.'

'Really?' Earl Padran ate his pastry and brushed crumbs from his fingers. 'I am told these margravates and baronies are squabbling amongst themselves. I'm told that more than half are ready to depose you as castellan, as soon as they can agree who will claim Hurat. Meantime, your garrison captains and many serving under them are Arafaze born, and they look homewards.'

Reske knew the few officers whose letters had betrayed split loyalties had been sent to defend the fortresses flanking the Mire. Thankfully, their letters had been sent straight to the castellan by recipients who wanted nothing to do with such treachery. Maixen had put the missives to further good use.

'Discarded documents found in fireplaces may say many things. Let me assure you before any more lives are lost, the Vale of Hurat's people stand together, from humblest to highest.'

'Ha! I told you not to trust that trash.' Firio of Ripat laughed sourly and held up his glass. 'Wine!'

As Senon filled the baron's goblet, Earl Padran's expression promised Firio nothing good. Perversely Reske's opinion of the man improved. Very slightly. He also wanted to know how Nindera had explained away deserting the nobleman in Hurat.

The Earl of Evarise folded his arms. 'What terms are you offering?'

Maixen smiled. 'Permission to withdraw your army unharmed to the western bank of the Fasil. We will not pursue you, provided you swear to keep Princess Idelina's quarrel with Princess Alriad out of the Vale of Hurat now and for all time. Neither royal lady has any claim to rule lands on this side of the Bastrys mountains. You and Princess Idelina will acknowledge the bloodline of the Earls of Hurat is extinct, and thus King Ganirin's settlement is void.'

'Who will govern these lands?' Earl Padran demanded. 'Who will defend the people from Mervante?'

The tension in the tent was matched by absolute silence outside. Reske wondered if the entire Hurat army was listening.

Maixen's smile widened. 'I assume you're waiting to hear your Mervantese allies are marching north from Gernet? You believe they will attack Chalus, forcing Earl Lystro to give battle, leaving you free to conquer Hurat. In return, you'll hand the castles guarding the Mire to King Tadiri with Idelina's thanks.'

Maixen stopped smiling. 'I'm sorry to disappoint you, my lord. The garrison at Gernet has been forewarned. The town is braced to repel any assault from Mervante. Though I doubt that attack will happen. King Tadiri will only send his forces north once your victory, or Earl Lystro's, is beyond doubt. If he can't claim his reward without shedding Mervantese blood, he'll do nothing but bide his time.'

Maixen spoke over Firio of Ripat's inarticulate protest.

'The weasel king also made an alliance with Princess Alriad and the Earl of Coylure. Earl Lystro believes Mervantese forces are creeping along the edge of the Mire as we speak. He expects them to sneak through the high ground on secret paths to muster at Sharrow and attack Hurat. Lystro is confident that will occupy me while he seizes Chalus and advances on the towns along the Dore. He'll be sorely disappointed. The Mire folk have promised me any Mervantese scouts will die before they can muddy their boots.'

Maixen leaned forward, earnest. 'Would you like me to summon a priestess, my lord, to prove I'm telling the truth? We honour our temple and our shrine in Hurat. Those who serve the Goddess and the God work together to serve the people. We will defend them from harm, as they defend us.'

Reske forced himself not to look at Mistress Nindera. The silence lengthened.

Earl Padran squared his shoulders. 'You cannot trust the Mire folk.'

'I can,' Maixen assured him. 'Their elders were willing to leave their endless marsh and stand before the altars in Scefet castle's sanctuary so the Goddess's servant and the God's could vouch for their truthfulness. You can read their sworn and sealed testimonies.'

Another silence lengthened. Baron Firio stirred as if he was going to say something, until he caught Earl Padran's fulminating glare. Nindera sat still and expressionless. Reske wondered what the murderous woman was plotting now.

'I might be persuaded to withdraw, on certain conditions,' Earl Padran said finally. 'Jedfal garrison will surrender its current stock of firing powder and shot for cannon and rampart guns.'

Maixen shook his head. 'We will not give you or Lystro of Coylure any means to wage your war. Hurat is and will remain neutral.'

'You will give us what we need, or we will take it.' Earl Padran's grip on his anger slipped.

'Try and see how far you get.' Maixen stood and walked to the tent's entrance. 'Weigh up a few considerations before you make rash decisions.'

'You cannot stand against us.' Earl Padran insisted, but he left his seat and joined Maixen.

Senon had stepped outside first. As the castellan and Earl Padran walked into the sunlight, Baron Firio hurried to join them. The young scrivener went too. Reske followed after a wary glance at Nindera who had not left her seat.

Outside, Maixen raised a hand. Firio of Ripat looked around for a response. Not seeing movement in the camp, he mocked the castellan. 'Dear me. Where have your servants got to?'

'The towers, you idiot,' Earl Padran snapped.

The earl watched the flags being raised to flutter boldly from Jedfal's turrets. Banners were released to flap against the gatehouse walls. Every margravate of the Tane was represented, and every barony of the Dore. Footsoldiers in every livery crowded the town ramparts and the castle's battlements. Jedfal's gates opened and a column of armed and armoured men and women marched out.

'My lord.' Maixen drew Earl Padran's attention to the garrison's fortress.

Footsoldiers swung rampart guns around on the battlements before pointing the weapons safely at the sky. Cannon trundled forward, their bronze mouths gaping. Three cavalry troops trotted out from behind the redoubt guarding the gate, as precise as a festival parade. Their mounts barely flicked an ear as the rampart guns fired a crashing volley. Jedfal's assembled defenders replied with a resounding cheer.

Reske watched Earl Padran calculating the chances of his travel-weary and wounded army defeating this array of fresh forces.

Reske really hoped Captain Grezel's chosen few had hunted down and slain any scouts who could tell the earl that mustering so many men and women in Jedfal had stripped the other Tane fortresses of all but a token guard. He hoped the shadowy folk who reported to Senon had silenced the spies who could have reported Hurat's townsfolk were moving helmets on poles and stuffed livery coats around their walls to create an illusion of defenders.

'Consider how bad your losses will be on your retreat to Hedvin, after you have tried and failed to rob us,' Maixen invited. 'Alternatively, you can lead your army back to Arafaze unharmed and pursue your quarrel with Lystro of Coylure elsewhere.'

Earl Padran rounded on him, wrathful. 'You're handing the crown to Alriad. You will live to regret that!'

'No, we're not, and no, we won't,' Maixen answered forcefully. 'I swear to you, the Earl of Coylure will quit Hurat lands as well or suffer the consequences. He's being told of Mervante's duplicity. He has our assurance we will not sell firing powder to you or anything else which we deny him. Do you think he'll try his luck and advance against Chalus? You know him better than I do. Or will he keep his current supply of powder dry and retreat with his army intact, ready to fight you on your return? Please, enjoy some wine while you think this through.'

Maixen didn't wait for any reply before he walked back inside the tent. Reske followed a few paces behind, as a good lackey should. Earl Padran and Baron Firio rejoined them to find Senon pouring wine into fresh goblets. Mistress Nindera had not left her chair, her expression unreadable. The young scrivener hastily resumed his seat and began writing.

Lord Firio emptied his goblet in a single swallow. Earl Padran picked up his wine and studied the garnet liquid through the faceted glass. Reske silently prayed to the God and the Goddess, and to any other power in this world or the intangible realm, that the earl didn't know something he and Maixen had overlooked. The grainlands were vast and trackless. A solitary Evarise horse and rider could have escaped Captain Grezel's vigilance.

Earl Padran put his wine down, untasted. 'You spoke of consequences if the Earl of Coylure refuses your offer?'

Maixen answered calmly. 'If he advances by land, every cannon along the Dore will blow his army to pieces. If he tries to ride the river downstream, our allies from the Mire assure me they can and will sink every barge that has his soldiers aboard.

Earl Padran cocked his head. 'You don't fear King Tadiri's retaliation, when he learns you have foiled his schemes? You truly think you can hold off Mervante without Arafaze aid?'

Reske saw he was genuinely curious.

'We trust in the Moon God and the Sun Goddess. They will defend us.' Maixen looked straight at Mistress Nindera.

Reske saw she understood him. Her lips thinned as she sought to hide her anger.

'So, my lord earl,' Maixen said briskly. 'Will you squander uncounted lives trying to seize lands which you will never be able to hold? You must know Hurat's people will resist an Arafaze occupation to their last breath? Why not go back to Hedvin before the equinox brings the autumn's rain? Wait in comfort until we see what Earl Lystro decides. If he tries to take Hurat, whoever wins that fight, your well-rested forces can attack the battered and bloodied victor before the first frosts. If Mervante's army sees you're victorious, they will march north as promised, and I imagine the Mire folk will desert us.'

Earl Padran allowed himself a reluctant half-smile. 'I sought opinions of your skills in Velasta. Do you know you are widely respected among those who command crown garrisons?'

'I am honoured by their good opinion.' Maixen bowed his head politely.

'I believe you are widely underestimated,' the earl said drily. He drank his wine and stood up. 'Very well. I will return to my encampment and you will have my answer by noon tomorrow. Meantime, I propose a truce to last until at least the dusk of the following day.'

'I agree, and thank you, my lord.' Maixen walked forward to shake the earl's hand.

The young scrivener was hastily packing his pens and papers away. Reske wouldn't give much for the chances those notes surviving unsmudged.

Senon reappeared in the tent's entrance with the visitors' cloaks. 'If you would follow me, my lord? Your horses will have been tended and watered, and food and drink offered to your escort.'

'Thank you. Good day, Castellan.' Earl Padran left the tent at Senon's side. The young scrivener sprang up to follow them.

'You will regret this day's work.' Firio vented his anger by sweeping his goblet off the table. The carpet denied him the satisfaction of it shattering. He took a step, ready to crush the crystal under his boot.

'Break that and I'll break your jaw,' Maixen said calmly.

Realising the castellan was serious, Lord Firio hurried out of the tent.

Mistress Nindera stood up. Maixen moved to block her path.

'We caught the killer you sent after Brother Alory. She didn't hurt him. We know why you wanted him dead. You're out to slaughter anyone who knows of the unseen world. But why did you have Margrave Vauset murdered?'

Reske watched Nindera intently. Would she claim the old margrave had hidden a talent for engaging with the intangible throughout his long life? Sister Jadewin insisted that was impossible. Which was well and good but didn't answer Maixen's question.

'Imbecile,' Nindera hissed with contempt. 'You have no idea what you're dealing with.'

She raised her left forearm, shaking back the lace at her cuff. Reske winced. He had seen maimed limbs before. This was different. Whenever, however, Mistress Nindera had lost her hand, no surgeon-priest had amputated whatever remained of her forearm, tidily sewing skin over sawn bone.

She thrust her uneven stump, scored with deep scars, at Maixen's face. 'Whatever you've been told about the intangible realm is not a hundredth of the truth. At best, the unreal can be barely contained. I have seen horrors the hidden brethren and the secret sisterhood cannot even imagine. I paid this price. Why do you think we abhor such magic, and those who use it so carelessly?'

She lowered her arm, tugging her cuff down to hide her injury. 'Pray you will be as fortunate as me when some nightmare escapes your complacent lover and slaughters innocents.'

Maixen didn't react. 'Why did you send that girl to murder Margrave Vauset?'

Nindera stared at the castellan as if he was some halfwit. 'He was the heart of Hurat's defiance. Without him, the nobility would yield. Princess Idelina must be crowned queen. Alriad will give the high temple's sisters free rein to browbeat the people with their conjured monsters. We have to end this lethal folly before countless people die. Now let me pass.'

Maixen didn't move. 'So you can murder more priests and priestesses?'

'A quick, clean death is more than these fools deserve for persisting in their arrogance. I will kill as many as I can.' Nindera laughed in the castellan's face. 'Are you going to call me before your assize for culling such vermin? What proof of my guilt can you show a justiciar when I refuse to answer your accusations? What witnesses can you call? Do you think the secret sisters and hidden brothers will let you drag their shameful deceits into the light?'

She narrowed her eyes. 'Do you think Earl Padran will let you detain me? Do you want to risk this truce which you have barely secured, after so much effort and loss? When you know you have no way to hold me?'

Maixen stepped aside. Gloating, Nindera left the tent.

Reske walked to the side table and poured himself some wine. He drank it and his stomach churned. 'She didn't ask about the girl.'

'She was a tool to be discarded.' Maixen joined him and reached for a glass. 'That woman used her because she knew she could see Alory's ... protector and attack the right priest. She never warned the poor child what the bird would do to defend him. In any case, Mother Finevre will never give her back.'

Senon appeared in the tent's doorway. Reske could see the master steward had questions about the steel-haired woman. He wished Maixen luck when the castellan tried to answer him truthfully without breaking faith with Jadewin and Alory.

'So,' Senon prompted. 'What now?'

'We get this furniture back to the margravine.' Maixen was admirably calm. 'Make sure that everyone in this camp, in the garrison and in Jedfal town stays alert. I'm confident Earl Padran will see it's in his best interests to return to Hedvin, but I wouldn't wager a bent copper penny on Firio of Ripat's good sense. He might try something spectacularly stupid.'

The castellan poured himself some wine. 'We'll doubtless have to wait until Earl Padran has learned what Earl Lystro has decided to do before we can be sure he will retreat. Then we return to Hurat at the fastest possible pace. I don't want King Tadiri making a fool of me by attacking because he learns the town is undefended.'

'I have every confidence in Mistress Quenild and Mistress Ticosa.' Senon turned to Reske. 'Your horse is ready, along with your gear.'

'Safe travels.' Maixen offered his hand. 'Send word as soon as you reach Velasta.'

Chapter Twenty-Nine

HURAT

28th Day of the Harvest Moon

Hurat's southernmost ferry tower came into view. Quenild heaved a heartfelt sigh of relief. They were nearly home, even if everything ahead was unfamiliar. She had never approached Hurat from this direction. She was also sick in every possible sense of travelling by road.

The first stretch of this journey had made her nauseous, as the coach followed the highway north from Gernet towards Sharrow. When they cut across the grainlands to shorten their route home, the rocking on rutted tracks had been ten times worse. Quenild would never again mock anyone whose stomach rebelled at river travel. At least sitting beside the coach's driver meant fewer stops for her to vomit into a ditch.

Ticosa was still travelling inside, making friends. Other passengers came and went when the coach stopped in the small towns to find refreshments and to harness fresh horses. No one had news of warfare sweeping down the Dore or the Tane. They were more interested in the equinox feasts and fairs. At least she and Ticosa would be home for the holiday, even if two days would give them scant time to prepare.

Across the great river, Hurat seemed peaceful enough. Though Quenild wasn't sure what catastrophe would look like, short of pillars of smoke and flames. Had Castellan

Maixen succeeded in whatever plan he had made when their news from the Mire had reached him? Assuming the news had reached him. Scefet's Captain Walsint had needed a lot of convincing to trust the Mire folk, and more still to accept their offer to escort his messenger on the fastest possible route through the high ground between the marsh and the grainlands.

Quenild trusted the Mire folk. Even so, that small party could have fallen foul of a landslip, storm-toppled trees or some other unforeseen disaster as they travelled those secret paths and passes. Lord Romer of Sharrow's men could have caught them, searching for their Mervantese allies.

She knew what Ticosa would say. There was no way to know, so there was no point in fretting. They had done all they could to help Hurat. Had it been enough? Quenild felt queasy again. She had not realised how many people lived outside the walls on the southern bank of the Dore. Tending their small holdings on either side of the highway, they would be easy prey for Mervante.

At long, long last, the coach reached the paved square by the chain ferry's tower. The driver pulled up the weary horses, and the lad who rode precariously on the roof unhooked the net spread over the travellers' bags and chests.

'Here we are,' the driver said cheerfully.

'Thank you.' Quenild did her best to sound grateful as she climbed down.

'I'll take that.' Ticosa snapped her fingers to get the lad's attention, reaching up for her blue leather bag.

'That's ours as well.' Quenild retrieved their second bag.

'Let me take those for you.'

Both women were startled to see Hurat's castle steward.

'The castellan's compliments and his apologies, but he must see you at once.' Master Senon sounded honestly sorry, but insistent. 'He needs the latest news from Gernet.'

'We'll see him after we have been home. I need a bath and fresh clothes,' Ticosa was equally emphatic.

Quenild saw the other coach passengers watching the three of them with keen curiosity. 'How did you know we would arrive today?'

Senon shrugged. 'People tell me things.'

Quenild saw passers-by slowing to listen. Everyone was avid for news. She reached for Ticosa's hand. 'Let's get this done and dusted. I'd rather not go home just to go out again.'

'All right. If we must.' Ticosa made no attempt to hide her irritation.

They walked to the ferry. Senon strode on ahead. Quenild and Ticosa followed him to the upper deck's benches. As the ferry began the slow crossing, being on the water reminded Quenild…

'Master Steward? Did *The Beech Tree* get back safe from the Mire?'

'Safe and sound,' he assured her. 'Ristal has your cargo stored in your warehouse.'

'Cargo?' Quenild didn't understand. They had left the barge empty at Scefet, when she and Ticosa had started their journey south to Avelsir in the lightweight Mire boats.

Senon reached inside his doublet and handed her a sheaf of paper. Quenild scanned neatly written columns listing substantial quantities of the Mire's rarest roots and herbs. Their broker's fee for trading three castles to the marsh dwellers left her lost for words.

Ticosa smiled sunnily. 'I did a little business while you, Captain Walsint and our new friends were discussing how best to alert Gernet's garrison without making King Tadiri's spies suspicious.'

Quenild didn't know what to say. All these years together, and the woman she loved could still amaze her.

The chain ferry reached the Hurat bank and they walked through the town. Their route took them tantalisingly close to home, but Senon was forging ahead carrying their bags. The women shared a rueful glance. Oh well, once the castellan heard their news, they would be free to do as they wished. Quenild savoured the prospect of time alone with Ticosa behind their own locked door. Bathed and perfumed, they would have no one to please but each other.

Soon enough they crossed the footbridge and went into the castle. Quenild would never have believed doing this could become so routine. In the castellan's tower, Master Senon left their bags with a young soldier and ushered them up to the audience chamber. Maixen sat at his long table, studying a letter. More despatches were stacked at his elbow.

Ticosa wasted no time. 'Well?'

The castellan looked up. 'The Arafaze earls have withdrawn from Hedvin and from Bastrys. Every scout's report convinces me they'll fight each other next spring, if nothing else decides whose queen claims the crown, but they'll do that on Arafaze land.'

Quenild had more urgent concerns. 'Is the Gorge open to trade? Will temples in Hedvin and beyond record purchases and payments? Will the black brothers validate contracts and hold copies in their archives?'

Maixen gathered his papers into a neat stack. 'Bastrys is no longer interfering with anyone's free passage up and down the Dore. Baron Zavire can't defy his Arafaze neighbours' fury about that any longer, without the Earl of Coylure's support. He also seems to have fallen foul of the new temple mother elected by the Bastrys sisters, but that is the Goddess's business. Mother Finevre assures me Hurat's sisters are reconciling transactions with temple records across Arafaze as they have always done. Father Memlin says the God's servants have resumed their former duties.'

Maixen left the table and walked towards the fireplace. 'Please, take a seat. I apologise for sending Senon to bring you here, before you could recover from your journey. Baroness Karlin of Evesk and Margrave Satrel of Stannar are expected any time today. Apparently decisions vital for Hurat's future must be made. I need to know how matters stand in every direction before they arrive.'

'What decisions?' Quenild demanded as she and Ticosa sat on the sofa.

'They didn't say.' Maixen leaned back against a window sill. 'Please, what exactly did you do in Gernet?'

'Someone had to warn your garrison captain to watch the road to the south.' Ticosa's grin dimpled her cheeks. 'The Mire folk convinced us any Mervantese trader going up and down the highway or spending time in Gernet would also be King Tadiri's spy. Any courier arriving with an urgent message from the marsh fortresses would be taken as proof Hurat's castellan had got wind of their master's plans. That would most likely provoke King Tadiri to attack.'

Quenild took her wife's hand. 'But who would look twice at two respectable merchants with a reputation for seeking out new markets and partners?'

'The Mire folk took us by boat to Avelsir and guided us across the grasslands to Gernet,' Ticosa explained. 'Your garrison captain had already fended off more than enough hostile Mervantese activity to make him suspicious of the weasel king's intentions.'

Quenild continued. 'He heard us out, and realised he was caught in a quandary. Preparations to hold off a determined assault couldn't be hidden. That in itself risked provoking the Mervantese to try seizing the town before its defences were complete. Any messenger he sent to Hurat to ask for your orders was sure to be pursued and killed. He had already lost two riders, found dead on the highway to Sharrow. Whatever letters they had carried were doubtless in the weasel king's hands.'

Maixen grimaced. 'It seems I did King Tadiri a disservice. I am in your debt.'

'We persuaded your captain to sit on his hands while we talked to the Mervantese traders visiting Gernet.' Ticosa widened guileless eyes. 'They were most interested in recent rumours from Hurat. Especially that we had heard Arafaze's rival earls were withdrawing from Bastrys and from Hedvin.'

'Did they believe you?' The castellan was curious.

'It didn't matter if they believed we'd floated down the Dore on an oak leaf.' Ticosa's dimples came and went. 'We'd be long gone before they learned different, but we reckoned that news might give King Tadiri pause for thought.'

Maixen was amused. 'He'll think he had a lucky escape. Until he sits and counts the days.'

Quenild was more interested in what lay ahead. 'What do you think he'll do now?'

'With luck, not a thing.' The castellan paused, looking out of the tower window. 'Both the princesses know about his double-dealing. Neither Earl Padran nor Earl Lystro will trust Tadiri again. He should think long and hard before attacking the Mire now the Mire folk hold those castles.'

'What do the nobles of the Dore and the Tane think about that?' Ticosa glanced guiltily at her wife.

Quenild shrugged. The castellan had said he was willing to pay any price.

Maixen rubbed a hand over his hair. 'I imagine that's one of the things Baroness Karlin and Margrave Satrel wish to discuss.'

A knock rattled the door and Senon came in. Two servants followed. The maid set out tea glasses and a tall silver pot on the low table in front of the fireplace while the lackey arranged plates of sweet and savoury pastries. A few moments later, the Baroness of Evesk and the Margrave of Stannar entered the room.

'Excuse us.' Ticosa rose to her feet.

Quenild stood almost as fast. 'We will leave you to your business.'

'Please, stay.' Baroness Karlin raised a hand. 'Senon tells us you are well-regarded and trusted by Hurat's merchants and artisans. Our business concerns everyone in Hurat town and the wider fiefdom. You may well have insights to contribute.'

She was smiling, so Quenild guessed the nobility weren't calling for Maixen to be flogged. She and Ticosa sat down again. The margrave and the baroness settled themselves in cushioned chairs as Senon served silver tea and pastries. Maixen was still standing by the window, apprehensive.

'I gather you have news from Gernet?' Margrave Satrel prompted him.

'There's no sign of a Mervantese advance. King Tadiri will know by now the garrison captain is fully prepared to repel his assault.'

Quenild braced herself for questions. Ticosa sat straight-backed and alert.

'Good.' Margrave Satrel moved swiftly on. 'Now, Castellan, as everyone knows, your oaths to the Arafaze crown died with King Venais. The bloodline of Hurat's earls is extinct, which leaves this town and the fiefdom without a suzerain. This cannot continue, for the sake of everyone's safety. We have discussed the matter at some length.'

His gesture took in Baroness Karlin and by implication the rest of the province's nobility. 'We all of us have spare sons and daughters, but we have agreed that no bloodline has a greater claim than any other to this town which King Ganirin built. Besides, if any of us claimed Hurat, there's every chance the townsfolk would resent being ridden over roughshod.'

Quenild nodded emphatic agreement. So did Ticosa.

Baroness Karlin inclined her head to acknowledge both women. 'But someone must command the garrison which guards this vital crossing, and oversee so much more. Law and justice must be upheld within Hurat's walls. After much thought and discussion, we have come to a decision.'

'Who will I have the honour to serve?' Maixen asked, impassive.

Margrave Satrel laughed. 'I owe you a saddle horse, Karlin.'

The baroness clapped her hands to get Maixen's attention. 'We want you, you fool. Who else has the garrisons' confidence? Who else will Hurat's townsfolk trust?'

'We can't be certain an Arafaze army won't return to threaten us some day, however this strife for the crown plays out,' the margrave said forcefully. 'You proved yourself by driving off Evarise and Coylure with the fewest losses possible. We trust you to do it again.'

'Though we believe Idelina and Alriad and their factions will tread warily, as long as you hold this castle and command the Vale of Hurat's garrisons.' Baroness Karlin reached for her tea. 'Setting you aside for an untested commander would be as good as inviting Padran or Coylure to try their luck. Not to mention encouraging King Tadiri of Mervante to probe for any weakness. We also have yet to learn if the Mire folk can be trusted.'

'What say you, Lord Maixen?' the margrave demanded.

The castellan was stunned. 'Lord?'

'Though we could not agree whether you should be acclaimed as a baron or a margrave,' Baroness Karlin mused.

Margrave Satrel grinned. 'So we decided to acclaim you as the new Earl of Hurat.'

Quenild thought Maixen looked like a man who'd been slapped in the face with a fish.

'Then no one leading an army from Arafaze can claim they outrank you. But we will not be swearing fealty to you.' Baroness Karlin finished her tea and put the glass on the table. 'I consulted Mistress Zile about the first settlement made with Ganirin of Arafaze, when he was acclaimed Earl of Hurat. She told me something interesting. According to her records, that title merely signified Ganirin would have unquestioned command when an army was mustered from the different fiefdoms across the vale. That ensured a single voice would guide tactics and strategy in time of crisis. It was only later that nobles already sworn to King Ganirin reclaimed the towns of the Dore and bound themselves to the Arafaze crown with new oaths of fealty.'

'You will be our equal, not our overlord,' Margrave Satrel said bluntly. 'Is that agreed?'

Maixen was still speechless.

Baroness Karlin continued, brisk. 'Let us say so, in principle at least. Mistress Zile will prepare an official proclamation for the first morning of the equinox holiday, together with letters to be sent to every garrison and town with full details of this new settlement. Copies will be displayed in every sanctuary, shrine and temple.'

The margrave turned to Quenild and Ticosa. 'We will be most grateful if you could look over the terms we propose, to make sure this new settlement serves the best interests of Hurat's townsfolk. You must not hesitate to raise any concerns.'

Now it was their turn to nod, lost for words.

'You will swear your oaths before Mother Finevre and Father Memlin, to be recorded, signed and sealed in the presence of the God and the Goddess. Copies of that document, and of this new settlement, will be sent to Velasta's high shrine, and high temple, as well as to the royal court archive,' Baroness Karlin concluded with evident satisfaction.

'Indeed.' Maixen was still stunned.

Quenild reached for her glass and savoured the silver tea's fragrance. It was hard to believe the dangers of this fraught year had finally passed by without the threatened storm breaking over their heads. Doubtless, Hurat would face new challenges, but after the equinox the Stag Moon would bring colder weather. The pace of life would slow into the quieter days of the Frost Moon. Peace should prevail at least until the ice broke next spring, and hopefully for longer. After that, Hurat should be well placed to face whatever the future might hold.

Then she remembered the question she'd intended to ask when they'd come into the room. 'Castellan, where's Alory?'

Chapter Thirty

VELASTA

17th Day of the Frost Moon

Rain spattered against the glass. The sky outside the pantry window was leaden. Velasta got the worst of all weathers, as far as Alory saw. Over halfway through the Frost Moon, and while the puddles on the terrace hadn't actually frozen, the days and nights were bitterly cold. The damp chill seeped into his bones.

Still, he shouldn't grumble. He spent most of his time indoors helping the Earl of Shirlat's housekeeper. He stepped carefully down from the stool and put the last of the sweet preserves from the back of the pantry's highest shelves on the table.

Mistress Hunys looked up from listing overlooked jars. 'Bless the Golden Mother for giving you such long arms.'

'What can I do for you now?' Hunys reminded Alory of his aunts, even if she was short and round and red-haired.

She considered this. 'Dust the plasterwork in the salons? You should be able to reach the ceilings and the cornices if I tie a feather duster to a broom handle.'

Before Alory could answer, they heard a key unlock the outer door at the side of the house. Reske took no chances.

'I'll swing the kettle over the heat.' Hunys put down her pen and stood up.

She met Reske in the doorway. He kissed her cheek.

'Any letters?'

'Not so far today. Let me have that cloak before you drip everywhere.' She reached under his chin, unfastening the clasp. 'Did you wipe your boots?'

'Always.' As Hunys went into the kitchen, Reske looked at Alory. 'I've found her.'

'Good.' Alory drew a resolute breath. This was why they had come to Velasta.

'She—' Reske broke off as they heard Jadewin greet Hunys in the kitchen.

The priestess came into the pantry. 'Is anyone watching the house?'

Reske shook his head. 'Not at the moment. They're strolling past, morning and evening, same as before.'

Alory was relieved. They were taking every precaution to convince royal spies, or anyone else who might be curious, that the Earl of Shirlat's residence remained shuttered, with only a handful of servants getting on with tasks best done while the mansion was empty. These servants were as loyal to Earl Debin as Reske, and they trusted him without asking questions about visitors from Hurat.

'How did you get on?' Jadewin asked him urgently.

'I've found her.' Reske looked at Alory. 'Are you ready?'

'As soon as I've washed my hands.' He showed them his grimy palms, hoping his grin hid his nervousness.

Jadewin's face was serious. 'The sooner we get this done the better. Princess Idelina is on her way back from Astyrie. She'll arrive in four or five days.'

Alory didn't doubt Jadewin's sources. The priestess left the house most days. Wearing her pale wool robe, she didn't have to sneak about like Reske. No passer-by would wonder why a sister might call at a servants' door.

'Are you ready?' Reske asked her intently.

'We are.' Jadewin's face was implacable. 'No matter what you learn today.'

Alory was already walking through to the scullery. He found Mistress Hunys emptying the kettle into a basin.

'Since you won't be waiting for tea.'

'Thank you.' The kitchen fire had barely warmed the water, but that helped the soap to lather. With his hands washed and dried, Alory went back to the others. Jadewin offered him a dry cloak.

'Thank you.' Alory was grateful Earl Debin had a nephew as tall and broad as himself. He hoped he would be able to thank the earl one day.

Reske was shrugging on his damp cloak. Alory followed him to the side door, fastening silver clasps under his own chin. He found fur-lined gloves in an inside pocket and gratefully pulled them on.

Outside in the yard, Reske turned towards the terrace behind the house. Alory followed him down the steps at the side, and along the edge of the ornamental garden where the noble family would take the air or entertain. A gate opened onto the narrow alley separating Shirlat land from the residence behind. Reske broke into a jog. Alory did the same.

Reske took a turn into a different alley, then another, and a third. Alory didn't try to keep track. He had studied maps of Velasta in Mistress Hunys's sitting room and he still couldn't get his bearings. His aunts had told him the city was huge, but he hadn't truly understood what that meant. Now he understood why Reske and Jadewin told him not to leave Earl Debin's house on his own.

If he lost sight of Reske, he'd never find his way back. Alory ran faster to catch up. Soon after, Reske slowed to a walk, and Alory saw a wide road ahead.

'How much further?'

'A fair distance,' Reske admitted. 'Aren't you glad of a chance to stretch your legs?'

Alory supposed so. 'The fresh air is welcome.'

Thankfully, it was barely raining. Even so, Alory could feel the cold seeping through dampness across his shoulders by the time Reske started looking warily around. Alory would have done the same walking these streets. Perversely, he felt more at home. Filthy gutters and grim-faced passers-by reminded him of Hurat's waterfronts, even if they were nowhere near a river.

Reske nudged him into an alley. 'See that tavern across the way?'

Alory studied the unsavoury drinking den. Ristal would tell him to steer well clear of such a place. His father would go straight through the door. 'She's inside?'

'She was earlier.' Reske stared at the tavern. 'Hopefully hiring brutes to hunt you, if Brother Belid's letter did its work.'

'Right.' Alory clenched his fists inside the earl's nephew's expensive gloves. They had discussed this plan time and again. 'Which way am I going?'

'Down there.' Reske's forefinger stabbed the damp air. 'Past the covered market.'

'Right.' Alory crossed the street, dodging between wagons and drays. He resisted the urge to look back at the alley's mouth. Reske would already be gone.

He pushed the tavern door open. Yes, his father would like this dismal hole. Sitting at a corner table, Mistress Nindera was totally out of place. The ruffians with her, two men and a woman, were right at home.

Nindera stared at him, too startled to hide her shock. Even without his priest's black robe, she recognised him at once. Alory didn't have to feign his own apprehension when their gazes met. No matter how often they had discussed this plan, something unforeseen could happen.

A fist thumped his shoulder, hard. 'In or out, shit for brains! Stop blocking the pissing door!'

Alory stepped back from the threshold to let the irate drunkard pass. Inside, chairs scraped the floorboards. Voices rose. They were coming after him. Which way was he supposed to go? That's right. Past the covered market.

He walked towards the sailcloth awnings over the multiple entrances to the wide hall. He mustn't go too fast or Nindera's ruffians would lose track of him. If he walked too slowly, they would get suspicious. Until Reske had warned him of such possibilities, Alory wouldn't have thought he could mess up being bait.

He sidestepped and dodged through the crowd on the footway. He passed the market and looked ahead, searching for the second turning on the right. Did those narrow alleys cutting between the wood and brick buildings count?

Alory glanced along the first alley and saw how many windows overlooked it. Being seen wasn't part of the plan. He carried on walking. His neck itched worse than a shirt full of lice, but he didn't look back. He mustn't do anything to make Nindera or her brutes suspicious. Reske had stressed that time and again.

Alory crossed the first side-street and walked faster. The sooner this was done, the better. The second street was pocked with rain-filled potholes. Workshops, emporiums and warehouses had been built shoulder to shoulder on his right-hand side. Those were more or less in good repair. On the other side of the road, broken barrels and split and splintered crates had been dumped among the tumbledown stables. Battered carts resting on scavenged bricks waited for someone who might or might not return to rescue them with mended wheels.

An improbably pearlescent cat appeared. Alory crossed the street. The cat, luminous as moonlight, trotted into an alley between the derelict stables. Alory followed it to a yard where huts and makeshift hovels made a maze for the homeless to hide in.

The cat vanished. Alory walked more slowly. He could smell a midden close by, as well as some hole used for a latrine. He didn't want to stumble into those unawares. He listened for any hint of the brutes coming up behind him.

When they had put this plan together, the young priest had wondered aloud why hirelings would follow him into a space which could so easily become a trap. Reske insisted caution would be outweighed by fear of Mistress Nindera's wrath, along with greed for her promised payment. She would seize this opportunity to have him killed.

A muffled grunt of mingled surprise and pain proved Reske was right. Alory turned to see Earl Debin's man with a gang of determined men and women, overpowering the ruffians from the tavern. Open hut doors showed where his allies had been hiding.

One swept a man's feet out from under him with a low, scything kick. The ruffian barely hit the mud before a second attacker rolled him onto his belly, wrenching his hands behind his back. The brute was gagged and swiftly trussed like a hog for the butcher. The other two hirelings had been subdued with equal ruthlessness.

Black-robed priests wearing silver masks had surged out of their hiding place to pin Mistress Nindera to the ground. An unknown brother deftly gagged her and dragged a black cloth bag over her head. A second priest knelt on the small of her back, looping rope tight around her elbows to bind her arms together.

Nindera fought them, twisting her body and kicking viciously. A third priest grabbed her boots and hauled her ankles off the ground. She wasn't wearing a scrivener's robe today. Her respectable matron's russet skirts slid back, revealing thick woollen stockings. A fourth brother tied her feet together.

Alory was relieved on several counts. No one could know if Nindera would come with her hirelings to see him killed for herself. Reske had been ready to follow her if she had left the tavern and gone a different way. They would have had to try to snare her some other time. Alory muttered a prayer of thanks to the Moon God for sparing them that.

The black-clad priests stepped back, dropping Mistress Nindera on the ground. Reske's allies dragged the trussed ruffians around so they could see their captured pay-mistress writhing furiously. The hidden brethren's instructions had been precise. Nindera's hirelings were to be gagged, but not blindfolded.

The priests stood in a line behind her. Their silver masks stared at the brutes. Alory saw his would-be killers' eyes bulge as a black carriage with curtained windows arrived, driven by another robed and masked priest.

The carriage pulled up. The brother who had hooded Nindera opened the door. The other three lifted her up and threw her inside. They climbed in and closed the door. The priest holding the reins guided the black horse carefully around the huts and hovels as the carriage left the yard.

Reske drew a knife. The bound woman made a choking sound, terrified. One of the men pissed himself. The other closed his eyes with a despairing moan.

'Don't be a fool,' Reske said, contemptuous. 'The Father of Night knows who's to blame.'

The three ruffians stared up with desperate hope. Reske reached down to cut the rope binding the moaning man's ankles.

'You may go. Make better choices in future. The Moon God will be watching.'

He freed the feet of the other two, sheathed his knife and led the Velastans away. Alory went with them, leaving the brutes lying in the filth, still gagged and with their hands bound. The priests had specified that as well.

As they reached the side-street, out of sight of the yard, the oldest man among the Velastans chuckled. 'My blood hasn't raced like that since I left the courier service.'

'You haven't lost your touch.' Reske reached inside his doublet and tossed him a heavy purse.

A young woman studied Alory, avid with curiosity. 'So who is—?'

'None of that,' the old man warned. 'Those fools aren't the only ones the Keeper of Secrets will be watching.'

He pointed past the young woman. A second black carriage waited further along the side-street.

Reske offered the older man his hand. 'Thanks again.'

The retired courier shook. 'I'm not asking questions, but I'll pray for good news before long.'

'And drink to better days ahead?' one of the younger men wondered hopefully.

The older man weighed the purse in his hand. Coin clinked. 'I think so.'

Alory waited with Reske as the Velastans walked off. 'I don't think we should keep our ride waiting.'

'No.' Reske walked towards the carriage. The masked priest holding the black horse's reins looked straight ahead. Alory was uncomfortably aware of awe-struck passers-by staring at the silent brother. Ill-disguised fear on some faces betrayed guilty consciences.

Reske opened the curtained door. 'After you.'

As soon as Reske joined him in the dimness, the carriage started moving. Alory realised they had reached the main road when he felt their speed picking up. He wondered where they were going. Did Reske know? Probably not. Either way, Alory didn't ask. Given the capital's sprawl, he settled in for a lengthy trip. Instead, the journey ended sooner than he expected.

'I'd say we've gone about two thirds of a league.' Reske reached for the swaying curtain before he caught himself, and folded his arms.

The coach moved slowly forward and stopped again. Alory heard the solid thud of a heavy bar securing gates. He looked uncertainly at Reske. 'Should we—?'

The silver-masked coachman opened the carriage door. Stepping out, Alory saw they were in the courtyard of a building very like the Tane Ferry Fever Hall back in Hurat.

A second priest stood beside the one who had driven them here. He offered Alory a long black robe and a silver mask.

Neither priest said a word. Alory stripped off his gloves and cloak, handing them to Reske. He hoped these silent brothers didn't see his hands were shaking. Putting on the mask and robe, he raised the hood. The robe was a perfect fit.

'I'll leave these in here, shall I?' Getting no answer, Reske shrugged and tossed the earl's nephew's cloak into the carriage and shut the door.

The two priests walked towards an entrance. Alory followed, and Reske followed him. They went into a sizeable hall and Alory barely swallowed a yelp when a masked priest stepped close and gripped his elbow. As he instinctively pulled away, his new black brother's hold tightened. The unknown priest's gesture indicated two vacant chairs at the end of the seats running around the walls. Regularly spaced candle lanterns burned above the hooded and masked brothers' heads.

Alory left the end chair for Reske and sat beside another unknown brother. The silent priest beckoned Reske. The Velastan pushed his cloak back off his shoulders and took his seat.

Mistress Nindera sat, shoulders hunched, on a chair in the centre of the room. She had the black bag over her head, though her arms had been freed. Her hand cupped her maimed arm's elbow. Her feet were hobbled with rope which would allow her a short stride if she dared to take it.

A priest rose from the seats opposite the door. 'You have been brought before the hidden brethren for judgement.'

Alory didn't recognise his voice, although that was no great surprise. He watched, tense, as another masked brother stood, walked over and pulled the bag off Nindera's head.

She blinked and squinted. Her steel-grey hair hung untidily around her shoulders as whatever combs or pins had secured it had been lost. She straightened her back and glared, defiant, at the priest who'd removed the hood. She didn't flinch when he produced a knife. Though Alory noticed she held very still when he slid the gleaming blade beneath the cloth tight against her cheek.

As soon as he cut through the gag, she ripped it away. 'I do not recognise your authority.'

The priest walking back to his seat showed no sign he had heard her. Other voices spoke from different sides of the room, cold and implacable.

'You conspired to murder the Moon God's faithful servants.'

'You coerced others to do your killing.'

'You committed the same offences against the Sun Goddess and her daughters.'

Nindera's lip curled in a sneer. 'You have no proof. You cannot—'

'Earl Debin's man!' A commanding voice overrode her. 'You served as a crown courier for more than twenty years, did you not?'

Reske stood up. 'I did.'

While his voice was steady, Alory saw the Velastan knot his fingers tight in the small of his back.

'As a courier, you were trained to recall and repeat confidential messages word for word?'

'That is correct.'

That was news to Alory.

'What did this woman who faces our judgement say to Castellan Maixen of Hurat?'

Reske lifted his chin, looking straight ahead.

'A quick, clean death is more than these fools deserve for persisting in their arrogance. I will kill as many as I can. Are you going to call me before your assize for culling such vermin? What proof of my guilt can you show a justiciar when I refuse to answer your accusations? What witnesses can you call? Do you think the secret sisters and hidden brothers will let you drag their shameful deceits into the light?'

Alory had no idea that a courier conveyed every intonation of the words they were ordered to echo. Even in Reske's voice, Mistress Nindera's icy disdain rang around the room. The young priest sensed magic in the air. These brothers were testing Reske's words with the enchantments Brother Talaven had taught him. Now the hidden brethren knew Reske told them no lies.

'That is sufficient. You may sit.'

Reske retreated to his chair. Alory saw the relief in his shoulders.

Nindera stood up. 'You have no—'

'You have not done this alone,' a voice behind her thundered.

Four brothers sprang to their feet, two on either side of the hall. Each pair seized the startled priest sitting between them.

They dragged their struggling brothers forward and threw them face down on the flagstones. The accused men froze as stern voices declared their offences.

'Brother Iseth. You have betrayed the Moon God, your brothers and our vows for gold and to serve your own ambition.'

'Brother Styred. You have betrayed the Moon God, your brothers and our vows out of fear and to save your own neck.'

Nindera sank onto her chair. 'You cannot—'

A door opened in the furthest corner of the hall. Alory hadn't even noticed it in the shadows. A masked and hooded priest entered, carrying a small table. Another followed with a coffer in his hands. The first priest placed the table in front of Nindera. The second put down the coffer and opened the lid. He took out three sheathed daggers and three cloth-wrapped bundles, all much the same size.

The brothers who had seized the first priest stepped forward to strip the accused of his robe and mask. In black doublet and breeches, the man crouched low on his hands and knees, his forehead on the cold floor. His rapid breaths rasped in the silence.

'Choose, Iseth,' a voice commanded. 'The needle or the knife.'

The accused man, Iseth, no longer anyone's brother, got slowly to his feet. He walked to the table, cowering as if he expected a beating, even though nobody came near him. He stood for a long moment, trembling, before he reached out, picked something up, and walked slowly towards the inner door. The priests who had seized him followed. Alory saw he had taken the dagger.

'Choose, Styred,' a different voice ordered. 'The needle or the knife.'

Alory knew this was entirely beside the point, but he couldn't help wondering how the hidden brethren decided who was going to say what, and when, in a meeting like this.

The second accused man didn't wait to be stripped of his robe and mask, handing them to his closest captor. He strode forward, took a cloth bundle from the table and walked towards the open door, straight-backed. Alory saw glistening tears on his cheeks. Reske stirred beside him, but before Shirlat's man could whisper a question, another merciless voice rang out.

'Nindera Kyse. The Sun Goddess and the Moon God grant us life, and they sanction death for those who shed innocent blood. Only you know the depths of your guilt. You may choose to pay the ultimate price, or you may hope to escape the vengeance of the unseen realm.'

'I – I don't understand.' For the first time, she sounded unsure.

A masked priest by the open door walked forward. He unwrapped the cloth bundle the man Iseth had left untouched. Alory still couldn't see what it was in it, but Nindera recoiled as if she had seen a scorpion.

'You – you—' She retreated, stumbling as the rope hobbled her stride. Knocking over her chair, she clutched her maimed forearm. 'You cannot—'

'Choose now,' a voice commanded, 'Or be confined until you do.'

Nindera was shaking her head, still backing away. Alory realised she was terrified. Priests rose from their seats, advancing to surround her. The steel-haired woman snatched the dagger from the table.

'You fools!' She circled slowly, threatening the oncoming brothers with the gleaming blade. 'You utter fools. You think you will escape when monsters tear down the veil and overrun this world? I only wish I could see you all die.'

Nindera slashed her own neck, under her ear. Blood sprayed high in the air. Masked priests rushed forward as she collapsed. A moment later, they carried her off through the inner door. Some of the brothers followed the captives. Most left through the door into the courtyard.

As the hall emptied, Alory had no idea what he should do. Soon he was surrounded by empty chairs, with Reske and one hooded brother. Blood smeared the flagstones between Nindera's chair and the table.

The priest pushed back his hood and untied his mask to reveal his deeply lined face. 'Thank you. Let us hope that's an end to this.'

Alory took off his own mask. 'What will happen to the man who chose the needle, brother?'

'I'm Terius.' The old priest offered his hand.

This was who Brother Belid had written to, sharing the crimes Hurat's hidden brethren had discovered. For a moment, Alory thought the older priest wasn't going to answer him.

Then he shrugged. 'What do you know of the nomads who roam the high plateau? Since you're from Hurat.'

'Very little,' Alory admitted. 'My aunts say they have no interest in trade. Idiots convinced they can persuade them to buy their special goods disappear or turn up dead and dismembered.'

He remembered something else. 'Don't they use needles to drive inked patterns under their skin.'

'Quite so.' Brother Terius walked to the table and unrolled one of the bundles.

Alory and Reske followed, careful to avoid the blood on the floor. The cloth held a selection of steel instruments with right-angled heads which bristled with varying numbers of needle-sharp points. Alory guessed the little hammer was used to hit their flat backs, to make those spikes pierce flesh. A block of solid ink had a faint blue sheen and brush marks showed where it had been moistened.

'This substance and these patterns make the nomads visible to creatures in the intangible world. Each clan has its own protector, designated by a specific design. Evidently the monsters rarely trespass on another's claim.' Brother Terius wrapped up the sharp instruments. 'They will, however, pursue anyone else they find marked and without a protector. We have found this a fitting punishment for brethren who betray their vows to safeguard the unseen world's secrets.'

His glance at Reske made it clear this applied to other people besides priests. Alory wondered how Mistress Nindera had learned what a nomad's inked skin signified. What else did she know that made death at her own hand preferable to such a fate?

Reske grimaced. 'There's no escape?'

Brother Terius shrugged again. 'Perhaps, if one travelled far enough to find a place completely deserted in both realms of existence.'

Earl Debin's man tried to hide a shiver and moved on swiftly. 'We have delivered Mistress Nindera to face the Moon God's justice as agreed. She can no longer influence Princess Idelina. Now the Sun Goddess's daughters must deal with those who have tempted Princess Alriad with promises of magic. We need you to give up Sister Hasrine.'

'As agreed.' Though a faint crease appeared between Brother Terius's grey brows. 'Provided she has not already made her choice between the needle and the knife.'

Chapter Thirty-One

VELASTA

18th Day of the Frost Moon

Jadewin watched the priestesses usher the last few worshippers out of the high temple. As one slammed the brass-sheathed doors, Jadewin wondered if the sister was venting her wrath over what she had heard. But was she angered by their temple mother's supposed betrayal, or furious on Elyka's behalf?

Jadewin walked along the corridor to the inner sanctum. Here in the capital, the Sun Goddess's massive gold and ivory statue stood under a glass and metal dome. As large as the room was, the heart of the high temple was crowded. Velasta's priestesses were eager to see who had written the first letter accusing their leader of misjudgement and malfeasance. Many more screeds had followed, leaving the high priestess with no choice. Mother Elyka must face her accusers or step down.

For a wonder at this season, the morning was clear and cloudless. The dome's windows were bright and sunshine filled the sanctum. Jadewin could see many more unfamiliar faces than she expected. Granted, she had set off for Hurat nearly a full year ago, but it seemed more women than usual had taken vows while she was away. Her stomach lurched with dread. Had the renegades recruited them, sharing their underhand schemes to give the crown to Princess Alriad? Would these newcomers support Mother Elyka regardless of anything anyone might say?

But this vote was the fastest way to remove the renegade from office without having to gather every priestess with knowledge of the unseen world from across Arafaze. Jadewin's trusted friends in the secret sisterhood, still true to their vows, assured her Elyka's renegades outnumbered them by some margin in Velasta.

Besides, while a full assembly of the secret sisterhood would undoubtedly condemn her, their verdict could never be shared. Elyka must be publicly disowned by the high temple's sisters to be discredited in court circles. Earl Lystro and Princess Alriad would have unarguable reasons to shun her after that.

Jadewin walked up to the golden bowl at the Goddess's feet. The silence was absolute as she knelt and sorted through the letters. Finding the one she had written, Jadewin rose and repeated her accusations calmly and clearly.

'As the Goddess's servants, we swear to stay out of any and all secular rivalries for power and influence. We swear never to use our knowledge of any individual's finances as a weapon against them. We swear we will not distort or manipulate trade for any purpose, no matter how noble those aims might seem. Our sister Elyka has done all these things and worse. She has persuaded sisters from this temple to conspire with her, and become forsworn. She has advanced Princess Alriad's claim to the Arafaze crown with no proof that this cause is righteous. She has promoted division and provoked quarrels where she should seek to heal rifts and find compromise. Sister Elyka is not fit to lead us as temple mother in Velasta or anywhere else.'

Elyka stepped forward from a knot of sisters behind the mighty statue. Jadewin waited with an expression of polite interest.

The older priestess was pale and the looseness of her clothing showed she had lost weight. It was generally believed the high temple mother had barely survived a life-threatening bout of onion-skin fever. Jadewin had tried to track that assertion to its source, but it had arisen in several places. Proving the story was a lie would take time and effort she could not spare.

Jadewin knew Elyka's recovery from her wounds had been slow and draining. Several friends among the secret sisters in Velasta wondered if the malice that fuelled the Lightning King's apparition could have caused some infection. Jadewin didn't know and she didn't care. The unyielding determination in Elyka's eyes was undimmed. This was the threat.

The older priestess addressed her sisters confidently. 'Princess Idelina has rejected the Sun Goddess's love and protection. She is capricious, unpredictable, spiteful. She shows no interest in the governance of this realm. You have seen how shamefully she has treated Earl Debin of Shirlat and his heirs. She is wholly unfit to be monarch.'

'Which is no concern of ours.' Unfortunately Jadewin saw too many faces around the sanctum seemed to disagree.

'Are we not sworn to promote peace and prosperity in the Golden Mother's service?' Elyka retorted. 'Princess Alriad's reign as queen would deliver these blessings to Arafaze's people, and much more besides.'

Jadewin tried to ignore thoughtful nods here and there. 'Princess Alriad's claim to the crown rests on assertions we cannot vouch for.'

'You cannot prove they are false,' Elyka shot back.

Jadewin was relieved to see the older priestess's sharp tone made a few sisters uneasy. 'The Goddess calls us to uphold the truth proven by her divine light. Not to let what cannot be disproved pass unchallenged.'

'Yet you accuse me of wrongdoing and expect our sisters to accept your unsupported word.' Elyka appealed to the gathering with outspread hands and convincing, sorrowful indignation.

Jadewin looked up at the Goddess's ivory face. Turning to Elyka, she held the older priestess's gaze with her own. As Jadewin saw her former teacher's self-possession falter, she made sure to hide her own vindictive satisfaction.

Elyka looked away, and Jadewin turned to the priestess by the sanctum's doors. 'Admit Sister Hasrine.'

She didn't need to see Elyka's shock. Murmurs of disquiet sharpened to whispers of anticipation. Silence fell as Hasrine walked in. Jadewin fought to hide her fears.

She knew she was shadowed by Elyka's acolytes, ever since she arrived in Velasta. She'd had to trust Reske's assurance that Brother Belid's unknown ally would deliver Hasrine to Sister Deyadir's erstwhile lover at sunrise today. She had to believe in Deyadir's faith in her friend. They could not do anything that risked the high temple mother suspecting this trap. But, unable to speak to Hasrine first, Jadewin could not be certain what the renegade priestess might say.

'Sister Hasrine, do you swear before the Sun Goddess and your sisters that you will tell the truth?'

'I swear it.' Even in the silence, Hasrine's words were barely audible.

'Sisters!' Elyka protested. 'Our dear Hasrine is clearly unwell. She requires nursing and rest, not this inquisition!'

Jadewin bit the inside of her lip. Hasrine had been thin the last time they met. Now the renegade was skin and bone. Her hair was dull and sparse, and her eyes were sunk in dark hollows. Clearly though, she could walk and she showed no visible sign of injury. Her pale wool robe was clean and had been recently altered to fit her. She wore her sunburst pendant. Even so… What had the hidden brethren done to her?

'Really, Elyka?' Hasrine stared, gaunt as a death's head. 'When you know what I have done to merit inquisition?'

Anger strengthened her voice. Jadewin hoped the priestesses standing closest could see the hatred in her red-veined eyes. Though Hasrine was shaking. How long would her strength last?

Elyka turned to the gathering. 'I must—'

Disapproval and open rebuke rushed around the sanctum, drowning out her words. Jadewin waited for silence before she continued.

'Sister Hasrine, did Mother Elyka send you to Hurat to gather information on influential people's debts, to be used to pressure them to support Princess Alriad's claim to the crown?'

'Yes.'

'I protest.' Elyka threw up her hands.

Jadewin ignored her. 'To your certain knowledge, did Mother Elyka send sisters from this temple to Bastrys to offer Baron Zavire forgiveness for his many financial offences in return for his support for Earl Lystro's army?'

'Yes.'

Elyka shook her head. 'Sister Hasrine can only answer for her own actions.'

Jadewin was mildly surprised the older priestess didn't notice how many sisters found her interruptions irritating. 'Did the Bastrys temple mother take any action to stop Baron Zavire blocking trade up and down the Dore?'

'No.'

'Once again, this is hearsay.' Elyka tried to sound wounded.

Jadewin thought she sounded venomous. She fixed her eyes on Hasrine. 'Did the Bastrys sisters take any action to stop Baron Zavire forcing merchants to yield their cargos to him, at great cost to themselves?'

'No.'

'To your certain knowledge, did—'

'I will not listen to this.' Elyka strode towards the door. 'No enchantment condemns me!'

Jadewin moved quickly to stop her leaving. 'You think we have forgotten to summon the Goddess's power? That's why you keep interrupting, to make sure I don't realise? Sister Hasrine, please step back a few paces.'

The renegade sister stood in a pool of sunlight. Her sunburst pendant appeared to simply reflect the Goddess's gift of this splendidly sunny day. Every woman present watched as she retreated into the shadows and her pendant gleamed bright gold.

'Sister, when you were in Hurat, were you aware of threats to murder the Moon God's priests? Threats which you did not share with the shrine father or with any other authority who might have protected our brothers. Was this on Mother Elyka's direct orders?'

'Yes, and yes.' Hasrine's pendant blazed like a living flame.

Elyka gaped at Jadewin, horrified. Jadewin knew her former mentor hadn't expected to be accused of offences that touched on the unseen realm. Truth be told, Jadewin had no intention of saying anything more. There was no need. She could see their watching sisters assume Elyka was simply astonished that Jadewin knew of this betrayal. They didn't need to know the details.

'Sisters.' Jadewin circled the Goddess's statue. 'I say Mother Elyka is unfit to lead this temple, or any other. Who believes she should step down?'

Hands shot up. There could be no question of the majority's condemnation.

'Who disagrees?'

Jadewin couldn't see a finger raised. If any of Elyka's acolytes were still loyal, they weren't prepared to be counted today.

'Who wishes to reserve judgement?'

Nobody moved.

Jadewin turned to the older priestess. 'Our sisters have spoken. You are dismissed.'

'And now you will offer to take my place,' Elyka sneered.

'Not at all.' Jadewin's pendant shone bright. 'I have no ambition to serve as temple mother, here or anywhere else.'

Her calm statement unleashed uproar. Sisters turned to those close by, gesturing and exclaiming. Others called out to friends and allies, waving to attract attention. Impassioned voices grew louder and louder, striving to be heard.

Jadewin watched Elyka walk towards the sanctum's doors, refusing to meet anyone's eye. She might have lost her position as high temple mother, and Jadewin would make sure word of Elyka's offences spread far and wide, but her one-time mentor subsiding into meek retirement was as likely as midsummer snow. Jadewin knew Elyka would already be devising a plan to repair her ruined reputation. More immediately, she must not be allowed to disappear before the secret sisterhood could be gathered to pass their own verdict on her undeclared offences.

Sister Hasrine's face was the colour of parchment as she stepped into Elyka's path. She leaned forward to whisper in Elyka's ear. The older priestess recoiled. Hasrine grabbed her arm with a bony hand, pulling her close with unexpected strength. A moment later, she released Elyka, pushing her own robe's sleeve back to show the older woman her fleshless forearm. Elyka's disbelief gave way to dread. Whatever Hasrine was saying, her gleaming pendant proved it was true.

Jadewin wasn't the only one who noticed their conversation. Silence fell as Elyka and Hasrine approached the great gold and ivory statue. Both women knelt at the Goddess's feet, with their hands clasped and their heads bowed in prayer.

Abruptly, Jadewin realised this was her best chance, possibly her only opportunity, to convince every sister of the importance of the task before them.

'We should not choose a new high temple mother today. This decision must not be made in haste. Before we come to a vote, we must discuss the failings that led us here, honestly and openly. Those sisters who offer to serve must ask themselves searching questions. Our new temple will have to find a path between Idelina and Alriad, offering counsel to both and making an enemy of neither. Whichever princess becomes queen, she will be handed power over countless people which she never expected to wield. Velasta's new high temple mother must be the Goddess's voice in her ear, for the sake of peace and good governance across the realm and beyond its borders.'

Jadewin was getting slightly light-headed, but she pressed on. 'She must command the trust of those nobles committed to Arafaze's best interests. She must recognise those who only pursue enrichment and aggrandisement. She must meet these challenges while ensuring we and all our sisters continue to serve the Goddess by safeguarding the health and wealth of those from highest to most humble, who look to every temple and sanctuary.'

Clouds passed over the temple, dimming the sunlight through the dome. The sanctum felt no cooler, but Jadewin saw many sisters shiver, troubled and uncertain. Still on their knees, Elyka and Hasrine were as motionless as the great gold and ivory statue gazing over their heads.

Somebody opened the sanctum's doors. The priestesses started to leave. Some walked alone, wrapped in their own thoughts. Others clustered in twos and threes, heads close together as they conferred.

'Sister?'

Jadewin jumped as a gentle hand touched her forearm. 'Sorry. Yes?'

The unfamiliar sister was about Jadewin's age and height, with a rosy complexion and masses of blonde curls. 'I'm Kilese, Deyadir's friend.'

'Oh, right, thank you.' Jadewin snatched a glimpse into the unseen realm to confirm this stranger shared their insight.

She saw more than she expected. She and Kilese weren't alone in the sanctum in the intangible world. A dark shadow padded across the floor to crouch beside the Goddess's statue. It appeared to be a huge cat and yet somehow, was not. Whatever the unnerving apparition was, its luminous green gaze was fixed on Hasrine.

Jadewin wondered how she was able to see the renegade priestess. Why would Hasrine look into the unseen world while she prayed? She blinked and saw the gaunt priestess hadn't moved. Elyka still knelt beside her in the tangible realm.

'Brother Terius will explain,' Sister Kilese assured her. 'He'll be here soon to ink Elyka. Neither she nor Hasrine will be permitted to leave the sanctum until they have faced the secret sisterhood's judgement.'

Jadewin wasn't entirely sure she wanted to know how the hidden brethren would ensure Elyka wouldn't simply walk away. Before she could pick one of the questions crowding her thoughts, she saw young Alory striding along the corridor to the sanctum.

He was grinning from ear to ear. Sudden suspicion prompted Jadewin to look into the unreal world. The fire bird was back, gliding on outspread wings an arm's length behind him.

'If you're done here, you should come back to the house,' Alory urged as he reached her. 'Reske's had a letter from the Earl of Shirlat. You'll never believe what it says!'

Chapter Thirty-Two

VELASTA

23rd Day of the Frost Moon

Korel made his way across the elegant salon. One of the assembled nobles waylaid the princess's chamberlain every few paces. Reske watched his friend shake his head, apologetic, easing past questions he simply couldn't answer.

As he reached Reske's side, the chamberlain took a glass of warm, spiced wine from a lackey's tray. The servants discreetly circling to offer refreshments were doubtless as curious as the invited guests, and had been selected with equal care. Servants who had learned the values of patience and discretion.

'Thank you.' Reske took a fruit-stuffed morsel of pigeon breast wrapped in bacon from a passing silver platter. 'Who are we waiting for?'

'Everyone we're expecting has arrived.' Korel sipped his wine. 'With their personal secretaries, as stipulated.'

Reske looked around as he chewed the savoury mouthful. Mentally ticking names off his list was easily done. Three times this many people wouldn't be a crowd in this vast room. Thankfully, generous fires in the hearths at either end of the salon kept the twenty or so people present comfortably warm.

The lords and ladies were talking quietly. Their conversations were further muted by the silk brocade curtains in shades of cream and pink, currently half-drawn to baffle drafts from the long windows that opened onto the mansion's garden in the height of summer. The luxuriously thick carpet underfoot had been woven to match, along with the upholstered chairs set back against the salon walls. A few of the lords and ladies had glanced at those, clearly hoping for a chance to sit, but no one dared to be the first.

Reske was satisfied. Sufficient noble witnesses were present, whose word would not be questioned. To prove they heard the truth, three priests and three priestesses stood on either side of the great salon. Today's news would spread rapidly through Velasta from the temples and shrines.

Even so, he was a little uneasy. 'I don't see Earl Akovin or Countess Rastial, Baron Masut or Baroness Hest. Did they decline the invitation, or not reply?'

'The countess and the baron declined with thanks. The earl and the baroness sent no answer.' Korel grimaced. 'My mistress will have a great many bridges to rebuild.'

The chamberlain had barely spoken when a discreet, high-pitched silver bell rang somewhere outside the salon. Korel left immediately through the closest servants' door. The murmur of polite conversation died away.

The tall double doors of the salon's main entrance opened a few moments later. Seeing every face turned towards her, Princess Alriad baulked on the threshold like a startled horse. Blushing an unflattering shade of scarlet, the older would-be monarch of Arafaze walked into the salon with her head held high.

She wasn't wearing one of the diadems she had reportedly favoured in recent months. According to Hunys and Reske's other sources, Alriad had come as close to wearing a crown as she dared for the midsummer feasts. Now her abundant and somewhat improbably chestnut hair was woven into elegant braids held high with diamond-studded silver combs. She had no way to know what was coming, but Earl Debin had always assured him Princess Alriad was no fool.

She wore a flowing gown of emerald green silk, embroidered with silver thread. Her diamond necklace, earrings and bracelets caught enough firelight to sparkle demurely. Walking at her side, with her hand resting on his arm, Earl Lystro of Coylure wore a doublet and breeches tailored from the same bolt of silk. A wide silver chain of flat links studded with diamonds curved across his chest, kept in place by the brooches on his shoulders. The couple's three daughters and two sons followed, wearing similar shades of green in fine wool broadcloth, and with markedly less jewellery than their parents.

Korel's glance sent servants to offer wine and dainties to the new arrivals. Reske saw a few nobles share discreet surprise at seeing the whole family present. The rest presumably realised it was in everyone's interests to have them here. The young lords and ladies of Coylure were of an age to assume adult responsibilities, and only a fool would ignore the sharp intelligence in their eyes.

Reske noticed Earl Lystro's wary glances at Alory. The young brother was standing with Brother Terius and a priest Reske didn't know. Did the earl recognise Alory? The lad swore he had worn his mask the whole time, when Lystro was confronted in his tent. There weren't many priests with his height and breadth of shoulder though. The earl and the princess both studiously ignored Sister Jadewin and the two older priestesses with her. Reske didn't recognise either of them, but both seemed shrewd and alert, at ease among the realm's exalted nobility.

The silver bell rang again so quickly that Princess Idelina must have been waiting to make her entrance as soon as her aunt arrived. Reske braced himself for some display of Idelina's well-known arrogance. Like Alriad, she couldn't know what was coming, but she must assume she had won the crown. She had been asked to host this gathering after all.

Princess Idelina walked in with her eyes downcast. She wore an elegant but plainly cut silk gown in deep rose pink, with a single necklace of gold and garnets. Her hair was simply gathered in a net of gold thread secured with garnet-topped pins. An expert hand with subtle cosmetics had made her face a beautiful, impenetrable mask.

Earl Padran of Evarise walked half a step behind her. He wore a doublet and breeches of bronze silk and a single heavy gold chain. Scanning the room to identify those present, he acknowledged Reske with a slight nod. Accepting a glass of warm, spiced wine, Idelina was talking to Korel. Reske saw the two unknown priestesses watch her intently.

Several nobles took a step towards Princess Idelina. Earl Padran's expression warned them off. Reske saw his eyes harden as laughter was hastily stifled over by the long windows. Princess Alriad had swiftly gathered the nobles she knew best around her. Earl Lystro stood a few paces away, talking to their children, who were trying to hide their apprehension. Earl Padran turned his back on the Coylure family and drew Princess Idelina into light conversation with the elderly and kindly Baron Ziverid.

Korel made another circuit of the gathering, assessing the need for further drinks and dainties. Passing Reske, he murmured. 'I hope your master knows what he's doing.'

Reske didn't answer. He could hardly admit to the same concern, as he watched Padran unobtrusively move Idelina towards the far end of the salon, exchanging pleasantries with the lords and ladies.

The silver bell rang and the assembled nobles couldn't hide their surprise when Dowager Queen Sefriya walked in. A few years younger than Princess Alriad, she wore a modest violet silk gown and gold jewellery set with amethysts. Her gold consort's crown was striking against her intricately woven white hair.

The Earl of Shirlat followed, escorting a woman Reske didn't know. Dressed in elegant charcoal grey, Earl Debin looked bone weary but his letter had assured Reske he had not been harmed during his imprisonment. At their brief meeting, Reske had satisfied himself that the earl showed no sign of physical injury. Assessing any lingering impact on his spirits of being threatened with death and disgrace for himself and penury for his heirs would have to wait.

Here and now, Reske wanted to know who this woman was. So did everyone else, judging by their murmurs. She was old, relying on the earl's arm for physical as well as moral support. Her white lace cap hid her hair, but her face was as wrinkled as a winter-stored apple. Her hand on Earl Debin's sleeve was swollen-knuckled from a lifetime of hard work. Round-shouldered, she moved stiffly, as if her back or hips pained her. Her plain black gown was several decades out of style, sewn from good quality cloth, carefully stored and rarely worn.

Whoever she was, Korel had been forewarned. He snapped his fingers and three lackeys fetched chairs, setting them in a half circle close enough to the hearth to benefit from the warmth. Earl Debin escorted the unknown woman to the central chair and sat to her right. Queen Sefriya took the remaining seat, smiling serenely.

The nobles didn't need asking to gather facing the new arrivals, Reske noticed Princess Alriad's fixed expression. The princess clearly found the old woman familiar, but was unable to place her.

'Good morning.' Queen Sefriya sat straight-backed with her hands in her lap and her slippered feet tucked under her chair. 'Like you, I have been sorely distressed by the divisions disturbing our realm's tranquillity. Unlike too many who sought to profit from this strife, I went in search of answers to the puzzles that plagued us.'

Sefriya's tone was steely. Startled faces told Reske the nobility were not used to this. He tried to recall if he had ever heard the dowager queen say more than brief greetings and thanks. He had only seen her a handful of times, at events where King Fedrin commanded everyone's attention.

'I do not know where the callous rumour started, claiming my husband was not King Serken's first-born child. I do not care to know,' Sefriya said coldly. 'Those who spread this gossip with no regard for my family's grief at our shocking bereavement may seek the Goddess's forgiveness, or the God's. My concern is establishing the truth beyond doubt, to settle this once and for all.'

She turned to address the priestesses by the door, and the priests standing by the windows. 'Good sisters and good brothers, please use your divine gifts to assure us that we hear the truth today and not lies.'

As the priests and priestesses moved closer, Reske saw recognition slowly dawn on Princess Alriad's face.

Queen Sefriya turned to the old woman. 'Please, tell everyone who you are and what you know of this matter.'

'As the Goddess and the God stand witness,' the old woman said dutifully to the priestesses and the priests. 'My name is Birna Kopar and I was a maid in Queen Misene's service until I married and left Velasta. I was one of her attendants when her only surviving children were born. The first of these twins was a boy, and the second was a girl, safely delivered in King Serken's presence, as he supported his wife through her ordeal.'

The old woman smiled with delight as her clouded eyes focused on Princess Alriad. 'You were my queen's joy and solace, after enduring so many losses. The God had finally favoured the king with a son and heir, and Queen Misene believed a daughter was the Goddess's gift to her.'

The old woman looked at the priestesses and the priests. 'I will answer any questions you wish to ask.'

'I do not believe that is necessary.' The shorter of the unknown priestesses stepped forward. Everyone could see the three women's sunburst pendants were shining bright gold. 'Brother Hetmar?'

'Sister Ruzil.' The third priest bowed respectfully to her. 'No lies have been spoken here.'

'Will the high shrine and the high temple acknowledge my daughter as the rightful heir to the Arafaze crown?'

Everyone heard the edge to Queen Sefriya's question. No one dared to glance at Princess Alriad or her husband, to see how they reacted.

'Gladly,' Sister Ruzil said calmly. 'Sister Drichet, Sister Jadewin, and I have been authorised by our sisters to speak for the temple in this matter. We have yet to decide who will lead us, now that Sister Elyka has been dismissed in disgrace for betraying the Goddess.'

Reske hadn't expected to hear the former high priestess so openly condemned. Judging by the ripple of surprise, neither had anyone else.

'The high priest will assuredly declare her as monarch.' Brother Hetmar's forthright agreement failed to quell the murmurs.

Earl Debin rose to his feet and everyone fell silent. 'My noble lords and ladies, let us be the first to acclaim Queen Idelina. Once we have done so, we must lead our peers in striving to heal our realm's divisions.'

Reske saw Arafaze's new and now undisputed ruler was standing with Earl Padran at the other end of the salon.

With a loud rustle of silk, Princess Alriad walked towards her niece. She sank low in a graceful curtsey an arm's length from her.

'Queen Idelina, I acknowledge you as unquestioned monarch of Arafaze. I pledge my loyalty to you and your children without reservation. I am profoundly thankful that my mother's faithful servant has been found to settle this question that vexed us.'

She rose without meeting Idelina's eyes and turned to the high temple's priestesses. 'I am deeply sorry I believed Mo– Sister Elyka's assurances that no such witness could be found. I regret beyond saying that I was persuaded by her arguments to claim the crown. My only defence is I believed I acted in the best interests of the realm.'

No one could miss the Goddess's servants' shining pendants attest to Alriad's sincerity. Reske did notice a few wry expressions. Conversations would follow about what she hadn't said, and a good number of further questions for the princess and her husband remained.

Alriad rejoined her family, leaving the new queen visibly uncertain what to do next. Earl Padran spoke quietly to her and they walked the length of the salon. The Earl of Shirlat stood to yield his chair.

The assembled nobles stepped forward. One by one, they bowed or curtseyed and promised their loyalty. Idelina's defensiveness slowly softened. Sister Ruzil and Sister Drichet were close enough for their glowing pendants to confirm the honesty of assurances on both sides. After pledging themselves to the queen, the lords and ladies were offered fresh glasses of sweet wine and platters of sweetmeats from Korel's seemingly inexhaustible pantries.

Reske joined Sister Jadewin by the fireplace at the far end of the room.

'High Mother Elyka simply didn't look hard enough for a witness to Fedrin and Alriad's birth?' Reske shook his head. 'So much strife could have been avoided.'

'Elyka didn't do a great many things which were her responsibility,' Jadewin said acidly. 'She should have consulted the sisters who attended Princess Olyshai's birth, and who nursed Idelina through the debilitating illness and melancholy that beset her afterwards. In her second pregnancy, Idelina should have been surrounded by those who would have cared for her and her unborn child with gentleness and understanding. Instead Elyka found excuses to send those sisters Idelina knew and trusted far away, within days of King Venais's death. Just as she sent those sisters who would never betray the intangible realm as far away as she could.'

'She made a mistake sending you to Hurat,' Reske observed.

Jadewin acknowledged that with a brief smile, but her eyes were serious. 'We have identified the renegades who helped Elyka terrify Idelina with phantasms of the Lightning King. We know who revealed magic's secrets to Alriad and Lystro of Coylure. Rest assured, every one of the forsworn will answer for their misdeeds.'

Reske stifled a shudder at the memory of Mistress Nindera facing the masked priests. He didn't ask what fate traitorous sisters would face. To his relief, Jadewin moved on.

'Earl Debin may be interested to know Sister Ruzil and Sister Drichet are both highly regarded among those who have offered to serve as Velasta's new high temple mother. Every sister who has stepped forward is committed to restoring unity and harmony across Arafaze and with our brother priests.'

'Do you...?' Reske tried to work out how to ask what he wanted to know.

'My sisters—' Jadewin held Reske's gaze as she stressed that word '—and I have concluded our brothers are correct to insist a shrine's leader's attention must not be diverted from his duties to the God, his brothers and the populace by any other obligations or responsibilities.'

Reske was relieved to hear it. 'That's good to know. So will you be staying in Velasta?'

Jadewin shook her head. 'Once the new high temple mother has been chosen, I'll go back to Hurat. With Alory, if I can persuade him to travel by road instead of waiting until the rivers thaw in the spring.'

Tall and confident, the young priest was discussing something with Brother Hetmar.

'Let me know when you're preparing to leave,' Reske said casually. 'I'll be glad to travel with you, with both of you, if that's agreeable. Castellan Maixen will want to know every detail of the resolution of this strife between the princesses.'

'Castellan Maixen?' Jadewin raised her eyebrows. 'You haven't heard there's a new Earl of Hurat?'

'I heard, but Earl Debin hopes that with the rival claims to the crown dismissed, tensions between Hurat and Arafaze can be settled without an irrevocable breach.' Reske made very sure not to look at Jadewin's pendant, in case the Goddess's magic could somehow reveal he was telling her the truth, but by no means all of it.

'I fear that raft has long since floated downstream.' The priestess glanced around the room. 'In the interests of restoring peace in court circles, the nobility in Velasta may be willing to dismiss Earl Lystro and Earl Padran's actions as follies far away, unworthy of further notice. That won't happen in Hurat. Folk along the Tane won't forget Margrave Vauset's murder, or those who died defending Vitry. Merchants and traders along the Dore won't forgive those in Arafaze who were willing to let Baron Zavire beggar them.'

'You may well be right,' Reske conceded. 'Even so, my master and others will strive to make amends.'

'I'll pray the Goddess blesses your endeavours, and I'll pass on whatever I learn which may be of help.'

The glint in Jadewin's eye told Reske this assistance would come with a price.

'Many thanks. Let me know what can I do in return.'

The priestess didn't hesitate. 'Court circles will agree it's in Arafaze's best interests for Alriad and Idelina to find common ground. It would be a disaster if they found that unity in fear of the intangible world and mistrust of magic. You saw Alriad trying to shift the blame for deeds done in her name onto Elyka. It's a short step to her telling Idelina renegade sisters led her astray with promises of magic to bolster her rule. If she claims she was too frightened to refuse them, I wouldn't bet against Idelina sharing how Nindera terrified her with the Lightning King.'

'True.' Reske couldn't deny it.

'That could become a catastrophe if they decide between them to reveal the existence of the unseen world. They would undoubtedly hide such a plan from temple and shrine, but you might hear a whisper of warning. Knowing what you now know.'

'I will stay vigilant. Remember, Brother Haber, her household physician, is one of Alory's brethren.' Reske had realised that was why Nindera had wanted the amiable priest dead.

'That's true.' Jadewin was relieved. 'He can help us find out who Idelina has already told and help us convince them to keep quiet.'

Reske didn't think that would be as easy as it might sound. 'Who should I tell if I hear something ominous when you're not in Velasta?

'I will introduce you to Sister Kilese. Now, if you'll excuse me, I'll see what Princess Alriad's daughters have to say for themselves.'

Reske watched the priestess join the young women as Earl Lystro looked on warily.

The Earl of Shirlat strolled over, collecting two glasses of wine from a passing lackey. 'Did your priestess friend have anything of interest to say?'

'She doesn't think much of our chances of drawing Hurat back into the Arafaze fold.' Reske saluted the earl with his glass and took a sip. 'Your very good health, my lord. Excuse me, I must ask. How am I to answer questions about your restoration to your rank and properties?'

Today's revelations would be the talk of Velasta for days, but Reske knew people would still be curious about what had happened to the earl.

'Tell them Queen Idelina has been gracious enough to forgive me, and I have accepted her apology in turn.'

Reske was startled. 'Forgiven you for what?'

'You do not know. As far as anyone else is concerned, the queen and I have settled the matter privately between ourselves.' The earl paused to make certain Reske understood him. 'Between you and me, I should have taken the time to try to understand the full extent of her fears and distress. I had no idea how she suffered after Princess Olyshai's birth. Obviously, I had no notion the woman Nindera had terrified her with monstrous visions of the Lightning King. That's why she fled Velasta. Then I came to Astyrie, thinking she simply needed a firm hand. I ordered her to do her duty to Arafaze and her children, and return to the high temple's care.'

The earl shook his head, rueful. 'She thought I was in league with High Mother Elyka. That's hardly surprising, given what we have learned. She lashed out, fearing for her own life and for her children. Unfortunately, hasty words can't be unspoken, when a soon-to-be monarch has passed judgement. That's water under the bridges, but...'

He sighed. 'Until you explained, I truly thought she had lost her wits. She started screaming, accusing me of sending monsters to murder her. I know others still doubt her soundness of mind, and of course, she cannot explain. That's another challenge she faces as she tries to win back trust and support.'

The earl watched Jadewin talking to the youthful heirs to Coylure. 'Is your friend going back to Hurat? And the boy? Do you think they will share more of this world of apparitions and monsters?'

'I hope so,' Reske said cautiously. 'In return for me passing on rumours of such horrors.' He explained Jadewin's concern, in case Alriad and Idelina united against those who had dealings with the unseen realm.

'That would cause difficulties,' the earl agreed. 'When you reach Hurat, tell Earl Maixen everything you've learned here. Assure him we'll share whatever else we discover which could threaten our peace, in whatever way, and I'll gladly accept his offer to do the same.'

'I will, my lord.'

Reske and Maixen had discussed their perilous new knowledge late into the night, before he left Hurat. Neither man could forget what they had seen, or unhear what they had been told. They agreed someone else needed to know the full extent of magic's involvement in the past year's events. Someone whose discretion they could trust absolutely. They had chosen Earl Debin even before they knew why Idelina had condemned him.

Jadewin could assure them that Elyka and her renegade sisters were no longer a threat. Hopefully Alory and his hidden brethren were safe now Mistress Nindera was dead. That was no guarantee knowledge of the intangible world wouldn't prompt dangerous ambition or murderous hatred in some of the hidden brethren or the secret sisterhood in the months and years ahead.

Maixen and Reske had stumbled on this secret by accident. From comments Alory and Jadewin had let slip, they clearly weren't the first and they wouldn't be the last. The priests and priestesses might be sure they could manage such situations.

Maixen and Reske didn't share their confidence. They knew of devious and ruthless opportunists who would try to use the unreal world for their own ends, if they discovered its existence. Neither man was willing to risk the chaos that would surely follow.

Someone had to stay vigilant. Someone besides those beholden to shrine and temple. For whatever reason, and Reske didn't presume to understand the Moon God's decisions or the Sun Goddess's choices, he and Maixen had been given this sacred duty.